BY A HAND

Kathy Shuker was born in northw ...
working as a physiotherapist, she s...... .... a
freelance artist in oils and watercolours. Writing took over her life
several years ago and *By a Hand Unknown* is her sixth novel, the
second of the Dechansay Bright Mysteries, each a standalone story
featuring art restorers Hannah Dechansay and Nathan Bright.

Kathy lives with her husband in Devon. Art is still a major passion
as are the natural world and music. Sadly, despite years of trying,
(and the tolerance of both husband and neighbours) mastery of the
piano, guitar and fiddle remains as elusive as ever.

To find out more about Kathy and her other novels, please visit:
www.kathyshuker.co.uk

Also by Kathy Shuker

BY A HAND UNKNOWN

Kathy Shuker

Kathy Shuker

A Dechansay Bright Mystery

Chapter 1

As if weary from a long day and too many visitors, the manor house had fallen silent, dozing in the fading light of an early spring evening. The paying public had left and the staff had long since finished for the day. Even the Gyllam-Spences had retreated into their private sanctuary. Carrie was alone, working late.

She left the dining room and walked into the exhibition room, flicked the light switch on and paused, savouring the peace. She liked being here after everyone else had gone. From the moment Ranling Manor opened to the public at ten each morning, a constant procession of people wandered through the rooms, pointing and commenting, asking questions and jostling for position. But Carrie preferred it like this: silent and still. The extensive art collection which the old manor housed – and which she had been employed to curate – was hers alone. She could pause and consider and simply think without interruption or distraction.

She twitched the protective fabric cloth back over one of the glazed cases housing watercolours and drawings, then headed for the far wall. Earlier that afternoon, she had replaced a painting with a fresh one from the storeroom. Now she checked the new hanging looked right and that the alarm cord was securely attached to it, then consulted her watch. It was after six-thirty already and she was tired. She'd had an argument with another member of staff that afternoon and still it lingered in her mind, leaving her restless and uncomfortable. And it had been such a petty thing. She glanced round the room once more and left, switching off the lights.

The oak-panelled hallway was empty. All day long a guide stationed by the big front door welcomed visitors, offering plans of the house and advice on the route used to view it. But now there was no-one. Carrie made for the door beside the old staircase which gave access to the private rear vestibule, then a soft groan had her stopping to look round and up the stairs. Nothing.

'Don't worry about the noises you'll hear,' Mortimer had said conspiratorially to her when she first arrived. 'The house talks to you sometimes. Just listen. Think what stories a house like this has seen, what secrets it could tell you. There's a lot of wisdom in an old house.'

Mortimer had a way of coming out with these strange remarks. He was the current Gyllam-Spence who owned and managed the estate, a seemingly pleasant but definitely odd man. Carrie listened anyway, but if the house had some wisdom or a secret to impart, it wasn't doing it tonight. At least not to her.

She put her key in the partition door but found it unlocked again and sighed with frustration. In the short time she'd worked at the manor, she'd been astonished at the lax security and no matter how often she mentioned it, Mortimer just laughed it off.

Letting herself into the workroom off the rear vestibule, she gathered her things together, picked up her notebook and bag and had just found her car keys when she heard another noise. But this one had definitely come from the huge storeroom next door where all the art works not currently on display were kept, and sounded like a book falling to the floor with a slap. But nobody should be in there at this time of night. Or at all: the storeroom was her responsibility.

She stood transfixed, straining to hear. Suppose it was a burglar who'd come in through the back door? That was often left unlocked too. Suppose he realised she was there? Barely able to breathe and scared to move, a threatening sneeze had her raising a desperate hand to her nose and her car keys dropped, falling with an ear-splitting clatter onto the stone floor. The echo hung in the room and she froze again. A few minutes later she heard the distinctive creak of the back door opening.

She cautiously opened the door onto the vestibule and peeked out. The back door to the outside was closed and the only light came through a long slit of window each side of it which offered a dull, insipid glow, enough to show that there was no-one there. Edging further out she found the storeroom door ajar and the room in darkness. She'd have sworn she'd closed and locked the door; she always did.

She sidled up to it, hooked a hand round the frame and flicked the light on. There was no-one inside but the old inventory book with the details of the collection had been moved. That was probably what had fallen. It should have been on the shelves and had now been put on top of the plan chest.

She glanced through its pages but there was no way of knowing what the intruder had been looking for and she pointlessly scanned the room. Did they find it, whatever it was? Some of the collection was tawdry and uninspired but there were real gems too, worth a lot of money. The only way to know if anything was missing would be to painstakingly check through every art work, piece by piece.

For a couple of weeks now she'd suspected that

something was wrong but she had doubted herself. She'd blamed the uneasiness of starting a new job, the unfamiliar location, the breakdown of her marriage and its emotional fallout. But there was no doubting what had happened here tonight, nor was she imagining the air in this room: it had been disturbed. The usually stuffy, stagnant space still held the indefinable energy of whoever had been there.

And what disturbed her most was that the only people who knew about the position and mechanics of this obscure internal room – and who had access to a key – were the people she now worked closely with every day: the Gyllam-Spences and Alan Foxhall, that slippery, two-faced man. It couldn't have been an outsider; that didn't make sense. Her worst suspicions had been correct.

Someone here was tampering with the collection and stealing from it. But who would believe her? She was the newcomer and she wasn't family, they had made that clear. If something went missing, she would be blamed.

*

Mortimer sat behind the desk in the manor office, his gaze resting on Alan who was telling them about a school visit planned for later in the week. Alan Foxhall was responsible for 'events' at the Manor, anything that could give them good publicity or, more importantly, some valuable extra income. He had been with them a couple of years and seemed to be good at his job, although Mortimer couldn't honestly say he liked the man, though in truth he hardly knew him. Alan didn't make idle conversation and, for all that he was the only member of the administration team who wasn't family, he exuded an irritatingly condescending manner.

'...And I've received several enquiries about wedding receptions this last week,' he was saying. 'Most of the couples

4

were asking about this summer, but two were planning ahead for next year.'

'Good, good,' said Mortimer. 'They need to come up with firm dates if it's for this year. I mean, we're in March already. Tell them we're booking up quickly. Are we?'

Alan produced a pained smile. 'It's April now, Mortimer. The third. And we're not really booking up yet but yes, I told them we were.'

It was their weekly Wednesday morning meeting, a chance to catch up and coordinate.

'Shouldn't we be putting our fees up this year?' said Toby. Toby was Mortimer's younger brother and seemed to think that their visitors could be endlessly squeezed for money. Probably because he spent so much of it himself.

Mortimer didn't reply. He'd noticed that he'd fastened his cardigan buttons in the wrong holes again and he started to unfasten them, one by one, and change them over.

'Mortimer, are you listening?' Toby's voice had gone up a notch, cross and impatient.

'Shouldn't we be putting our fees up,' said Mortimer distantly. 'Yes, I heard.'

'And what about ticket prices? Inflation is running high. We mustn't get left behind.'

'We haven't.' Mortimer managed to fasten the last button in the appropriate hole and looked up at his brother. 'I do keep a check on these things, Toby. We can't afford to price ourselves out of the market. They'll go elsewhere.'

'Well I keep a check on it too and I know of a couple of places that charge more than we do.'

Mortimer ignored him. Toby was all mouth. He supposedly managed the ticket office and did the publicity but seemed to do precious little of either. The estate worked in spite of him, not because of him.

5

'Remember I've got a couple of conservators arriving tomorrow to work on some pieces from the collection,' Mortimer said.

'What pieces?' demanded Toby. 'You never said.'

'I think I did,' said Mortimer mildly. 'They've been booked for a while. Anyway, you wouldn't know if I told you, Toby. You never have anything to do with the collection.' He looked over at Carrie, their new curator, a rather diffident young woman. She had arrived late to the meeting, looking flustered and ill at ease. There again, she often did. 'I'll meet them first and sort a few things out but perhaps you'll go through the necessary work with them, Carrie? Explain the ins and outs of what needs doing?'

Carrie appeared distracted. She kept glancing round the room, studying people's faces. He frowned.

'Is that all right, Carrie?'

'What, oh yes, the conservators. Sorry. Of course, I'll see them. Yes.'

'But why are they coming here?' complained Toby. 'It must be more expensive than sending the artworks away.'

'I've told you before: I'm not doing that again. The last time I sent a painting away, I never saw it again. And the insurance money doesn't compensate: they never give you what it's worth. Anyway I negotiated a deal with the man who runs the restoration business, Timothy Blandish. They're staying at The Boatman in the village and he promised they'd be discreet. *And* quick. Can't remember their names off hand but I've got them here somewhere...'

He ferreted through a teetering pile of papers on the desk in front of him, sending several fluttering to the floor, grabbed one of the remaining sheets, peered at it, then looked round for his reading glasses.

'They're on top of your head,' remarked Sid.

Sidony Pettiver was Toby's ex-wife. She was in charge of the house guides, training them and organising their rotas. She was calm and efficient. Someone needed to be.

He offered her a grateful smile, disentangled them from his hair which he wore long and tied in a ponytail, and perched them on his nose.

'Hannah Dechansay and Nathan Bright. So there we are. Hopefully they should get here by lunch-time.'

Mortimer glanced round the room over his glasses. Rosamund, his niece who worked in the office fielding phone calls and answering general queries, had got up and was picking up the errant papers one by one and replacing them on the pile.

'Thank you, Rose,' he muttered.

'Where are the conservators going to work?' Sid enquired with her familiar challenging glare. 'We aren't closing any rooms off are we? I hate having to do that.'

'No, no. In the workroom, I thought.'

'The workroom?' queried Carrie. 'My workroom? But...'

'I didn't know it was *your* workroom,' said Rose waspishly.

'No, I know. I meant...'

'I realise it's where you base yourself Carrie,' interposed Mortimer, 'but I don't know where else would be suitable. You've got work tables in there and some natural light. They asked for both of those things. It won't be for long.' He shrugged, not remembering too clearly now how long that Blandish chap had said it might take, only the price tag. 'You can squeeze in here for the duration, can't you, when you're not sorting through the collection? Plenty of room to go round, isn't there?'

He looked expectantly at Rose and Alan who both had a desk in here and generally seemed to tolerate each other.

Neither voiced any support however.

'Is there any other business?' he asked loudly. 'Problems?'

He wished he hadn't asked that. He didn't want to know about any problems, not this morning.

'Are these conservators only working on those pieces you mentioned to me last week?' asked Sid. 'Nothing's coming out of the show rooms, is it?'

'No,' said Carrie, 'but I did change that painting we discussed from the exhibition room yesterday: the Watteau for the Ingres. And I wrote out some information about the replacement for the guides. Rose was going to type it out for them.' Carrie pointedly looked across at Rose.

'Yes, yes, I'll do it this morning,' Rose said impatiently.

'Good. Right. Time to get on then.' Mortimer rose to his feet and gathered up his sheaf of papers, ready to take them back into his study next door. There was a general scraping of wood on the stone floor as chairs were moved and put back in position.

Rose joined him before he could reach the door and put a hand on his arm, making the bangles on her wrist jangle.

'What are these people like, Uncle Mortimer?' she asked breathily.

'I've no idea, Rose. Why?'

'I just wondered, you know, since they're going to be among us for, what, days on end.'

'Weeks, dear.'

'Really? That long. So didn't you ask?' She shrugged. 'I mean. Are they old or young, you know, that kind of thing? They don't sound married.'

He offered an indulgent smile. Rose was always on the lookout for eligible men. Any man really. He blamed her father. When Toby wasn't ignoring her, he was heavy-handed

8

and critical. It had made her prickly and insecure.

'I don't know. We'll find out soon enough, I imagine.'

'Oh Uncle Mortimer, you are hopeless.'

'Yes, my dear, so you've said.'

Rose turned away as Carrie came up.

'I'm sorry about the workroom, Carrie,' he offered. 'Can't be helped, I'm afraid.'

'No, no, it's fine. I'll manage. Mr Gyllam-Spence...'

'Do call me Mortimer. You make me feel so old.'

Carrie produced a weak smile.

'In fact, you look rather tired yourself,' he remarked. 'Something bothering you?'

'I didn't sleep well last night. In fact, I wondered if I could...' She broke off and glanced sideways towards Alan who was watching them a little too closely. 'Actually no, it's fine. I'll make sure I'm around when the conservators arrive tomorrow.'

Mortimer regarded her pensively as she left the office. She was very diligent. Perhaps too diligent for her own good, he thought.

*

Late that afternoon, in the reception area of the Blandish Fine Art Conservation studios in Oxford, Hannah Dechansay and her colleague Nathan Bright were sorting out the final arrangements for their visit to Norfolk. Their huge 'Blandish' trunks, carefully packed with all the equipment they expected to need, had long since been picked up by the carrier and were already on their way.

Although Timothy Blandish had set up his base and workshops in Oxford, his business specialised in offering a more personal service. If someone was nervous of parting with a piece of art or preferred a discreet, private service – and could afford it – then a member of the team would be dispatched to work on site. Timothy sent his restorers to all parts of the UK and across western Europe, wherever the client was. Indeed he went to some trouble to seek out and cultivate exactly the right clients.

Usually only one member of the team went on an assignment however and Hannah wasn't happy that Nathan was going to tag along on this one. He had worked for Timothy for more than seven years and Hannah for only one which Nathan seemed to think gave him seniority. But they were both the same age – thirty-nine – and her CV was as good as his. Better, well, more varied anyway; she had moved around a lot. The point was: she liked working alone. She didn't welcome interference.

Daphne, company receptionist and Timothy's long-suffering secretary, was now in the process of recounting what she knew about the manor. Hannah liked Daphne: she was kind, straightforward and efficient, with a store of useful information, especially about the wealthy and well-to-do whose lives she followed in the pages of the glossy magazines.

'Interesting family,' she was saying. 'There have been Gyllam-Spences at Ranling Manor since the late eighteenth century. Their wealth was built on a thriving trade in wool, then the family diversified into shipping and started collecting art and fine things. It went from there, each successive generation adding to the collection. Apparently it's quite varied: paintings and drawings, plus a few bronzes – some well-known artists, others more obscure. And of course it's open to the public – the half of the house that houses the collection and a chunk of the grounds. Six days a week.' Daphne's tone became wistful. 'Sounds like a lovely old place and a wonderful setting, right at the heart of the Broads with beautiful gardens and a stream meandering around the

10

boundary. You do get to visit the most amazing places.'

'We do,' agreed Hannah. 'I'm sorry we can't take you with us.'

'So am I. You're booked into the inn in the village of East Ranling. It's called The Boatman and it's about two miles from the manor.' Daphne dropped her voice. 'I'm afraid they're the cheapest rooms. Timothy didn't want too much expense. He was hoping they'd put you up at the house but no joy there, I'm afraid.' She shrugged and affected a brighter tone. 'And here's a map of the layout of the place and where you should park. I made two copies.'

'Ah, thought I heard you.'

Timothy's shrill voice assaulted them as he emerged from his office.

'All set for Norfolk? Mr Gyllam-Spence has agreed to my costing but wants to be informed if there's any unforeseen expense. He's a man after my own heart: believes in economy. Do some quick assessments when you get there and let me know what you find. He's keen to get the work done quickly and I don't want to give him any reason to complain. Nathan has experience with drawings and you can concentrate on the oils, Hannah. That'll keep it snappy.' He looked from one to the other. 'Keep me informed of progress, won't you? Lots more jobs waiting when this one's over.'

'Yes Timothy,' said Nathan.

Hannah simply nodded.

Timothy returned to his office and closed the door. There was silence.

'Says the same things every time,' remarked Hannah, softly aggrieved.

'We'd be disappointed if he didn't,' murmured Nathan.

Hannah flicked him a long-suffering look then turned back to Daphne.

11

'What do you know about this Gyllam-Spence man?' said Hannah.

'His name's Mortimer. He's fifty-eight and single and widely considered to be eccentric. No wife but there are other Gyllam-Spences living and working with him there. Oh, and he has a thing about trains.'

'Trains?' queried Nathan.

'Model ones, *you* know.'

'Ah.'

Hannah grinned. 'Sounds like fun.'

'Well, don't have the kind of fun you had in Provence last year.' She looked at them both severely. 'Behave yourselves and don't get involved in any trouble.'

'Where's the pleasure in that?' Nathan raised one quizzical eyebrow and left, making his way back up to the workshops on the first floor.

Hannah met Daphne's gaze and rolled her eyes.

'I can't believe Timothy's put us to work together again,' she muttered.

'He did say he would.'

'Yes but *Nathan*. And stuck in Norfolk with him.'

'Oh he's all right. It's just, you know, he's got...'

'Issues,' finished Hannah. 'Yeah, I know. His brother, Sam.' She leaned forward on to the reception desk and dropped her voice. 'Does he ever talk to you about it?'

Daphne shook her head. 'Not really. He's a man. What do you expect? If you want my opinion, you'd be better off not poking that particular wasp's nest.' She raised a warning finger. 'And just make sure you keep out of trouble.'

'A manor house in the depths of Norfolk. Come on, Daphne, what kind of trouble could there be?'

Chapter 2

It was just after one in the afternoon when Nathan arrived at the manor only to find Hannah already there, sitting in her little red Mini in the private parking area round the back. He'd taken a wrong turning in Milton Keynes, forcing him to make a short detour, and had been obliged to follow a tractor for the last two miles. Hannah raised her eyebrows as his car swept in alongside hers and offered a wry grin. She said nothing when they got out but he could read the amusement in her eyes which was worse. He should never have bragged about his map-reading skills, oh and did she need any help to find her way there.

Their instructions were to come round to the main entrance of the house. Ranling Manor had been built in the seventeenth century, a large, elegant two-storied property set in ten acres of equally elegant grounds. The front gardens were laid to lawn either side of a path while the public access and parking were discreetly placed on the western side, screened by trees. The front door was heavy, wide and imposing. And open. Though still early in the year, a constant trickle of visitors was filing in. Hannah and Nathan followed on.

In order to open it up to the public, the house had been neatly divided either side of its central hallway into show rooms on the left and residential quarters for the family on the right. The same had been done on the first floor. The broad main staircase still stretched from the entrance hall to the public bedrooms but the private quarters had its own winding run of stairs at the rear, allowing the two sides of the first floor to be completely self-contained. Downstairs the office, the hub of the day-to-day administration of the estate, lay to the right of the entrance hall and, with a door at each end, worked as a stepping stone between the public and private rooms.

Mortimer Gyllam-Spence was all smiles when he met them.

'You've found us then. Well done.' He beamed and shook their hands. 'A bit out in the wilds aren't we but that's all part of our charm as I'm sure you'll find out. So, a quick overview. This is our nerve centre, so to speak. Rose here runs the office. If you need the phone or the fax or maybe just information, she's your girl.' A young woman with blonde hair smiled in their direction, looking up at them through her eyelashes. 'Alan seems to have wandered off, I'm afraid.'

Mortimer surveyed the office as if Alan might suddenly materialise.

'Anyway, we're open six days a week, closed on Mondays. There's a wide range of fascinating art works to see and we've tried to keep the furniture and décor as authentic as possible. The grounds are delightful too. I'm sure there are maps somewhere for you to see what's what.'

He explained a little more about the running and layout of the manor, briefly introduced them to Sidony, a woman in her fifties who scrutinised them with a searching gaze, then took them down the main hallway and through a door to a room at the back.

'And this is Carrie, our curator,' he said. 'Hasn't been here long but she's doing a grand job, sorting us out.' He offered Carrie an apologetic smile. 'We're a bit... well, dis-organised, aren't we? Anyway, I think I was supposed to be somewhere else ten minutes ago. She'll explain about the pieces you're going to be working on and all the other things I've forgotten.'

Carrie was fine-boned and pretty, her golden-brown hair fastened in a solid plait down her back while odd wisps escaped fetchingly around her face. She wore a long, loose, printed cotton dress with puff sleeves and flat, slip-on shoes. She seemed out of place somehow, as if she'd been transported through time from the sixties. Nathan could imagine her with flowers in her hair, maybe with a guitar hanging round her shoulders, singing songs about love and peace. But he quickly realised he was being fanciful. However ethereal she might appear, Carrie was business-like and efficient.

The room they were going to be working in was what Carrie called the 'workroom', right at the back of the house, a few paces from the rear door. She had put the work out ready for them and now gave them a list of the pieces and the issues she had identified as their problems.

'I'm having another key made to this door,' she added. 'Please lock it when you finish each day. I'll get one for the door from the entrance hall to this rear vestibule too. It should be kept locked to stop the public from wandering but often isn't. People forget. There's a washroom across the hall under the stairs for you to use. The door next to it gives access to the rear of the private quarters.'

'Mortimer said we'd be given a key to the back door,' said Hannah.

'Yes, it's the quickest route to our car park through the private gardens. I'll chase that up for you too. Mortimer's a bit, shall we say, absent-minded? If you've got any queries, just ask. I'll be around or in the office.'

She offered a brief, hesitant smile and left them to settle in. Their trunks had arrived and had been moved into the room, ready. They unpacked some basic kit and spent the rest of the afternoon assessing the work.

It was five-thirty by the time they drove to the village and found the inn. A pub more than a hotel with just six letting rooms, The Boatman was double-fronted and built in a decorative pattern of small red bricks. It was old and quaint with a faded, traditional décor but boasted a delightful position facing the river. Most of the village in fact seemed to stretch out on a long loop of the River Ant.

In early April demand for the inn was low and it was still closed for the afternoon. A bored-looking young woman with a froth of curly blonde hair answered the bell and showed them their rooms which were upstairs at the rear, side by side, and shared a communal bathroom.

Hannah and Nathan exchanged a look.

'Food's served from seven,' the girl added in a flat, disinterested voice and left.

They arranged to meet downstairs for a meal and separated to unpack.

The lounge bar had half a dozen people in it by the time Nathan bought himself a pint of bitter and grabbed a table by one of the front windows. On the other side of the lane in front of the inn a couple of boats were tied up on the long stretch of quay where a number of tables and benches stood empty. A chill wind and the suggestion of rain in the air had driven everyone inside. Nathan's thoughts wandered, far ranging, drifting back to a past he had chosen not to think about in a long time. It occurred to him that he'd been naïve not to realise this might happen.

'Penny for them?'

He frowned and looked round, dragging himself back to the present. Hannah had put a glass of white wine down on the table and was slipping her slim frame into the seat opposite.

Her short, spiky dark hair, still wet from the shower, had been towel-dried and roughly fingered up into floppy peaks.

'Hi. Room all right?'

'Yes thanks. Basic but clean. Yours?'

'The same. I've stayed in a lot worse.' He glanced out of the window again. 'I was just thinking about holidays. Family holidays. We used to come here a lot when we were kids. Not to this village exactly but to the Broads. It's such a network of rivers and lakes, we used to love it, me and my brother.' He nodded, unconsciously smiling as the memories began to play again. 'Dad would hire a boat and we'd mess about for hours on the water.' He looked away abruptly, picked up the two menus propped up in a wooden holder on the table and handed her one. 'Let's order, shall we? I'm starving.'

They spent a few minutes in silence studying the menus then Nathan went to order at the bar. He returned with a wooden order marker, shaped like a sailboat, resumed his seat and picked up his beer.

'So... here we are. Again.' He took a mouthful and sat back, looking at her across the table. 'Hopefully it'll be less eventful than our stay in Provence.'

'I hope that's not why he's put us together again: so you can keep an eye on me.'

'Don't be absurd. It's just basic job planning.' He shrugged and took a pull of beer.

'I won't be watched and spied on, Nathan.'

'Don't flatter yourself, I've got better things to do.'

There was a charged silence.

'Timothy seemed to think it would be eight to ten weeks work,' said Nathan. 'From what we saw this afternoon, that's probably fair.'

'Maybe. Though a couple of the paintings look as if they might be time-consuming.' She took a sip of wine. 'Timothy

17

doesn't judge so much on the time he thinks it'll take as the time he'd like it to take.'

He gave a wry grin. It was true. 'What did you make of Mortimer with that grey ponytail and a cardigan that looks like it was knitted for a seven-foot giant? It nearly came down to his knees.'

'I liked him. Living in a place like that all your life might make you a bit odd.'

'I'm not sure. I think maybe he likes the image. His eyes look alert enough to me. I suspect he doesn't miss much when he chooses.'

They were both silent again. Nathan reflected that they hardly ever agreed on anything.

'You know the best places to go then,' Hannah remarked. 'I've never been to Norfolk before.'

Nathan pulled a face. 'Not any more I don't. It's been years.'

He saw Hannah planning to respond and he guessed what she might ask next. He regretted ever mentioning his brother and those family holidays. He didn't want to talk about it.

'Carrie seems to know her stuff,' he said instead. 'I thought she was quite impressive.'

Hannah grinned. 'I'll bet. And it helps that she's pretty.'

'Is she?'

'Oh come on, don't pretend you hadn't noticed.'

'OK, yes, so I'd noticed. But I was more struck by something else. Didn't you see it? Something was bothering her.'

'What?'

'How should I know?' Nathan tried to find the best way to describe his impression of her. 'She looked edgy. Preoccupied. Maybe Mortimer isn't as easy-going a boss as you think he is.'

18

'You're imagining things.'

'I might have known you'd say that.'

'Maybe she's done something she shouldn't have and keeps thinking she'll be found out.'

Nathan shook his head. 'Nah. It wasn't guilt. It was more like she was scared or confused… Oh good, here comes our food.'

The conversation lagged and they never returned to it. But, going to bed that night, the young curator drifted back into Nathan's thoughts. Of course she was pretty. But it was the expression in her eyes that had stayed with him. Hunted, he realised, that was the word that described it. She looked hunted.

*

There were four oil paintings and eight drawings needing attention. On the Friday morning Hannah and Nathan picked up where they'd left off the previous afternoon, assessing the work involved, taking photographs and making notes. With their trunks open beside them, hinged vertically like a door, they had access to a wide range of equipment. The workroom was a good space: large and rectangular with two decent-sized tables and one west-facing window. Hannah had chosen the table nearest the window, claiming her greater need for natural light since she would have to colour-match any infill painting. They both had lamps in their kit but she wanted to take advantage of the daylight and, for once, Nathan didn't demur.

Hannah appreciated both the airiness of the room and its position. It was in a kind of no man's land, off the rear vestibule and away from the noise and bustle of the public rooms. And Mortimer had encouraged them to use the door under the staircase to access the family kitchen.

'Make yourself hot drinks when you want them. Netta

won't mind. She's our housekeeper and cook,' he'd added fondly. 'Been with us for years. Very accommodating. I'll introduce you just now.'

He hadn't introduced them – he'd probably forgotten as soon as he'd said it – but, half way through the morning, Hannah found her way to the kitchen and made coffee for Nathan and a mug of tea for herself. There was no sign of Netta and she took the drinks back to the workroom to find Carrie there, talking to Nathan. He was smiling idiotically back at her as if he'd just been promised his all-time dream holiday.

Carrie looked round, suddenly awkward.

'Oh, hi Hannah. I've just brought the keys for you.' She gestured towards a small ring of three keys, lying on Nathan's table. 'And I was asking if you could make sure you draw the curtains before you leave so no-one can see what's in here.'

'Sure.' Hannah set Nathan's mug of coffee down.

'Mortimer's kind of… well, he doesn't always consider security.'

Carrie produced a forced smile and slipped back through the door. Like a sylph, thought Hannah: insubstantial and soundless. It wasn't hard to see why Nathan liked her: she was charming and vulnerable with her floaty dresses, her pale skin and wistful expression. She was the sort of woman every man wanted to fuss over and protect. A perfect model for a Pre-Raphaelite painting.

'See,' said Nathan. 'Edgy.'

Hannah shrugged and regained her seat.

'Come on, it's hardly surprising that she worries about security. I mean, just look at what I've got here.' She gestured a hand to embrace the work put out for her. 'Perugino, Rubens, Bazille, Guardi. What about you?'

'Ottavio Leoni, Giovanni Battista Tiepolo, Turner, Ruskin, and many more.'

'Exactly. Quite a responsibility.'

'I suppose. She was just filling me in on the family. You know Mortimer's brother Toby that we met yesterday? The publicity man? He was married to Sidony, the woman organising the guides. They're divorced now. And that young woman in the office, Rose, is their daughter. And they all live here too. Cosy, huh?'

'Sounds like a recipe for trouble to me.'

By late that afternoon, they'd finished their assessments and, while Nathan faxed them through to Timothy from the office and made a call to order the mountboard he needed, Hannah took the opportunity to have a look around.

The front door was closed and the guide had gone. She picked up one of the house plans from the guide's welcome table, glanced at it and wandered into the library opposite. Two leather, wing-backed armchairs were angled towards a neat tiled fireplace, and glass-fronted bookshelves lined two of the walls. She turned to study a painting on the wall to her left, a stern-looking man with impressive mutton chop whiskers. The floor was carpeted and she didn't hear Mortimer coming to stand beside her.

'My grandfather, Edward Gyllam-Spence.'

Hannah smiled an acknowledgment. 'He looks... forbidding, if you don't mind me saying so.'

'I think you're right. A man of ambition. He knew what he wanted out of life and wasn't afraid to go in search of it. But a philanthropist too, though he didn't have the means he'd have liked with which to do it. Not like his own father.' He moved a couple of steps further along the wall. 'And this is *my* father, Henry. He tried to live up to his father's ideals. I suppose we all do.'

Hannah studied the picture only briefly. Like the first, it was a run of the mill portrait by a proficient but not exceptional

21

hand. She looked at Mortimer instead. He was studying the painting with a curious expression on his face which quickly evaporated when he realised he was being watched.

'Is everything all right, Hannah?'

'Fine, thank you. Nathan's in the office, faxing our first assessments to Timothy.'

'I see. Any special problems?'

'Nothing we can't sort out. Would you mind if I take a look around the collection?'

'No, no. In fact, let me show you. We've got the place to ourselves after all. Come next door. There's a couple of pictures in here I'd like you to see. By the way, I've just remembered where I've heard your name. You're not related to the artist Eric Dechansay by any chance?'

'He's my father.'

'Really? Lives in Paris I believe, yes? Quite a pedigree, my dear.'

He led the way into the drawing room and to a full-length, gilt-framed portrait of an elegant woman, her long dark hair fastened up on her head, a serene expression on her face.

'My great-grandmother, Cecilia. A handsome woman and a strong character.' Mortimer took another step or two. 'And here's her husband, my great-grandfather. Another Mortimer. Both painted by...'

'John Singer Sargent. Wonderful.'

He turned to look at her and smiled. 'Of course, you'd recognise the hand at a glance, I dare say.' He returned his gaze to the portrait. 'My great-grandfather believed he'd made it when he commissioned these portraits. But he never got a title, sadly, and that was what he really wanted.' He became pensive. 'That was sort of how the whole collection started. My wealthy forebears wanted to be accepted into polite society. They wanted recognition. Trade and fortune weren't

22

considered enough, you see.'

'And you,' said Hannah, 'would you like a title?'

'Me? No.' He quickly laughed the suggestion off then regarded her shrewdly. As if deciding he had maybe already said too much, he took her arm. 'Come with me, there's a rather fine Holbein over here which you might like. It's only small but excellent, I think.'

He proceeded to take her on a tour of the rooms, pointing out features of which he was particularly proud. As he did so he became someone else, she felt, less personal and more of a performer, a ringmaster perhaps presenting his best acts to an expectant public. In the exhibition room he showed her a Friedrich, a Fantin-Latour, a Watteau and a Rossetti, as well as the drawings currently on display on a table under glass and a number of small bronze figurines. He pointed out the original seventeenth century oak wall panelling and winked when he told her that some of the rooms had a secret compartment hidden behind it. The kitchen, pantry and utility rooms had been kept, he said, as they were in Victorian times. Then he took her upstairs. All the rooms, up and down, housed a range of fine wooden furniture of different eras: Georgian, Late Regency and Victorian.

They returned to the main hallway just as a man of perhaps thirty or thirty-two came out of the office, shrugging on his coat. He had a fair complexion and sandy hair, already thinning at the front, and he was frowning, his mouth set in a tight, impatient line. He looked surprised to see them and stopped short.

'Ah Alan,' said Mortimer. 'You weren't around yesterday when I introduced our restorers. This is Miss Dechansay.'

'Hannah,' she corrected, and considered offering the man her hand but something in his manner stopped her.

'Alan organises all our events: weddings, celebrations of

one kind or another, and coordinates school trips. That sort of thing.'

Alan nodded at her, barely changing expression, but his eyes examined her intrusively. 'Yes, I've just met your colleague. I hope you won't find it too difficult working here. We're quite a close-knit unit, aren't we?' He embraced Mortimer with a look. 'Used to our own little routines. Anyway, I'm running late. Sorry, must go.'

He walked briskly away and through the door to the rear vestibule.

'Well, yes…' agreed Mortimer. '…we aren't…'

'I see we're all working late tonight.' Sidony joined them from the office. 'Excuse me for butting in. Mortimer, Rose is going to the post. Have you got any letters waiting to go?'

He hesitated. 'Do you know, I think I might have.'

'I'll be off then,' said Hannah. 'Thanks for the tour.'

She found Carrie in the workroom again, installed in her chair, while Nathan leaned against his work table, arms folded. They stopped talking as she came in and Carrie jumped up.

'I'm in your place.'

'It's not a problem. I was just going to get my bag and go. I'll probably start work in the morning, get the ball rolling, if that's all right?'

'Of course.' Carrie looked surprised. 'I don't usually work weekends but the house will be open as usual.'

'Hannah's a workaholic.' Nathan cast her an amused glance. 'Though it might be a good idea to get started.'

He's trying to impress her, thought Hannah. Or just annoy me.

'I should be going too,' Carrie said. 'Don't forget to lock the door when you leave.'

Nathan offered her a quick smile as she left.

'Getting quite pally,' remarked Hannah.

24

Nathan shrugged. 'Just talking. Where have you been?'

'Mortimer's been showing me round, telling me about his grand forebears. He even told me about his model train set-up. He's got a den in the garden with it in. I've been invited to take a look some time.'

'Now who's getting pally? Did he offer to show you his etchings too?'

'Oh come on, it wasn't like that.' She grabbed her shoulder bag from the back of the chair. 'In any case, he's old enough to be my father.'

Nathan grinned but she ignored him and left him to do the locking up.

*

Carrie paused by the front gate of her rented cottage and looked back over the road to the river. The cottage was a small semi-detached dwelling on the edge of the village, adjacent to a large boatyard. Beyond the two cottages, the road wound inland and a narrow private lane gave access to three or four other properties further along the river: grand houses with large gardens and waterside frontage. Carrie thought of the two little cottages huddled side by side as the poor relations but didn't care. Lane End No 1 was all she needed at the moment, precious for being all her own space.

A boat motored past, a cruiser she had been told it was called, but there wasn't much traffic on the river yet. 'Wait till the season starts,' her neighbour, an elderly widow called Joan, had told her. 'Then you'll see the difference.' On the far side of the water lay a nature reserve where footpaths wound between stands of trees, round marshy ground and swathes of reedbeds, all hugging the banks of a lake known as Ranling Broad. Now, in the weak late afternoon sunshine, a variety of bird calls piped and whistled to her on the breeze. It was all new to Carrie, both fascinating and at times rather eerie; she was a city girl.

She turned back to the house and opened the gate. Joan was standing at the window next door as usual. She appeared to spend much of her life in silent watching. She waved now and Carrie lifted a hand in acknowledgment as she walked up the path. A letter was waiting for her, dangling by one trapped corner from the letter box in the front door. At a glance she could tell it was from Nigel, and she put it down on the side and put the kettle on. She needed to soothe the day out of her system before she could face that.

It wasn't until the mug of tea was half drunk that she plucked up the courage to read the letter. It was like so many that had gone before.

Darling Carrie,

I miss you. I know I've done some stupid things but I never wanted to hurt you. I've changed, please believe me. There is no-one else, only you. There never was. I don't know what I was thinking but the affair didn't mean anything. It wasn't even an affair – that makes it sound more serious than it was. It was a fling, started in a moment of stupidity and weakness – my vanity, I suppose, puffed up by her attention. Perhaps it was insecurity, I don't know, but I've learned my lesson now. It didn't make me feel better, only worse.

So I'll say it again – there is only you in my life. This separation was supposed to be a trial. Well, it's proved to me what's important and I know I want to be with you. Please say you feel the same way and come back. It'll be different this time. I promise. Get in touch, please?

With <u>all</u> my love,
Nigel

26

Carrie put the letter down and gave a long, shuddering sigh. She felt tears on her cheeks and brushed them away with the back of her fingers. She wanted to believe him but finding out about his affair had rocked her world too violently and it still hadn't come back to rest. How do you believe someone who has repeatedly lied to you? How do you get the trust back? Is it even possible? She kept asking herself the same questions but never came up with the answers.

She finished her tea and sat, a knot of scenes from the past twisting through her mind. She got up with a sudden need to respond, found some letter paper and sat down again to write.

Dear Nigel,

She stared at the paper for several minutes. How to explain how she felt? She didn't even know herself, it was so confused and raw, such a mixture of longing and hurt and weariness. Perhaps she should just tell him to stop. Stop these constant entreaties. Leave her alone. But was that what she wanted?

She threw the pen down. She didn't know. She was desperate to be allowed to embrace this fresh start but a small part of her did still want to go back to him and try to recapture their early days together. Nigel used to be the person she'd go to when something bothered her. He was good at listening, at helping her to get things in proportion. Like this thing with the intruder in the storeroom. If she could only talk to him about it, see what he thought, just get it out there and off her chest.

It had rattled her. Ever since she'd half expected someone to approach her about it, to explain, or maybe to warn her not to mention it. They must have known that she was the person in the workroom next door – it was her space. It was of no importance, they might have said, and she would have been reassured. Maybe. But no-one had said anything which made it feel more ominous. She had the sensation that she was being watched, tested to see if she would toe the line and keep mum about it.

On the Wednesday she had spent a long time looking through the collection in the storeroom and it had only confirmed her suspicions. She ought to tell someone but didn't know who. Who could she trust? Nathan came into her mind. She hardly knew him, but she had chatted to him a couple of times already and he'd been easy to talk to. It had started with a shared interest in Old Master drawings and gone on from there. She was surprised and a little embarrassed that she'd already told him about Nigel's affair, about her separation and how nervous she'd been starting this new job. Hannah, on the other hand, with that spiky hair, quick manner and those big, inquisitive eyes, she was less sure of.

She grabbed a chocolate bar, put on jeans and a pair of trainers, and set off for the nearby bridge which gave access to the reserve. Joan had told her about a rare bird called a crane, which had recently been seen there. It danced apparently – some sort of courtship ritual that even the young ones practiced as they were growing up. It's a wonderful thing to see, Joan said. So Carrie had looked them up and found out that cranes mated for life and were a symbol of longevity. She had been quite taken with the idea of seeing one and had started going over to the reserve after work each day. It was a new routine, a way of switching off and doing something different – part of this fresh new start she was determined to have.

As she walked, she resolved to speak to Nathan alone when the opportunity next presented. She would tell him about the intruder and canvas his opinion. He could be trusted, she decided, and, for the first time in days, she felt a spark of optimism.

Chapter 3

The first few days Hannah and Nathan worked at the manor were uneventful. Nathan started work on a sheet of drawings by John Ruskin, nature studies of different leaf forms in graphite on white wove paper. It was one of the more straight-forward jobs waiting for him, requiring the image's removal from an old soiled mount. The tape used to attach the sheet to the mount was acidic and had caused the paper to stain and discolour, though fortunately the sketches weren't yet affected. Hannah had chosen a less problematic piece to start with too, the Frédéric Bazille, a view in oils of Montmartre in Paris, which she'd said simply needed a good clean.

They settled into a routine of sorts, carefully keeping to their own personal space. They had worked in the same room at times back at the Oxford workshops but not this closely. This more intimate environment needed boundaries, though Hannah always worked with a personal cassette player pumping music in her ears anyway; she said it blocked out distractions and helped her concentrate. Nathan glanced across at her sometimes. She would be nodding her head to some unheard beat or rhythmically waving a hand while pausing to lean away and study the painting as a whole.

She was a curious woman. She didn't give much of herself away which was unusual in his experience. Her work was good and he liked that, liked her passion for it too. After they'd been together in Provence the previous summer, he'd thought he'd started to get a handle on her but now, after more than a year working in the same place off and on, he still didn't feel he knew her. Vivacious and smart – with large blue eyes – she was admittedly attractive in a careless 'like me or lump me' kind of way. But she was bloody stubborn, self-sufficient *and* pugnacious. He'd have bet good money – if he'd had any – that she didn't play nicely with the other children when she was a kid. Or maybe he brought out the worst in her. His ex-fiancée used to accuse him of that.

The mountboard Nathan had ordered, five large sheets of it, arrived on the Thursday morning, a week after their arrival. Rose came down to the workroom to tell him that it was in the office and that it needed removing because it was in the way. She said it nicely. In fact, she came too close for comfort to say it, lingering and smiling up at him. And she offered to help him move it but he said he was fine, thanks.

He manoeuvred it back through the door to the rear vestibule and into the workroom, propping it up against the wall. Hannah looked up.

'Good timing,' he remarked. 'I'm about ready to cut a new mount.'

She frowned and pulled her earpieces out. 'Sorry?'

'Good timing,' he repeated, with a nod to the packaged mountboard. 'Do you want a drink?'

'Please. Tea.' She offered the suggestion of a distracted smile and turned back to the painting on her foldaway easel.

Carrie was in the kitchen, tipping milk into a mug of coffee, when he walked in. Their paths hadn't crossed for a few days.

'Oh hi.' Her expression looked awkward or perhaps anxious. 'How's everything?'

'Fine thanks. I've managed to get the mount and tape off

that Ruskin. And the adhesive that was left behind too. That was the hardest part. A bit of cleaning too.'

He was talking too much, filling the silence. She probably didn't want to know any of this. In fact, she looked embarrassed, perhaps regretting telling him so much about herself the other day.

Netta, the housekeeper, bustled in. She was in her fifties, a round-faced, round-bodied, genial woman who had taken Hannah and Nathan's occasional visits to the kitchen in her stride, even offering them biscuits to have with their drinks and making them sandwiches for lunch.

'Well, hello. Busy in here today, isn't it?' she said comfortably, glancing from one to the other.

'I'm just going actually.' Carrie raised her mug in explanation of her presence, offered a tentative smile, and left.

'And I'm here to make some drinks.' Nathan reached for the kettle. 'Can I make you one, Netta?'

'No, no, but thank you for asking.' She leaned against the units beyond him, looking towards the door which Carrie had left slightly ajar, and dropped her voice. 'Nice girl but I'm not sure she's finding it easy to fit in here. Bit of an outsider, you see.'

Nathan switched the kettle on and prepared two mugs, putting a spoonful of coffee in one and a teabag in the other.

'What makes you say that?'

'Well, you know, she's from London, isn't she, and it's a very different world here. Country people are never in quite such a hurry.' She smiled knowingly. 'I dare say you're a city boy too so maybe you don't know what I mean.'

'No, I think I do. I spent a lot of time round here when I was a boy.'

'Did you indeed? How lovely. Well, I think it's all a bit strange for Carrie. And she's got lots of new ideas for the manor. This old place has been run the same way for donkey's years and it's worked perfectly fine. Why change it now is what I say. It upsets people.'

The kettle boiled and Nathan dispensed the hot water into the mugs.

'Has someone been complaining about her then?'

Netta grunted with an ambiguous shake of the head. 'She is pretty though,' she conceded as he added a drop of milk to the mugs. 'And quiet. She means well, I'm sure.'

'Yes, I'm sure she does.'

He smiled a farewell and left. Rose was walking briskly back up the long private hallway which led to the office at the front. She'd been listening outside; he was convinced of it. Back in the workroom, he carefully shut the door, put Hannah's mug of tea down on the work table beside her, then perched on the edge of the table, carefully avoiding her equipment. Hannah thanked him, pulled the earpieces out again, and switched off the stereo. He let his gaze roam over the painting she was cleaning and took a sip of coffee.

Hannah was frowning at him. 'Everything all right?'

'Hm, maybe. Have you noticed how Rose always seems to be watching and listening?'

'She certainly watches you quite a bit. I think maybe she's smitten.'

'Don't make me laugh.'

'It's true. There's no accounting for taste.'

'Very funny. I saw Carrie in the kitchen. I thought perhaps she wanted to talk but Netta came in and she couldn't leave fast enough. It seems she might not be popular in some quarters here.'

'What makes you say that?'

'Netta described her as an outsider. Thinks she wants to change things too much. I sensed undercurrents. I feel kind of sorry for her. She's recently separated, you know – her husband cheated on her – and she's trying to make a fresh start. It can't be easy.'

'No, it can't. Poor thing.' Hannah picked up her mug and took a thoughtful drink of tea. 'But she is an outsider, isn't she? Like we are at the inn. Haven't you noticed how people stop talking and look at us when we go in? It probably takes years in a place like this to be accepted as a local.'

'I suppose so. But we won't stick out so much when it gets busier. There are already more boats mooring up now than when we arrived. The river'll be teeming with them in a week or two. We should do that while we're here: hire a boat.'

Hannah looked at him as if he'd finally lost his senses. 'We should? Do you know how to manage a boat?'

'Of course. More or less. I told you: we used to do it all the time when we were kids. Dad let us steer.' He grinned. 'Well, sometimes.'

'Nathan, you keep talking about your brother but you've never told me how he came to disappear. I mean, did he…?'

'That's because I don't know,' he said abruptly. 'People always ask that but if you're not living with someone, how do you know what's going on? They don't reply when you ring one day. So you try again the next. And the next. Nothing. And then you realise that something's wrong. That was it. He'd disappeared. Eleven years, twelve coming up and still nothing. End of story.'

He pulled away from the table and walked to the window. It offered a view over a cobbled yard with a huddle of potted plants near the farthest wall. He didn't really see it.

'Did you know that tens of thousands of people go missing every year and thousands of them never show up again. Every year. So where do they all go? How can you slip through the cracks like that? More to the point, how can you do that to your family?' He turned back. 'You see, that's why I don't talk about it. What is there to say? Anyway, I've got work to do.'

He felt her eyes on him as he took his coffee back to his own work station. He knew he'd overreacted. He was the one who had started the conversation about his family and Hannah was bound to want to know what had happened. But Sam was a running sore that Nathan kept trying to cover over. Unsuccessfully. He didn't need reminding.

*

Several days passed before Carrie was able to speak to Nathan alone. There had been earlier opportunities, odd moments when she had seen him in the passageway or wandering round the public rooms on a break one day, studying the displays. She'd thought the opportunity had come early in the week when he came into the kitchen, but then Netta had appeared and she needed more than a snatched minute. She needed time to explain and the privacy to do it when there was no-one else around.

It was the end of the afternoon on the following Thursday when she saw him alone again. The front door had been closed to the public and the guides had gone, leaving the manor in that strange limbo, like a small town after the fair has passed through. She saw Nathan wandering into the exhibition room and casually followed him. He flipped back the fabric cloth over a glazed cabinet to look inside and she slipped in alongside him. He was studying a drawing by Bellini and looked up in surprise, then smiled.

'Hi Carrie. All right?'

'Yes, fine. You?'

'OK, thanks.'

'Good… good. Look…' She glanced round. There was

no-one else in the room but she wasn't sure who was still about, who might be listening. Better to be out of the house to do this. She flashed him what she hoped was an innocent smile. 'Is Hannah with you?'

'Hannah? No, she's gone. We came in separate cars today. She was feeling a bit groggy today. Why? Did you want her?'

'No, no. Good. I mean… I'm sorry she's not well. Are you leaving in a minute? Could I walk with you to your car? There were a couple of things I wanted to discuss with you.'

'Of course.' His eyes narrowed as the strangeness of the request sank in. He dropped his voice. 'Are you sure you're all right?'

'Yes.'

'OK.' He flipped the cloth back over the display. 'Come on then.'

They walked out into the hallway just as Alan emerged from the office.

'Carrie?' He glanced between them but barely acknowledged Nathan. 'I thought I heard your voice. I've got a school on the phone. They want to book a tour with one of your talks. Come and have a look at the calendar, will you?'

She went into the office with him and Nathan followed.

Rose was at her desk and her gaze flicked between Carrie and Nathan. Her lip curled.

'Well, well. Going to catch up on some evening homework together?' she enquired.

'I was just asking Nathan's advice about something…' said Carrie, a little too quickly. '…that is, the way we should be storing the drawings.'

Even to her own ears, it sounded fake and she felt her cheeks flush. She turned away and studied the calendar then fixed up possible dates with Alan. She heard Nathan asking Rose if she could recommend any restaurants in the area that he could try.

'Nothing too pricey, mind. We don't get paid that much.'

'The Dog and Duck's good, over at Shepingham,' said Sidony, who had come in behind them. 'They do a great roast on a Sunday and they're quite reasonable.' She gave Nathan a puzzled smile. 'But surely you get paid expenses?'

'Let's just say they're kept on a tight rein.' Nathan raised his eyebrows. 'You haven't met our boss.'

'If your conditions aren't good enough, you could always come and be a room guide here. The last one we took on hasn't got a clue. I can't see him lasting.'

'I'll bear it in mind.'

Mortimer poked his head round the rear door of the office and looked surprised to see them. 'Are you all here for a reason?'

'No Mortimer.' Sid produced a cherubic smile. 'No reason. We just love our work so much.'

'And we were just going.' Nathan looked back at Carrie. 'All done? We can discuss those drawings on the way to the car.'

They left the house in silence. Carrie glanced back in the half-light towards the rear door.

'They know there's something going on,' she murmured.

'Why? What is going on?'

She didn't immediately reply and they turned, following the path as it weaved between a shrubbery and the beginnings of a fruit orchard.

'That's what I need to talk to you about. You see, I'm new here and I don't know anyone, no-one I can risk confiding in, that is. It's a tricky thing, you see. I mean, I don't want to make accusations if I'm wrong. But I don't think I am wrong.'

She stopped walking suddenly, aware that she was rambling and avoiding the issue, sounding foolish.

36

Nathan stopped too and looked at her earnestly. 'You can tell me.'

She looked round but could see no-one. Even so, she dropped her voice.

'It was more than two weeks ago, just before you arrived. I was late finishing work. I'd been checking on a painting I'd hung that day and I went back to the workroom. I could hear a noise but thought I was just imagining it then I dropped my keys and the noise stopped. Someone was in the storeroom next door.'

'Who was it?'

'Well, that's the thing: I don't know. I didn't see him.' She glanced round again. 'Can we keep moving?'

'Of course. But you think it was a man?'

'I don't know. By the time I went round to look there was no-one there but the door was ajar. I always lock it. I'd locked it earlier that afternoon after replacing the picture I'd taken down. Someone had been in and hurried out when they heard me.'

Toby suddenly appeared in front of them, coming round another stand of shrubs from the parking area. Carrie visibly jumped and barely managed a response to his greeting.

'Night,' she heard Nathan say.

They reached her car and she looked round.

'Do you think Toby heard me?' she whispered.

'No, he couldn't have. Look, Carrie, there's probably a really innocent explanation. Why don't you tell Mortimer about this?'

'I don't know what to do. Suppose it was one of the family? I'm the outsider here. I mean, it could have been Alan but he's more one of them than I am. It must have been someone with access to the key that's kept in the office. And no-one's said anything about it but, if it was innocent, why be so furtive? The thing is, I've been going through the collection and there's definitely something wrong. Some of the drawings...' She shook her head, clearly distracted. 'And there's something else...'

They could hear footsteps coming towards them from the house.

'That'll be Alan,' she said breathlessly. 'Going back to his cottage. It's down that path there, past the trees. Quick, can we meet up at the weekend, away from here? Then we can talk properly.'

'Sure. What about The Kings Arms in Ramsby? Twelve o'clock on Saturday.'

'Yes. Don't tell anyone what I said,' she hissed.

She got in her car and had to sit a minute to let the hammering of her heart settle down before she could start the engine and leave. But at least she'd spoken to Nathan. He'd know what she should do.

*

But Nathan didn't know what to think. Carrie was obviously frightened of something or of someone. He hardly knew her and yet she had decided to confide in him which was both touching and a little unsettling. What did she expect him to do? Her story about the person in the storeroom was certainly odd but there was likely to be a rational explanation. Perhaps she was making something out of nothing. Perhaps the recent break-up of her marriage had played on her mind too much. It was hard to imagine something sinister going on at Ranling Manor, though they were a curious bunch of people he had to admit. Still he liked Carrie and he was happy to meet up with her. She'd probably feel better just for talking about it and realise she was making a mountain out of a molehill.

He chose not to tell Hannah about the planned meeting.

He knew exactly what she'd say. Instead he told her he planned to go exploring old haunts on the Saturday while Hannah said she was going to Norwich. In the end they didn't even see each other at breakfast.

He arrived at The Kings Arms just before twelve and stood outside for a good quarter of an hour. When Carrie didn't appear, he went inside but there was no sign of her there either. He found a table by the window looking out over the front car park and entrance, got himself a half of draught beer and waited, checking his watch every few minutes. At twelve forty he ordered a sandwich to keep himself going and waited again, making excuses for why she might be late. Still she didn't come.

By one forty-five he was sure she wasn't coming and left. Maybe she'd had second thoughts, had perhaps decided she was overreacting and didn't want to pursue it. Maybe she felt embarrassed. Or perhaps she'd been taken ill and not felt up to coming. She could have rung the pub to say so but might have fallen asleep and forgotten. There were a lot of maybes. And he didn't know where she lived, nor her phone number and, even if he did, wasn't convinced he'd be chasing her about it. It wasn't the first time he'd been stood up. He'd see her on the Monday and clear the air with her.

And yet he felt uneasy.

On the Sunday, challenged by Hannah about his pre-occupied behaviour at breakfast, he was tempted to tell her but passed it off. Carrie had warned him against involving anyone else and it was probably nothing anyway.

But Carrie wasn't in work on the Monday morning and, after looking for her in vain, Nathan ended up in the office.

'She just hasn't turned up,' Rose said dismissively. 'Must have overslept.' She regarded him accusingly. 'Why do you want her?'

'Work stuff,' he said, and returned to the workroom.

When Carrie didn't materialise by mid-morning Rose was told to ring her home phone number. There was no reply. At Mortimer's insistence, Toby drove into the village to check on her but there was no response to his ring on the doorbell and no sign of any activity at the house. Joan, the next-door neighbour, informed him that she hadn't seen Carrie since the Friday. She had come home slightly earlier than usual and had gone out again soon after.

'I was out the front, brushing the path. She said she was going for a walk. Wanted to clear her head, she said. I was watching the telly after that and didn't see her come back. You don't think something's happened to her, do you? It's strange I haven't seen her all weekend. Maybe she's been taken ill in there.'

Mortimer called the police.

It was fortunate that the manor was closed to the public, Mortimer told his senior staff. He summoned them all to the office in the afternoon, including Hannah and Nathan, to tell them that the police had broken into Carrie's house but that she wasn't there and didn't appear to have been there for a couple of days. Her bed had not been slept in.

'They're making enquiries,' he said. 'But it's very worrying. Apparently her car is still parked at the back and her bag and personal things are still in the house. So if anyone has any information about her since she was here on Friday, they'd like to speak to you. Someone will be here shortly to interview us.'

There were grumblings and asides. Hannah and Nathan looked at each other, then withdrew to the workroom.

'What can have happened to her?' said Hannah.

Nathan took a moment to check no-one was outside the door and closed it firmly again. He turned to face Hannah.

'I'm worried. I was supposed to meet her on Saturday lunch-time but she didn't turn up. I waited for a while but she never came and I heard nothing.'

'You didn't tell me you had a date.'

'It wasn't a date. It was…' He shook his head. 'I don't know what it was. We fixed it up on the Thursday.' He hesitated but, for all that Hannah drove him crazy, he thought he could trust her. So he told her the little he knew of Carrie's concerns about the intruder. 'She didn't want to talk about it here and suggested meeting somewhere else. But it never happened.'

'You'd better tell the police.'

'I will. But there's not much to tell.' He paused. 'She wasn't happy.'

'Maybe she's gone back to her husband. Just left, had enough.'

'You heard Mortimer. Her things are still at the house. Her car hasn't gone. Anyway, I don't think she was ready to go back. If ever.' He thumped an angry hand against the wall by the door. 'You see, someone else has just disappeared. Gone.'

They got back to work but the atmosphere was thick with unspoken questions and concern. Nathan struggled to concentrate. When the policewoman came to see them, he waited until he could speak to her privately then told her about the missed rendezvous and about Carrie's account of the intruder who might not have been an intruder. The story seemed more far-fetched in the telling and, while the policewoman listened attentively, he wasn't sure she believed it.

'And have you any idea where she might have gone?' she asked. 'Did she seem distressed in any way?'

'Well, yes, she seemed anxious. Of course she would.'

'Because you say she was scared?'

41

'Yes.'

'Did she say who she was scared of?'

'No. She didn't say it; it was just my impression.'

'I see. Was she an anxious sort of person normally, would you say?'

'I don't know. I only met her for the first time the week before last.'

The policewoman nodded, expressionless. 'She recently separated from her husband. Did she seem depressed, would you say?'

'I don't know. No, I don't think so.'

'Well, thank you for your help, Mr Bright.' She nodded and left.

It had been a frustrating conversation. He sensed more behind the non-committal words than she was prepared to say.

The police examined the contents of Carrie's house, made house to house enquiries, and began a search for her in the locality. It wasn't an easy place to search. The reserve on the other side of the river was watery and wild, the network of footpaths winding through trees and shrubby ground with streams and standing water seemingly at every turn. Then there was Ranling Broad itself, accessed from the river by a narrow canal and popular with the boating community. But it was a large body of water to search.

And beyond all that were fields and ditches and woods. East Ranling was just a pimple of human development among miles of farmland and wild countryside. She could have been anywhere, or perhaps, a police officer was heard to say lugubriously, she had gone off with someone and was miles away.

But on the following Thursday afternoon they found her body, caught up in weed and debris at the side of Ranling Broad. She had been dead for days.

42

Chapter 4

In Mortimer's huge shed, deep within the confines of the private gardens and masked by a run of copper beech hedging, he sat at his work table, meticulously painting the woodwork on the outside of a tiny model shop. It was a greengrocer's with an inset glazed entry door and, in front of the shop window, a display rack of fruit and vegetables. The fruit and vegetables were going to be tricky and time-consuming to do but he preferred to buy his scenery models naked, so to speak. The activity and satisfaction of painting them pleased him. Once upon a time he'd been passionate about producing his own art – watercolours and sketches – but these days his art materials were relegated to a corner of his den and painting scenery was his favourite way of switching off.

There was a firm double rap on the shed door and he looked up, glancing at the clock on the wall: it was six-thirty on the Friday. Whatever the time, he would answer that knock; he knew it well. He put the model and the paintbrush down and walked to the door, turned the key and let Sid in, locking it again behind her. Mortimer didn't want just anyone to be able to wander into his den at will.

Sid didn't say anything. She walked across to his work table, glanced at what he was doing, then sat in one of the battered old armchairs nearby and looked at him.

'So...' she said as he came across to join her. '...you're

hiding away in here.'

'I'm not hiding. I always come over here.'

'These aren't normal times.'

He turned away, staring over towards the table and his half-painted model. 'I can think better in here. Anyway what else is there for me to do?'

'And has your thinking brought forth any fruit?'

He didn't answer. He doubted if she expected him to. He had known Sidony since they were both young, forty years and more. Sidony Pettiver was the only daughter of a well-to-do local family. Her older brother had been one of Mortimer's best friends. As teenagers they had all gone to the same social events, all very county and privileged, except that none of those families had had the wealth they'd once enjoyed and the war had left no-one unscathed. The world had changed. Still, for a brief time, smitten, Mortimer had dated Sidony. Then it had all gone wrong and she'd married Toby instead.

He looked back at her. 'Coffee?'

Without waiting for a reply he picked up the kettle and took it to the sink in the corner. Sid always drank coffee with a drop of milk and two sweeteners, had done for years. She carried the sweeteners around with her. He made himself one too and returned to the table. Sid was watching him with that shrewd, eye-narrowed look he knew so well as if she were trying to read his mind. He hoped she couldn't. Damn it, he never knew what she was thinking, not the private stuff.

He put her mug of coffee – with the teaspoon still in it – down on the little coffee table in front of her and took the seat opposite.

'That detective they sent from Norwich…' He fixed her with a look. 'He's asking so many questions. Why should any of us know anything about it?'

'It's his job.' Sid tapped two sweeteners into her coffee

44

and stirred it round. 'Routine stuff, I imagine. Carrie spent a lot of time here after all. Hardly knew anyone else, I don't think.' Sid frowned. 'To be honest, I don't really know who she knew. I feel bad that I didn't take more trouble to get to know her.'

'None of us did. It's not your fault and no-one knows what happened. That Chief Inspector Crayford said they'd know more when the post-mortem results came through. Then there'll be *more* questions. They're waiting on a time of death.'

Sid didn't reply and he watched her face. She looked unusually pensive. Where was the usual forthright woman who never hesitated to tell him how he should run the manor, or whose plain speaking often caused issues with the house guides? Sid never suffered fools – or lazy people – gladly.

'Have you any idea what might have happened?' he ventured.

'None.' She examined his face again. 'You?'

'No. An accident, I assume.' He picked up his coffee and took a sip, then sat back, still with the mug in his hands. 'But now we have to stay closed tomorrow and probably beyond while they continue to poke about and ask questions,' he added peevishly. 'Now. Right after Easter. Anyone would think it had happened here.'

'You're upset,' stated Sid.

'Of course I'm upset,' he said savagely. 'She was a nice woman. Young. Smart. Pretty. It's such a waste. I never thought...'

He stopped abruptly. He'd never been involved in a police investigation before and he was rattled. That they should have come to this. Desperate to distract himself, he put the coffee down and got up to survey his half-painted model and the paints on his table, looking for potential fruit and vegetable colours. He could mix the subtler colours as necessary.

'I think your little speech to the staff this morning was good,' Sid said reassuringly. She took a mouthful of coffee. 'They need your guidance at a time like this. Especially having to pass through those television crews and reporters camped out by the gates.'

'I asked them to be discreet.' Mortimer suddenly turned and looked her full in the face. 'Are they being? You have your ear to the ground more than me. Are they behaving themselves? We don't want any scandal and gossip. The phone calls I've had to field from the press – my God Sid, it's not the sort of publicity we need.'

'They're behaving fine, considering Rose has been flirting with that detective sergeant, but she always does. I don't think she even realises she's doing it.'

'You really should take that girl in hand.'

'You think I haven't tried?' she cried. 'It's Toby's fault. He always spoilt her. And she's silly about men. She just cannot grasp the idea that the more she throws herself at them, the more they back off.'

Mortimer grunted. 'And what about those two conservators? The inspector wasn't saying much. A bit cryptic I thought, but I got the impression that the man – what's his name?'

'Nathan.'

'Yes, him. That he and Carrie had become friendly. Do you think he's said anything?'

'You mean you think he knows something?'

'I don't know.' His voice rose. 'I don't know. Maybe he's involved.'

Sidony nodded thoughtfully. 'I must say, Carrie didn't seem to quite fit in here.'

They looked at each other a long moment. He returned to

46

his seat and they both drank their coffee. Sid glanced over at the railway circuits laid out on the fixed trestle tables across the room. Two trains were endlessly circling on different tracks, occasionally running side by side or crossing over each other on flyovers amid an idyllic and totally imagined countryside setting.

'So where are you going to put that little shop?' she asked as if the previous conversation had never taken place.

*

It was a different group of police officers now. The female officer Nathan had spoken to when Carrie first went missing was no longer around. A specialist detective unit from Norwich had descended on them instead to deal with her unexplained death. Having made some preliminary enquiries on the Friday, going over ground that the first officers had already covered, they returned on the Saturday and Chief Inspector Crayford installed himself in the library behind the old, leather-covered desk, and interviewed each of the house staff in turn. His sergeant, a younger man with a polite manner but a steely gaze was sitting at a slight remove, taking notes.

Nathan and Hannah had been asked to stay available and had come in and installed themselves in the workroom as usual. It was the middle of the afternoon by the time the inspector spoke to Nathan. A tall, thin man in his forties with a fast-receding hairline, he looked jaded.

'I gather you don't usually work here, Mr Bright. You work for a specialist restoration company, is that right?'

'Yes. Blandish Fine Art Conservation. Hannah – Miss Dechansay – and I are only here to do some restoration work on a few art works in the manor's collection.'

The inspector referred to his notebook.

'And I see that when you spoke to one of our colleagues,

you suggested Carrie Judd was apprehensive about something.'

'Yes. She'd heard someone acting suspiciously in the storeroom next to where she worked. It was after work hours and she'd locked that room up as usual.'

'The room where the items not currently exhibited are kept?'

'Yes.'

'Did she mention it to Mr Gyllam-Spence?'

'No. She felt awkward.' Nathan shrugged. 'In case it was one of the family.'

'Acting suspiciously in their own home? Did that make sense to you?'

'I don't know. Look, the thing is…' Nathan hesitated. '…when she checked out the storeroom afterwards she said something was wrong.'

'Something was wrong? That's rather vague. Did she say what?'

'No. I was supposed to meet her on the Saturday to talk about it but she never arrived.'

The inspector nodded in that way some police officers did, as if you might be telling the truth, or then again, you might not.

'So how well did you know her? Was there some romantic attachment between you?'

'No. I hardly knew her.'

'But she confided in you?'

'She… I think it was because we'd spent some time talking about the drawings I was going to work on.' It sounded lame, he knew. Nathan couldn't really explain it himself. That was the best he could do.

'I see. You said previously that she seemed particularly anxious.' He waited.

Was that a question? thought Nathan. 'Yes. Well, perhaps confused.'

'Confused? I see. Depressed, do you think?'

'No.'

'You seem very sure. Did she talk to you about her husband?'

'Only to say they'd split up.'

'So when did you see her last?'

'On the Friday, I saw her around the house a couple of times, but not to speak to. Hannah and I work at the back in the room Carrie generally used.'

He nodded. 'And when did you make this arrangement to meet?'

'On the Thursday.'

'Did she have any friction with anyone recently that you know?

'I don't know but I doubt it: she was easy to work with.'

'And where were you on the Friday evening, Mr Bright?'

Nathan frowned at the suddenness of the question. It wasn't one he'd been expecting.

'In the village. Hannah and I ate at The Boatman. We're staying there for the duration.'

'You were together all evening?'

'Yes. Till bedtime.'

'Did you go out again later?'

'No. I went to my room and slept.'

The inspector closed his notebook. 'Well thank you for your help, sir. You won't be going anywhere for the time being, I trust?'

'No, I've got a pile of drawings to work on.'

*

Hannah looked up as Nathan opened the door of the workroom

and walked in, carefully closing the door behind him. For once she'd not put the cassette player on, wanting to be aware of what was going on around her. Too unsettled.

'I think I'm under suspicion,' Nathan said tersely and slumped into his chair.

'Suspicion of what?'

He shrugged. 'Doing something terrible to Carrie, I imagine.' He snorted. 'Me. They probably think the story about Carrie's concerns was just me trying to cover my tracks.' He sighed. 'It sounded pretty feeble to me to be honest. I don't damn well know anything. Anyway, they want you next. They're in the library.'

'Is there anything I should know?'

He shook his head. 'Just answer what they ask. Keep it simple. If you're not careful you end up saying things in a way you don't mean.'

Hannah walked to the library in some trepidation. The door was open when she got there and the sergeant was standing in the hall, waiting for her.

'I'm Sergeant Harris, Miss. In here please.' He indicated the chair opposite the desk.

'Miss Dechansay.' The inspector looked up from the papers in front of him and observed her. She saw him take in her spiky hair, the leggings and the dusty, paint-dabbed overshirt she was wearing. 'Just a few questions. Perhaps you can help us get a picture of Carrie Judd. You work with Mr Bright and you've been here...' He glanced at his notebook. '...three weeks now?'

'Just over.'

'Had you met Miss Judd previously anywhere?'

'No.'

'You did both inhabit the art world though and I under-stand it's a small one. Everyone knows all the other players.'

'Not all of them.'

He nodded, just the once.

'And your relationship with Nathan Bright?'

She frowned. 'He's my colleague.'

'There's no romantic entanglement?'

She almost laughed. 'No. He's my colleague. Work is work. We usually work alone but he's had a lot of experience with works on paper. I mostly work with canvas and panel paintings. That's why we're here together.'

'I see. Did you think that Mr Bright had an attachment to Carrie Judd?'

'He'd hardly known her any time.'

'Attachments can form quite quickly.'

Hannah shook her head. 'I don't think he'd formed one.'

'And yet he'd arranged to meet her on the Saturday lunchtime. Did you know that?'

'Yes. When she didn't turn up and he was worried.'

'Ah.' Again the nod. 'Did he tell you about Carrie's concerns?'

'Yes.'

'Did she say anything to you about them?'

'No.'

He smiled.

'Did I say something funny?' she demanded.

'No, no, I'm sorry. I'm just not used to people answering my questions so directly. So tell me, what did you make of Carrie?'

'You want my opinion?'

'Yes.'

She thought for a moment. 'I think that Carrie was a hard-working, professional woman. If she was concerned, it must have been for a reason. She didn't seem like the kind of person to make it up.'

'And did she seem anxious usually? Or depressed?'

Hannah frowned. 'Jumpy perhaps, not anxious, and no, she didn't seem depressed.'

The slow nod again. Hannah could hear the sergeant scribbling in his notebook.

'Thank you. And where were you on the Friday evening when Carrie was last seen? Just a routine question Miss Dechansay.'

'With Nathan. We had a meal at The Boatman then went for a walk to clear our heads.'

'Where?'

'Along the waterfront.'

'What time did you part?'

'I'm not sure. Maybe half ten, a quarter to eleven. We went back to the inn and got some hot drinks from the bar. There's a couple of armchairs in the snug off the lounge bar, more comfortable than sitting up in the rooms.'

'And did either of you go out again?'

'No. I mean I didn't and I think I'd have heard if Nathan did. He's in the room next door and the landing floor creaks.'

'Did you not sleep?'

'Not straight away. I usually read for a while before settling.'

'I see.' He smiled again, more warmly this time, which surprised her. Suddenly he looked quite human. 'Thank you, Miss Dechansay.' He stood up and reached towards her over the desk. 'Here's my card if you think of anything else that might be useful. I imagine you'll be contactable at The Boatman or here if we need to speak to you again?'

'Of course.'

She returned to the workroom. Nathan fixed her with a beady gaze as she entered.

'Well?'

52

She didn't immediately respond but walked over to sit in her usual place and turned to face him before she spoke.

'Scary, isn't it, being questioned like that? Makes you feel guilty even when you're not.'

'They think I knew her better than I'm saying.'

'He asked me that too but I said not.' She glanced at the door and dropped her voice. 'You didn't, did you?'

'Hannah.' He glared at her. 'Of course not. You think I'm lying?'

'No, no.' She shook her head. She didn't know what she thought but she didn't truly doubt Nathan's honesty. 'It's just this...' She waved a hand vaguely towards the door. '...it makes you start to question everything. Anyway, let's do some more work before we pack up.'

She turned on her seat to face the Bazille on the easel, put her earpieces in and switched on the stereo. Usually her music – pop, classical, jazz, reggae, whatever the mood dictated – helped to soothe her, to keep her thoughts steady. But it didn't help today; it was a struggle to concentrate. As she jettisoned one dirty swab and picked up a fresh one, dipping it in the cleaning solution, she glanced over at Nathan. He was struggling to focus too, his gaze fixed, a hand occasionally being pushed roughly back through his hair.

Like her, he was probably thinking of Carrie, found floating in filthy, boggy water like something discarded and unwanted. Hannah had hardly known her and yet still she felt the woman's sudden death as a shock, a loss, a crack in the natural order. She'd been younger than Hannah; she'd been knowledgeable, conscientious, attractive and courteous. And now she'd gone. Just like that.

*

The police stayed around for days, both in the village – where

53

they had set up an incident room in the village hall – and intermittently at the manor where they continued their interviews, speaking to the café and gardening staff, following up any leads or discrepancies. The press and television reporters had got their story and gone but the gossip circulated around East Ranling like a winter flu. Both the regulars at the pub and Brian and Alice March who ran it assumed that Nathan and Hannah would be able to furnish first-hand accounts of the tragic incident and of how the investigation was progressing. After all, they worked at the manor; they must know something about it.

But they knew little. What they did eventually learn, other than the brief mention now made on the television evening news, came from Netta, whose sister, Irene, was the caretaker and key holder for the village hall. Irene was apparently also the sort of person who made it her business to be indispensable and to know things. She took in regular provisions of tea, coffee and biscuits for the officers. She baked them a cake or two. And she kept her ears and eyes open and occasionally asked the odd question on the sly, mostly of the less experienced staff.

'She can get anyone to talk, can Irene,' said Netta, slightly embarrassed, 'to let slip things they didn't mean to. Now you mustn't tell anyone what I'm telling you. I don't think it's public knowledge yet.'

It seemed that the police were coming to the conclusion, for lack of any evidence to the contrary, that Carrie's death was an accident, that she had gone for a walk to explore the reserve, fascinated by the story of the crane, but, unused to the terrain and its perils, she had lost her footing and fallen into the Broad. She had then got caught up in weed and been unable to extricate herself. After several days in the water, buffeted by debris and nudged against stones and reeds, her body had not offered up as much information as they might have hoped. There was no definitive evidence of any struggle and no-one had been found who had seen Carrie after she crossed the bridge. There appeared to be no motive for murder nor had she left a suicide note. It was thought to have happened on the Friday evening – no-one had seen her since – though, since the body had spent nearly a week in water, the pathologist couldn't be precise about the time of her death.

A full week went by. By the following Monday, a Bank Holiday, a week and a half after Carrie's body had been found, this information became the standard gossip in the village. On the Tuesday afternoon, amid rumours of the police scaling back their investigation, Rose came to the workroom to inform Nathan that Mortimer would like to see him in his study if he could spare a moment.

'What *have* you been doing?' Rose said to him coyly. 'Uncle Mortimer almost never asks people to go to his study.'

Nathan didn't reply, exchanged a look with Hannah, and made his way there, past Rose who still hovered in the passageway.

Mortimer's study lay at the front of the house, adjacent to the office. It was a cosy, narrow room with one wall of book-shelves and the rest oak-panelled. A small fireplace in the furthest wall had an arrangement of dried flowers in front of it. Its window gave a view to the front but was sheltered from inquisitive visitors' eyes by a discreet hedge and a trellis. Mortimer was sitting behind a mahogany desk and motioned Nathan to the chair on the other side, facing him.

There was a brief silence while Mortimer fiddled with the arms of his reading glasses on the desk, frowning darkly.

'You wanted to see me?' prompted Nathan.

'Yes… yes, I did.' Mortimer looked up suddenly and fixed Nathan with a disconcertingly accusing look. 'No doubt

55

you've heard that the investigation into poor Carrie's death is being scaled back, pending any new information that might come to light. There'll be an inquest eventually of course.'

'I had heard something like that.'

'Yes, well, I shan't beat about the bush. I want to know why you told the police that story?'

'What story?'

'You know what story: the one about Carrie seeing some prowler and yet not seeing him. That something was amiss with the collection.'

'I told it because that's what she told me.'

'Why didn't she come to me if she was concerned?'

'I don't know.'

'Well it's damned awkward. I don't know where she got that idea. The police asked me a lot of questions about our collection. Chief Inspector Crayford wanted me to look through the storeroom and check if anything was missing.' He gave an embarrassed laugh. 'But, you must understand, the inventory isn't always absolutely up-to-date. Carrie's predecessor was a good man but he did get rather lax in his later years and I'm not exactly good at paperwork myself. And then of course art works are sometimes lent elsewhere. One drawing got badly damaged by accident a couple of years ago and couldn't be saved. These things happen. The point is, I've had a look and I told them that I don't think there's anything missing. It all looks just the same to me.'

Mortimer stopped short.

'The upshot is, I asked you here to put your mind at rest. And I want you to stop repeating this story. Gossip like that, completely unfounded, can do all sorts of damage. We really don't need it. It grows and gets exaggerated and the next thing people will be doubting our care and security. No-one will risk bequeathing us their precious art works again.' He fixed

Nathan with another look. 'You of all people will understand how important reputation is in the art world.'

Nathan nodded.

'You do understand? No more hearsay.'

'I understand.'

'After all, what did she actually see? Anyone? Was it someone she recognised? Did she name names?'

'No. She didn't see anyone. I think…'

'That's what I thought, Nathan. That's what I thought. She was jumping at shadows. The poor girl had been under a lot of stress, you see: separation, a new job, a new place to live in. It had obviously taken its toll. Such a tragedy though. A lovely girl. I think perhaps you were getting quite close to her… No? Even so, you must be upset – as are we all.'

Mortimer's frown returned as he stood up and came round the desk, sticking out his hand. Nathan got up too.

'Thank you for coming, Nathan. I'm glad we've got that little issue cleared up.'

They shook hands firmly but Mortimer held on to Nathan's hand just a moment too long.

'You should have told me, before the police, you know. Still…' He released his hand with the ghost of a conciliatory smile. 'I suppose you've heard that it's the funeral tomorrow? Somewhere out by Cheshunt in Hertfordshire, I gather.'

'Yes. Hannah and I are planning to go.'

'Yes, yes…' Mortimer said distractedly, going back to his desk. 'Me too. I never know what to wear. Black always makes me look like one of the undertakers. Must be my face.' He muttered the last remarks as if he'd already forgotten Nathan was still there.

Nathan returned to the workroom and sat down. He was aware of Hannah looking across at him but said nothing and tried to focus on the job in front of him. He'd finished tidying up the Ruskin, had cut a new mount for it and had already stowed it away in its protective folder. Now he was working on the Ottavio Leoni, a fine portrait in black, red and white chalk on a blue-grey paper. Dating back to the early seventeenth century, it was fragile and very thin in places. He'd cleaned a little light soiling off it and now needed to strengthen the thinned paper and repair a tear in it a few centimetres from the top. Narrow strips of Japanese tissues were laid out on the table before him and he was preparing a starch paste to fix them in place.

But his mind kept wandering, to Carrie and the terrible manner of her death, to Mortimer and the strange interview. The next thing he knew, Hannah had impatiently pulled her earpieces out and was glaring at him.

'So are you going to tell me?' she demanded.

He reluctantly met her accusing gaze. 'He thinks Carrie was imagining things.'

'He said that?'

'More or less. He hasn't found any problem with the stored collection.'

'And that's why he asked to see you?'

Nathan shrugged. 'It seems.'

He looked down and moved some tissue paper around. He knew Hannah was still watching him but after a moment she gave up and turned back to her easel. She was cleaning the Perugino now, an oil on panel, an image of the Archangel Raphael with a staff in his hand and a fish at his feet. Apparently one of the pieces of wood forming the panel was slightly warped and causing movement of the paint surface. Hopefully the problem would keep her occupied for a while and give him a chance to think.

Was Mortimer's behaviour truly eccentric or was it contrived and how could he be so sure that Carrie didn't have

58

a genuine reason for concern? Had he really searched through the collection to check for any anomalies? Come to that, would he recognise one if he saw it?

Nathan finished mixing the paste and started smearing a little on one of the strips of tissue, trying to push it all out of his head. He had far too many questions and none of the answers.

Chapter 5

Carrie's funeral was held at a small church in a picture postcard village north of Cheshunt in the Home Counties. According to Mortimer, Carrie's estranged husband had made all the arrangements. Nigel Judd had moved back to the area where his parents still lived and was renting a place nearby. Since Carrie was an only child and her parents were now both dead, he had decided to hold Carrie's funeral at the local church and have her buried in the graveyard there.

Rose had insisted on accompanying Mortimer and his surprise had been evident but she didn't know why. She thought it her duty. She was a Gyllam-Spence after all. Mortimer, and even her own parents, might consider her trivial and hedonistic – and maybe she often was – but she liked to think there was more to her than that. Too often she felt excluded and yet there was a chance she would be the owner of the manor one day. Maybe. If her father didn't produce a legitimate son and heir with whichever woman happened to be the current love of his life.

The outdated terms of the estate's trust insisted that the property went to a male offspring when there was one. Though Rose rather doubted that Amanda, her father's current girlfriend, was likely to become the next Mrs Gyllam-Spence – their relationship had all the hallmarks of the countless inconsequential flings he'd had before. In the shorter term, her father would inherit the manor if Mortimer pre-deceased him. Would he rely on her help to run the place, give her some responsibility? She doubted it.

She and Mortimer sat at the back of the church and watched the pews quickly filling up in front of them. Rose hadn't expected this many people to come. She loved watching people and listening to them. It was one of the other reasons why she'd wanted to come. At an early age she had decided her own family was not a typical one and she was fascinated by other people's relationships, by their ambitions, by how they manoeuvred their way through the hurdles of life. It seemed Carrie had been popular before she came to Ranling Manor; these couldn't all have been her relations. Old colleagues perhaps, maybe school friends. They were well-heeled, prosperous she guessed, and they looked genuinely stunned, speaking to each other in hushed tones.

Rose had never been on particularly friendly terms with Carrie – she'd thought the woman distant and standoffish – but it didn't change the fact that it was awful that she'd died. And in such a horrible way. Rose preferred not to think about it. She saw Nathan and Hannah arrive and watched them sit near the back on the other side. Hannah looked round and saw her and they exchanged a brief, meaningless smile, but Nathan was fixedly staring ahead, not looking at anyone. Were they a couple? It didn't look like it.

'We won't stay for the reception,' Mortimer muttered in Rose's ear.

'Don't you think we should?' she hissed back.

'No. Doesn't seem appropriate somehow. Anyway, we should get back. There are things to do.'

She sniffed, disappointed. She was curious to meet some of these people. She'd also hoped to speak to Nathan. The man intrigued her. He was older than she was but she liked that. He

61

was good-looking in an old-fashioned sort of way and his glasses gave him an intelligent, dependable air. He also did an interesting job; he went places.

The funeral procession came in and Rose watched the husband walking behind the coffin, a fair-haired, fairly thick-set man, looking stiff and very alone. The service started and Rose tried to concentrate. She was wearing a pair of new black, high-heeled shoes and they were killing her.

With the service over, everyone spilled out into the cemetery for the interment. Afterwards, in the slow dispersal of the mourners from the graveside, Rose saw Nathan and Hannah go over to speak to Nigel Judd. Or rather, Hannah did. Nathan stood at a slight remove, saying nothing. That was interesting: it looked as if Hannah knew the widower.

'Are you coming, Rose?' said Mortimer, breaking into her thoughts.

'Aren't you going to speak to Carrie's husband?'

'No. Come on.'

Rose raised her eyebrows; it wasn't like Uncle Mortimer to be curt. But he'd already set off for the car park and she tottered after him.

*

It was busy in The Boatman that Wednesday evening. The local football club and their supporters had piled into the public bar and were apparently holding a competition to see who could talk the loudest. The lounge bar was quiet by comparison though the chatter and laughter echoed through. Hannah and Nathan sat opposite each other at the table in the window.

Nathan was monosyllabic and Hannah watched him warily. They hadn't eaten together the previous evening. It seemed that neither of them wanted to be trapped into routinely spending the evening with the other. Sometimes one or other of them made an excuse to eat later or go somewhere else but tonight they had drifted back together with the magnetic attraction of opposite poles and were sitting in virtual silence. Nathan had hardly spoken since their brief conversation in his car on the way back from the funeral. The meeting with Nigel Judd had been the trigger for yet another argument.

'You might have told me you knew him,' Nathan had said peevishly.

'I didn't know I did. That is to say, it wasn't until I saw his name on the order of service that I wondered. Then I saw him come in. You never told me his first name so I didn't put two and two together. Why would I? In any case, I can't say that I know him.'

'But you dated him, you said.'

'Only once and it was years ago. We didn't click so I didn't pursue it.'

'He was very friendly considering you dumped him.'

Hannah screwed up her face in exasperation. 'Because it wasn't like that. I don't think he was interested either. We were introduced by a mutual friend. Clearly not a great friend considering I have no idea now who it was.'

'Well he seemed quite keen to be friendly now, asking how you came to be there, what you were doing, where you were staying.'

'He was being polite.' She stared out at the passing landscape. 'And curious, I suppose. It's always odd when you meet someone after a long gap. How chance throws you together again. It makes you think.'

Nathan glanced at her. 'Think what?'

'I don't know. How things turn out. Coincidences, that sort of thing.'

He hadn't pursued it. Now, despite her sporadic efforts at making conversation, he remained largely taciturn. Usually he was talkative, chivvying, perky, quick to offer an opinion, whether he knew what he was talking about or not. Sometimes – often – she found it maddening but this introspective mood bothered her more. It wasn't normal.

With their meals finished, he sat staring at the pint of draught beer he'd half-drunk as if he might see some revelation in its amber depths.

'Come in number twenty-two,' Hannah said eventually.

He frowned, dragging himself from somewhere far away. 'What?'

'Where are you? It's like sitting with a plaster statue. Sorry, I know you're cut up about Carrie. I'm pretty upset about it myself. It's awful. But there's something else bothering you isn't there? Talk to me.'

He took another pull of beer and set the glass down with a sigh. He stared at it long enough to make her wonder if he was going to reply, then did.

'I can't believe that Carrie has just been written off. The police aren't pursuing it and Mortimer is treating her like she was a crazy woman and warning me off.' He shook his head. 'It's wrong, that's all. It's wrong.'

'He was warning you off? You didn't tell me that.'

'Oh it was all very gentlemanly,' he said tersely, lip curled. 'But we mustn't spread gossip, must we? We mustn't tarnish the glowing reputation of Ranling Manor. Hell, Hannah, they're already behaving as if Carrie was never there, as if she didn't matter.'

Hannah frowned, thoughtfully sipping at the remains of her wine.

'It's not good enough.' He thumped the table making the cutlery jump and rattle and people look round. 'No-one's going to bother to find out who was messing about in the storeroom that night. More to the point, no-one's going to bother to find out who killed her.'

'Shh.' She glanced round and paused to let the atmosphere settle. 'You don't believe that it was an accident?'

'No.' He leaned forward, speaking softly. 'Do you? I mean, come on: it can't be a coincidence, can it? Carrie hears an intruder and arranges to tell me all about it. The next thing she's found floating in Ranling Broad. Then Mortimer's trying to cover it up.'

'Are you trying to suggest that Mortimer was the intruder?' She laughed. 'Oh come on. Why would he meddle with his own collection? Anyway, he's harmless.'

'Is he? On what do you base that assessment? In any case, he may nominally own the collection as the oldest son but he can't do anything much with it. The collection's held in trust and the trustees have to be consulted about any sales or whatever.'

'Who told you that?'

'Sidony.'

'Even so. You've seen him. He's in a world of his own most of the time: family history and pictures and model trains.'

'Maybe. But remember Carrie said there was something wrong with the collection.'

'Yes. So?'

'Alan came up on us and she never had a chance to explain what she meant. But what would that suggest to you?'

'Well in the art world, if a picture's described as "not right" or "wrong", it usually means the attribution's not correct, that it's by a different hand to the one claimed.'

'Exactly what I thought. So possibly a forgery.'

'But not necessarily. Perhaps just a mistaken attribution.'

'Could be. But if you put it alongside suspicious

65

behaviour in the storeroom, it suggests a very different scenario, doesn't it?'

'Such as?'

'Suppose someone's taking pictures and replacing them with fakes? Not all at the same time, but one by one. A trickle if you like. Who'd notice?'

Hannah met his gaze.

'A new curator?'

'Exactly.' Nathan sighed again and ran a hand through his hair. 'I keep rerunning that last conversation through my head, looking for something to latch onto, wondering if I misinterpreted her or I'm misremembering. But I keep coming back to her odd behaviour and the same old phrases.'

Hannah took another mouthful of wine.

'You're feeling guilty,' she said.

He recoiled slightly as if she'd tried to hit him.

'No, I'm not. Well… maybe a little. I keep thinking that I might have been able to do something if I'd realised sooner that there was a real threat.' He took another mouthful of beer and looked away. 'The thing is, I knew what she was going through. I understood her state of mind. When she told me about how her husband had cheated on her – and with someone she knew – it was painfully familiar. My fiancée did that to me too. It leaves you feeling like you can't breathe.'

Hannah stared at him, taking in this rare piece of personal information. She knew he'd been with a girl for a long time, had been engaged, and that it had come to an abrupt end. She'd never been told the details.

'But Carrie's death wasn't your fault, Nathan. None of it was. You barely knew her. You offered friendship and agreed to see her. What more could you have done?'

'I don't know.'

'And the chances are that it was an accident,' she added

66

gently. 'You couldn't have stopped that.'

'Do you really believe that?'

'It's possible.'

'Or someone might have followed her...' Nathan paused, glancing to see who else might be able to hear him. 'Suppose she stopped to look out across the water and someone came up on her from behind. If it was someone she knew, she wouldn't have felt threatened. Either way, she could have been pushed.'

A middle-aged couple staying in another of the rooms walked in and they fell silent again, watching the couple find a table nearby then go to the bar.

Hannah wrinkled up her nose.

'It sounds pretty far-fetched. I think you should let it go, Nathan. Mortimer's already warned you off. You're just going to get into trouble.'

'This, coming from you, Miss Trouble herself? Besides, I thought you said Mortimer was a pussycat.'

Her eyes narrowed. 'I did not say that. Not exactly.'

'Well I can't let it go, OK?'

'Fine. Fine,' she said crossly. 'Snoop if you must but for God's sake let the dust settle, will you?'

She stared at him long and hard then leaned forward.

'And you'd better be careful. Or maybe they'll find your body floating in some murky water somewhere too.' She sat back. 'Or more likely Mortimer will complain about you and Timothy will blame me for being a bad influence.'

*

The Thursday was dry and sunny, though an easterly wind blew straight across the flat, broad lands from the North Sea, chilling the air and nipping at exposed flesh. By six-twenty, when Hannah ventured out wearing jeans and a jacket, the sun had disappeared behind a high bank of cloud, dropping the temperature still further. She pulled up her collar and set off.

She had a mission. With the conversation from the night before constantly niggling at the back of her mind, she had decided to see for herself just how easily Carrie could have fallen accidentally into the Broad. In any case, after working all day on the Perugino, she thought the walk would do her good.

There were two bridges over the river which gave access to the reserve. One, at the northern end of the village, carried both cars and pedestrians; the other, to the south, was a footbridge and Hannah headed for the latter. It was the one Carrie would have used, not far from the house she'd been renting. It gave onto a dirt path, wide enough for two to walk abreast, that wound between shrubs and trees, the oaks just in fresh spring leaf, the willows and birches often arching over her head. Birdsong lilted from the depths of the trees and an occasional butterfly fluttered past. A lone walker passed her going the other way but otherwise it was quiet and remarkably peaceful. Hannah thought she could see why Carrie might have chosen to regularly come this way: a chance to clear her head and shrug off her demons.

At a fork in the path a small wooden signpost indicated that Ranling Broad and a hide were to the right and a butterfly garden was to the left. She turned right and kept walking. Turning a bend, the trees suddenly opened up on her left and she saw the Broad with the water chopping and frothy in the wind. Geese had collected on the far side while a handful of ducks nearby eyed her up speculatively. And here was the hide alongside a stretch of path close to the water's edge leading to a wooden landing stage. A small cruiser was tethered to a mooring post and a sign advertised wildlife boat tours of the Broad.

Hannah stood on the boarding and looked down into the

water. Weed grew from the lake bed and eddied eerily in the currents as if performing a dance to some unheard music. The main path turned inland from here but a narrow track of worn ground beyond the boarding still ran alongside the water and Hannah took it, ducking the hanging branches and stumbling once on an exposed tree root. Pausing once to look into the water, it was unnerving to see how quickly the ground fell away from the bank and those weeds, still dancing below the surface.

A few minutes later she was back on the main path. Presumably if she kept walking, sooner or later she would reach the other bridge. It was more winding than she'd expected and just when she was toying with going back the way she'd come, she was brought up short. The path had looped back to the Broad again, not far from the canal which gave access from the river, and this time there was no boarding, just dirt and scrub. A couple of bits of police tape still dangled from the trees on each side and flapped in the breeze, and the ground had been scuffed by untold feet and heavy equipment.

So this is where they found poor Carrie, she thought, and the reality of it struck her like a blow. It was desolate and chilling.

And she wasn't alone. A pale, sandy-haired man was standing there, staring at the water, as still as stone. He looked round at the sound of her steps and his disconcertingly pale eyes widened. It was Alan Foxhall.

'Evening,' said Hannah.

'Evening.'

His face was expressionless, but then it usually was.

'What a sad sight,' she said. 'I didn't realise this was where she was found.'

'No. Indeed.' He hesitated and glanced around. 'Nathan

not with you?'

'No.'

'Just out for a walk then?'

'Yes. A bit of fresh air. You?'

'Me? Killing time. Grace, my fiancé, works for the trust which runs this reserve. I came to give her a lift back. She should be finishing soon.' He fixed Hannah with a look which came across as a challenge. 'I'll walk back with you.'

The cloud had become louring and rain threatened so she reluctantly fell in with him. It wasn't a comfortable walk. He didn't speak again and she had the strong impression that he thought his silence would force her to talk. To say what exactly? She said nothing.

They reached the main entrance to the reserve where a timber building stood with a sign saying *Reception* over its open door. Alan left her and headed to the car park, saying he'd wait in the car. Hannah poked her head round the door. It was a small shop for wildlife-related gifts and books, as well as a reception space with a wooden counter, a rack of information leaflets, a hot drinks machine and a blackboard where the day's wildlife sightings were chalked up. On one long side and up four steps, it also doubled as a hide, offering bench seats by glassless windows which looked out over a stretch of marshy ground.

'Hi,' said a young woman with short amber hair. 'I'm afraid I'm closing up in a minute.'

'That's OK. I'm sure I'll come again.' Hannah took a step inside and glanced at the blackboard. It offered a list of names, birds presumably, most of which she'd never heard of. No crane however.

'See anything special?' the young woman asked.

'No. No, I was just walking really. To be honest, I'm not very knowledgeable about wildlife. I'm not quite sure what I'd be looking for.'

'No problem.' The woman turned to the rack and picked out a few information leaflets. 'Here. These will tell you a little about the most common wildlife we see here.' She smiled. 'For the next time you visit. Everyone has to start somewhere.'

'Thank you. You must be Grace. I'm Hannah. I'm working at the manor at the moment.'

'Oh right, I know: you're one of the restorers.' She offered a warmer smile.

'That's right. I've just bumped into Alan. He's waiting for you in the car.'

For the blink of an eye, Grace's expression changed, then she smiled again and thanked her.

Hannah walked back into the village, wondering what exactly to tell Nathan over dinner that night. It would be fair to say that Carrie *could* have slipped into the Broad by accident though she doubted that he would believe her. Nathan was on some sort of trail of redemption and she knew a little about that; nothing she said would change it. So she wouldn't tell him about seeing Alan, not yet anyway. It had looked suspicious, the way he was staring at the water, and she didn't want Nathan to do anything rash.

And, for all she might pour cold water on his theories, she wasn't completely convinced herself that Carrie's death was an accident.

*

Hearing raised voices as he approached the office on the Friday morning, Mortimer's heart sank. He hadn't slept well, had been late coming down for breakfast, and had hoped for a quiet morning. It was just after nine and there should have been a calm spell until the visitors were let in at ten, bringing their bustle, questions and confusion with them.

Mortimer had no problem with the paying public: they had exchanged their hard-earned money in return for an interesting tour of the house and its contents. They deserved that. But there was always a small minority determined to stray where they weren't supposed to and others who became difficult and abusive for surprising – and sometimes even imaginative – reasons. And then there was just the invasiveness of it. Notwithstanding that the family had its own private quarters, there was something suffocating about strangers swarming over both house and gardens, whereas this first hour offered a breathing space, a chance to check that all was in place and sort out any problems before the mayhem started. Arguments he could do without.

He pushed the door back and ventured in. His brother, Toby, was there with Rose.

'What I spend on Amanda has nothing to do with you,' Toby was saying angrily. 'You're a grown woman and you've got your own income now. You can't expect me to give you handouts. In any case, I don't have much spare myself.'

'You seem to be able to splash it about when you want to. What about that trip up to London with her last month? Dinner and the theatre and some swanky hotel for the night.'

'I'd put money on a good horse at Cheltenham this year if you must know.'

'Ha,' scoffed Rose.

'Toby, Rose, please, must you?' said Mortimer, as Alan walked in through the door from the hallway. 'Do we all have to listen to this?'

'I'm sorry Uncle Mortimer but that Lanson woman is always showing off, telling me what Dad's bought her and the places he's taken her, trying to suggest she's more important than I am. And it's not about the money. She's not much older than I am. It's disgusting.'

'It's really none of your business.' Toby pointed one accusing finger. 'Anyway I've seen you flirting with older men. You're not so fussy yourself so don't come that with me.'

'Enough.' Mortimer glanced uneasily between them. 'Haven't you got any work to do?'

'As it happens, I have.' Toby puffed himself up, straightening his shoulders. 'I've got a meeting with a magazine journalist. I won't mention any names yet till it's a done deal but they're thinking of doing a feature article on the manor. I don't want to jinx it but it could be a significant spread. I need to get down to Ipswich for eleven.'

'Oh? That sounds interesting.'

Mortimer thought of pressing for more information. Toby had talked this sort of big game before but nothing much usually came of it. He suspected his brother used a story like this as an excuse for going off and doing God knew what. Having returned to the manor and what he called the 'family business' some ten years previously, his property development business having folded, he had claimed for himself the job of publicity manager. It was a cushy number for him. Mortimer figured he just liked the title and his efforts were spasmodic to say the least. Still, cross-questioning had never worked with Toby; he had too agile a tongue.

'Well don't let them make it all about the loss of our curator will you?' he said instead. 'We don't want that association played up. Most unfortunate.'

'Certainly not. What do you take me for?' Toby produced his oily smile. 'No, don't answer that, dear brother. See you later.'

He exited into the house, presumably to get ready to go out, clearly unruffled by his daughter's criticism.

Now Rose trailed reluctantly to the desk by the window, casting a glance towards Alan who was already ensconced at his own desk in the corner.

'Anything happening today I should know about?' Mortimer asked.

Alan gave him a regular printout of events scheduled to take place the following month but Mortimer invariably either lost it or forgot to look at it. Then he'd find himself surprised to be engulfed by a party of giggling schoolgirls or shocked to see a wedding marquee going up on the lawn at the back.

Alan looked round with his lizard-like, unblinking gaze. 'No, nothing special today.'

'Good, good.'

'Do you really think it'll be a problem, Uncle Mortimer?' said Rose.

'What?'

'Carrie drowning like that. Is it going to be a problem? I mean, will it keep people away?'

'No, I shouldn't think so. Some people will come just to see where she worked and where it happened.' He paused and frowned as the idea took hold in his mind. 'Ghoulish really.'

'It is. But it *was* horrible.' She pulled a face and was silent a moment, then appeared to shake it off and turned. 'How's Grace, Alan? I was in the village last night, going to see Debbie, and I saw you and Grace heading to the minimarket. She looked upset.'

His eyes narrowed. 'No, she wasn't upset. Why should she be? But I'll tell you who I saw last night.' He paused, waiting for them both to look at him. 'One of those restorers. On the reserve.'

Alan certainly had Mortimer's full attention now.

Rose frowned. 'What was he doing there?'

'It wasn't the man. It was the woman. Hannah. I was killing time, waiting for Grace to finish, so I went for a walk and I came across where Carrie's body was found. You can't

74

miss it: there are still a few bits of police tape there. And there was Hannah, standing staring at the water like she was mesmerised by it.'

'Oh now that is ghoulish.' Rose wrinkled up her nose. 'Why would she be interested?'

Alan shrugged.

'Outsiders,' he said dismissively. 'They can't leave things alone, can they? Always have to poke their noses in and interfere.' He offered them both a brief, meaningful look and returned to his diary.

'Curiosity, I suppose,' Mortimer said distantly, unsure what to make of this information.

He rather liked Hannah. It had occurred to him more than once that she was the kind of daughter he might have had if he and Sidony had stayed together. There was something in the set of Hannah's face which reminded him of Sidony – a straight manner, a stubbornness of jaw but also a softness in the eyes when she smiled. Did he need to question her about what she was doing at the reserve? Wouldn't that look kind of obvious?

He pushed the thought away.

'I suppose I'm going to have to find someone to replace Carrie.' He flicked a glance between Alan and Rose. 'Or maybe not. Maybe it would be better to just get someone in now and then when we need them.'

Neither of them expressed an opinion which he took to suggest agreement.

*

Rose was still in the office later that morning when Hannah turned up, asking to use the phone.

'I need to speak to my boss,' said Hannah.

'Why, what's the problem?' asked Rose.

75

Hannah eyed her up before she replied. People did this to her all the time and Rose hated it. As if she didn't need to know. Well, maybe she didn't but she wanted to.

'Now that I've got the dirt and varnish off the Perugino,' said Hannah slowly, 'I've found that the warping of the panel is worse than I'd realised. It's making paint crack and flake off.'

'Oh. And your boss needs to know this?'

'He likes to be kept in the loop. Timescales, that sort of thing.'

Rose pointed her to the phone and, on an impulse, left the office and walked through towards the workroom. She pulled her jumper down and straightened her hair with her fingers then knocked on the door and immediately put her head round it.

'Nathan, *ciao bello.*' She produced what she hoped was her best smile. 'Mind if I come in?'

'Er, no. Is there a problem?'

'No, no problem. *Nessun problema.* Only I've been really curious to see what you're doing down here. Do you mind?'

She crossed to stand by his work table and stared down at the drawing in front of him. It was a graceful, full-length image of the Virgin Mary, in what looked like pencil on white paper. She'd probably seen it before but she wasn't sure.

'What are you doing to this?'

Nathan raised his eyebrows at the question then looked back at the picture and began talking like a teacher.

'At some point it's been allowed to get up close and personal to a pastel drawing and the coloured pastel has transferred itself to the white paper. See? Here, here and here. It needs to be removed. As well as spoiling the simplicity of the work, pastel can attract mould. If it's not needed it has to go.'

'Oh OK. So how do you do that? With a rubber?'

'Not exactly.' He glanced up at her with the suggestion of a smile. 'I'll try to get as much as possible off by simply blowing it off with this air-bulb, see? For stickier areas, I can brush. This one is very soft-bristled.' He picked up a brush and showed her. 'In a couple of places the colour has ground more into the paper. As long as it's somewhere away from the drawing, I can use this vinyl eraser powder to help lift it. It's like the white vinyl eraser you might buy but more discreet to use. You gently rub it on with a fingertip, then brush or blow it off.'

'Fascinating. And is this what you do all the time, smarten up old drawings?'

'No. I work on all kinds of pictures. Sometimes I work on oil paintings like Hannah.' He nodded his head in the direction of Hannah's easel where the Perugino stood. 'Hannah's just gone to ring our boss.'

'Yes, I saw her. So I suppose you travel to all kinds of places in this job?'

'Yes, wherever the work is.'

'Abroad too?'

'To Europe sometimes.'

'That must be difficult for your girlfriend. Or wife, if you're married.'

He laughed shortly. 'No such problem.'

'I see.' She smiled again and perched her bottom on the edge of the table. She was wearing a tight skirt and it rode up to display a little thigh. 'It must be exciting to travel. I'd love to do that.'

'Haven't you ever been anywhere?'

'Not really. Dad had this property development business down in Hampshire. We often used to go to the Isle of Wight and we went over to Brittany once. Dad went away on business

77

– to all sorts of places – but we didn't go with him. I think we cramped his style.'

'Still, you could do some exploring of your own now, choose where you want to go.'

'By myself?'

'Or with a friend.'

'I suppose. I'm going to evening classes to learn Italian.'

'Oh? Planning a trip to Italy?'

Rose shrugged. 'I'd love to. Have you been there?'

'Yes, a couple of times.'

'Lucky you.' She hesitated, trying to gauge his mood, curious to know what he thought. 'Wasn't it sad about Carrie? I suppose she might have done it deliberately, mightn't she – you know, jumped into the water? She never looked happy. But then you can't come somewhere like this and assume you can change everything. I mean, this place managed without her for centuries, didn't it?'

'Is that what she did, tried to change everything?'

Rose pulled a face and shrugged again. 'I don't know. I just got that impression from odd things that were said. You know, just generally.'

'Well, I've no idea what happened. Look Rose, I really need to get on with this.' He gestured to the drawing. 'My boss is keen on schedules.'

'Oh, all right.' She wriggled herself down off the table and smoothed her skirt down, cross with herself. She always seemed to say the wrong thing. 'I didn't realise I was in the way.'

'No, I didn't mean that.' He smiled at her. He had a nice smile with eyes that crinkled up, not like Alan who looked like a vulture when he smiled. 'But I do have to concentrate. I can't afford to make a mistake or I'll be out of a job.'

Mollified, she smiled back and walked to the door but

stopped before she got there.

'That Hannah's a bit odd, isn't she? I mean, yesterday, going to look at where Carrie died? Kind of a creepy thing to do.'

He turned to look at her but hadn't replied when the door opened and Hannah walked in. She glanced at Rose, then at Nathan, then back at Rose. The two women nodded at each other and Rose withdrew, pulling the door to behind her. She paused by the door though and listened.

'You didn't tell me you'd been to see where Carrie was found,' Nathan was saying in an accusing voice.

Rose walked back to the office, smiling to herself. She liked Nathan but she wasn't too keen on Hannah.

Chapter 6

Norwich, the county town of Norfolk, was originally an Anglo-Saxon settlement and its subsequent wealth was built on the wool trade. Now a thriving, bustling city, it boasts one of the largest medieval cathedrals in England and still has, at its heart, a warren of narrow, cobbled streets. This much Hannah had learned on her first visit. She had called in at the tourist information office, acquired a map and a guide book and had visited some of the most notable sites. But it also offered the biggest choice of shops in the area so that Saturday she had decided to return and indulge in a little shopping.

It was also good to get away and be alone. After Rose's visit to the workroom the day before, the atmosphere had been so taut, it had felt as if it might crack.

'I didn't go to see where Carrie was found,' Hannah had protested to Nathan. 'I went to see what the place was like. If you must know, I wanted to see how easy it would be to fall into the Broad accidentally.'

'Oh really? And?'

'And if you weren't used to the place, and perhaps it was overcast or dark, it could happen.' She shrugged. 'I'm just saying, it could happen. Then I saw the remains of the police tape and realised that was where Carrie was found. I don't know how Rose knew though. I suppose Alan must have told her. He was there, standing, just staring at the place.'

'Alan? And you didn't think to tell me that either?'

'Do you tell me everything you do? We don't live in each other's pockets, Nathan.'

After glaring at each other, they had both retreated into their work, barely speaking again for most of the day. It felt childish but there was no way Hannah was going to apologise; she had nothing to apologise for. But she did make a mental note never to tell the ubiquitous Rose anything. That girl liked acquiring information and she used it to manipulate people. And now Nathan had gone off doing God knew what. Well, she hoped he had a nice day. With any luck he would work the bad mood out of his system.

The roads were busy. Hannah eventually found a parking space and made her way onto the thronging streets. She browsed in and out of shops, treated herself to a magazine and a new paperback, then found herself by the market square in the centre where stalls sprawled across a swathe of the slope up to the council buildings at the top. It was just the sort of place she liked to poke about. There were fruit and vegetable stalls, fresh bread and cakes, hardware and garden plants, but what really caught her eye were the brightly coloured clothes hanging from rails on coat hangers, some spinning in the breeze. Hannah was wiry with skinny legs. She wasn't elegant and knew she never would be. On the contrary, she felt her happiest in jeans or leggings with a big sweater or shirt, in dungarees or an oversized cotton dress with patch pockets. And she loved bright colours.

She started to pick through the stalls, happily losing track of time, and was standing with a coat hanger in hand, a pair of baggy cotton trousers in a gaudy fake patchwork design with cinched in ankles dangling from it, when a woman's voice spoke behind her.

'You could get away with them, I'm sure, but I couldn't.

81

Not with my waistline.'

Hannah turned abruptly to see Sidony, who smiled.

'Sorry if I gave you a shock.'

'Hello Sidony. No, it's fine. I was miles away.' Hannah hung the trousers back on the rack.

'Oh Sid, please. Call me Sid. Everyone does.' She glanced towards the rejected trousers. 'And don't let me disturb your shopping.'

'You're not. I'm not sure they're quite me. With legs like mine I'd probably look like a clown. In any case, I've already bought a pair from one of the other stalls and I don't really need any more.'

'I don't need half the clothes I buy but it never stops me. Are you alone? What about a coffee? Let me buy you one.'

'Lovely, thank you. But I'll have tea if you don't mind. I don't drink coffee.'

'Oh yes, I think Rose said.'

Sid led the way to a coffee shop down one of the side streets, away from the noise and frenzy, and they sat in an upstairs room by a window looking down on the street below. Hannah's mother would have approved of Sid. She was elegant. Her waist might have spread a little but her clothes were always neatly tailored, her make-up tasteful and her white-grey hair immaculately cut and flatteringly layered. She had an attractive, even face and a direct gaze.

'So what does Nathan do while you spend your money in Norwich?' said Sidony, stirring two sweeteners into her coffee.

'I have no idea.' Hannah shrugged. 'He used to come to Norfolk on holiday apparently and I think he's enjoying revisiting some old haunts.'

'I see. I'd thought perhaps you were more than just colleagues.'

82

Hannah's eyes narrowed. 'No. We just work together.'

Sidony produced the suggestion of a smile. 'Don't take offence. I didn't mean anything by it.' She sat back in the chair. 'How's it going? I imagine poor Carrie's tragic death has made it difficult for you. I still can't quite take it in.'

'Me neither. But we're plodding on.'

'Is Nathan all right? He seemed to have got to know her quite well.'

'I don't think he had a chance to know her well. We hadn't been here long enough.' Hannah paused. 'Have you had a number of different curators over the years?'

'A few, I suppose. Graham had the job before Carrie and he was here when Toby and I came back to the manor. I take it you know that we were married?'

Hannah nodded.

'Graham had already been at the manor for years by then. When he retired there was a short gap until Mortimer hired Carrie and she thought Graham's approach had become out of date. Isn't that always the way with new blood?'

It was a casual remark, apparently without inflection. Hannah drank a little tea and found Sid's probing eyes on her as she put the cup down and looked up. She felt she was being examined and thought she'd retaliate by doing a little examining of her own.

'Did Carrie rock the boat then?'

Sid gave a short laugh. 'I don't know about that. I suppose there's always a frisson of trouble when a pretty woman joins a workforce. Laws of nature. Alan took rather a shine to her to start with, even asked her out, I think.'

'I thought he was engaged?'

'Exactly. She didn't accept, sensible girl.'

Hannah nodded thoughtfully. 'Can I ask you a personal question?'

83

'Try me.'

'Isn't it hard to still be living and working under the same roof as Toby? Wouldn't it have been easier to work somewhere else?'

Sidony took a slow sip of coffee, then sat back again and looked at her, pursing up her lips thoughtfully.

'Is that what you'd have done? Gone, left a good job and all your associations. It would be like giving in, don't you think?' She rocked her head slightly side to side. 'I suppose if I was still in love with him, it would have been easier to go. But that died years ago. Toby is serially unfaithful. He's currently dating Amanda Lawson, one of the house guides. I might as well tell you because you're bound to hear it from someone. Amanda thinks it'll be different with her, that they'll have a sweet, rosy future together and that she will be important to him and to everyone else because of who he is.' Sid shook her head with a wry smile. 'She's fooling herself. Toby is only interested in himself. He'll cheat on her eventually and so it will go on.'

'And how does Rose feel about all this?'

Sid's expression closed down and she leaned forward to pick up her coffee cup.

'I'm not entirely sure. She doesn't confide in me.' She drank a mouthful of coffee and replaced the cup on the saucer. 'When she was young she was always daddy's girl. Always wanted him more than me. Perhaps that was my fault: she and I were never quite singing from the same page. Do you have children, Hannah?'

The abruptness of the question took Hannah by surprise. 'No.'

'In that case it may not be easy for you to understand.'

'I had a mother. We weren't always singing from the same page either.'

'Perhaps you do understand then. I love Rose – she's my daughter – but we're not close.'

They sat for a moment in silence, finishing their drinks. Sidony finished first and considered Hannah with her cool, scrutinising gaze.

'I gather Carrie told Nathan that she thought someone had been in the storeroom one night, acting suspiciously.'

'Something like that,' said Hannah carefully. 'But Mr Gyllam-Spence doesn't seem bothered by it. He thinks everything's as it should be in there.'

'And why shouldn't it be? There's no sign of anyone having broken in, is there? I don't really understand why Carrie was so bothered about it – assuming anyone was actually there. I believe there's nothing missing, nothing out of place. The poor girl was clearly living on her nerves and blew it out of proportion. She should have spoken to Mortimer about it anyway if she was worried. Why didn't she?'

'I don't know.' Hannah hesitated for the blink of an eye. 'Who has a key to the storeroom?'

Sidony shrugged. 'Mortimer. Carrie had one of course. But there's one in the box in Rose's desk in the office too. There's a spare key for everything in there.' She produced another wry smile. 'I really don't think you should be looking to point fingers.' Now a moment's hesitation as if she were toying with revealing something private. 'It isn't easy, you know. There isn't the money there used to be. Just because the collection has many valuable pieces in it, it doesn't make Mortimer a wealthy man. And ticket sales barely cover costs. If we didn't have all the functions and events...' She stopped suddenly as if she thought she'd said too much. 'Well, I'd better let you get on with your shopping.'

She reached down to her handbag, stowed by the chair in a shopping bag and lifted it to her lap to pull out a vanity mirror and check her make-up. She dabbed at the corner of her mouth with a tissue and replaced the mirror.

'Sid, why did you tell me all this?' said Hannah.

Sidony snapped the handbag closed and regarded her silently for a few disconcerting seconds.

'It bothers me how easily rumours start. A place like Ranling Manor with its history and its privileged occupants is always going to provoke gossip and, God knows, Toby doesn't help that. But rumours about the sad death of a young woman or spurious suspicions about the looting of the collection, that sort of nonsense we can all do without. Mortimer is foolishly eccentric but he's a good man and I don't want to see him hurt. The manor and its collection mean everything to him.' She paused. 'You understand? There's nothing going on at the manor, just a bunch of people trying to keep their heads above water.' Her voice became quieter but harder and more insistent. 'Don't go spreading baseless rumours, Hannah, nor your friend. Just stay out of it.'

Sid got up, shrugged her jacket on and picked up her shopping bag.

Hannah stayed in her seat. 'Thank you for the tea,' she said with deliberate politeness.

Sid nodded and walked away but Hannah didn't move. It occurred to her that Sid was both a clever woman and a smooth talker. And she knew a great deal more about what went on at the manor – in public and in private – than she let on.

*

Nathan stood in the red phone box along the street from the inn and put his available silver change out on the shelf. Not for the first time, he thought how much easier this would be if he owned his own mobile phone. They were developing rapidly – he'd been reading about all the latest brands in a magazine only the other day – but they were still kind of big to lug around and signal coverage was patchy. And they were pricey too, though feeding money into public phone boxes wasn't exactly cheap either. At least this one was reasonably clean. The things phone boxes got used for didn't bear thinking about.

He dialled the number and waited, listening to the peals at the other end, and checked his watch: five past seven. His mother rarely went out in the evening so he assumed she would be there. In any case, he'd got into a routine of ringing her on a Monday night so it was likely she'd be waiting.

He heard the phone being picked up and his mother saying the number. The pips went and he quickly pushed coins into the slot.

'Hi Mum. How are you?'

'Oh good, Nathan darling.' She had that familiar breathless, anxious tone again. It had started when Sam had gone missing all those years ago and still came back even now, whenever she got stressed. 'I'm so glad you called. If you hadn't I was going to try to ring you at that place you're staying. What is it? I've got it written down somewhere.'

'The Boatman. Why, what's the matter?'

'It's Samuel,' she said on a rising note, as if it had been a foolish question. 'Lyn – you remember Lyn?'

'Yes, I remember Lyn.'

Lyn and her husband had owned the Norfolk holiday cottage Nathan and his family had stayed in several times back in the day, an annexe adjoining their own home. They'd had no children and had spoilt Nathan and Samuel every time they'd stayed. His mother had struck up a friendship with Lyn which had lasted over the years. Now, both widowed, they kept in touch with letters in Christmas cards and an occasional phone call.

'Lyn sent me her local newspaper,' his mother said. 'You know the one for the Broads where we used to stay. We used to buy it sometimes, didn't we?'

Nathan's heart sank. 'Yes, but Mum…'

'She does it sometimes if she thinks there's something that'll interest me, take me back I suppose. Anyway, this one had a special section for a festival they had in Pollersby. You know that village? You must do. We went there once, I'm sure we did. Apparently, it was their May Day celebration with maypole dancing and morris dancing and a fair and I don't know what. Anyway, the thing is, she particularly wanted me to see it because she thought she recognised Samuel in one of the photographs. And it is him, Nathan, she's right.' His mother almost laughed. 'Can you believe it? I can hardly believe it myself but I'm sure this time. It's him.' She paused. 'Thinner of course, a bit gaunt in the face, but we can do something about that, can't we?'

She waited and Nathan felt once again the full weight of her expectation. He had been here so many times before that he'd lost count and every time his mother would end up gut-wrenchingly disappointed, slapped back into a torpor which would take her weeks to get over. Over the years and still even now, well-meaning friends would regularly contact her to say they'd seen Sam on a train pulling out of a station. Yes, it had to be him. Or they'd seen him on a street in London, or Scotland, or when they were away travelling in South Africa or the States. They were always convinced that it was Sam and it always came to nothing.

And how would any of them know what Sam looked like now? Lyn certainly wouldn't; she hadn't seen him since he was a spotty teenager. Probably not even his mother would find it easy to recognise him now. Assuming that he was still alive. Nathan always qualified his thoughts in this way. In his heart of hearts, he doubted his brother was and he refused to get excited and feel the loss all over again. But how could he say that to his mother?

'Does the article mention him?' Nathan enquired carefully, aware that he was treading on glass in bare feet as usual.

'The article? No. No, it's all about the village celebrations of course. He just happened to be there, in the background of one of the pictures. By the pub. You know how these things are. But you're over there now, aren't you? You must go and look for him, Nathan. I'd send you the article but I don't want to part with it or risk it getting lost in the post and you're bound to be able to get your own copy somewhere there, aren't you?'

She read out the date on the newspaper. It was already a week and a half since it had come out. It wouldn't still be available to buy. He supposed he might be able to see a copy at the newspaper offices, wherever they were, but what was the point? Another grainy photograph of a complete stranger and, in spite of his determination to quell any hope, he would feel the agony of yet another disappointment.

Nathan composed himself, searching again for the right soothing but sensible words to say to his mother.

'I'll see what I can do, Mum. You do realise it's likely to be someone who happens to look a bit like Sam. We've been here before, haven't we, and we've ended up disappointed. It's painful. I don't want you to get your hopes up too high.'

'Oh darling, that won't happen this time, I'm sure. It's Sam, it must be.' She hesitated. 'And I know you get upset too when it comes to nothing,' she added softly. 'But it'll be all right this time. Trust me, this time we can bring him home.'

They talked a little longer: about her knee which had been a little swollen and painful – 'I think I twisted it' – and about his job at the manor – 'It sounds like a fascinating place. Did we ever visit it when we stayed over there?' They never had visited Ranling Manor, Nathan assured her, not when there were two young boys to amuse who wanted to mess about in boats. 'And Dad too,' he reminded her. 'You remember how he preferred to be out and about; he didn't care much for looking at exhibitions and old furniture.'

The call ended and Nathan made his way back to the inn. He met Hannah in the lounge bar and they sat with a drink while they considered the menu and the specials. After seeing little of each other all weekend, their forced proximity at work had brought about some thawing of the ice between them. He knew he'd overreacted to being told that Hannah had walked through the reserve. He also sensed that Rose liked to say things and twist it to her own ends and, at work that morning, he'd said something to that effect to Hannah.

'I suppose I should have mentioned it,' she'd conceded and they'd let the matter drop.

Now Hannah was looking at him expectantly.

'Did you manage to speak to your mother?' she asked.

'Yes, thanks.'

'How is she?'

He hesitated and feigned further interest in the menu which he already knew virtually by heart.

How was his mother? Where could you start to describe the situation? He didn't like to talk about it. He didn't want people's sympathy or their trite efforts to make him feel better. And yet, after negotiating these conversations with his mother, he sometimes felt as if he might explode if he didn't speak. All the things he wished he could say but had forced himself to bottle up would come rushing out anyway, bursting from him.

It was the interminability of it which drove him to distraction. He felt like they were on a giant hamster wheel, going round and round but never getting anywhere. And of course it was his mother's anguish which cut him in two. It was infuriating that she allowed herself to believe every time, that she never learnt from the previous pain, and yet he admired her for never giving up hope.

He put the menu down.

'She's OK. She's twisted her knee and it's a bit swollen. Otherwise...' He sighed. 'A friend has sent her a newspaper that's local to somewhere near here. There's a piece about an event in Pollersby.'

Hannah frowned. 'I recognise the name from the map. Is it north of here?'

'I think so. I don't remember it much. Anyway, one of the photographs in this newspaper includes what she thinks is a shot of my brother Samuel.' He shook his head and took a long draught of beer.

'What makes her think he would be over here?'

'She believes he's anywhere where someone has supposedly seen him. It doesn't matter where it is or how unlikely. Her friend Lyn who lives near here thought the picture looked like Sam so Mum does too. I can't tell you how many times I've been through this. I just wish she'd...' He gave a shuddering sigh. '...let it all go, let Sam go and try to live a life for herself now.'

Hannah nodded slowly. 'I guess it's the not knowing that haunts you. There's no closure, is there. No way to grieve and move on.'

He was struck by her tone. There was nothing sickly sympathetic about it, rather it actually suggested understanding which was unusual in his experience. Of course Hannah knew about loss and grieving: she had coped with her mother's dementia and then lost her not long before starting this job. She'd been pretty haunted by it herself. Perhaps she still was.

91

'Exactly,' he said. 'That's it. If we'd found out that he'd died, it would have been hellish but this constant hope and disappointment...' He didn't bother to finish the sentence. 'Let's talk about something else. In fact, why don't we order? I'll go. What do you want?'

'Chicken curry please.'

Back at the table they were both silent.

'I bumped into Sidony on Saturday,' said Hannah. 'We had a drink together in fact. It seems she and Rose aren't close.'

'She told you that?'

'Yes. I asked her how she coped with living and working at the manor, given her divorce from Toby.'

'Bold,' remarked Nathan. 'I like it. What did she say?'

'That she wasn't going to give up a good job and her "associations" as she put it when she doesn't care about him now anyway.'

'Fair enough.'

Hannah nodded thoughtfully. 'She also said that the manor only staggers along, that without the functions and extras they'd struggle to make ends meet. Interesting, I thought.'

Nathan raised his eyebrows. 'That was remarkably forthcoming. What did she want?'

'She wanted us to be good people and not stir the waters too much. My words, not hers. She's scared of rumours that'll impact the business.' Hannah sat back holding her glass of wine. 'You know, I think she has a soft spot for Mortimer.'

'Rose was asking about my job, how much it allowed me to travel. She's led a pretty restricted life from the sounds of it. I actually felt sorry for her.'

'Oh, that's dangerous. You're probably the most exciting thing that's happened to her in ages, Nathan Bright. She's banking on you taking her away from Ranling Manor and putting the world at her feet. You'd better watch out or in no time she'll be fixing dates with Alan to hire a marquee and have your wedding reception at the manor.'

Nathan pulled a face. 'Oh please.'

'Which reminds me,' said Hannah. 'Sid told me that Alan had tried it on with Carrie but got nowhere.'

'Really? I thought he was engaged?'

'He is.'

'Well, well. I wonder if that's important.'

Hannah regarded Nathan over her glass of wine. 'It'd be interesting to have a good look round the storeroom ourselves, wouldn't it?'

'Ourselves? Excuse me, I thought you'd written the whole thing off as an accident?'

'No-o, I'm keeping an open mind. There's a key to the storeroom in some sort of box in Rose's desk in the office. I asked Sid who had access to one.'

'You shouldn't have done that. You'll make them suspicious of us.'

'They already are. First Mortimer with you, then Sidony with me.'

'It'd take time to look round properly. I'd have to do it alone while you distracted them. Both of us in there would be too obvious. What could you do?'

'Me? Nothing. I am not starting a fire. Not even in a waste paper basket.'

'That wouldn't work anyway. Too many smoke alarms. We'd have the fire service descending on us.' Nathan took another pull of beer and sat back. 'I'll think of something.'

They were both silent again. He saw a smile pulling at the corners of Hannah's mouth.

'Well, at least you're not so grumpy now,' she said.

'I'm never grumpy. I've never been anything other than my usual charming self. What do you mean?'

She didn't reply but the smile broadened. Damn her. He did feel better actually. He realised she'd probably done it intentionally, distracting him from his lugubrious thoughts about his mother and Sam by talking about the Gyllam-Spences. It didn't change the fact that, for some reason, Hannah could make him swear black was white just to contradict her.

Chapter 7

This had been Sidony's idea. It was Saturday night and Mortimer sat at the head of the dining table, gloomily surveying the assembled party. Sid was sitting at the other end, facing him, and caught his eye from time to time as if warning him to behave. She wanted him to play the perfect host, had insisted that he make an effort.

She had called on him in his private lair on the Tuesday evening to tell him her plan. He had been sticking foliage on trees. His railway landscape lacked trees, he had decided, maybe even a small wood. There were a few dotted around but not enough. It looked bare, as if some terrible blight had stricken the area.

'We should invite our two restorers to have dinner with us,' she'd said.

'Why should we do that?'

'Firstly, because it would be the hospitable thing to do. They're stuck living in a pub for the duration and it's not very homely, is it? Plus, they're our guests.'

'No they're not. They're... well, they're our employees, in a way.'

'Now you're sounding like a snob.'

'I'm not a snob.'

'I know. But you sound like one when you say things like that.'

'But it's true. And I don't have to prove it to them. I've been very courteous and welcoming.'

'We need to be even more welcoming.' She hesitated. 'Ever since Carrie's tragic death, there's been an atmosphere here, Mortimer. You can't have missed it. Everyone's understandably edgy. And then there's that story about someone ferreting about in the storeroom. I know, I know, don't look at me like that. I'm sure there was nothing to it. But my point is: it might be a good idea to make our relationship with these people more social and less functional. It would defuse the situation a little, make it more relaxed. They seem to want answers when there aren't any questions to ask. But people are less suspicious if they get a chance to know you. They're much less likely to tell stories or create waves. We don't want any trouble do we?' He looked at her doubtfully. 'I'm only talking about dinner, Mortimer. I'm not suggesting you adopt them.'

'I've already chatted to Hannah. I showed her round the public rooms soon after they arrived.'

'And you think that's enough?'

She'd looked at him pityingly. He liked to think there was some affection in it too but he wasn't sure. After all these years, Sid was still a mystery to him; she played her cards so close to her chest. He didn't remember her being like that when they were both young, but marriage to Toby would be likely to change anyone. In any case, he had agreed to the meal. He was always going to give in to her sooner or later. Did she know that and bank on his agreement? Probably not. He hadn't told her how he felt about her since she'd gone off with Toby all those years ago.

And now here he was, presiding over dinner with these strangers. He hated dinner parties at the best of times; he'd much rather be sticking foliage on trees. That's why Sid kept looking at him.

They'd already eaten the starter, a salmon mousse with toast, and now the main course – pork loin with apple sauce and duchess potatoes – had just been served, plated, by Netta with the assistance of her niece, Rita, who helped out on a part-time basis and for special occasions, glad of a bit of extra money. There were eight of them round the table. On Mortimer's right sat Alan with Rose beyond him and then Nathan. Hannah sat to his left, next to Toby and then Grace. Sidony had organised the seating.

'I'm splitting them up,' she'd said. 'Divide and conquer. Makes them less likely to present a united front.'

Toby had wanted to invite Amanda but Mortimer had put his foot down and Toby had reluctantly capitulated. There was going to be enough tension round the table, Mortimer thought, without adding Toby's latest mistress to the mix.

Rita was now putting two large bowls of vegetables on the table, one of carrot batons and one of savoy cabbage and Netta came behind her with two gravy boats. She looked round anxiously to see what she might have forgotten, then left, bundling Rita out before her and closing the door.

Mortimer offered red wine which everyone accepted apart from Hannah who was driving and claimed she was happy with water. While the vegetables were being passed round, Sidony turned to her near neighbour.

'I'm so glad you could come, Grace. I haven't seen you in a while.'

Grace flicked a quick glance across at Alan who was spooning carrots onto his plate, then offered a brief smile. 'Thank you for asking me.' She accepted the bowl of cabbage Toby passed to her. 'Spring's always busy on the reserve.'

'I imagine it is,' responded Sid smoothly. 'Have you seen anything of this fabled crane that everyone's talking about?'

97

'Oh yes, he's about. But you usually only see him when it's quiet. We're hoping he might attract a mate.'

'I must come over sometime.'

'The best times to come are early or late. After that poor woman's body was found in the Broad, it's brought in all sorts of morbid onlookers.'

An awkward silence fell and glances were exchanged.

'That's what you said would happen, isn't it, uncle Mortimer?' said Rose, apparently oblivious to the mood.

'Something like that, Rose,' he mumbled, aware that Sid was watching him again.

They finished serving themselves. Mortimer's mother had always insisted on saying grace but that hadn't been done since she'd died and, as soon as everyone was served, Mortimer picked up his cutlery.

'Right. Everyone done? Let's eat.' The sooner this was over, the better.

For a few minutes, all that could be heard was the scrape of silver cutlery on china plates.

'So do you sometimes manage to get back home at the weekend?' said Sidony to the two restorers. 'You don't usually work weekends, do you?'

'We do sometimes if there's something we want to get on with, you know, for continuity.' Hannah glanced over at Nathan. 'We don't generally try to get back home. It's quite a long way just for a weekend.'

'Cross country,' agreed Toby. 'Always the slowest routes.'

'How do you all manage to get time off or take a holiday?' said Hannah. 'It must be very full on here.'

'We have a kind of rota,' said Mortimer.

'Informally,' added Sidony. 'Everyone chips in to keep the place running. I try to organise a more efficient rota so it's fair for everyone but no-one seems to keep to it.'

'You don't keep to it yourself.' Toby flicked her a dark look. 'You nip off up to that flat of yours in London, soon as blink. You can't complain about everyone else.'

'I wasn't complaining.'

'So long as everyone does their work *and* gets a break,' intervened Mortimer quickly, 'it doesn't matter, does it?'

There was another silence. Mortimer became aware of Alan looking sidelong at him. Alan and Grace had come over early and let themselves in – Alan had a key to the back door, after all – so when Mortimer had come out of his study, ready to go and receive his guests, he'd found Alan in the hallway outside. Why was he there? And had he heard anything of the phone call Mortimer had been making? Mortimer tried to remember exactly what he'd been saying at the time but wasn't sure.

Nathan broke into his thoughts. 'Didn't I see some posters for special events you've got planned for the Spring Bank Holiday weekend?'

Toby nodded vigorously, still chewing, then swallowed. 'Glad you saw them.' He turned to wave his fork at Mortimer. 'You see, the posters do work.'

'But we need more up,' said Alan. 'East Ranling's covered but I didn't see any in Ramsby the other day, or Shepston.'

'I thought you were doing all the neighbouring villages,' protested Toby. 'I can't be everywhere.'

'I have been doing other things.' Alan looked at Toby with frank dislike. 'You are responsible for the publicity, are you not?'

Mortimer raised a pacifying hand. 'I don't think we need to discuss these things now, do we, Toby, Alan? It's Saturday night and we have guests.' He turned to Nathan. 'Yes, it's a regular event we have for Spring Bank Holiday. There'll be a big marquee on the lawn with a craft fair running all weekend and falconry displays too.'

'And don't you have a Punch and Judy show too?' asked Hannah. 'I used to love them when I was little.'

'That's right,' said Sidony. 'We try to keep a sort of old-world theme to these events when possible, keeping them in line with the history of the place.'

Hannah put her cutlery down and picked up her glass of water. 'It must be such a responsibility looking after this wonderful collection. Do you think you might still add to it?'

Mortimer realised everyone was looking his way and the silence grew and became uncomfortable. He paused eating.

'Well, I hope we might. As I think you know, we occasionally get work bequeathed to us. That's always quite exciting.'

'Oh yes, we're always open to offers.' Toby grinned and took a long swig of wine. 'What he's trying to say is there's not the money now, you see, unless we're given something. Though our forefathers never turned down a good offer either, as far as I can tell. In fact, one suspects that the first Gyllam-Spences acquired some of their pieces in highly dubious ways.' He winked across at Hannah. 'Not that I'm suggesting we do that.'

Rose giggled.

Mortimer glared at them both. 'The collection was started in the eighteenth century. There was in fact considerable wealth at the time which came from the wool trade and then shipping. Of course the collection was paid for. There's still paperwork for some of the art purchased, even from back then.'

Toby smirked at Hannah. 'Some of it.'

'I don't believe that any of the old significant collections

100

have paperwork for absolutely everything.' Alan flicked Toby a dirty look. 'Some of it is bound to get lost through the years. It makes the collection no less important or treasured.'

'Tell us about your work,' said Sidony loudly, embracing both Nathan and Hannah with a smile. 'All the pieces you must get to see – it must be fascinating. Very varied I imagine. Or do you specialise and become very expert in a particular field?'

'Not really,' said Nathan. 'We have to be quite versatile but there are areas which some of us have had more experience in. Though there's always something new to learn.'

'We try to keep on top of the latest developments in restoration,' Hannah added.

Rose turned to Nathan alongside her and offered him a winning smile. 'Like you specialise in drawings.'

'Not exactly but I've done quite a bit of work with them.'

Sid turned to Hannah. 'And you're working on our Old Masters.'

Mortimer wasn't sure he liked all this talk about art and restoration. In an effort to defuse the situation, Sidony was trying too hard.

'I'm sure they don't want to spend their evening talking about work,' he said. 'They get enough of that all week. Tell me, have you had a chance to explore our beautiful slice of Norfolk?'

The conversation moved on to particular places of interest to see. Nathan knew some already; Hannah had never been to the area before. The subject kept them all safely occupied until the dessert – a French apple tart with cream – was served.

'Which part of London are you based in?' Hannah asked Sidony. 'I worked in London for a while and had a flat in Finchley. It was only a shoebox really, because rents were so high but still it was great to be able to visit the galleries and museums or take in the occasional play.'

'West Hampstead,' said Sidony. 'My flat's pretty tiny too but, as you say, it means you can get out and see things.'

'It's not so tiny you couldn't squeeze a guest in,' complained Rose. 'You always want to go alone.'

'That's not true. The last time I asked you, you wouldn't come.'

Rose looked sulky. 'That was because...' She glanced sideways at Nathan. '...it doesn't matter.'

Sid smiled towards Hannah. 'But it is nice to be alone there sometimes with only yourself to please. There are always people about here.' The smile faded as if she thought she'd said the wrong thing. She looked down and ate a mouthful of apple tart.

'I have my den,' Mortimer said, to cover for her. 'I please myself there.'

'I wasn't aware you didn't please yourself everywhere.' Toby fixed him with a look. 'Though you certainly make yourself scarce when it suits.'

'And this from the man who's hardly ever here,' said Mortimer bitterly, waving an impatient hand towards his brother. He stopped short, diverted his hand to his wine glass and managed something approaching a laugh in Nathan and Hannah's direction. 'Don't mind us. Families, eh. Always argue, don't they?'

By the time the meal had ended nearly an hour later and the conservators had refused coffee and gone back to the inn for the night, Mortimer wasn't sure they'd created quite the impression Sid had had in mind.

After seeing his guests off, Mortimer found Grace waiting to see him in the hallway, before she and Alan left too.

'Mortimer, have you been able to find someone to take a look at our roof? Another tile came off last week and it leaks

102

worse than ever when the wind blows the rain in.'

'Really? Oh dear. I am sorry, Grace. I'll see what I can do.'

Alan was waiting along the hallway, pale eyes fixedly watching, expressionless. Indeed, Mortimer was sure that it was Alan who had prompted the diffident Grace to ask the question. It occurred to Mortimer suddenly that Grace was scared of Alan. Why had he never noticed that before? He also suspected that Alan could be a ruthless man if there was something he wanted. Or if he were crossed.

*

Hannah was back at her easel on the Monday morning staring at the flaking Perugino. When consulted, Timothy had expressed his usual dismay at any suggestion of a delay in his neatly planned schedule but, after he had spoken to Mortimer, she had been given the green light to proceed. Trying to flatten the warped section of panel which had caused the paint to flake in the first place would only have created worse problems, as would trying to pin it to stop it warping further. It was going to be a slow job but Hannah had settled for stabilising the paint surface and hoped that the worst of the warping had already happened. The painting was nearly five hundred years old after all.

As she carefully used a tiny brush to ease a little diluted adhesive under a fragment of loose paint, she wondered what would happen to the collection now that Carrie had gone. The young woman had understood the care these fragile artworks needed. She'd mentioned her hope of introducing better humidity control and storage procedures, had complained that the art was being neglected and needed a radical plan to stop it deteriorating further. Change. Had that been the reason she had become so unpopular? Or was all the innuendo about her 'new broom' approach started by someone simply to create a gulf between her and the rest of the staff; it weakened her position and made her more likely to be ignored. It was the way bullies worked. Someone might have been using it as a tactic to cover their pilfering.

She pressed gently with a clean soft brush on the paint she'd just stuck down, firming it into place, and glanced across at Nathan who was now cleaning the Barocci – a head study executed in black, red and white chalk. He was absorbed and concentrating but his mood seemed to have lifted in recent days. In her car, returning from the dinner party on the Saturday night, they had inevitably engaged in a post-mortem of the meal.

'What did you make of that, then?' he'd said. 'Talk about a warring family. They're all at each other's throats. And Mortimer seems particularly twitchy. What's he up to?'

'Why should he be up to anything? Wouldn't you be twitchy if your family was bickering around you?

He didn't respond. Maybe referring to his family wasn't such a good idea.

'Did you clock that Sidony has a place in London and goes there often?' he said a couple of minutes later.

'Ye-es. So?'

'So, if someone is taking drawings and replacing them with forgeries, they'd have to be able to offload them. London would be the obvious place.'

'Now you're suspecting Sidony?'

'I'm just saying. You can't trust what they're telling us, any of them. There's a little too much righteous indignation and defensiveness when anyone questions the integrity of the collection.'

'True.' She paused, thinking it through. 'Sid might be trying to do something to keep Mortimer afloat.'

'Or just financing her lifestyle. She wears quality clothes, that woman. She doesn't do cheap.'

'Maybe. But has it occurred to you that, according to your theory, there would have to be two people involved at the very least, one to steal and another to create a replacement? Unless, of course, one of your prime suspects here at the manor happens to be a closet artist, brilliant enough to be able to fake an Old Master drawing.'

He was silent. She flicked a glance sideways at him as she drove but there were no street lights on these country roads and she couldn't read his expression.

'Except that the art work doesn't have to be brilliant, does it?' he said eventually as they turned into the car park of The Boatman. 'I mean, not so good that a specialist would be taken in. These art works have presumably been authenticated already. Unless the estate decides to sell one, they aren't going to be re-examined. The forgery just has to fool the people here for a while. But you're right about needing two people to make it work. Good point. I've been so busy wondering who was doing the stealing and who would have been prepared to kill Carrie over it that I never got that far.'

Now, peering through her magnifying lens, Hannah eased a little more adhesive under another flake of loose paint while Prokofiev's *Romeo and Juliet* coursed into her ears from her stereo. She was slowly nodding her head to the *Dance of the Knights* when Nathan came to stand beside her easel. She gave the paint a quick firming prod and pulled out her earpieces.

'What?' she said impatiently. She loved this piece of music.

'I've got it.' He moved round to lean against the window sill.

'Got what?'

He glanced towards the door and dropped his voice.

'How I can get into the storeroom and look around. This weekend. It's their Bank Holiday event, remember? They'll all be so wrapped up in it that no-one's going to be bothering about us. I figure we make ourselves visible at the event over the weekend, smile nicely and look like we've put the whole Carrie business behind us, then work the Monday the same as usual. Except that I'll get the key to the storeroom and finally get to see what's going on in there.'

'And what do I do?'

'Cover for me if anyone comes looking and asking questions.'

'Oh great. Thanks.'

Chapter 8

The Bank Holiday events always brought crowds of people to Ranling Manor.

Rose liked it. Normally the house was like an old ship, she thought, beached and left to dry out, creaking and groaning, but the holiday events created a buzz, transforming the place for the weekend, as if they were hosting a huge garden party. Alan had organised special tickets for those who only wanted to visit the attractions in the gardens and locals poured in as well as visitors from further afield.

This year, they were helped by dry weather and some fitful warm sunshine. All the family and staff were expected to be on hand to help out: Toby was in charge of the public address system, announcing events and encouraging people to patronise the café; Sidony moved around, marshalling her guides and helping out at the ticket office; Alan acted like a wandering trouble-shooter, walking briskly between event venues with a two-way radio in hand, very full of his own importance. Even old Netta helped out at the café for a couple of hours each afternoon.

Rose wasn't sure what her uncle did exactly but she had a soft spot for Mortimer and forgave him. He wasn't one for big gatherings. He'd disappear off to his den as soon as he got the chance while the rest of them got on with it.

'No time off for good behaviour here,' Rose had remarked

coyly to Nathan earlier in the week. 'It's all hands on deck for special events like this. You will come, won't you?'

'Definitely. But we'll have to work the Monday. I don't think our boss has heard of Bank Holidays.'

She laughed. 'I'll be helping out at the café. Make sure you call in. I'll be looking out for you.'

And he did come, visiting the café on both the Saturday and the Sunday afternoons, buying tea and a piece of cake from her on each occasion. He looked like he was enjoying himself, said he wanted to make sure he saw everything. And, best of all as far as Rose was concerned, he did it without that other woman. On her break, Rose had seen Hannah – she of the superior manner and challenging gaze – wander round the displays and the craft fair by herself. She'd even stood at the back of the crowd of children sitting to watch the Punch and Judy show, shouting at Punch and laughing just like the children. Strange behaviour for a grown woman. And those clothes she wore: a vividly-patterned flounced skirt, a bright blue sleeveless tee-shirt and a clunky pebble necklace. It was hardly surprising that Nathan wasn't interested in her.

But, in spite of herself, Rose found Hannah intriguing. She was confident and self-possessed; she gave the impression of being in control. More than that she didn't seem to care what other people thought. Rose rather envied that.

*

On the Monday morning the conservators were back at work. Hannah, the earpieces of her music player rammed in her ears as usual, had said she'd virtually finished stabilising the loose paint on the Perugino but Nathan could see her scanning it now with a raking light, checking the surface for anything she'd missed. She was nothing if not thorough and he appreciated that about her. Nathan, however, struggled to settle, his mind going ahead to his foray into the storeroom later. He spent the morning cleaning the chalk dust and eraser crumbs off his work table, then cutting a fresh mount and backing board for the Barocci.

He'd decided to leave his exploration until early afternoon when the biggest crowds descended, the gardens were thronging and the house was at its quietest. That would give him roughly three hours before people came back in. Would that be long enough? It had to be. The only variable was Mortimer. He'd been seen early in the afternoon on both the Saturday and the Sunday, sauntering around the gardens, acknowledging the people he knew, saying a polite and gracious word here and there, but not staying. Having shown his face and graced the public, Mortimer had slipped away early. To his shed perhaps and his beloved trains. Or maybe he had somewhere else to go. Either way, it was a risk Nathan had to take.

It was just after one when Nathan left the workroom, crossed into the private side of the house and wandered as nonchalantly as he could up the hallway to the rear door of the office. He had rehearsed a variety of excuses if someone happened to be there but thankfully it was empty and the door to the public hall was closed. He could hear a tour guide on the other side of it explaining to a visitor the layout and order of the rooms to be visited. He crossed to Rose's desk. It had seven drawers: one in the middle over the kneehole and three on each side. He slid each one out in turn until he found a box – a lockable, hinged metal affair which mercifully had the key in the lock. It wasn't hard to see why Carrie had despaired of Mortimer's security. There were maybe eight keys in it of varying sizes and the larger ones were all labelled. He found the one for the storeroom, slipped the box back in the drawer and returned the way he'd come.

The key tuned noiselessly in the lock – perhaps someone had taken the trouble to oil it recently – and he slipped inside, locking the door behind him and flicking on the light.

According to Carrie, some works were never shown publicly because they were deemed too fragile; others were put on display on rotation with works already on view; a few seemed to have been stored and then forgotten. The whole space was disordered anyway, she'd said, and it was hard to find anything. She'd laughed.

'This place is kind of archaic,' she'd said. 'You'll see. Lots of old-world charm maybe but it needs dragging into the nineties.'

Her words and her laugh echoed through Nathan's head now, as if she were still standing there beside him. It felt surreal to remember that she was dead. Horrifying. The thought brought him back to the present and the importance of what he was doing. He scanned the room.

It was a large rectangular space with a racking system from floor to ceiling on the far wall for framed and unframed paintings, both canvas and panel, and a deep shelving unit against the wall to his left, stacked with box files. To his right was a huge plan chest with eight shallow drawers and another narrow shelving unit. He had no idea where to start, especially since he wasn't even sure what exactly he was looking for. A glance at the writing on the box files suggested they held the paperwork for the art works: their provenance, gallery exhibits, authentication letters and valuations.

But there had to be an inventory. Carrie had made passing reference to one, that it was woefully inadequate and that she was going to redo it. There was a loose-leaf file folder on top of the plan chest and he picked it up. This was clearly Carrie's work: dividers had been inserted and labelled for a succession of chronological art periods, though it only went as far as the

Baroque. She must have been planning on preparing another. Sadly there was only information in it for a handful of artists; it was very much a work in progress.

But there was a chunky hard-backed exercise book lying flat on the edge of one of the lower storage shelves. *INVENTORY* had been written in capital letters on a sticky label applied to the front where it was peeling from one corner, and a quick flick through revealed pages of hand-written scrawl by a succession of different hands with new additions to the collection added apparently haphazardly at the end. This must be the one Carrie had inherited with the job. It did look chaotic. How was this going to help?

He noticed however that each of the drawers of the plan chest had a small sticky label on the end of it. The top one had A – D written on it; the second had E – H and so on down each drawer to the bottom. He put on a pair of thin cotton gloves and pulled out the drawer next to the bottom, labelled Q – T. It held a range of works on paper in assorted media, many mounted and contained in clear archival pockets but some were simply held in paper folders, acid-free hopefully. He'd seen a work by Giovanni Battista Tiepolo in the inventory, noted simply as *Head of an Old Woman,* and he found it – it was mounted and backed – and he pulled it out and laid it on top of the chest. Now he saw how this worked.

He returned to the inventory and painstakingly began to cross-reference each work, searching in the respective drawers. It was a slow and tedious job. A lot of the work was of little more than average quality, some of it clearly produced quickly to satisfy the commercial market of the time. Some of Mortimer's ancestors had shown more acquisitiveness than taste. On the other hand there were some real treasures in here and occasionally he found himself becoming distracted by a particularly accomplished work, enjoying the craft of it and the confidence of the lines, then had to remind himself that he was looking for something 'wrong' or maybe something missing. Time was pressing: this wasn't an art show for his benefit.

In a few places in the inventory he found notes written in pencil, done by a newer hand, presumably Carrie's – reminders to get a work freshly mounted or stored differently. The watercolour by Richard Parkes Bonnington that he was due to work on had 'arrange to have on view' written alongside it with a question mark. He was more than half way through the inventory book and his eyes were starting to tire, his concentration wavering, when, in the middle of reading the entry for a work by Annibale Carracci – a preparatory drawing of a young man for an altarpiece – something caught his attention and he brought the book closer. There were fragments of a pencil rubber both on the sheet and caught in the fold of the pages, the pale grey or off-white residue left behind after something has been erased. He held the book underneath the light. Definitely. And if he tilted the book slightly, he could make out the faint marking of what had been there before: against the entry for Carracci was a question mark. And it was the same distinctive mark Carrie had made on the Bonnington with a slight backward slope and an exaggerated curly top.

He frowned, then searched in the top drawer for the drawing and pulled it out, still in its clear protective pouch. It had been done in red chalk, heightened with white, on buff paper. Nathan stared at it a moment but left it on the top and returned to the inventory. A couple of pages later he found more eraser residue – he was looking for it now – and the unmistakeable imprint of another erased question mark, this time against the entry for a charcoal drawing of a young woman by Peter Paul Rubens. Nathan laid it next to the Carracci and stood looking from one to the other.

The skin began to prickle at the back of his neck. Carrie was right: there was something wrong about both these drawings. He felt that indefinable discomfort about them, like a nagging ache that's hard to pinpoint but won't be shrugged off. He couldn't be certain – he wasn't an expert – but his gut was telling him they weren't right. According to the inventory, the Rubens came into the collection in 1894. He flicked back: the Carracci was acquired in 1912. Of course, even if they were fakes, it didn't prove that someone had recently taken the originals. Mortimer's ancestors might have been duped by a smooth-talking dealer. He could imagine the sales patter: *This is a wonderful work, sir. This sort of piece doesn't come on the market very often. It's been in a private collection for more than a century in fact but now the owner's keen to sell to cover some debts. The thing is – well, I'm sure you understand – he doesn't want publicity.* People were deceived by that sort of line all the time. But Nathan didn't believe it, not after what Carrie had told him, not after seeing her question marks erased.

He returned to the inventory and held it under the light as he turned the pages. There was no need to cross-check every item now. He needed to look for more question marks and, a few pages on, he found one. This time it was against a red chalk drawing entitled *Portrait, Unknown* by Michelangelo Buonarroti and again it had been rubbed out. Now there was a name to conjure with. Even the great man's drawings could command a high figure. It was described as a drawing of a man's head in red chalk and highlights. Nathan began a search through the top drawer but it wasn't there. He tried searching under M. Still no joy. In desperation, he looked through all the drawers but there was no sign of the portrait. And there was nothing in the inventory to suggest that it had been loaned or damaged or sold either, so where was it? And who had been back to erase that question mark?

He heard a voice in the hall outside and immediately caught his breath and glanced at his watch: four twenty. Those were the unmistakeably soft, dry tones of Mortimer. Was he planning to come in here? The key was still in the door, blocking the keyhole, so if Mortimer tried his key in the lock, he'd guess straight away that there was someone inside.

Nathan quietly replaced the two drawings from the top into whichever drawer was still open and eased it back into place. He toyed with switching the light off but that might attract more notice.

He picked up the pouch containing the Tiepolo.

'I hope you don't mind me tracking down the key,' he planned to say. 'I wanted to have a look at your other Tiepolo. It'll help me with context for the one I've got to work on.'

Was it plausible? Enough, maybe, though not for locking himself in, especially after the warning he'd had. Nathan strained his ears to listen. It sounded like Mortimer was talking to Netta but he couldn't make out the words. Then a sticky couple of minutes later, it went quiet. Nathan put a hand to his chest and took a long, deep breath. He replaced the Tiepolo and the other two drawings in the appropriate drawers then studied the inventory again. *Portrait, Unknown* seemed to have been exhibited intermittently until a few months ago.

He flicked slowly through the remaining pages of the inventory but found no more of Carrie's question marks. It was twenty to five and he needed to be out of there, needed to get the key back in the box before anyone noticed it was missing. In any case, he knew now what had spooked Carrie. The issue was what to do about it.

*

Showered and wrapped in her dressing gown, Hannah was

sitting at the tiny table in her room, staring at an almost blank sheet of paper. She and Nathan had both arranged to have their mail forwarded to the inn and, spread out on the table to her right were two sheets of tightly handwritten pages from her sister, Elizabeth. It was six forty-five and Hannah had been trying to write a reply for half an hour already. It was never easy. Elizabeth was a teacher, three years older than Hannah, and they'd never had much in common. Now Elizabeth had written to say that she and her husband, Ian, had moved home. Again. They had been living in Knutsford in Cheshire but had recently bought a huge barn conversion in a village nearby.

Elizabeth had been fulsome in its praise:

> *Oodles of character but with every modern convenience. We love it. You won't believe the vaulted ceiling in the sitting room. You must come and see us when we've settled in. It's been too long. I did try ringing to tell you but you're never there, are you? I hope this reaches you wherever you've gadded off to this time.*

Hannah's reply so far hadn't got beyond *Dear Elizabeth,* and *Congratulations on the new house.* What else was there to say? Elizabeth and Ian had no children and poured all their love and attention into their home. Elizabeth had been teaching at the same school for years and Ian was a solicitor, a partner in a local legal practice. Their house was all about entertaining and creating the right impression for their guests, often his clients. Elizabeth's idea of wall art was any kind of print which matched the décor. Which was fine: it was their home. Hannah didn't care what they chose to do except that Eliza insisted on making derogatory comments about Hannah's life choices.

There was another one in the current letter:

*How can you stand fiddling away at dirty, moth-eaten
paintings all day? You could have achieved so much more,
Hannah. And how are you going to meet anyone and settle
down when you never stay anywhere long enough? You
know Mum hated you moving around all the time. It's not
too late for you to have children. She'd have liked that.
Especially since I was advised not to try for a baby.*

Rereading it, Hannah let out a grunt of frustration, dropped her
pen on the table and stood up just as someone knocked on her
door. She pulled the dressing gown tighter across her chest and
walked across to stand behind it.

'Who is it?'

'Me.'

She turned the key and pulled it back. Nathan walked in
saying nothing, glanced round, then sat heavily on the side of
the bed. Hannah closed the door, relocked it and turned to
examine him.

'You're wet.'

'Full marks for observation. It's raining.'

'Right. And now you're making my bed wet.'

He glanced down as the comment seemed to flicker
briefly across his brain but he didn't move. She turned the
chair by the table round and sat to face him. Returning to the
workroom that afternoon, he had refused to tell her anything
about what he'd found in the storeroom. Rather, he'd mimed
zipping his lips while glancing meaningfully at the door then
simply resumed his work. She'd left just after five and hadn't
seen him since.

'So,' she said, 'are you finally going to tell me what you
found this afternoon?'

'Don't get touchy. You know we can't talk there. There's
always someone hanging around and I needed some time to

116

think. I went for a walk.'

'In the rain?'

'Yes, in the rain. Haven't you ever walked in the rain when you needed to clear your head?'

She pulled a face. 'Maybe.'

'Then I went to the phone box and rang my mother.'

'Of course, it's Monday. How is she?'

He shook his head. 'Still going on about that newspaper piece, wanted to know what I'd found out. I haven't even thought about it.'

'You should though. I mean, just to...'

'No.' He cut her short. 'There's too much else on my mind. Anyway, I'm still hoping she'll let it go.' His glance took in the writing paper and envelope on the desk. 'Sorry, I'm disturbing you.'

'Not really. I'm trying to write a letter to my sister. It's like trying to do a self-appendectomy using a blunt penknife.'

'Oh.'

He looked disinterested; he'd barely heard her.

'OK, so tell me.'

'Well, it's exactly what I suspected.' Nathan ran a hand through his wet hair. 'There's a drawing missing. By Michelangelo.'

'Michelangelo? Wow, even just a sketch by him would be worth serious money. Are you sure?'

'Of course I'm sure. I looked everywhere. And it can't just be bad record-keeping. Carrie had drawn a question mark in pencil next to its entry in the inventory and someone has been in and rubbed it out. But I could still see the imprint.'

'You're sure it was rubbed out recently?'

'It was definitely Carrie's question mark – hers are distinctive. And she didn't rub it out herself. She's dead, remember?'

117

They were both silent.

'So what are you going to do about it?' said Hannah.

'I don't know. I'd bet everything I own that someone has taken it to sell. Someone probably intended to replace it with a copy but with all the commotion and the police hanging around, they changed their minds.' He paused and frowned. 'Or…' He rocked his head side to side. 'Or maybe they haven't got round to it yet. Maybe they need it a while to make the copy.'

Nathan had been staring at the wall opposite. He turned to look at her.

'There's something else. There are two drawings there which look wrong – there's just something about them. It's exactly as she said. She'd marked those too and those marks have been erased as well. There might be others that aren't right that she either didn't notice or didn't mark. I didn't have time to check every one in detail and, honestly, I wouldn't necessarily know. And I didn't have time to look at the oil paintings either but it's easier to fake a drawing. It's also easier to secrete unframed works in and out of the building.'

Hannah didn't respond.

'So,' he prompted, 'what do you think?'

'I think it's going to be difficult to prove,' she said slowly. 'The police wouldn't give you the time of day for a story like that. And if you kick up a fuss about it, without any real evidence to back it up, Mortimer is clearly going to deny it. He'll claim an error again, or a misplacement, damaged goods, anything rather than get bad publicity. It'd be your word against his.'

'So we have to find some proof. We owe it to Carrie.'

She stared at him. 'You do realise how hard that's going to be? There won't be a paper trail. There's a lot of wheeling and dealing goes on that never gets anywhere near a gallery or

118

an auction house – dealers who know the collectors with special interests, including those who won't ask too many questions.'

Nathan shrugged. 'There'll be something. People always make mistakes. Something small maybe but it'll give them away in the end.' He paused and raised one quizzical eyebrow at her. 'It's not like you to back down from a challenge.'

Hannah sighed inwardly. He obviously wasn't going to let this go. She suspected it wasn't just about Carrie. It was as much to do with his missing brother which clearly weighed heavily on him. Maybe doing this was some kind of atonement for feeling he'd let his brother down. Or maybe for thinking he'd let them both down.

'It would be useful,' she said, to herself as much as to him, 'to know where they all were – Toby, Alan and the rest of them – on the Friday when Carrie went missing.'

'Certainly, but how will we find that out, short of raiding the police records? I assume they asked everyone else the same questions they asked us. *We* can't very well ask them.' He adopted a high, strangled voice. 'Excuse me, Alan, but where were you when Carrie was being murdered?'

She produced a pained smile. 'Well certainly not like that. But it is amazing how much people like to talk, especially about themselves.'

'That sounds like your province, not mine.'

Hannah laughed shortly. 'On the contrary, I think Rose would love to talk to you.'

Nathan groaned.

'As for places where a piece of art could be fenced,' she added, 'there's a gallery up the road here in the village. I went in once. It had some decent pieces, especially watercolours, but everything they sell is new work, a lot of it aimed at tourists. It's too close for comfort anyway. Though it might be worth checking out the local auction house, finding out if anything has been sold on recently, just in case they weren't shifted privately.' And it'll keep you busy, she thought. Make you feel like you're doing something.

'I doubt it. That'd be too close as well. In any case, it's probably the kind of auction house where they sell old furniture and pianos with half their strings missing. It won't be any good to us.'

'Well that's where you're wrong, smarty pants. I saw an advert from them in the local paper last weekend. Swinyard Auctioneers – an old family firm. They're just a few miles away and they've got a specialist art sale this Saturday. They have one every quarter. I think they've got viewing all week.'

Nathan bowed his head in silent acknowledgement. 'Then we should go and take a look.'

Chapter 9

It would be useful to know where they all were... on the Friday when Carrie went missing.

Hannah's own words rattled round her head on an annoying repetitive loop. Why had she said that? Why was she allowing herself to get sucked into this? She acknowledged that there was a serious wrong to be righted but wasn't convinced they were the right people to be doing it. If Carrie was killed to stop her talking, they could be treading on very dangerous ground, especially since Nathan tended to go at things like a bull in a china shop.

Still, left alone, he'd only get himself into trouble. And she was intrigued.

It's amazing how much people like to talk, especially about themselves.

She had often been surprised at how readily complete strangers, given a sympathetic ear, had trusted her with their personal stories. And it had occurred to her that Netta knew a great deal about the people in the manor and that her sister, Irene, made it her business to know a great deal about everything. They'd be a perfect source of information, approached the right way. Netta had confided to her once that she and her sister got together every Thursday after work and treated themselves to afternoon tea at the tea rooms in the village.

'It's open till six during the season,' she'd said, 'and it's a bit quieter for that last hour. Have you been in? They do a delicious chocolate fudge cake.'

It could be a perfect opportunity to get them talking; Hannah just needed an angle, a reason to 'bump into' them. She managed to get an appointment with the village hairdresser for four o'clock on the Thursday afternoon, started work early that morning and was back in East Ranling with time to spare. Coming out of the hairdresser's some fifty minutes later, she saw Netta and her sister heading up the road to the tea rooms. She gave them a few minutes, then followed on. Glancing in the tea shop window, she could see a few people enjoying a late afternoon tea but it wasn't busy and she went in.

It was a quaint place, the sort of old-fashioned tea shop that paid homage to a more gentile past and a slower, more ordered way of life. Decorated in pastel pinks and greens, every table was spread with a white, lace-edged cloth and place settings of stainless steel cutlery and floral china plates. Shelves on the wall to one side were filled with teapots in every style and size and a glazed chiller cabinet at the rear held a mouth-watering assortment of cakes.

Hannah stood for a moment, eyeing up the available tables. Netta and Irene were sitting near the back at a large round table set for four and she looked across, managed to catch Netta's eye, and went over to greet them. Netta introduced her sister who immediately insisted Hannah join them.

'Well, if you don't mind? Thank you.'

'You don't want to sit alone, do you?' Irene watched beadily as Hannah settled herself into her seat. 'It's good to finally meet you. Netta's told me all about you. You're staying at The Boatman, aren't you, you and that other restorer?'

'That's right. I've just been to the hairdresser's and thought I'd treat myself afterwards.'

Both women glanced up at her hair which had been neatly trimmed and blown dry into its usual spiky style. They refrained from comment.

'And your young man, where is he?' said Irene.

'You mean Nathan? He's not my young man. We just work for the same business.'

Irene nodded, expressionless. 'What a thing it was that happened to that curator girl.'

'Yes, it was a terrible shock. We hadn't known her long but she seemed very nice.'

'Oh she was,' agreed Netta. 'Such a tragedy. Look, here's Sheila to take our order.'

'You'd better choose your cake from the cabinet,' Irene instructed Hannah. 'We know what we want.'

Sheila returned to the kitchen with their order leaving a brief, awkward silence in her wake.

'Have you heard any more from the police about it?' Irene fixed Hannah with an interrogating gaze.

Hannah shook her head. 'I don't suppose they know any more.'

'There have been drownings before of course and they always make you wonder just what happened.'

'Oh?' said Hannah. 'Did you think it was suspicious then?'

'We shouldn't really talk about it.' Netta flicked a barbed glance at her sister. 'Mr Mortimer doesn't like gossip.'

'But these things happen, Netta, as Mr Mortimer knows only too well. Remember young Robert all those years ago.'

Netta flicked her sister a warning look and Hannah was on the point of asking who Robert was when Sheila returned with cups, saucers and a huge pot of tea. She came back a minute later with their chosen slices of cake: chocolate fudge for Netta and Hannah, and lemon drizzle for Irene. It was Irene who immediately took charge, marshalling the distribution of cups and pouring tea.

'You're going to love that cake,' she informed Hannah in a tone that brooked no argument. 'Sheila's cakes really are the best.'

Conversation faltered as they started eating. Waiting a couple of minutes, Hannah paused to take a sip of tea, then embraced the two women in a confidential look.

'It can't be easy having your home open to the public,' she said. 'I don't think I'd like it. Mr Gyllam-Spence told me he escapes to his den in the garden. In fact, he invited me over sometime to see his train layout.'

'Well, you are honoured.' Netta stopped eating and looked at her with a new respect. 'He doesn't usually like people disturbing him over there. To be honest, he doesn't always get the understanding and support he needs in my opinion.'

'You're thinking of Toby,' said Irene. 'He's never been one to do anything useful if he could find a way round it.'

'You've known them both a long time then?' suggested Hannah.

'All our lives really. There have been Gyllam-Spences at the manor for generations.'

'Mort... Mr Gyllam-Spence hasn't had any children, has he?' said Hannah. 'Does that mean that the manor will eventually go to Rose?'

'In the end perhaps. Mr Toby's the next in line.' Netta finished her cake and dabbed her mouth with the paper napkin. 'If he doesn't have any sons I think Miss Rose might inherit. Though I don't know how she'd cope with it. A nice girl I'm sure but head in the clouds most of the time.'

'She's still young,' offered Irene. 'She'll settle down when she meets the right chap. Wasn't she going out with that boy from The Hawthorns? The people who run the equestrian centre?'

'That's over, Reenie. I don't think she's seeing anyone at the moment.' Netta leaned forward and dropped her voice again. 'She tries too hard, see. Scares them off. And really there's no need: she's pretty and she's from a good family.' She straightened up, gave them a meaningful look, and drank a mouthful of tea. 'There's a girl here in the village she's very friendly with.' She glanced towards the window as if the girl might come in at just that moment. 'Not a great influence in my opinion.'

Irene finished eating and Hannah became aware of them both watching her as she tackled the remains of her cake. She ate it quickly and sat back.

'Delicious,' she announced and they both looked pleased, as if they'd made it themselves.

'So you travel all over, do you, doing this art restoration work?' said Irene.

'Sometimes. We're based in Oxford but if artworks can't be moved or the owner prefers that they aren't, we go to them.'

'Very interesting I'm sure.'

'It can be. Though sometimes I think I move around too much. It must be nice to settle into a community like you have here, somewhere where you know everyone and everyone knows you.' Hannah picked up her tea cup and flicked a casual glance between the sisters. 'The police who came to investigate Carrie Judd's death must have caused quite a stir. They were outsiders, weren't they?'

Netta nodded. 'From Norwich. All over the place they were, asking questions, looking into everyone's business. It was very unsettling.'

125

'Just doing their job.' Irene finished the last of her tea and put the cup down with a flourish. 'It was quite interesting actually. I helped out at the village hall where they set up their incident room, you see. They were very organised, I'll give them that.'

'Did you get to see what they did then?'

'Oh yes.' The two neighbouring tables had already emptied but Irene leaned towards Hannah conspiratorially. 'I wasn't supposed to see but I was curious and I kept my eyes open. Then I got friendly with a young policewoman who explained a few bits to me – like the stuff they put up on their boards, you know? And how they ask questions about the person who's passed and about people's whereabouts when it happened. Just like they do on the telly, in fact.'

'How fascinating. Did they speak to people all round the village then?'

'They talked to the girl's neighbour and others living that end of the village. But they seemed more interested in the manor and the people she was working with. I suppose you all knew her better.' Irene looked at Netta. 'We didn't see her round the village much, did we?'

Netta shook her head with a pained expression. Undaunted, pouring everyone a second cup of tea, Irene continued, regaling Hannah with an account of the things she'd both seen and been told.

Half an hour later, walking back to the inn, Hannah saw Nathan sitting on a low brick wall near the tow path, staring out over the water. She went across and sat down beside him making him look round, surprised.

'Hi,' he said. 'Where did you come from?'

A number of ducks, noticing the new activity, paddled towards them in hope of food, a small flotilla of ducklings tagging on behind.

'Cute.' Hannah watched them for a minute then turned to look at him. 'The tea-rooms. Guess who I've been talking to.'

'I give in. Who?'

'Netta and Irene.'

'About what?'

'They have afternoon tea there on a Thursday and I joined them. Irene makes it her business to know everything so I nudged her for a bit of information.'

'Wasn't she suspicious?'

Hannah shook her head.

'Irene likes to share. She kept saying: "I shouldn't really be telling you this but..." and "You won't pass this on, will you?" and told me anyway. She's probably told the whole village already.'

'What exactly?'

'OK, so on the Friday night when Carrie disappeared Mortimer had gone to the cinema in Norwich. Alone. He didn't get back until late. Netta said films are a bit of a thing with him and he often goes. Toby stayed in with a bottle of wine. Again he was alone.'

'Presumably he'd been let down by Amanda then,' said Nathan. 'Or perhaps that relationship's already history.'

Hannah shrugged. 'Alan was at the darts night at the inn then home with Grace, and Rose went to the hairdresser's – Friday's their late-night opening – then went round to a friend's house and stayed over. Sidony went up to London to her flat.'

'And these alibis were checked out?'

'I suppose so. She implied they had and I couldn't question her too closely. The police didn't pursue any leads so they must have. Which means Mortimer, Sid, Rose and Alan all have an alibi but Toby doesn't.'

'Not necessarily. Sid might not have gone to London and

Mortimer only has an alibi if someone at the cinema remembers him.'

Hannah sighed. 'What is it with you and Mortimer? He might have the ticket still.'

'Do you keep your cinema tickets once you've left?'

'No. No, I don't. I'm just saying he might have. Sid might have her train ticket too.'

'True. And I'm just saying there's some wriggle room in all these alibis and I suspect the police haven't pursued them too closely. This family's treated like royalty round here, like they couldn't do any wrong. I'm not sure it gets us anywhere.'

Hannah stood up and glared down at him. 'I thought you wanted me to get people talking so I did.' She started to move off but he grabbed her wrist.

'What?' she demanded.

'Thank you. No, really, it's useful.' He let her go. 'We could maybe talk about it over dinner?'

'OK.'

She left him to it, making her way back to her room in the inn. She felt very tired suddenly. All this diplomatic questioning was very draining. She kicked off her shoes and threw herself on the bed. It was a few minutes later, her mind beginning to switch off and the suggestion of sleep creeping up on her, when she remembered that she never did ask who Robert was.

*

Nathan drifted back to the inn a few minutes later. It was after six and he stopped in the bar for a drink. There were several tables occupied outside but it was quiet in the lounge and he took his pint over to a table near the fireplace and sat, staring into mid-air, his mind sifting through the information Hannah had given him, wondering where exactly it took them.

'I thought I might see you here.'

He looked up to see Alan Foxhall standing by the table, clutching a glass of bitter.

'Is Hannah around?' Alan added.

'I'm not sure. Can I help?'

'Not really. She left work early, didn't she? I saw her go.'

His tone was thick with criticism.

'That's because she started early, before you and the others were in.'

Alan's eyebrows rose. 'And why was that?'

'Does it matter?'

'I suppose not.' Without asking permission, Alan sat down in the chair opposite. 'But what would make her do that?'

Nathan met his unblinking gaze and paused before replying. 'An appointment at the hairdresser's in the afternoon – not that it's any of your business. I didn't realise that you were scrutinising our timekeeping. Did Mortimer tell you to do that?'

'No. You mistake me. I was just curious.'

'Indeed. Excessively curious. Then perhaps you might remember in future that we work our hours and then some and we get the job done, so it's our business when and how we do it. We have no need of a self-appointed foreman.'

Alan's mouth twisted unpleasantly into a sardonic smile.

'Mortimer is… shall we say, lax? I see it as my responsibility to make sure no-one takes advantage of him.'

'So you are self-appointed. But I see no credible reason for you to be suspicious of Hannah.'

'They're suspicious times, you have to admit. And you're not above throwing a bit of suspicion about yourself, I understand.' Alan picked up his beer, languidly drank a mouthful, then got to his feet. 'Perhaps you could pass a message on to Hannah when you see her? Carrie Judd used to give talks to some of the school parties that come round and now… well, as you can imagine we're at a bit of a loss. I was discussing the problem with Mortimer and he suggested that Hannah might step into the breach while she's here, share her experience so to speak.'

'I'm not sure our boss would be happy about that.' Nathan rather doubted Hannah would be either. 'She's already got a lot of work to do.'

'But that's all sorted.' Alan looked triumphant. 'Mortimer rang your employer and he was most accommodating. He said he was more than happy for you to help out. Indeed he said Hannah had done some similar speaking engagements before. Anyway, if you'd just tell her, she can ask Mortimer about it when she's back in work. The next school visit is in about ten days.'

He offered the suggestion of a nod and walked away, taking the door through to the public bar and Nathan watched him go with distaste. It felt as if the air had been left tainted. What was it about that man that he disliked so? He said all the right things but it was the way he said them, in an affected, smart voice while metaphorically sticking two fingers up at you.

And why had he come? He didn't need to find Nathan to mention the talks: he could have told Hannah the next morning. It was an excuse to nose about, to show that he had his eye on them, to check they weren't up to anything. Did he really expect to find anything out or was it just a warning? And was he doing it of his own initiative or because he'd been told to? It would be useful to know more about him but there seemed no point: Alan had one of the best alibis for the evening Carrie disappeared. He was at the darts club then home with Grace. It was a crying shame.

Chapter 10

Swinyard Auctioneers sat on the outskirts of the nearby sleepy market town of Spedham. The business occupied what had once been a range of farm buildings but which had now been converted and adapted and the Swinyard family had been selling a range of items there for more than sixty years. An auction took place once a week. The firm did house clearances and did often sell old furniture and unplayable pianos, but their dedicated art sale every three months had developed a reputation in the area, attracting both dealers and private buyers, all hoping to pick up a bargain. Or a 'sleeper' perhaps – a forgotten work found in a dusty old house, something that others hadn't recognised as the special piece that it was.

Nathan and Hannah had agreed to check out the saleroom together on the Saturday morning. Although the sale didn't begin till two, viewing was only available until twelve. Then the display would be cleared and chairs laid out for the auction. Hannah had said she needed to do something beforehand and arranged to meet Nathan there at eleven fifteen. But here he was, parked up and still waiting outside the door of the main saleroom and there was no sign of her. It was already eleven twenty-five. At this rate there'd be little chance to poke around and ask questions before they were kicked out.

Nathan shifted about impatiently; it wasn't like Hannah to be late. Compulsively punctual was her own description of herself. He looked at his watch again: eleven-thirty. He couldn't wait any longer.

'Sorry I'm late.' Hannah was running towards him from the car park clutching a plastic carrier bag, her shoulder bag thumping up and down against her hip. She stopped just in front of him, panting. 'Really sorry. It took longer than I expected.'

'What did?'

'I'll tell you later. We'd better get in, hadn't we?'

A handful of people were browsing inside. The old barn had been renovated and the walls plastered and painted. It was a clean, serviceable space but had none of the sleek finish and expensive pinpoint lighting of the specialist fine art auction houses. Framed paintings hung at intervals on the walls, both oils and watercolours, and several trestle tables were spread with mounted paintings and drawings, neatly wrapped in cellophane and numbered. Four easels spaced around the room held what the auctioneers presumably deemed the most notable and valuable lots, and three members of staff were in attendance: two, wearing white coats, for security, and one, in a dark grey suit, to answer questions. The suited guy was expounding something about one of the oil paintings in a keen, animated way to a grey-haired lady. He had a round, open face and a chuckling laugh and reminded Nathan of his most genial uncle. Not the kind of person, he thought, to knowingly fence stolen pictures.

They each grabbed a list of the lots for sale and started to wander round. There wasn't much that excited their interest; there were a lot of tired, generic oil paintings, mostly Victorian, produced to cater to the burgeoning middle class of the time with a desire to decorate their homes. There were a couple of older, Baroque pieces, both in poor condition, and Hannah did pause to admire a small, loosely painted

132

watercolour with a big, dramatic sky over a green, bucolic landscape.

'Someone trying to imitate Constable would you say?' she murmured. 'Nice anyway.'

He pulled a face. 'Desperately needs remounting. Look at the foxing.'

They moved on to the tables, scrutinising the drawings and unframed watercolours.

'There's nothing here that really stands out.' Nathan became aware that one of the security men was watching them. 'We must look suspicious,' he muttered.

'It's you,' Hannah muttered back. 'You're looking at everything as if you've got a bad smell under your nose. Why don't you speak to the guy in the suit? He's free now.'

'And say what?'

'I don't know.' She shrugged. 'Do you ever make private sales, maybe.'

Nathan glanced round. 'OK.'

He approached the man who offered a smile. 'Can I help you sir?'

'Yes. Morning. I was just wondering if you ever sell any paintings privately, I mean, not in the auction?'

'No sir. Everything that comes into our hands goes through the auction house. Was there something in particular you were looking for?'

'No, no, not really.' Nathan hesitated. 'But, if I did want to find work by a particular artist, say, is there a dealer around here you could recommend to source it? As a collector, if you know what I mean?'

The round, friendly face clouded.

'I'm not in a position to do that, I'm afraid sir, but reputable dealers do advertise. You'll find them in the Yellow Pages.' He hesitated and eyed Nathan up speculatively. 'It

133

would be wise to be wary of back street dealers.'

'I see. Thank you.'

Nathan returned to Hannah and they left. He was glad to get outside.

'That was unpleasant,' he remarked. 'No doubt he thinks I'm a crooked investor now. Whatever, I don't think there's anything being fenced through there.'

'You're right, this feels like a reputable place and an Old Master drawing would stand out a mile anyway. Still, it was worth looking.'

'I'm sure that whatever's being peddled is being done privately, on the sly, probably through one of the back street dealers the guy warned me about. Though how to find him – or her – I don't know.'

They reached the cars and stopped. Hannah had managed to park her Mini next to Nathan's Ford Escort.

'So are you going to tell me what made you late?' he said.

'Yes, right. The thing is, I've been thinking about your mum...'

'My mum? Why on earth would you...?'

'Let me finish. She's fretting about that newspaper report, isn't she? She thinks it's important and you're avoiding the issue but you know she's going to ask you about it again on Monday.'

Hannah opened the plastic carrier and pulled out a newspaper.

'So I went to the newspaper offices to get a back copy of it. Here.' She thrust it at him. 'The report on Pollersby's May Day celebrations is in the middle pages. Lots of photos.'

'What the hell?' Nathan's face creased up in disgust as he took it from her. 'You shouldn't have done that.'

'Why not? You weren't going to and it wasn't going to go away, was it? Now you can tell her that you've seen it and that

134

it's a false lead.'

'You're interfering in something you don't understand. Why do you have to meddle? It's none of your business.'

'Because I'm the one who's here listening to you fretting about it every week.' Her voice rose. 'I was only trying to help. You can't keep running away from it. Trying to ignore it won't work.'

'How come you're such an expert on my family? Anyway as I recall, Hannah Dechansay, your relationship with your mother was hardly a bed of roses. And how often do you speak to your father? At least I talk to my mother regularly. Who are you to lecture me on filial duty?'

Hannah glared at him. For a moment he thought she was going to hit him. Then she got in her car and drove away, wheels throwing up the gravel as she sped out of the car park.

Nathan threw his head back and sighed, then slowly, reluctantly opened the newspaper at the middle spread. He scanned the pages, squinting at the photographs, reading the captions underneath, trying to figure out which one was supposed to magically show his missing brother. He'd pushed the issue so far down in his mind that he struggled now to remember exactly what his mother had said about it. He'd probably blocked the words even as she was talking.

They were typical newspaper images of a village event, grainy and indistinct, a crush of people having a good time and caught in mid-movement, dancing, shouting or turning away: the May Queen surrounded by her entourage processing through the village; a bunch of children dancing round the maypole; lengths of trestle tables groaning under plates of food; and a shot of the forecourt of The Fisherman and Dog where a group of morris dancers were in full cry. That must be the one; his mother had mentioned the pub. He brought the newspaper closer, studying the crowd of people gathered to watch them. This was absurd. How the hell could you recognise anyone from a picture like this?

He closed the newspaper up impatiently, folded it roughly in two and threw it onto the passenger seat of his car as he got in, then sat for a few minutes, doing nothing, just staring through the windscreen, as a procession of images from the past scrolled through his mind: scenes from his childhood playing with his younger brother, arguments and fights as they muddled their way through adolescence, strained telephone conversations in the last weeks and months before he disappeared.

He suddenly grabbed the newspaper again and opened it to the centre spread, peering at the morris dance picture again and at one particular man in the crowd who stood watching the dancers. His stomach tied in its familiar knot. How could you tell? Damn Hannah for doing this.

*

Rose glanced along the tables on the quay outside The Boatman. It was the first of June, the moorings were all taken and people sat in raucous groups, drinking, chatting, laughing, enjoying the fine sunny evening. But there was no sign of her friends. She turned away, crossed the road and went inside the public bar of the inn. A bunch of men were clustered at the bar clutching their pints, putting the world to rights by the sound of it, and a couple of tables were occupied but her friends weren't there either. Rose had a horrible feeling that she'd got the time wrong. It was just before seven; maybe they'd agreed seven-thirty. Unless they were in the lounge bar, of course. She got teased sometimes for being 'posh' and 'Miss La-di-da' so she tended not to go in the lounge bar herself in case her friends made fun of her for it. Still, there was no harm if they weren't there. She wandered through.

But they weren't there either – just a handful of people she didn't know – so she went to the bar and bought herself a glass of white wine, then stood around, wondering where to take it. She noticed the archway to the snug. She hadn't been in there in years and casually walked over to glance inside. One person sat there, occupying one of the wing-back armchairs, reading a book, some kind of long drink on the table in front of her. Hannah.

Did she ever suffer from being called la-di-da? Would she care if she did? It didn't seem likely. On an impulse, Rose went in and sat down in the armchair the other side of the table.

'Hi,' she said, more aggressively than she'd intended.

Hannah looked up and surprise registered in her face.

'Hi.'

Rose put her glass down. 'I'm waiting for some friends. We're going to a party. Someone's birthday.'

'Nice. In the village?'

'Yes.'

Rose noticed one of the tourist maps that were ubiquitous throughout East Ranling; every business seemed to have a rack of them.

'Thinking of going on a trip somewhere?' Rose indicated the map.

'Not especially. I was just curious to see what was around, if there was anything nearby I should visit.' Hannah scrutinised her. 'Have you ever been on one of those wildlife boat trips on the Broad?'

'Yes, ages ago though. It was quite good. Are you thinking of going?'

'Yes, maybe.'

Rose picked up her glass again, took a generous sip of wine and sat back.

'You're not married or engaged or anything?'

'No. No, I'm not. Why?'

'Have you been?'

'I've been close a couple of times but it didn't work out.' Hannah regarded her calmly. 'You?'

'No.' Rose hesitated. 'I met an Italian guy a couple of years ago and we dated for a while. He was over here working, trying to improve his English. It seemed pretty serious.' She shrugged. 'Then he went back to Italy and we exchanged letters for a while. He said he liked it here, that he might come back. Or I might go there.' She flicked Hannah a sidelong look. 'It doesn't seem to bother you, being alone, I mean.'

Hannah leaned forward and picked up her glass. 'It doesn't really. I've come to the conclusion that being with the wrong person is far worse than being alone.'

Rose drank some more wine and digested this idea. She thought of her parents and supposed it was true. But how did you find the right person to be with? Hannah clearly hadn't yet and maybe never would now. Her slight build made her look younger but close-up Rose thought she looked older, maybe in her late thirties.

'I guess you did a lot of training for your job, right?'

'Yes. An art history degree then a course in art conservation.'

'Was it worth it, do you think, all that work?'

Hannah pursed up her lips. 'I think so. I learned a lot and it's useful. It gave me choices and I've got an interesting job.'

Rose nodded. 'So where's Nathan tonight?' she asked suddenly.

'I don't know.' Hannah raised her eyebrows.

Rose thought she saw amusement in those big, challenging eyes and was offended. There was nothing funny in the question.

The landlord, Brian, appeared in the archway.

'Ah Hannah, good. I've got a man on the phone called Nigel Judd. Do you know him? He wants to speak to you.'

'Yes, I know him.' Hannah was frowning. 'Why? What does he want?'

'I've no idea. I said I'd see if you were here.'

'Oh all right. Thanks.' She put her glass down. 'I'll come now.'

Rose watched her follow Brian through to the lounge bar and just stopped herself from going along too. Nigel Judd? She'd love to know what that was about. She listened intently but the phone was behind the bar and too far away for her to pick anything up.

Hannah returned a few minutes later and bent over to pick up her glass.

'Well I hope you enjoy the party,' she said, looking down at Rose. 'I think I'd better find myself a table and order a meal.'

Rose quickly got to her feet.

'Wasn't that Carrie's husband? What did he want?'

'Oh, nothing important.' Hannah was dismissive. 'He just wanted to ask something.'

Rose returned to the public bar to wait for her friends and sat musing on the phone call and Hannah's curious behaviour. Nigel and Hannah. Maybe there was more going on there than met the eye. Maybe Hannah wasn't so nonchalant about being single after all.

*

Hannah got in her car at eleven-thirty on the Sunday morning and set off to meet Nigel. His phone call had come out of the blue.

'Ah, good, I've tracked you down,' he'd said when she picked up the phone. 'You said you were staying at the inn in

139

the village. There only seems to be one.'

'There is. How are you doing?'

'Oh you know, a bit up and down. The thing is, Hannah, I wondered if I could come over and see you?'

She was silent, taken aback by the question. There were so many reasons why she didn't think that was a good idea.

'I've been going through Carrie's things,' he continued. 'You know what it's like: it's been kind of difficult and I've been putting it off. The thing is, I've found a notebook.'

'A notebook?' That piqued Hannah's interest.

'Yes. It looks like a workbook really. All sorts of scribbled notes. There may be stuff in there that relates to her work at the manor. I thought perhaps you could have a look at it and see whether it's of any value to them. I'd prefer to show it to you than the people there first in case they just bin it. They didn't seem that interested in her, if I'm honest. And if you think it's no good to them, I'll have it back.' He paused. 'I know it's stupid to keep these things but I can't quite... Anyway, I thought I could be with you by late morning tomorrow. Would it be OK to drop it off? Will you be at the inn?'

Hannah still hesitated. She was happy enough to look at the notebook for what it was worth but she didn't think Nigel should come to The Boatman. It would create talk and rumour. Suspicion too maybe.

'I was planning to go out tomorrow, Nigel. But I could meet you somewhere.' Her thoughts flicked to the tourist map, trying to remember the names in the advertisements. 'There's a place south of here called Acle. It'd be easier for you to get to. There's a pub not far from there called the Labourer's Rest. It does Sunday lunches apparently. Say twelve o'clock. I'll wait in the car park.'

And now here she was, going to what felt like a potentially

uncomfortable rendezvous. What did she remember of Nigel from that one date? Not much. He was an accountant; he liked numbers. And he'd been a little too attentive, stifling even. She remembered thinking quite quickly that it wasn't going to work: there had been no meeting of minds, nothing that they had in common.

She arrived a couple of minutes early but Nigel was already waiting for her, standing leaning against his car. She parked nearby and went over to meet him. They both smiled and nodded awkwardly at each other.

Nigel was pale and drawn. She put out a sympathetic hand and touched his arm.

'How are you Nigel?'

'Oh, you know, all right. Like I said on the phone, it's been kind of difficult.'

'I can imagine. I am sorry. Any problems getting here?'

'No, none.'

'Good. Shall we go in?'

The pub hadn't long opened and wasn't yet busy. Some of the tables were reserved but they were able to find a table for two, tucked away privately in a corner and they got drinks – soda and lime for Hannah and a beer for Nigel – and both ordered a roast dinner.

'I thought you might be busy today,' said Nigel, 'that perhaps you and Nathan had plans.'

'No, we tend to do our own thing at the weekends.'

He pointedly glanced at her left hand. 'Not married or engaged then?'

'No. Too contrary for that,' she said lightly. 'That's what my mother used to say anyway.'

'I don't believe her.'

The waitress came to the table, inviting them to go to the carvery and Hannah was spared the need to respond. They joined the queue and returned to the table a few minutes later with plates of roast beef, Yorkshire pudding and a medley of vegetables. They began to eat. Hannah wanted to ask about Carrie and how they came to be separated but didn't feel she could. But Nigel soon stopped eating and began talking and she didn't need to. He picked up his beer and sat back in the chair.

'You didn't get the chance to really know Carrie did you? She was a very special person.'

'She seemed it.' Hannah stopped eating too, rested her cutlery down, and gave him her full attention. 'Tell me about her.'

He hesitated and swallowed, as if trying to get his emotions under control.

'She was kind and honest but self-contained. She was a bit like you, you know? Arty, passionate about what she loved, inhabited a world that was kind of different to mine. She wasn't interested in numbers or anything like that. She did like crosswords though.' He smiled sadly. 'And she loved going to the theatre, all kinds but especially Shakespeare. Most of the time I couldn't make head nor tail of it and she'd patiently explain it to me.'

'How did you meet?'

'At a party at a friend's house. I'd noticed that she'd come alone and was looking kind of sad. Then she drifted away into another room. When she didn't come out after a few minutes, I followed her in. There was no-one else in there and she was standing by the window, staring at her reflection in the glass. We got talking. She'd recently lost her dad. She seemed really glad to have someone to talk to.' He frowned. 'I used to be good at listening.'

He took a needy mouthful of beer. 'It was my fault, you know, that we were separated. Six years we'd been married and everything was fine.' He frowned. 'Better than fine, I realise now, but I didn't know how lucky I was. Then she got wrapped up in a big project at work, some major exhibition she was helping to set up, and I was busy at work too and stressed. We never seemed to have any time together just to relax. Then there was this girl at work. Well, one thing led to another and I had a stupid fling. I mean really stupid. It never meant anything to me… or to the girl. I'm not excusing it; it was wrong. I loved Carrie. I did really. I told her it would never happen again but she...'

He took another swig of beer then wiped his lips with the back of his fingers. He looked up into Hannah's face. What little colour he'd had seemed to have completely drained away.

'...she said she couldn't trust me any more.'

'She was probably in a state of shock when she said that, Nigel. She just needed time and space to get her head round it and think things through. She might have come round.'

'Do you think so?' He shook his head sadly. 'But I'll never know, will I?'

Hannah offered an understanding smile but struggled to know what to say.

'You mentioned her notebook?' she prompted.

'Yes, I've got it with me. I can't understand much of it but then I wouldn't. Anyway, she used her own kind of shorthand. They were notes to herself, not for other people to read.'

'I see.' She glanced at his plate. The beer was going down but not much food. 'Come on, eat some more. I bet you're not eating properly at home.' Now she sounded like her mother.

Nigel played around with a little more food then gave up, pushing the half full plate away and cradling the dregs of his beer, looking introspective. Hannah finished eating and picked up her soda.

'Did Carrie talk to you much after she moved to East Ranling?'

Nigel took a minute to focus on her. 'No, not really. We spoke over the phone a couple of times.'

'Did she talk about her work here?'

'No. Yes, well a bit. I didn't understand the half of what she did. But I don't think she was sure she'd done the right thing taking that job.'

'Why, what did she say?'

He shrugged. 'Something about being the outsider, that she didn't fit in.' He paused, looking cross now. 'And some guy was giving her grief. That's all she said.'

'Did she say who?'

'No. Anyway, that's one of the reasons I didn't want to go back to the manor with the notebook. I don't want to have anything to do with them. But she was very proud of her work and I thought maybe she'd have wanted them to see any special notes she'd made or...'

His voice trailed off and he reached into the inside pocket of his jacket on the back of the chair to get the notebook. He held it for a moment as if having second thoughts, then passed it over. It was a long, thin hardbacked book, easily pushed into a pocket or handbag.

'See what you think.'

'OK. We'll take a look and if you give me your address I'll send it back to you if there's no need to pass it on. There probably won't be. It'll be things she thought she might do, plans for the collection perhaps.'

The words hung in the air, only emphasising a future that would never come to pass, a young life cut short. Hannah inwardly squirmed and wished she could take them back.

They made desultory conversation after that. Nigel asked what Hannah had been doing these recent years and was sympathetic when she told him about the passing of her mother. She asked after his work and if he liked where he was living now. It was a struggle to keep it going and eventually they parted. Hannah didn't head straight back to East Ranling but drove around for a while, checking out a couple of places she'd seen on the map that morning, visiting another wildlife reserve and then stopping to drink tea at a roadside café with a view over a river. She spent time there, trying to clear her head. The conversation with Nigel had been unsettling; he was a tortured soul and nothing anyone said was likely to help him at the moment.

She left the notebook in her handbag, reluctant to even think about it yet. The words *some guy was giving her grief* kept running through her head.

*

Nathan hadn't intended to go to Pollersby but found himself driving there all the same, the newspaper which Hannah had given him dumped on the passenger seat beside him. He'd gone to Horning first, trying to revisit the pleasure of his childhood trips there but the newspaper article had put his head in the wrong place. It had thrust him forward, away from the carefree days of his youth to the tormented months and years after Sam disappeared and, no matter how hard he tried to quell them, the memories refused to go back in the box.

Now he'd seen that picture, he had to go and look. He had no choice.

He arrived around half past twelve. Pollersby was a pretty village. A similar size to East Ranling but more compact, its river frontage smaller and the bulk of the older settlement – including the pub – clustered around an ancient village green. Nathan parked the car, grabbed the middle sheet from the newspaper, folded it up small and pushed it into a pocket of his linen jacket. He went to explore. The green had clearly been used for the maypole dancing and he recognised The Fisherman and Dog from the photo. A hard forecourt in front of the pub, where a number of customers were already sitting at wooden tables, was where the morris dancing had taken place. There was a pleasing buzz of talk and laughter as he drew near and a general air of activity in the area but nothing approaching the crowds he'd seen in the newspaper. He went inside.

His eyes took a minute to adjust after the sunshine outside. It was an old inn, low beamed, with a traditional long wooden bar and stools dotted at intervals in front of it. He edged onto one of the vacant stools, ordered a half of bitter from the young woman tending bar and sat for a few minutes, glancing around, taking in what sort of a place it was. Why on earth would his brother be here of all places? There again, why did he disappear in the first place? And this was as likely, or as unlikely, a place as anywhere else.

Nathan took a mouthful of beer, savouring it slowly. There wasn't much activity at the bar. Only one other guy sat there, an old bloke with a shaggy grey beard, nursing a pint of cider from the look of it. Nathan waited until the bartender reappeared then produced the newspaper from his pocket and unfolded it.

'Excuse me, have you got a minute?'

She came over to face him across the bar. She couldn't have been more than twenty-two or twenty-three, her hair bobbed and blonde, cut higher at the back, her kohl-lined eyes curious and expectant.

'Were you working here over the May Day celebrations?'

'Ye-es,' she replied warily. 'Why?'

'Would you be able to tell me who this guy is, standing outside here, watching the morris team?'

He thrust the sheet of paper in front of her and pointed out the man. The girl screwed up her eyes, leaning forward to peer at the photograph, then shook her head.

'Nah, I'm not sure. It's not a very good picture, is it?' She walked to a doorway which led to the back rooms of the pub and shouted. 'Ian? Are you free? There's a guy here wants to know if you know someone.' She turned back to Nathan. 'Ian's the landlord. He might know him.'

The bearded chap at the other end of the bar and the people at a couple of tables not far away all looked up. Nathan felt himself examined. So much for trying to do this discreetly.

Ian appeared and came to stand facing him. He was a big man with bulging muscles and the kind of nose that suggested he might have played rugby in his youth.

'Yes?' He fixed steely eyes on Nathan's.

'I wonder if you recognise this man watching the morris dance the other week?'

Again Nathan proffered the newspaper article and pointed. He watched Ian study the image without expression then straighten up and give him with the steely look again.

'I'm not sure I know him. Why do you want to know?'

Nathan shrugged. He wasn't going to tell the story to this suspicious stranger, especially with half the pub listening in.

'It was just chance. I saw the article in the paper and thought I recognised him as someone I went to school with. Haven't been in touch for ages so I thought I'd look him up.'

'Uhuh. What was the name of this schoolmate of yours?'

Nathan hesitated. 'Sam.'

'Sam,' repeated Ian. His eyebrows rose then he curled his upper lip and shook his head. 'Doesn't mean anything to me.'

'But you do know who this man is?' Nathan pointed at the photograph again.

'Can't say that I do. I might have seen him before. I see a

147

lot of people, especially on days like that.' Ian nodded at the photograph and wandered away.

Nathan took another mouthful of beer and left. He was sure the landlord did recognise the man in the picture but he clearly wasn't going to tell him. He strolled down to the riverside and glanced along the quay. Several boats were moored up. No doubt most of their occupants were now enjoying lunch at The Fisherman and Dog. He sighed and sat down on a bench overlooking the water. He'd known this would be a wild goose chase but he supposed Hannah was right: he'd had to follow it up. After a few minutes watching ducks and swans prospecting for food, he became aware of his stomach rumbling. Rather than return to the pub, he remembered seeing a small tea room on the other side of the green and made his way back towards it.

Passing the forecourt of the pub, a middle-aged couple stopped him and the man spoke.

'We were inside just now when we overheard you asking about someone you know. We didn't catch it all but perhaps we might be able to help if you showed us the photograph. We've lived here quite a while now.'

'Thank you.' Nathan unfolded the newspaper article again and showed it to them. 'It's this guy here.'

They both stared at the image, eyes puckering. The woman straightened up, shaking her head.

'Is Ian new here then?' asked Nathan.

'Not very. He's just tricky sometimes. I'm sure he loses custom the way he talks to people. He's not so bad with locals, mind.'

The man was still examining the photograph. He tapped it with a forefinger.

'I think I do know your man. He lives on a boat but only stops here now and then for a day or two. I've seen him come

148

in the pub for a meal and a drink. The next thing you know, he's moved on.'

'What's his name?'

The man chewed on his lip, trying to recall. 'I'm not sure. I've never spoken to him. He keeps himself to himself.'

'Sam?' suggested Nathan.

'I don't think so. John maybe. Or Joe. Something like that.'

'Well thanks anyway.'

'If you left us your phone number, we could let you know if we see him again?' said the woman. 'Would that help? I'm Glenys, by the way, and this is Paul.'

Nathan gave them his name and the number of The Boatman as a point of contact and thanked them again. He doubted he'd ever hear any more about it. It was another dead end.

*

'I'm sorry.'

She'd found Nathan. He was sitting in the snug downstairs at the inn and looked up in surprise as Hannah spoke. She sank into the armchair opposite, dropping her bag on the floor alongside. It was early evening on the Sunday, earlier than they would normally eat, but it was pretty clear that Nathan had already been there some time. He had a half-drunk pint of beer on the table in front of him and a paperback book open on his lap. She'd tried his room before coming down and got no reply.

'I shouldn't have gone looking for a copy of the news-paper,' she added now. Over the course of the afternoon, she'd had time to reflect on the whole newspaper debacle and realised she'd been tactless. Which wasn't unusual. 'I wanted to help but I did it all wrong.'

Nathan nodded slowly, closed his book and put it down on the table.

'I'm sorry too. I overreacted. I shouldn't have made those remarks about your parents. That was mean.'

'No, well... families are complicated, aren't they?'

'You can say that again.' He hesitated then stood up. 'Can I get you a drink?'

She smiled. 'Thank you, yes. I'll have a medium white wine please.'

He returned a few minutes later, put the wine on the table in front of her and sat down again.

'Thanks. Book any good?' She nodded at the paperback.

'Not bad. What have you been up to?'

Hannah glanced round. There were just two other people in the small room, a couple near the wall on the other side.

'I went to meet Nigel in Acle.'

'Nigel?' His explosive response made the couple look round. He dropped his voice and looked at Hannah suspiciously. 'Why?'

'Because he rang. Here. Yesterday evening. And asked to see me.' Hannah glanced towards the couple but they'd lost interest again and were talking. 'He had a notebook that he'd found in Carrie's belongings.'

'You're sure he didn't just want to see you?'

'I'm sure. Hell, Nathan, he's just lost his wife. Anyway, he just didn't.'

'All right. So what kind of notebook?'

'A workbook, the sort of thing you jot reminders to yourself in – things you need to do or hope to do. I've only glanced at it. It really is just jottings, some of which only Carrie would have understood but he seemed to think there might be something in it that the people at the manor would need to know. Though I doubt they'd be interested. The truth

150

is Nigel's a lost soul at the moment, trying to make sense out of something that has no sense.'

She leaned over and pulled it out of her bag. 'This is it.'

Nathan flicked through a few pages, frowning. 'She really did have terrible handwriting. Still, it might be worth looking at. I'll keep it shall I? Is that all he wanted?'

'Yes. But he talked a lot – about Carrie. He's pretty messed up about her, as you'd expect. I didn't know what to say.' She took a sip of wine. 'What have you been doing? Or have you been here all day, reading?'

'No, I went out. I went to Pollersby and took that newspaper piece with me.'

'Uhuh.' She waited. 'And?'

'And nothing. Another dead end. The only people who said they recognised him seemed to think his name was John or Joe. At least I can tell Mum that I looked into it.' He paused. 'Thanks anyway.'

Hannah nodded. She was on the point of saying that if Sam had wanted to disappear he might very well have changed his name, but she stopped herself just in time. She picked up her glass and sipped at the wine.

'I had an idea.' She leaned forward. 'There's a guy I know in London, an art dealer. He has his ear to the ground when it comes to pictures changing hands. He might have heard of some Old Master drawings being moved. I thought I might go up and see him, maybe next weekend. In fact, I figured if I work a few long days this week, I could go Friday afternoon and stay over.'

'We should both go.'

Her eyes narrowed. 'That makes more of a thing of it.'

'You don't think that asking if any under the counter deals have been going on in the art markets won't make a thing of it anyway?'

151

'Loads of deals in the art world are "under the counter". Besides, the thing is, he's...' She hesitated, searching for the right words. '...he might be more likely to talk freely if it's only me.'

'Is this guy a crook?'

'No, no. Just... OK so maybe he's a bit of a wheeler-dealer.'

'You mean you won't ask too many personal questions.'

'Exactly. I need to keep it... general.'

'How the hell did you meet someone like that?'

'It's a long story.'

Nathan leaned forward too until she could see the untanned skin in the creases round his eyes.

'Hannah, Carrie was murdered, we both know that, don't we? You are not going alone.'

152

Chapter 11

Mortimer walked over to the control panel and switched on, setting both trains in motion. Over the years, this simple hobby from his childhood had developed and slowly consumed him. Half the capacious shed was now given over to the trestle tables supporting his fictitious terrain and tracks and he had meticulously painted the walls against which the tables stood with a trompe l'oeil landscape to match. The two main circuits of track were connected with junctions and points, and were supplemented by a couple of sidings where he kept extra carriages and tenders. The outer circuit was the simpler of the two, rising gently up an embankment to a hillside station before turning and descending to another station near the control panel. The inner circuit was a more complicated double loop incorporating a tunnel, two stations and three bridges. He stood to watch the trains move off, still feeling the calm satisfaction they always gave him.

It was just after five and he was expecting Hannah. She had come to his study to see him on the Friday, wanting to ask about the talks he'd asked her to give, but he'd been about to go out to meet someone.

'Just a chat about a possible bequest,' he'd told her. 'Though, of course, it might not come to anything.'

Lying didn't come easily to him but he was surprised at how good he was becoming at it of late. He'd even had the presence of mind afterwards to suggest this meeting here in his den after the weekend. An idea had come to him about something she might be helpful with but he wanted time to think it through.

Now he reached into the bag of aniseed balls in his pocket, took one and was still sucking on it thoughtfully when he heard a knock on the door and went across to open it.

'Hannah, come in, come in.' He closed the door behind her, then pulled the bag of sweets out of his pocket and offered it to her. 'Aniseed ball?'

She looked surprised, then grinned and took one, popping it in her mouth.

'I haven't had one of these in years. Mm, I'd forgotten how good they are.'

'I love them. There's a shop in the village sells old-fashioned candy from big jars – perhaps you've seen it? Sid keeps telling me they're bad for me, though. Too much sugar, she says, so I ought to cut down.' He offered a guilty smile. 'We don't always do what we're supposed to though, do we? Anyway, I'm sure you're not interested in my digestion or my teeth. Come over, have a look around. Can I make you a drink? You don't drink coffee, do you? Perhaps something stronger?'

He walked over to a cupboard by the sink and bent over to look inside.

'I think I've only got whisky and maybe some brandy. Yes, that's all, I'm afraid.' He straightened up. 'I'm not a big drinker.'

'Have you any tea?'

'Yes, yes. No milk though, just that whitener stuff.'

'Black tea would be fine, thanks. No sugar.'

Hannah had approached the edge of the model and was watching the trains, a smile teasing her lips.

'This is brilliant,' she murmured. 'What fun.'

'You like it?'

'Of course.'

He filled the kettle and came over to join her. He felt absurdly pleased. So few people seemed to understand his passion which is why he rarely encouraged anyone to come here any more. He'd had enough patronising smiles to last a lifetime. Especially from Toby.

'It's all run from there, is it?' She nodded towards the control panel.

'Yes. I've got separate controls for each train. You see, I can make one slow down to stop at a station.' He demonstrated. 'That's a locomotive called the *Evening Star*. It was the last steam locomotive to be built by British Railways. On the other track is a Class 8F locomotive. See how the firebox glows when it's moving? Here, do you want to start the train off again? Pull it out of the station. This knob here.'

Hannah turned the knob and the train moved off again; her smile broadened.

'Can you buy all this scenery then or do you have to make it?' she asked.

'You can buy a lot of it but I like to make as much as I can, or at least paint it myself. It's part of the pleasure in doing it.'

'Yes, I can see that.'

'Can you?' He looked at her, brows furrowed, then smiled. 'Well good.'

The kettle boiled and he invited her to take a seat and went to make the drinks, placing her tea down on the table beside her. He sat down, clutching his mug, but it was still too hot and he put it down.

'So,' he began, 'you wanted to ask about the talks? Didn't Alan explain?'

'Not really. I'm not sure what I'm supposed to be talking

155

about. I'm a conservator, not a professional art historian like Carrie. I'm not comfortable about doing it.'

'Now come, Hannah, you're being falsely modest. You know far more art history than most of us I'm sure. You're worrying about it too much. Your boss said you'd given talks before.'

'Not in this sort of situation I haven't.'

'You'll be fine. Just mention the history of the collection and how it came to be acquired; it's all there in our house guide anyway. I saw Carrie taking a trip round once. She showed them the main exhibits and explained how they related to the era in which they were created, something like that. Honestly, so long as you make it interesting enough for the kids to enjoy, it doesn't matter. Tell them about some of the techniques used. Tell them what used to go wrong. Children like to hear about disasters. I suppose we all do – makes us feel less inadequate ourselves.'

Hannah nodded slowly, eyeing him up shrewdly. 'OK, I'll see what I can do. But I won't be here that long. Who's going to do the talks when I leave?'

'That's a very good question. Yes.' He picked up his coffee, sipped it and sat back, still holding the mug. 'I've been thinking about that. Well, not that exactly. More about whether we could perhaps manage without a curator. Maybe just get someone in now and then to sort out issues.'

'Do you not think you might have more problems with the collection degrading if it's not regularly checked and cared for?' said Hannah. 'And that doesn't solve the problem of the talks.'

He laughed. 'No, of course. How sharp you are.'

Perhaps too sharp, he thought, and wondered how far he could trust her.

'Though Sidony might do it well,' Hannah was saying. 'I

heard her talking to some visitors the other day and she's very eloquent, *and* knowledgeable.'

Mortimer sighed, in spite of himself. 'Yes, she is. I suppose I might suggest it to her.' He offered Hannah an arch look. 'Sid is a formidable lady, don't you think?'

'Yes.' She paused, interrogating him with a look. 'You said there was something you wanted to talk about too?'

Mortimer took another sip of coffee then leaned forward to put the mug down. This had seemed like such a good idea in his head and now he wasn't so sure. Twice he opened his mouth and closed it again before finally managing to speak.

'It was about Sidony that I wanted to talk in fact.' He cleared his throat, rubbing one hand nervously over the other. 'You see, Sid and I used to be an item, oh years and years ago. Then it... well, we drifted apart and after a bit she got engaged to Toby and that was that. When they got divorced, I thought she'd leave but she didn't. I suppose that, against all reason, I hoped that meant she might still care for me. Does that sound foolish?'

'No. Not at all.'

'No?' He half-smiled, then stood up suddenly and walked restlessly up and down the little seating area.

'The thing is... it's been years now and there's no sign she does but I still can't help hoping.' He stopped walking and stared down at Hannah. 'I wondered if you might be able to give me a woman's point of view. You're like her in some ways, you see. But she's been behaving differently of late. She spends more time away in London, for example; she seems more remote.' He began pacing again. 'I think maybe she's met someone else... which is only understandable. After all, she's still a very fine-looking lady.' He stopped walking again, frowned, and fixed Hannah with a penetrating gaze. 'You've chatted to her. She even bumped into you in Norwich, I understand, and you had a drink together. So what do *you* think?'

Hannah stared at him as if he'd lost his reason. He'd wondered that himself a few times recently, the things he'd been doing. The time and her silence dragged on. He felt like he was waiting for the verdict of a judge.

'She hasn't told me anything about having met someone,' Hannah said slowly. 'But she wouldn't, would she? She hardly knows me.'

'I thought women talked about things like that.'

'When they're close, they sometimes do. But...' Hannah shrugged, frowning. '...have you told Sidony the way you feel?'

'Told her?' Mortimer scoffed. 'No, of course not. I'd embarrass her, wouldn't I, if she's not interested any more, and ruin the friendship we've got. And of course she isn't interested.' He walked away, throwing out his arms sideways and shouting: 'Why would she be?'

The words seemed to bounce back and forth before fading to another silence. Mortimer stopped walking suddenly and looked back. Hannah was watching him warily.

'I don't know what to say,' she said.

Mortimer took a deep breath to calm himself down and returned to drop carefully into his seat. 'No, no, of course. I shouldn't have asked you. I thought you might... But no, of course.' He paused then added, 'But thank you for listening. I'd appreciate it if you didn't mention any of this outside these walls.'

'No, of course not.' Hannah drank a little more tea, put the mug down and got to her feet. 'Thank you for the drink. I'll think over what you said about the talk. And I should mention that Nathan and I are going to work long hours this week so we can take Friday afternoon off. We'll start early in the mornings to make the time up.' She paused, challenging him with a look. 'I understand Alan Foxhall has been questioning our timekeeping.'

'Has he? Well that's not come from me. No, no, you arrange your work as you see fit. It's not a problem.'

'Good.'

'Back to see family in Oxford no doubt.'

Hannah smiled briefly and a couple of minutes later she was gone.

Mortimer cleared away the mugs and poured himself a whisky. What was Alan up to? He took too much on himself that man.

He took a sip of whisky and enjoyed the soothing warmth of it. He already regretted the conversation with Hannah: he had revealed too much of himself. He'd half-intended to ask Hannah to try to quiz Sid about her private life but he'd changed his mind at the last minute. Some things you just couldn't talk about. Or shouldn't. She was smart, Hannah – which he liked ordinarily – and she was sympathetic, perhaps deceptively so, but those big eyes and that encouraging smile had led him to be indiscreet. He'd lost control there for a few minutes. How easy it was to give yourself away.

*

While Hannah stayed behind to see Mortimer about her talk, Nathan finished what he was doing and left promptly. He drove back to the village, parked behind the inn and walked up the road to the Thayne Gallery. With its summer opening hours it didn't close until six and he was curious to check out the place and see what they had on offer.

It was a double-fronted shop, deeper than it looked from the outside, with another exhibition space at the rear. Bright and well-lit, the front room was hung with a mixed selection of modern work, some quite loose and impressionistic, but before Nathan had a chance to look at anything properly, a man loomed up on him from the recesses of the shop offering an obsequious smile.

'Good afternoon, sir. I'm Edgar Thayne. Is there anything in particular you're looking for today?'

The man was fortyish, with just the beginnings of grey hair at his temples and a close-cropped dark beard.

'Not especially, I just wanted to browse a little.'

'Certainly sir. Do ask if there's anything you'd like to know about our artists. This space is given over to up-and-coming progressive talent; the rear room is devoted to more traditional works.'

Nathan thanked him and looked round. He liked some of the modern pieces but he was looking for a present for his mother and they were all too big and too expensive. In any case, she wouldn't appreciate them. He went into the back room. The walls were hung with oils, acrylics and watercolours, most of them Norfolk views. Hannah was right: some of the watercolours were good. Looking through the mounted pictures in the browser, he found a small one of an old-fashioned wooden boat with a red sail, gliding up a river banked each side with reeds. It was simple and atmospheric with an expanse of rose-tinted clouds in a big sky. He pulled it out and turned it over to check the price.

'Charming sir, isn't it? I might be able to offer a small discount.' The Thayne guy had appeared in the doorway again, the smile still in place.

They did a deal. Nathan knew his mother would love it and his conscience pricked him. He sauntered back to the inn along the tow path. It was a sunny evening and the moorings were busy. Getting near the inn, someone at one of the tables on the quay had stood up and was waving at him. With a sinking feeling he recognised that it was Rose and he reluctantly went over to speak to her.

There were three of them at the table and Rose introduced the couple sitting opposite as her friend, Debbie, and Debbie's boyfriend, James.

'Join us,' she said. 'It's too nice to sit inside.'

He hesitated.

'Oh come on, join us. We haven't got anything infectious.'

'All right.' He managed a weak smile. 'But only for a minute, I'm afraid. I've got some things I need to do.' He sat down on the bench seat beside her.

'All alone?' she enquired. 'I saw you walking up the street. Where's Hannah?'

'I don't know.'

Rose raised her eyebrows and grinned foolishly. It occurred to him that she'd been drinking for some time.

'You've bought something.' She nodded at the package he'd put down on the bench beside him and looked at him expectantly.

'It's a small watercolour I got in the gallery.'

'Oh nice. Can I see?'

'Sorry, I'd rather not unwrap it now. He packed it up for me quite securely, ready to post.'

'Oh. The man himself, was it? Or his side-kick?'

'Edgar Thayne he said his name was. Do you know him?'

'Of course. The gallery's been there as long as I can remember. His father used to own it but he died a few years ago.'

'I guessed he was the owner. He did seem very proprietorial.'

'Proprietorial? I can barely even say it. Nathan, I do love the words you use.' She called across the table to Debbie who was giggling because James was nuzzling her ear. They both looked drunk too. 'Would you say Edgar Thayne was proprietorial? I think that means he's essentially full of himself.'

Debbie pushed James away. 'He certainly is. Stuck-up is the word I'd use. Thinks he brings a bit of class to East Ranling.' She smirked at Rose. 'Not that you need more class of course.'

'Yeah, yeah, that's me: classy.' Rose laughed and looked back at Nathan. 'It's true. Edgar's a bore and looks down on the rest of us – silly snob – and I'm from the manor. Not that we're so hot, are we? I mean, the things that go on in that place. Though he does suck up to Uncle Mortimer of course, but then everyone likes Uncle Mortimer. Anyway…'

She reached into her bag and pulled out her purse.

'Here Nathan.' She proffered a five-pound note. 'Let me buy you a drink. You'll have to get it yourself though because I'll probably spill it. Dad's had another win on the horses and for once he gave me some.' She lowered her voice conspiratorially. 'Wanted to get me off his back no doubt.'

'That's kind of you but I really do need to get on. Stuff to do. Sorry.'

It was several minutes more before Nathan managed to finally extricate himself and get back to the inn. He met Hannah by the stairs and they went up to their rooms together.

'How did you get on with Mortimer?' he asked.

Hannah pulled a face. 'It looks like I'm stuck with the talks for now. He made a couple of suggestions for them. I'll just have to wing it.'

Nathan told her about his visit to the gallery and his run-in with Rose and her friends.

'My God, she was smashed. Sounding off to the whole village about what a snob Edgar Thayne is – which is probably

162

true, mind you. Did you meet him? Then she said something curious about the manor: *Not that we're so hot. The things that go on in that place.* Do you think she knows something?'

'It sounds like the sort of thing Rose would say just for effect. Posing.'

'I hate to think what'll become of the manor if she inherits it. But I'm sure you're right about the gallery: it's not the kind of place you use to fence Old Master drawings. Very modern.'

'And of course you couldn't take my word for that,' said Hannah. 'OK, OK, I'm only joking. Can I see which picture you bought?'

They'd arrived at their rooms.

'Sure.' He unlocked his door and invited her in. 'You mentioned how good some of the watercolours were and Mum likes atmospheric watercolours. And, of course, she has fond memories of this area.' He laid the picture on the bed and peeled off the brown paper in which it was wrapped, propping it up on the top of the chest of drawers. 'What do you think?'

'Yes, good.' She scrutinised it. 'It is good. She'll like that.'

'Thanks. Yes, I think she will.'

When Hannah had gone, he put the painting away in his wardrobe, undecided whether to post it on or wait until he saw his mother in the flesh. But tonight he'd have to ring her and tell her that the newspaper photograph was a dead end. Perhaps he should post the picture on after all.

He threw himself on the bed and stared up at the ceiling, mentally rehearsing what he would say to her, knowing the pain it would bring.

Chapter 12

On the Friday afternoon, with their weekend bags packed, Hannah and Nathan travelled up to London by train, having left Nathan's car at Hoveton and Wroxham station. They sat facing each other over a table. Nathan was travelling backwards because Hannah preferred to see where they were going rather than where they'd been and Nathan said he didn't care.

She settled back in the seat as the train gathered speed, watching the fields rush by, her mind still full of the work they had been doing all week. The Perugino was as stable as she could make it, was freshly varnished and back in its frame, and she had started work on the Rubens which appeared to be a preparatory oil sketch the artist had made for a bigger painting. It needed a thorough clean before she could tackle the questionable previous restoration. Nathan had taken a Turner watercolour out of its frame and had been checking it for mould, cleaning it and cutting a fresh mount. And Hannah's evenings had been spent fretting over the talk she was due to give to the school party the following week. If anything they'd both worked longer hours than usual and they needed a weekend away, even if they did have a serious purpose for going.

With two and a half hours to kill, Hannah had brought both a paperback and a magazine and started reading the book;

Nathan had a book too but put it to one side and browsed the newspaper he'd bought at the station. After twenty minutes of glancing across its pages, he folded it up and put it down. She noticed but carried on reading.

'This friend of yours whose flat we're staying in,' he said, 'you're sure she's not going to be there?'

'I told you: she went away yesterday, jetting off to sunny Spain.'

'Lucky her. And how do we get the key?'

'Her neighbour's got one and I have a code word so she'll let me have it.'

'Very MI6.'

He looked out of the window and was silent for a couple of minutes. She resumed her reading then felt his eyes on her again.

'So you lied when Mortimer suggested we were going back to Oxford to see family?'

She gave in, closed the book and put it down. 'I didn't *lie* exactly; I just didn't reply. I sort of nodded.'

'I think that counts as lying. It's fine. I'm guessing we'll both have done a lot more lying before this is through.' He looked at her with an expression of mingled amusement and challenge. 'Like saying what a great weekend we had back home when someone asks us. And they probably will. We're being watched.'

'You're saying I should have told him we were going to London?'

'No. No, I'm not.'

'Good. Have you finished with the paper?'

'For now, yes.' He handed it over.

'Do you mind if I do the crossword?'

He snorted. 'What, the easy one or the cryptic?'

'The cryptic.'

'Be my guest. I can't do them. I didn't know you liked them.'

'I used to do them all the time when I was a kid. I did one a couple of weeks ago and I'd forgotten how much I enjoyed them. They're a good way to switch off.'

Hannah tried to concentrate on the clues but Nathan was still watching her.

'You didn't tell me much else about that meeting with Mortimer,' he said eventually, 'except that the train layout was good.'

'There wasn't much to say.'

He regarded her a long moment. 'I don't suppose he'll invite me to see it. I haven't flashed my big blue eyes at him.'

She gave him a withering look. 'Neither have I.'

The conversation in the den had run through Hannah's head several times since her visit. Mortimer's sudden outburst had taken her by surprise; she'd had no idea he harboured such intense feelings for Sidony nor did she want to get involved. But what lingered most in her thoughts were his efforts to justify not replacing Carrie which had prompted her first doubts about the man. Had the girl been a nuisance to him? Had she guessed what he was doing, selling off his own collection maybe? Perhaps to keep afloat, knowing that the trustees wouldn't look kindly on it, would think the general integrity of the property had to be maintained at all costs?

But Mortimer, sneaking about and pushing Carrie into the Broad? Hannah couldn't imagine it. Not that absent-minded and kindly man. Still she didn't feel like sharing the conversation with Nathan: he'd be bound to jump to conclusions. She forced herself back into the crossword.

'An anagram: fires tiler.' She frowned. 'For a word meaning manure? Yes, got it: fertiliser.'

Pleased with herself, she smiled, writing in the solution.

That gave her a few letters and would start her off. Nathan stared at her as if she'd fallen from another planet, then picked up his book and started reading.

*

Hannah woke early the next morning, surfacing slowly from a dream. She'd been out shopping with her mother in Cheltenham and they'd stopped to have lunch in a small restaurant. Her mum was unusually chatty, laughing even, because suddenly Hannah's father had come to sit at the table and was holding forth the way he did, telling improbable stories, waving his hands expressively and winking at his daughter. Then he'd just got up and walked away and they were both waiting for him to come back…

Hannah opened her eyes suddenly, exhilarated, happy even and yet unaccountably edgy. Her mother was alive. And her dad was there too – the dad who was never there. But of course it was all wrong; none of it made sense and slowly reality sank in. No, her mum had died more than eighteen months ago, her brain frozen with a rapidly progressive dementia. And her father hadn't had any contact with his ex-wife for years before that and lived in Paris. Hannah saw him only rarely. She felt the familiar disappointment settle on her. She kept having these dreams, even now.

There was light in the room and she sat up, glancing round, trying to ground herself. Of course, she was in Rachel's flat. She could hear the sounds of the city already up and moving outside: the thrum of traffic; a delivery van reversing; a car horn impatiently sounding. She looked at her watch: it was ten to six. Nathan was asleep on the sofa in the living room next door because the flat only had one bedroom. She lay down again, trying to relax, and the conversations of the previous evening ran through her head.

Nathan had been more relaxed since they'd arrived. The change of scene maybe, away from the tensions at the manor, had been the catalyst needed. He even seemed to have lost some of his guilt and angst about Carrie and was more like his usual talkative self. Over dinner at a restaurant nearby, he'd suggested they take in a play or a show the following night.

'Unless you had other plans?' He regarded her levelly. 'Or don't want my company?'

She met his gaze. 'No. No plans. Sounds good to me. Assuming we can get tickets.'

He stared at her, a smile teasing the corners of his mouth. He'd noticed that she'd only half-answered, of course he had.

'There are always returns,' he said. 'Let's see what we can get.'

By the time they'd finished eating and had shared a bottle of wine, an easiness had settled on them, a rare mood of concord. Hannah felt bold enough – or perhaps careless enough – to risk bringing up the subject of his brother.

'I get the impression you used to be close to Samuel.' She gave a half-laugh. 'Not like me and Elizabeth. We never seem to get it right. Ever. So tell me about your brother. I'd like to know. What's he like?'

He said nothing and she wondered for a moment if she'd completely misjudged the mood but when he did speak the words came freely.

'He was my kid brother.' He produced a light shrug and the suggestion of a smile. 'So naturally he was a pain in the backside. He's three years younger than me so inevitably as a kid I thought I knew much more than he did and he ought to listen to me. Which of course he didn't.'

Nathan was fingering the dessert spoon he hadn't used, staring at it as he moved it back and forth.

'He was a clever kid, that's probably why. Maybe too

168

clever: he never seemed to be able to channel himself into anything. He'd flit from one interest to another and, just when you thought he'd found his calling, he'd get bored with it and move on.' He looked up at her suddenly. 'He could play the violin like you can't imagine. No really, he was good. He was also good at gymnastics. And he was academic.'

'So what did he end up doing? You told me he had a job when he disappeared.'

'Disappeared.' He snorted derisively. 'Makes it sound very supernatural, doesn't it, or like something from a sci-fi movie. The thing is, it felt like that. There and then not there. Gone, just like that.' He shook his head. 'Sorry. You were asking about his job. He studied for a joint honours degree, part of which was in English Literature, then did teacher training and got a job teaching English at a secondary school. He hadn't been doing it long. I don't think he was happy. It wasn't like he'd felt a mission to be a teacher, he just didn't know what else to do. I guess I should have seen some warning signs but I still don't know what they were.'

Nathan pushed his hair back with a restless hand.

'He always sounded the same on the phone: bright, breezy, a bit cheeky. He sent Mum flowers for Mother's Day and rang her specially. He didn't talk about the job much, it's true. He did say something about maybe getting some serious tuition on the violin and trying to get a job with an orchestra. I'm afraid I didn't pay much attention. He was always talking about some new project or other.'

'Did you look into orchestras after he left?'

He flicked her a look. 'What do you think?'

'Of course you did. Sorry.'

He shrugged. 'Don't be.' He smiled. 'I like that you're interested. Really. I know I get a bit... difficult about it sometimes.'

169

Hannah frowned now, remembering that smile, and the clink of their glasses. It had been a good evening. Surprisingly good.

A couple of minutes later, restless, she was up and slinging a cotton dressing gown over her nightie. She needed a pee and a cup of tea and she cautiously opened the door onto the living room. The still, humped shape on the sofa appeared to have had a fight with his bedding overnight; it wasn't clear who had won. It didn't move anyway, not until she emerged from the bathroom a few minutes later and found Nathan peering at her through one open eye.

'What time is it?' he muttered.

'Six o'clock.'

He groaned.

'I'm going to make tea. Do you want some?'

He grunted an affirmative and she ambled to the kitchenette at the other end of the room to put the kettle on, then put two slices of bread in the toaster and switched it on.

'Are you eating too?' Nathan had appeared beside her in his pyjamas, hair dishevelled, chin stubbled.

'Yes. I'm starving. Why, do you want toast too?'

'Uhuh.' He stretched his head and neck back and something crunched. 'That sofa's going to cripple me.'

'Well, you did insist on coming.'

'Wouldn't have missed it for the world.' He looked at her sidelong. 'You know, that's a clever hairstyle you've got. You can't tell the difference from your usual style even when you've been rolling around the bed all night.'

He reached up and touched her hair and she automatically put her hand up to catch his wrist.

'What are you doing?'

'You've got something in your hair.'

He brought his hand down and she was still holding his

wrist as he opened his fingers and showed it to her: a small white feather. Their eyes met and locked, her hand still on him. She released him suddenly. The kettle boiled and she quickly moved away.

'Check that toast isn't burning will you?' she said.

They had arranged to meet Anders Bianchi, Hannah's dealer friend, in a pub in Bloomsbury at twelve noon. Travelling on the underground to get there, hanging from the ceiling straps side by side, Nathan pressed Hannah to tell him more about the man.

'It's an odd name,' he said.

'Half-Italian father, Norwegian mother but grew up in the UK.'

'OK. So how do you know him exactly?'

'He was the dealer a friend of my father's used to sell his paintings.'

'So he mostly deals in new work?'

'He deals in what he thinks he can sell,' she hedged.

'Wherever it comes from?'

'I didn't say that. I think he's pretty straight.'

'But you don't ask too many questions?'

She rolled her eyes at him but didn't reply.

'And you got to meet him how?'

'I lived here in London for a while, remember? My father came over for an exhibition of his work in one of the private London galleries. He took me out to dinner and this guy was sitting nearby and, well, we all ended up in a pub afterwards while they caught up. You know how it is. My father doesn't come over to the UK very often.'

'So he doesn't deal for your father?'

'No… I don't think so… not any more anyway. My father hasn't always…' She became cross. 'How should I know? As you so kindly pointed out: I don't speak to him very often.'

171

'But you can trust this bloke?'

'Yes.'

She hoped she was right. Fortunately Nathan didn't pursue it any further and they arrived at the pub with a few minutes to spare.

It was an old, low-ceilinged tavern which dated back to the eighteenth century. Although it had been opened up into one large room at some time in the past, it retained a broad chimney in the middle with a fireplace on either side of it and wood-framed stained-glass panels further subdivided the room into more private spaces. Several tables were already occupied and there was a low rumble of conversation. Hannah looked round but couldn't see Anders so they bought drinks from the bar, found a table by a screen on the far side of the chimney where they still had an eye-line to the door, and waited.

Anders was five minutes late and came in looking edgy. He'd lost weight since she'd last seen him and wore a light grey suit, a size too big for him, and an open-necked striped shirt. His grey hair was cut very short and a prominent vertical crevice ran down each cheek but he smiled when he saw Hannah coming to meet him.

'Let me buy you a drink,' she said.

'Thanks. A whisky – with a lot of soda. My stomach isn't what it was.'

With his drink in hand, she took him back to the table and introduced Nathan.

Anders shook his hand. 'Pleased to meet you. Any friend of Hannah's is a friend of mine.' He sat in the vacant chair and settled back, scrutinising Nathan before turning his attention back to Hannah. 'How's that rascal of a father of yours doing, girl? Haven't seen him in too long.'

He spoke precisely, like someone who had worked hard to lose his regional accent but it was still there, just below the

172

surface, stretching the vowel sounds now and then, occasionally clipping a word. Hannah had never managed to pinpoint it. South London maybe? Essex?

She produced a laugh. 'I haven't either. I'm afraid my trips to Paris are few and far between.'

'Yes, well, perhaps when they finally open the channel tunnel – if they ever do – it might be easier.' Anders hesitated looking expectantly now from Hannah's face to Nathan's and back again. 'You didn't explain much on the phone. What's this all about then?'

'Hannah says you keep track of art sales.' Nathan moved in quickly before she had a chance to speak. 'That you know people, know what's being moved, maybe even where to.'

'I might do. Sometimes.' Anders looked at him suspiciously. 'Why are you asking?'

'We were wondering if you'd noticed a particular movement in drawings recently?'

The dealer frowned. 'What sort of drawings?'

'Good ones,' interposed Hannah. 'Like Old Master drawings?'

'Oh you mean *serious* drawings. There's always some movement. You know the art market, girl. People buy and sell all the time. It's a commodity for a lot of them; they're playing it like they play the stock exchange. Of course, for a few, it's about acquiring a special collection. Those are the ones obsessed with a particular artist or art movement. I like them: they're real art lovers.'

'And they're prepared to pay a lot for it too, I imagine,' remarked Nathan, 'but aren't always bothered about where the pictures come from.'

Anders turned back to fix Nathan with a look, eyes narrowed. 'Are you sure this guy's a colleague, Hannah? He sounds more like a copper to me.'

173

'No, he's not.' Hannah flicked Nathan a baleful glance. 'He's just suffering from sleeping on a sofa last night. The thing is, Anders, someone we know thinks that a couple of their drawings have been replaced with forgeries.'

'A Rubens and a Carracci,' interposed Nathan.

Anders produced a low whistle. 'Nice.'

'Exactly,' said Hannah. 'So naturally that suggests that the genuine ones have been sold on.'

He regarded her warily. 'And is this person looking to get them back?'

'No-o,' said Hannah slowly, glancing at Nathan again. 'She doesn't want the trouble and attention that would bring. You know how these things can get blown up in the press. But knowing what was going on might help her protect the rest of her collection, make her more diligent if you like.'

Anders took a thoughtful mouthful of his whisky and soda and nodded. 'That makes sense.' He sniffed, glancing casually round at the nearest tables. There was just one occupied: a man and a woman were poring over an A to Z of London. He leaned forwards, putting his elbows on the table. 'There has been some talk.' He paused, regarding each of them in turn. 'Nothing specific, you understand. I mean I couldn't name names.'

And wouldn't even if you could, thought Hannah. 'What sort of talk?' she asked.

He tilted his head on one side with a grimace. 'Drawings and paintings, just one here and there, good names but nothing so huge that it attracts too much attention – nothing like an oil of Monet's water lilies would, for example. That'd be too well known, too expensive. There's a suggestion that it's a network, a few different forgers, see, but all co-ordinated. Course it's all just talk.'

'A network?' said Nathan. 'Which means what exactly?

174

Countrywide? International?'

Anders shrugged and took another mouthful of his drink. 'UK I think but it's all gossip, nothing you can pin down. They're clever these buggers, you can be sure of that, selling in different places, using different people. It's a nice little earner.'

'To say the least. But illegal.'

'Well of course, if it can be proved.' He sat back in his chair. 'But you know how it is with artworks: it's all about expert opinion and the experts don't always agree. And if it's a good forgery, I mean really good...' He raised eloquent eyebrows. 'Assuming it ever gets that far of course.'

'Have you heard of a Michelangelo drawing selling recently?' demanded Nathan in a low voice.

'Michelangelo?' Anders mouthed, then snorted. 'That'd be getting a bit greedy, wouldn't it? Might be noticed.' He rocked his head side to side, puffing out his lips. 'Though I suppose if you've got a buyer lined up already...' Shrewd eyes examined Nathan's face. 'Lost a Michelangelo has she?'

'We don't know,' said Hannah firmly. 'We're just making general enquiries.'

Anders turned back to her and fixed her with a long, hard look. 'Well you be careful who you make enquiries of, my girl, because the word is that there's some in this network are ruthless and none too fussy about who gets hurt along the way, *if* you get my meaning. I'd keep out of it if I were you.' He turned his attention to his drink, downing the remainder in a long draught. 'Afraid I've got to go. I need to be somewhere else.' He put a hand to his stomach and belched. ''Scuse me. Stomach's not what it was.'

He stood up and looked down on Hannah. 'You look after yourself, young lady, and give your father my best when you see him next.' He turned his gaze on Nathan. 'And you, young man, watch she doesn't get into trouble. What you've been talking about isn't a game for amateurs.'

*

'*She*?' said Nathan, after Anders had gone. '*She* doesn't want the trouble and attention? Do you really think that changing the personal pronoun will hide the identity of who we're working for? He wouldn't have to ask far to know would he?'

'You're the one who went blundering in with *Hannah says you know people* and obsessive collectors *aren't bothered where the pictures come from.* Talk about tactless. I was just trying to cool the situation. I thought he was going to do a runner.'

'There didn't seem any point dancing around the issue. That was why we asked to see him in the first place, wasn't it?' He glared at her accusingly. 'You said you trusted him.'

Hannah glared back.

They ordered sandwiches and ate them, intermittently trying to dissect the conversation, trying to work out where it left them. Nathan had hoped that Anders would give them a name, something to go on, but all they knew now was that it was probably a big operation rather than just a small-time local crook. That made it harder to investigate. It also made it riskier and Anders' warning hadn't passed Nathan by; he didn't want to put Hannah in danger. But if he said that, she'd be even more likely to do something rash so he kept it to himself.

They split up for the afternoon. While Nathan headed to the British Museum, Hannah went to the National Gallery.

'I know, I know,' she said. 'It's a busman's holiday but I can't resist it.'

After meeting up back at the flat late in the afternoon, they got back on the tube in the early evening, stopped at Leicester Square and grabbed a meal at an Italian restaurant before heading to St. Martin's theatre. It was the thirty-ninth year of the staging of Agatha Christie's *The Mousetrap* and Nathan had managed to get tickets. Neither of them had seen it before and they were unusually united in their enjoyment.

Coming out a couple of hours later, there was the usual shock of returning to reality after the stillness of the spectacle inside, made worse by the bustle and noise of the streets.

'Do you want to get a taxi back?' said Nathan.

'No, shall we walk for a bit? There's no hurry and I've missed the atmosphere of the city streets.'

They sauntered along, weaving through the crowds on the pavements, sometimes getting separated by the throng. Nathan took her arm at one point to stop her from being pushed into the road and he kept his hand protectively there. He noticed that she didn't object either. They'd been walking for maybe twenty minutes when he spotted an old pub on the other side of the road.

'Let's stop and have a drink,' he suggested.

He'd expected it to be quiet and quaint and give them a chance to relax and talk but it was crazy in there. As well as the crush and babble of people there was pop music playing and a pinball machine beeping loudly in one corner. At the bar men stood three deep, either putting the world to rights with their friends or trying to elbow their way to the front to buy a drink.

'Let's find somewhere quieter.' Hannah had to raise her voice to make herself heard. 'I can't think in here.'

'You're right. We'll go.'

He turned to leave but a movement at a table to the left of the door caught his eye and he automatically glanced across. A man had just taken a plastic carrier bag containing something from the person sitting opposite him and was now bending over, stowing it quickly and furtively in a tatty old leather briefcase on the floor by the side of his chair. The other person, without speaking, was already on his feet and about to go.

Nathan saw the seated man straighten up again and quickly looked away. With his hand on Hannah's back, he shepherded them both out of the door.

'What's the matter?' said Hannah.

'Nothing's the matter.'

'You look like you've just seen a ghost.'

'Not exactly.' He encouraged her to walk along the street with him. 'I've just seen Toby Gyllam-Spence.'

'What, in there?' She jerked her head back towards the pub.

'Yes, near the door. And he was just given something by another man. Very shifty.'

'Money?' suggested Hannah.

'Probably. Unfortunately, I'm pretty sure he saw me too. He saw us both.'

Chapter 13

'They say the fire started in the kitchen then tracked up the back staircase to the first floor. It's a mess.'

Mortimer felt Sidony's eyes on him and looked up. It was Sunday lunchtime. Toby had gone away and still wasn't back and there were only the three of them there: Sid, Mortimer and Rose. Mortimer didn't miss his brother – he was only too glad when he wasn't there – but it grieved him that he used the place like a hotel.

'The Boatman. Are you listening to me, Mortimer?'

'Yes, yes. The Boatman. The fire started in the kitchen and it's a mess.'

'That's where Nathan and Hannah are staying,' said Rose. 'It's lucky they went away.'

'Indeed,' said Sidony, 'but that's my point: there's a problem now. Netta was telling me. It's the talk of the village apparently. The landlord says that he's going to have to be closed until checks are carried out on the structure and they can organise repairs. Even when he can open again, he thinks the back rooms upstairs will be out of use for a while. His priority is getting it all safe and getting the bar and kitchen functioning.'

Mortimer nodded. 'Terrible,' he murmured. 'Brian and Alice have put a lot of work into that place.'

'You're missing my point, Mortimer. We need to offer

accommodation to Nathan and Hannah for the remainder of their stay.'

'What, here?'

'Yes. Where else did you have in mind?'

'Are you sure that's necessary?'

'I think it's a great idea,' said Rose.

'Of course you do,' said Mortimer acidly, stressed and speaking without thinking. 'You'd like to get him here and all to yourself.' Rose glared at him and started to protest but he turned back to Sidony. 'There are costs to be considered.'

'Oh really, a few meals,' said Sidony, 'not much else. We'll manage, I'm sure. Negotiate it with their boss if you're so bothered about it. They won't be paying for The Boatman after all.'

'That's true. Yes, I suppose you're right. I'll arrange it.'

'I'll help.'

He tried to smile at her but couldn't pretend he was happy about it. Still he had other things on his mind and they ate in silence for several minutes.

Netta had just brought in a trifle for dessert when the phone rang.

'That's the house line,' said Rose and immediately started to get to her feet.

Mortimer stopped her. 'It'll be for me. I was expecting a call.'

He hurried back along the passage to his study, carefully closing the door behind him, and picked up the receiver. It was for him, a call that had been promised by the previous Friday.

'You're making a lot of excuses,' Mortimer said testily after listening for a few minutes.

He listened again. More excuses.

'I thought we had an agreement,' he insisted.

He closed the call and stared at the phone. 'Damn you.'

He put a hand to his forehead. It felt hot and clammy. The pressure to live up to his father's expectations and keep the manor going was going to be the death of him.

*

'No, it's fine.' Hannah put down her overnight bag and glanced round her allotted room at the manor. 'Perfect, thank you. This is very kind of you.'

'Not at all,' said Sidony. 'These are difficult circumstances and we're only too glad to be able to help. Now, have you eaten? We had our main meal at lunchtime today but there's bound to be something in the kitchen if you want it.'

'Maybe we could have a sandwich,' said Nathan. He was standing just outside in the passage.

Sid turned and embraced them both in a look.

'Do help yourself from the kitchen, and to hot drinks or whatever. Netta's gone home long since. We thought you might like to use the snug to sit in. It's at the end of the passage on the right opposite the kitchen. It's not used much and I'm sure you'd both prefer your own space. There's a sofa in there and a television. Oh and there's a small bathroom you can both use here.' She pointed to the door opposite, then hesitated. 'I'm afraid there are no keys to the doors – there used to be once, I suppose, but I've not seen any. Not that you should need one. A woman called Joy comes in once a week on a Thursday to clean. Netta and Rita change the bedlinen on a Friday. Right, Nathan. You're next door.'

Sidony left to show Nathan his room. She was definitely a cool, calm customer, thought Hannah; she didn't seem to allow anything to faze her.

She looked round. The clothes and personal effects that she had left in her room at The Boatman had been bundled into a couple of black bin bags and now sat forlornly on the floor.

181

It had been a shock to return to the village to find the inn silent and charred. The fire had long since been put out but the damage at the rear was very evident. The fire service, concerned for the stability and safety of the rear staircase, had retrieved Nathan and Hannah's belongings which fortunately had not been affected. And now here the two of them were at the manor. Mortimer had left a message with Brian and Alice, inviting the two restorers to stay. They hadn't seen him since their arrival however; Sidony had done all the honours.

She waited until she heard Sidony leave Nathan's room and walk back along the passage, then went round and knocked on his door. He opened it almost before she'd finished knocking, glanced up the passage and stood back to let her in, closing the door behind her.

'This is an interesting development,' he said softly. 'I wonder where everybody else sleeps? I think we're over the kitchen here. At least you've got a window.'

'I'm surprised they're letting us stay. They're not keen, I'm sensing.'

'Noblesse oblige. They probably didn't feel they had a choice.'

Hannah sat on the side of his bed. She felt very weary suddenly.

'I know you thought Toby looked suspicious in the pub last night,' she said, 'but the more I think about it, the more I think it was probably just some win on the horses. He wouldn't do business about a large-scale fraud in a pub, would he, and we know he's a gambler.'

'Exactly and gamblers usually lose. They're often skint which is a prime motive for a bit of theft and fraud. We can't rule him out. Which reminds me...' He delved into his overnight bag, pulled out Carrie's notebook and sat down beside her on the bed. 'I was looking through this on the train

182

and I saw something. Wait a minute.' He flicked through the pages, pressed the book open and handed it to her. 'What do you make of this?'

Hannah scanned the sheets. There were notes about a couple of the oil paintings on display and a suggestion that the frame on one of them needed attention. Also a reminder to look something up, perhaps for her talk to a school party. Hannah continued to read down.

'Here,' said Nathan, stabbing the opposite page with an impatient finger. 'See. *BADN*. What do you suppose that means?'

'OK, OK, I'm getting there.'

There were two questions marks before the initials and a short sentence after them: *Sees a chart is ruined*. Hannah stared at it, shaking her head. Carrie's writing was pretty sloppy.

'Does it mean anything?' She paused. 'I think it might be an O. *BAON*.'

'Really?' He peered at it again and pulled a face. 'No, I think it's a D. But what about the other bit, what do you think she's referring to? What chart?'

'I've no idea. Something in the storeroom? A layout of the place? Or is there a drawing that's a kind of chart?'

'I don't think so. It means nothing to me.'

'And ruined.' Hannah stared at the entry, brow heavily furrowed. 'Something that needed our attention maybe?'

Nathan shrugged. 'Beats me. You know, she noted somewhere else that she was musing on suggesting the two rooms – the workroom and the storeroom – were knocked into one. Thought it would make a better use of space and give more ventilation.'

'I wonder if she ever put that to Mortimer?' mused Hannah. 'Though the building is probably listed which might be an issue.'

'I don't know. Look, can we go down and grab some sandwiches? I'm starving.'

'Sure. Can I keep this now?'

Nathan grunted an affirmative but was already up and heading for the door.

*

They heard from Timothy on the Monday that Mortimer had already negotiated a reduction in the fee for their work in exchange for their board and lodging. So they were expected to eat at the manor every night.

'Great,' said Hannah when Nathan told her. 'We will be popular.'

Nathan glanced towards the door of the workroom and dropped his voice. 'Look on it as an opportunity. We might find out more living here.'

'More than we want to know, I suspect.'

'That's the idea,' he said drily, 'positive thinking.'

It was a strange place to live. Hannah quickly became aware of what she thought of as the sticky quietness of it. There were sometimes other people about – Sidony was at breakfast the next morning, for example – but mostly they weren't evident. There would be the sound of a voice coming from somewhere else in the house or a series of footsteps, echoing down a passage perhaps, a snatch of music or a television programme. The residents, either by design or by accident, seemed rarely to be in the same room, or even indeed in the same house, more than strictly necessary. Netta informed her that the whole household rarely all sat down to eat together in an evening; there was always someone missing, sometimes two or more. So Netta, who usually went back to her little cottage along the lane from two till six, had got into

184

a routine of preparing what she called 'versatile' food which could be quickly cooked, reheated or even eaten cold if someone came in late and wanted it.

It quickly became obvious that there was no mystery about how someone could sneak art works out of the manor. Anyone could do something on the sly in that house without the others being any the wiser.

*

On the Tuesday evening only Rose, Toby, Nathan and Hannah sat round the dining table and, in virtual silence, ate a beef casserole together. Rose had tried to start up conversation a few times but each time it had quickly died for lack of interest and she was feeling frustrated. She wanted to get to know Nathan better and she wouldn't get a better chance than this, would she, with him staying on site? But there were too many people. And Hannah.

Netta came in to offer them apple crumble with cream for dessert and, as soon as it was eaten, Hannah excused herself and went back to her room, claiming a need to read through her notes before giving her talk to the school party the following day.

Rose cheered up and picked up the bottle of wine that Toby had opened. Neither Nathan nor Hannah had drunk much so there was still a couple of glasses' worth left in it. She offered it to Nathan who politely refused so she poured some into her own glass. Her mother kept telling her she drank too much but Sid wasn't there to scold tonight. In fact Rose had no idea where she was.

'I'll finish that, thanks Rose,' said Toby.

She poured the last of it into his glass. She was waiting for him to go upstairs and leave them alone – he didn't usually linger after a meal – but he got up, crossed to the sideboard and took a cigar out of one of the drawers. On an apparent afterthought, he turned to brandish it at Nathan.

'Want one, Nathan?'

'No, thanks. I don't smoke.'

Toby grunted, produced a lighter from his pocket and, still standing, lit up, drawing on the cigar with clear satisfaction.

'Coffee?' Netta offered from the doorway. 'Oh Mr Toby, you shouldn't be smoking in here. You know Mr Mortimer doesn't like it.'

'Oh absolutely Netta,' responded Toby drily. 'We mustn't upset Mortimer, must we? Tell you what, I'll take it upstairs. I don't want coffee anyway.' He turned to Nathan. 'Why don't you come upstairs and join me for a nightcap? Mortimer can't stop me smoking in my own room and I've got a rather fine brandy up there.' He hesitated, turning to his daughter. 'Sorry, Rose. A man's meeting. I want to have a word with Nathan in private.'

'OK, thanks. I will.' Nathan offered Netta an apologetic smile. 'No coffee for me either tonight, thanks Netta.'

Nathan is so polite, thought Rose, so unlike most of the people she knew. She found it completely charming.

Toby knocked the rest of his wine back and invited Nathan to follow him, leaving Rose sitting alone with Netta bustling about clearing things off the table, tutting to herself. After a couple of minutes, Rose got up, told Netta she'd take her wine to her room, and made for the stairs. She paused at the top but there was no-one in sight. Toby's bedroom was half way along the corridor on the left and she picked her way along to it, carefully avoiding all the places where the floorboards creaked. Her father had closed the door but Rose's hearing was good and with no other sounds to distract her, she could hear her father's bullish voice quite clearly.

'What about that brandy?' he was saying. 'Or I've got

whisky if you prefer. A malt.'

'No, brandy would be good, thanks.' Nathan was only just audible.

There were the clinking sounds of a decanter and glasses and a creak as her father sat in one of the chairs. Rose drank a mouthful of her wine and waited.

'Must be an odd job you do,' Toby remarked. His voice was pinched; he was clearly pulling on his stupid cigar while he talked. 'I mean, moving around like that. See all sorts of people, I imagine. Do you ever find it difficult, not getting drawn in?'

There was a pause before Nathan replied. 'Drawn in? What do you mean exactly?'

'Oh you know, taking sides, getting involved, that sort of thing. You're only human.'

'I certainly am. But no, I don't find it a problem. Not yet anyway.'

'You liked that Carrie girl though, I'm guessing. Must have been a bit tricky for you.'

Rose's wandering attention was caught again; she leaned closer to the door.

'I liked her well enough,' said Nathan. 'She seemed very good at her job but I couldn't say I got to know her.'

Toby grunted and there was a short silence. Rose dared take another gulp of wine.

'In some ways, I think it's easier for me.' Nathan's voice was languid, casual. 'I move on. You have to work cheek by jowl with the same people year in, year out. Can't always be easy.'

Toby laughed. 'You're right there. You know of course that I was married to Sid? Of course you do. It's no secret, especially with Rose there to keep reminding us.' There was a pregnant pause. 'Like our Rose, do you?'

Nathan made no immediate response. Rose could barely breathe, waiting to hear what he'd say.

'Are you a matchmaker now?' said Nathan.

'Relax. I was just asking. She likes you. Anyway, I feel sorry for the girl. I'm not sure bringing her back here was the best thing we could have done, especially with the way it worked out.'

Rose frowned, her ear pushed up against the door, but it had gone quiet again. Her father was drinking probably or sucking on the cigar.

'Ever been married, Nathan? No? Well, it's not good when it all goes wrong, let me tell you. It changes people. Look at our Sid. She was never what you might call easy-going, but these days...' Another pause. '...she's a bitter, vindictive woman. And what a temper. Threw a glass of wine over the woman I was with when we first split up. Ranted at her. Completely lost it. You wouldn't think to look at her in her power suit, so cool and efficient, would you? You don't see the half of it. Ruthless and hard as nails these days.'

Rose's frown deepened. She and her mother didn't get on that well but she didn't like her being described in that way. It wasn't fair. When she'd been a child, Sidony was the person who had made sure she was clean and fed, who looked after her when she was ill, or hugged her and rubbed her knees when she fell over. She'd been a competent but never effusive mother. Later, when the marriage had broken down, Sid had retreated into her own world. A bit aloof maybe, authoritarian too. But ruthless? No. Her father was an oaf.

'And she's gone all secretive lately too,' Toby was saying. 'I'm sure she's up to something. Making plans she doesn't want to share perhaps. I've seen her get like that before. Anyway, more brandy?'

There was a creak as he got to his feet. He must have

knocked back the first and barely tasted it.

'No, I'm fine thanks.'

For the first time ever it occurred to Rose that drinking too much wasn't very attractive. Her father did it all the time and look how that had turned out. Nathan didn't. She looked accusingly at the remains of the wine in her glass.

'And yet you still manage to all live here together,' Nathan was saying, 'which must make it even more difficult. Did you never think of going away again, maybe trying something new?'

Toby's seat groaned again as he sat down. Rose could smell the cigar smoke filtering under the door.

'Capital,' he said. 'That's the problem. I don't have any. In any case, this is the ancestral home. I believe I have as much right to be here as my brother.'

'You say that as if Mortimer didn't share your opinion.'

Toby snorted. 'Mortimer and I have never seen eye to eye... about anything. Except that we both fancied Sid when we were young. She was a real looker back then *and* from a good family. Quite the catch. But she took up with Mortimer early on. Imagine. She was only about eighteen then of course. I don't know what she saw in him but they were pretty close for a year or so.' He stopped suddenly, as if for effect. 'Then of course the thing with Robert happened.'

'Who was Robert?'

'Oh, didn't you know? Robert was Sidony's elder brother and big friends with Mortimer when they were young; they were of an age, you see, did all sorts of things together. Then he and my brother went out boating one day. They were maybe twenty-one, twenty-two. Some people who saw them before they set off said there was an argument on the quay, a row even, really heated. And it wasn't the first time by all accounts. Anyway, Robert never came back. He drowned.'

'That's awful. What happened?'

'Mortimer *said* it was an accident.' Toby emitted a scornful noise. 'Well he would, wouldn't he? And it's amazing what being the heir to a place like this can do for you. The police never pressed the point – recorded it as an accident so there you are. Whatever it was, his relationship with Sidony didn't last. That's when she and I got together.'

Rose frowned. She didn't know about her mother and Mortimer. And she'd heard about Robert's death but had never heard that Mortimer was implicated in any way. Was he? She was shocked. Not kind, gentle, rather odd Uncle Mortimer. Anyway, why tell this so particularly to Nathan?

'She held it against him?' prompted Nathan.

'What do you think? Of course nobody talks about it, never did. Mortimer could never do any wrong; he's always been the darling of the family. Of the whole village.' He laughed unpleasantly. 'Just look at Netta. She thinks the sun shines out of him. It's Mr Mortimer this and Mr Mortimer that. But you've seen him.' A brief pause. 'He's not the pussycat everyone thinks and I should know.'

There was a charged silence after this remark.

'Did I see you in London by any chance last weekend?' asked Nathan. 'In a pub. We'd popped in for a drink but it was so busy we didn't stay.'

'That's right. I thought it was you. And with the delightful Hannah too.' Another pause. 'And yet weren't you both supposed to be going back to Oxford?'

'Last minute change of plan. A friend of Hannah's was going away and offered her London flat to us for the weekend. Too good an offer to refuse. We'd been to the theatre that night. *The Mousetrap.* Very good. Ever seen it?'

'No.' Toby snorted. 'Sounds like a cosy weekend though. And yet you insist there's nothing between you.'

190

'We're friends,' Nathan said evenly.

Rose felt like interrupting and assuring her father that the two restorers were indeed only friends. Hannah, after all, was meeting Nigel Judd on the sly. Not that her father ever listened to what she said.

'I suppose you must have wondered what I was doing there too,' he said now. 'I'd had quite a win on the horses as it happens. I was celebrating my winnings. I don't always use the regular guys for my bets, you see. If you know the right people you can get better odds, if you know what I mean. In fact, I could give you some tips if you're in the market for it.'

'Thanks, but I'm not much of a gambler.'

'No? And yet I'd got the feeling that you were. One for taking chances, that is.'

'In what way?'

'Oh, just an impression. Though I wasn't just talking about the horses. If you know what you're doing, you can back your hunches on all sorts of things. Especially a smart, educated chap like you.' He hesitated. 'I could put something your way if you're interested. I know people. Of course, it's not without its risks.'

Rose heard the house phone ringing downstairs. There were no phones upstairs despite her frequent appeals to Mortimer to install one, so she knocked back the last of her wine and hurried to the stairs and down. The nearest phone was in the sitting room and she grabbed the receiver.

A couple of minutes later she was back upstairs and knocking on her father's door, walking in without waiting for a reply.

'There's someone on the phone for you.' She fixed Nathan with an accusing look. 'It's a woman.'

'Right. Thanks. And thanks for the drink, Toby.'

Nathan was up and already walking to the door.

191

'I took it in the sitting room,' said Rose. 'It's a bit late to be ringing, isn't it?' she added to his departing back as he hurried downstairs.

*

Afterwards Nathan lied about the call. When Rose asked about it at breakfast the following morning, he claimed it had been his mother, that she'd tripped and fallen and was a bit shaken. Even as he was saying it, he regretted it. Hannah was there too and was watching his face, concerned.

'Is she all right?'

'Yes, she's fine. She just needed to talk a bit, get some reassurance. Nothing broken. I'd given her this number the night before in case of emergencies.'

Rose didn't challenge his story fortunately. It seemed that Toby had kept her talking up in his room and she hadn't heard the conversation.

Getting in his car on the Saturday morning, he still felt bad about the lie. Hannah had been cheery and bright-eyed at breakfast, glad to have got her talk out of the way and relieved that it had gone down well. To celebrate, she'd decided to visit the sea and, having looked at a map, insisted that there were several nice places an easy drive away. She looked expectant as if she thought he'd be up for the trip too but he'd told her he wasn't interested, that there was an archaeological site he might visit to the west instead. He'd been kind of short with her and it was another lie. He had other plans for the day.

He still remembered the phone call vividly. He'd been anxious that it might be his mother but as soon as the woman spoke he knew it wasn't. A breathy voice, fussy and rapid.

'Nathan? Nathan Bright? Oh good. I'm sorry it's late but I've been trying to track you down. I rang the number you gave me but the man who answered said you weren't there any

192

more, that there's been a fire or something.'

'Ye-es. Who is this please?'

'Sorry, yes of course, it's Glenys. You left us your phone number at The Fisherman and Dog in Pollersby. Do you remember? You were looking for someone you thought you'd been to school with? Well, he's back. His boat – it's called the *Sally Ann* – is moored up here and we saw him in the pub earlier this evening. We promised to let you know.'

She'd fallen silent then, undoubtedly waiting for a response but Nathan had been too stunned to give one. He'd forgotten about the photograph, had told his mother that it had come to nothing, that it was just another false lead and he'd sidelined it in his own head.

'Hello? Are you there?'

'Yes, sorry. Thank you for letting me know.'

'Do you want us to say something to him, tell him you're looking for him?'

'No.' He'd said it too urgently, too brusquely. 'No,' he repeated more softly. 'Thanks anyway. I'd rather just turn up and, you know, reintroduce myself quietly, no fanfares. It's been a while.'

'I understand.'

Putting the phone down he'd already decided he wouldn't go, for what would be the point? He could do without all that stress and heartache again. But here he was, setting off for Pollersby, having argued with himself ever since and determined not to discuss the matter with anyone, not even Hannah; it was a private thing.

He arrived in the village at twenty past eleven. He hadn't hurried and he didn't now, parking the car in the village car park and sitting in it for several minutes, still trying to talk himself into doing it. The pub had just opened when he got there but he didn't go in, just carried on walking and picked

193

up the tow path by the side of the river, checking the name of each boat as he went along the line of moorings. There was only one left now, tied up at the end, and he heard whistling coming from it as he drew near. He saw the boat's name – *Sally Ann* – barely registering it, because he recognised the tune being whistled, *Yesterday* by the Beatles. He felt a frisson of anticipation, or maybe apprehension. He didn't know what to think or feel any more, didn't know where his head was on this emotional merry-go-round. It was a song he and his brother used to sing along to when they were young. But then again everyone did, didn't they? It meant nothing.

He came alongside and paused, scanning the boat. It was an old cabin cruiser with a boxy cockpit at the rear and, to judge from the windows in the hull, accommodation in cabins below. It sat lower in the water than the more modern boats but looked to have been recently painted.

The whistling came from somewhere inside; there was no-one visible.

'Hello,' he heard himself call out. 'Anyone aboard?'

The whistling stopped and there was silence. Nathan became aware of the calls of birds in the trees and shrubs behind him, then the drone of another boat's engines as it passed by on the river, its wash making the boats bob up and down at their moorings. Someone laughed on one of the boats further along and said something unintelligible. Still there was silence on the little cruiser.

Was that a face he saw at one of the windows, not long enough or clear enough to identify who it was or even its sex? Either way it had gone. He had been spied on and ignored. It made him impatient and cross. This was absurd; he only wanted to speak to the man, to say hello and goodbye and draw a line under it all.

'Hello,' he called again, more stridently this time.

'Anyone home?'

A figure slowly emerged from below and stood on the rear deck: a tall, thin man, bearded and wearing jeans and a tee-shirt. His hair looked dark but he wore a peaked cap and, with the sun behind him, Nathan struggled to make out the features. His brain was automatically cross-referencing what he could see with both what he remembered and with all the photographs of Sam as a youth. There might have been a similarity but so much time had passed, he couldn't be sure.

The man didn't speak but stared at him too, then glanced up the tow path and back again.

'Hi,' he said, then paused. 'You'd better come aboard.'

Nathan hesitated, frowning, then grabbed the guard rail either side of the entry and climbed on board.

They stood facing each other, both staring. Nathan could now make out the features: the slightly narrow-set eyes and the long nose – exaggerated perhaps because the man's cheeks were hollowed out, his cheekbones very prominent. The hair was longer than he remembered but it curled around the ears in a familiar way and the height was right. The posture was familiar too – the slight tilt of the head to one side as if listening for a cue. And now he could see the recognition in the man's gaze too; he kept pressing his lips together hard as if trying to control them.

'Nathan?' the man said eventually.

Nathan didn't speak but stepped forward and wrapped his brother in his arms, holding him tight. After a brief hesitation Sam hugged him back and for several minutes they just held each other and didn't speak. Nathan couldn't speak. When they finally released each other, he stepped back and looked away, brushing tears from his cheeks, spent, confused, conflicted. Dazed even. He looked back at Sam, and suddenly the frustration and anger of all these last years welled up inside

195

him and finally burst out.

'What the hell have you been doing?' he spat out. 'Where have you been? Gadding about on your little boat, having a great time, were you? Didn't it occur to you that we'd be sick with worry about you? For God's sake, Sam, what were you thinking?'

He half-turned, throwing out his arms to the side in a gesture of frustration, needing to move and dissipate this energy, this overpowering fury that was flooding through him and made him want to hit something.

'No, don't tell me: you weren't thinking. You just followed your own star and to hell with everyone else.'

'It wasn't like that.'

'So how was it, Sam, hm? Tell me, how was it?'

'Not here,' said Sam. 'Come inside.'

Nathan stopped pacing. 'What?'

Sam checked along the tow path and towards the other boats moored up.

'Come inside,' he repeated. 'Have a drink. I'll explain then. Please Nathan. Please.'

Chapter 14

Hannah didn't see Nathan again for the rest of the Saturday. If he was in his room when she returned from her trip to the coast, he made no sound. He'd been off-hand with her at breakfast, vague about what he planned to do and snapped at her when she teased him about it. The easy camaraderie they had shared in London the previous weekend already felt like a world away. They were back to business as usual – though he wasn't usually rude.

When she went down to dinner at seven-thirty, Mortimer sat alone in the dining room, playing with the stem of a glass of white wine. He smiled when she came in and half rose to his feet in a chivalrous gesture, though she wasn't convinced he was pleased to see her. Since his outburst about Sidony, he had been more distant, less inclined to make conversation.

He invited her to have a glass of wine and the next minute Netta bustled in with a small roast chicken on a carving dish.

She glanced round, put the dish down and frowned at Hannah.

'I was hoping Mr Nathan might have come in late,' she said. 'I haven't seen him about today. Is he all right?'

'He sends his apologies. He's fine.'

Hannah hoped he was. She had no idea.

'Ah well, this chicken'll be all right cold if he wants it later.'

Mortimer carved the meat for them both and they made occasional desultory conversation while they ate but he left, with gracious apologies, as soon as he'd had his crème caramel dessert. Hannah took her dishes back to the kitchen then spent the remainder of the evening in the snug. Around ten thirty, she heard measured, careful footsteps making their way up the staircase by the snug door and, going to her room soon after, saw a light under Nathan's door and stopped outside. A moment later she turned away and went on to her room.

She still hadn't seen him by the time she went out on the Sunday morning. It was a fine, sunny day and she wandered along the river then took the farther bridge over to the reserve. It was busy. The sun had brought people out, strolling the paths, stopping now and then to listen to the birdsong or scanning the trees to spot the source of it. She meandered on, her thoughts inexorably returning to Carrie and the last time the young woman had walked this way.

Earlier in the week, Nathan had told her about his conversation with Toby and the suspicious offer: *I could put something your way.* Apparently he'd backtracked almost as soon as he'd said it and the phone call from Nathan's mother had brought the interview to a sudden halt. Had he really been about to cut Nathan in on the fraud or did he have something else going on?

Hannah was frankly stumped. Everyone's behaviour gave cause for suspicion but they were no nearer to finding out who was involved than they had been at the start. Toby had badmouthed both Sidony and Mortimer and the story about Robert was unsettling but Toby was hardly a reliable witness. And now Nathan seemed to have lost interest and was avoiding her. He was a big help.

She sat for a while in the hide looking out over the Broad, watching the waders and ducks as they foraged for food. A marsh harrier soared high above, its huge wings spread wide as it wheeled and dipped. But the image of Carrie's body floating in the water loomed into her mind and she got up, too restless to stay, and walked on until she reached the reception centre.

It was busy and there was a queue for the drinks machine so Hannah idly browsed the racks of gifts for sale: key rings and tea towels; posters and maps; stationery and mugs; and a range of guides to the flora and fauna of the area.

She picked up a notebook and a ballpoint pen and took them to the till. There were two people on duty, a man and a woman, neither of whom she had seen before, and she paid, then climbed the steps to the lookout over the Broad. Grace was sitting there alone and looked up in surprise as Hannah slipped onto the bench next to her.

'Hi,' said Hannah. 'I didn't know you were working today.'

Grace smiled. 'I'm not. I just...' She shrugged. 'I sometimes come here anyway. It's peaceful.'

'I agree. You know, I still haven't seen the crane.'

Grace looked amused. 'Patience. You have to spend hours watching to see these things. Of course there's an element of luck too.'

'I'm beginning to think it's just a story, that it doesn't exist.'

'Oh it does exist. Trust me. I've seen it. It's stunning – definitely worth the wait.'

They sat for some minutes in companionable silence, looking out over the water. Glancing sideways at her companion, Hannah sensed something wrong. She had noticed before that there was something sad and wistful about the young woman but now she looked shuttered, oppressed even, and she had a ring of bruising on her left wrist.

199

Grace saw her looking and immediately pulled the sleeve of her cotton sweater down.

'I should go.' She got to her feet and slipped the strap of her bag over her shoulder.

'Are you alone today Grace? I mean, is Alan waiting for you? Only I was thinking of getting some lunch and I'd love some company if you're free.'

'He's away for the weekend,' Grace said slowly. 'It's a darts club trip. They go every year.' She paused, fingering her sleeve, but her expression had visibly brightened. 'Where are you going?'

'I don't know: the inn or maybe the tea-rooms. They do light lunches, don't they?'

'Yes.' Grace paused again, clearly fighting some internal battle. 'Let's try the tea-rooms. I'm less likely to be...' She shrugged the end of the sentence away, already moving towards the stairs.

A family group left the teashop just as they arrived and Hannah and Grace took the one free table in the corner at the rear, ordering sandwiches and a pot of tea for two. They made stilted and patchy conversation while they ate, Grace regularly glancing towards the window, or at the door every time it opened and the bell rang. When they'd finished eating, Hannah started talking about the reserve, prompting Grace to tell her what wildlife she'd seen recently and the young woman slowly relaxed.

Replacing her teacup on its saucer, Grace stroked the tablecloth and looked round the room.

'It's nice here,' she said, with a soft smile of satisfaction. 'Ordered and clean and kind of innocent.' She became embarrassed. 'Sorry. Silly thing to say, isn't it? But I haven't been here in ages.'

'How long have you lived in East Ranling?'

'Just over three years, when Alan got the job at the manor.'

'Did you know anyone here?'

'No. My family's from Nottingham but my folks split up and I don't see anything of them now.' She hesitated. 'Alan doesn't like me going back.' She glanced again towards the window as if he might be there, watching her, then she looked down and dropped her voice. 'He doesn't like me going out and seeing people.'

'Making friends, you mean?'

Grace nodded but wouldn't look Hannah in the eye. Hannah poured them both a second cup of tea.

'I know you're supposed to be engaged, Grace,' she said softly, 'but you don't have to stay with him – not if you're not happy.'

'I'm fine.' Grace poured a tiny drop of milk into her tea and stirred it round several times unnecessarily. 'I mean, well… you know…' She started to mumble. 'I have thought about it, but it's not easy.'

'No, I can see that.' Hannah drank a mouthful of tea. 'Is he not always… kind to you?'

Grace shook her head. She put the spoon down then suddenly looked up.

'He forged his references to get this job, you know. He was accused of stealing from his last employer but it wasn't proved. Not enough evidence or something. They just sacked him – didn't want to call in the police and get the bad publicity. I didn't know to start with. I found out later.' She hesitated, eyes apologetic and pleading. 'I didn't know, you see, what he was like. It took a while for me to see. He's… rough sometimes, difficult to please, but he can be very persuasive when he wants.'

Hannah nodded. His kind always were, she thought.

That's how they manipulate people, especially women. She'd known a man like that once.

'Grace, you know the weekend when the curator, Carrie Judd, disappeared. Wasn't Alan supposed to be with you on that Friday? He was at the dart's club and then home with you, is that right?'

Grace hesitated again, flicking a glance round then eyeing Hannah up warily. Eventually she leaned forward.

'No. He told me I had to say he'd been there. He didn't come home till the next morning. He doesn't always. I think maybe it's another woman.' She paused. 'Honestly, I don't care,' she added fiercely, lifting her chin. 'I'm glad when he's not there. I suppose that's wrong of me.'

'Of course it's not. In your shoes, I'd be thrilled if he wasn't there. He has no right to say who you can and can't see. He doesn't own you. And for God's sake don't feel guilty about how you feel. He's the one at fault, not you.'

They finished the last of the tea and got up to go. Standing on the pavement outside, ready to part, Grace put her hand on Hannah's arm.

'Don't tell anyone I had lunch with you, will you, please? Promise? He'll be cross if he finds out. And don't pass on what I said. He'll know it came from me.'

'Of course not. Look Grace, you really should leave him.'

'He won't let me.'

'Go when he isn't there. Have you got any money?'

'A little. I've been saving up without telling him.'

'Good. Then don't stay. There are lots of jobs in conservation and wildlife management all over the country and you've got experience. Plus you're passionate about your work and good at communicating it. Employers will appreciate that. Go far away. He'll soon forget about you and look for someone else to torture. Think about it.' She pulled the pen and pad she'd bought at the reserve out of her handbag and wrote on one of the sheets, pulling it off. 'And if you need any help, here's my address and phone number in Oxford. We won't be here too much longer but you can call me. If I'm not there I can still pick up my messages. If you need to, you could stay with me for a bit till you find something. Truly. Don't feel alone.'

They parted and neither of them noticed the man watching them from the doorway of a shop further up the street.

*

It was just after four in the afternoon and Hannah was sitting reading in the snug when Nathan walked in. The sound of the door opening made her look up.

'Hi.' He came closer and stood, looking down on her.

'Hi.' She frowned up at him but he didn't move or say anything. 'What?'

'I'm sorry.'

He paused as if he expected her to respond in some way.

'Uhuh,' she offered, and waited.

'I've been kind of... not myself,' he said eventually. 'I... well, you know. I just wanted to say that.'

'I see.'

He made as if to go then turned back. 'Do you fancy going for an Indian tonight? We could give our apologies here. I don't want to stay in.'

She regarded him meditatively.

'All right. Where?'

'I passed a place today – twenty minutes away by car. It opens at six and looked quite big. If we go early I doubt we'll need to book.'

'Fine.'

'I'll drive. Let's leave about six thirty, shall we?'

She heard him climb the stairs up to his room and went back to her book.

*

It was just before seven when they got to the restaurant and getting a table wasn't a problem. The building had once been a sprawling roadside café but had been refurbished and now boasted a warm, sophisticated décor against a soundtrack of soft music. They studied the menu while working their way through a stack of poppadoms, then Nathan ordered a chicken jalfrezi and a bottle of Indian beer while Hannah chose a chicken biryani and a glass of white wine.

Nathan wasn't forthcoming. When the food arrived he said he'd had some issues to clear out of his head over the weekend and apologised again for his abruptness the previous morning. He said he'd spent the Saturday touring round and had had a long lunch at a riverside café; details were non-existent.

'And today?' she asked.

'Much the same really. Keeping my bad mood to myself. You should be grateful.'

'I am.'

She told him about her trip to the coast the day before, that she'd ended up in Cromer and eaten ice-cream on the beach, that she had dined alone with Mortimer the previous night.

'Really? Did he say anything?'

'Very little. I don't think he could wait to get away.' She finished the biriani and folded up her napkin. 'I did have an interesting lunch today though. Very interesting in fact. But if I tell you, you've got to promise to keep it to yourself. I said I wouldn't tell anyone.'

'I'm not anyone.'

She raised her eyebrows and waited.

'OK, yes, I promise,' he said impatiently. 'What's the big secret?'

'I met up with Grace.'

'Grace? Alan's Grace?'

'In a manner of speaking.'

She explained how they'd met that morning and the turn of the conversation over lunch.

'So it turns out Alan doesn't have an alibi for the Friday night Carrie went missing. But the problem is we can't do anything about it because if I tell the police what she said, he'd know and he'd take it out on her.' She hesitated. 'Or she'd deny she ever said it because she's scared witless. I keep thinking about it, trying to find a way round it. It's progress of a kind but, in itself, it doesn't prove anything. And I'm worried about Grace too. She's desperate.'

'She needs to get out of there.'

'That's what I told her.'

They didn't bother with dessert and were back in the car before nine. The drive home passed in silence. Nathan parked the car in the manor car park and turned off the engine.

'What is it you're not telling me, Nathan?' Hannah's voice sounded loud in the sudden silence.

'What on earth do you mean?'

'Oh please, don't stonewall me. I thought we'd got beyond this. It stands out a mile that there's something going on but you keep avoiding me and making excuses.' She waited but still he said nothing and in the end she flung the car door open angrily, stretching a leg out. Then she felt his hand gripping her arm and stopped.

'Hannah, please. Listen, I'm sorry. Yes, OK, you're right. Don't storm off. I'll try and explain.'

She retracted her leg, closed the car door and turned to look at him. He released her arm and sighed.

'I've been confused,' he said.

'OK. I get that. So tell me about it. Maybe I can help.' It became obvious suddenly and she realised she'd been stupid not to have understood before. 'It's something to do with Sam, isn't it?'

'Yes.' He ran his hand through his hair. 'I went to Pollersby again yesterday. That phone call in the week wasn't from my mother; it was from a woman I gave my number to in the village last time. She said she'd let me know if the guy in the photo came back. Well he did. I didn't intend to go but then I kind of had to. I didn't want to tell anyone; I needed to be sure and that's why I lied.' He paused, flicked her a glance then looked down, staring at his hands. 'I really didn't think it would be him but I had to go.'

'And it was him?' she prompted.

'Yes. I still can't quite believe it. It's as if I dreamed it. After all this time…'

'But he was all right?'

'Yes. Kind of.'

'Well, that's good isn't it? Though I suppose it was really emotional. In fact I can't begin to imagine how it would feel. Wonderful and yet kind of hurtful too. If he's all right I guess it could be really hurtful – that he never told you, I mean.'

Nathan turned to look at her. 'Yes, that's exactly how it was. So hurtful I felt winded, like I'd been punched. If he'd had some terrible accident, had had amnesia or something or… I don't know, anything, I'd have understood but it was nothing like that. He was alive and well and just doing his own thing.'

'Did he explain what had happened?'

'Yes. A little. He lives on a boat now. That's where I found him, moored up. He looked different. Well, it's been twelve years so he would. He was always a tall, wiry kid but now he's skinny. Gaunt really.' He snorted. 'He's grown a

206

beard and his hair's receding. My kid brother's going bald and I can't...'

He stopped suddenly and swallowed, lifting a hand to cover his mouth.

'He told me he ran away because he owed some money. Not just some money, a lot of money. He'd got into gambling. We didn't know. He said it got out of hand pretty quickly and suddenly he owed all this money and to some heavy guys, and they weren't the sort who took kindly to people who didn't pay their debts. His salary as a new teacher simply didn't come near to paying off what he owed and he was desperate that these people didn't track his family down; he particularly didn't want them visiting mum. So he left.'

'He must have been scared out of his mind to do that.'

'Yes, I suppose so. Anyway, he keeps moving around now, doesn't stay anywhere for long, just in case. It's a warren of waterways round here so there are lots of places to moor up. He does odd jobs as and where he can.' A weak smile. 'I told you he was a man of many talents. He said there's work out there if you're prepared to do it. People always want something done, hedges cut, rubbish cleared, walls and windows painted. But when you think of all the things he could have done...'

Nathan stopped talking and stared out of the windscreen at the slowly dimming light. Another car drove in and parked further along. They both turned their heads and watched Sidony get out. She either didn't see them or chose not to look and took the path to the back of the house and walked out of sight.

'Are you going to see him again?' ventured Hannah.

'He said he'd be around for a few days then he'd be off but back in a week or two maybe. I gave him the number here to phone.' He frowned again. 'I'm not sure he will though.'

'No?' She hesitated. 'Did you manage to make up?'

'I don't know.' He tapped an agitated finger against the steering wheel. 'I'm angry, Hannah. And I'm confused. God, I'm confused. I love Sam. He's my brother and I've always loved him. And of course we bickered and fought as kids but he was my pal, a part of me almost.' Nathan let out a long, slow breath. 'But finding him like this... I don't know, I can't get my head round it. I still feel...' He hesitated. '...betrayed. Perhaps that's the wrong word but I can't get past the hurt. Why didn't he come to me for help? Years of drifting around, running away, wasting himself. How could he do that and not think to contact us at all? Not even a word to tell us he was all right. And the way mum's been fretting – it's often made her ill.'

He put a hand to his forehead and rubbed at the skin, up and down, up and down. 'I know we'd drifted apart those last couple of years before he left. We'd taken different careers, lived in different places. Perhaps I should have done more to stay in touch with him.'

'You shouldn't blame yourself.' She put her hand on his free one. 'You didn't do anything wrong. You were always there for him if he needed you; he knew that. You're not responsible for his choices.'

He nodded, pursing up his lips, and looked down at her hand. She quickly withdrew it and they sat in silence for several minutes.

'We should go in,' Hannah said eventually.

They let themselves in the back door, passed the workroom and went through the door under the stairs to the private hallway. There was a light on and the faint sound of the television came from the sitting room. Sidony perhaps.

Hannah paused by the kitchen door. 'I'm going to make myself a cup of tea. 'Do you want anything?'

'No, I think I'll go up.' Still he didn't move. 'Thanks Hannah. I mean, you know, for listening.' He turned away suddenly, walking briskly up the stairs to his room.

Hannah took her tea upstairs, the conversation still running through her head. Half an hour later, sitting propped up in bed, she picked up Carrie's notebook and began to flick through the pages. Finding out that Alan had blatantly lied about the Friday night was indicative maybe but she needed something more concrete to go on. There had to be something in among all the notes in this book, some kind of clue.

It wasn't an easy search. Carrie's writing was spidery and erratic. In among her regular writing she sometimes added notes in a margin or crammed at the top or bottom, afterthoughts perhaps on pages apparently chosen at random, wherever she could find a space. Eventually Hannah came to the entry Nathan had pointed out: two question marks then *BAON sees a chart is ruined*. Or was Nathan right and it was a D not an O? She looked at other examples of Carrie's capital Ds and Os. No, she was convinced it was an O. But did it have any significance? She couldn't see how it related to anyone at the manor, let alone Alan. It was just odd.

She fell asleep a few minutes later with the light on, and the notebook fell out of her hand and closed.

Chapter 15

Nathan woke early on the Monday morning feeling hot, sticky and edgy. He had no idea what the time was. Without a window in his room it was disorientating. He stuck out an arm, fumbling on his bedside table for the travel alarm clock which went everywhere with him, and peered at its luminous dial. Ten past five. He collapsed back into the pillow. He'd been dreaming about something but couldn't now remember what it was, though it still seemed to linger somewhere deep in the recesses of his mind. It was something uncomfortable, something he didn't like. So why bother to try to remember it? Yet it felt important somehow; he needed to get a hold on it. After a few minutes he gave up. He couldn't.

He thought about the evening with Hannah instead, of how he'd blurted out the whole story of his meeting with Sam and had become emotional. How embarrassing was that? Though she had been surprisingly understanding. God, how awkward. Hannah of all people. And yet it had been a help to talk about it. He rolled over, trying to clear his head, and succeeded in dozing a little until it was time to get up.

It was a relief to get back to work. The preceding week he'd been working on the drawing by Tiepolo, a pen and brown wash image of an old man, described in the collection's listing as an apostle. Peter perhaps. The ink used was probably ox gall which, being acidic, had eaten into the paper over time and accounted for the holes he'd needed to fill. Using rag paper of the same colour and tone, chosen from the supply in his trunk, he'd torn it into strips and soaked it, then begged the use of Netta's blender to process it till it was smooth and could be meticulously pressed into the tiny gaps. She'd been surprised at the request but hadn't objected and the paper had been left to dry and set over the weekend.

Now, back at his work table, he examined his handiwork and was pleased. There might be other places in time which would wear through – the paper did look fragile – but that wasn't his problem now. He needed to take a few photographs and record the job then cut a fresh mount and backing board to protect it.

He glanced across at Hannah. After some discussion with Mortimer the previous Thursday, she was carefully removing paint from the old heavy-handed restoration on the Rubens sketch, an image of the Roman gods Venus and Mars. Someone in the past had decided to prudishly drape flowing garments over Venus to cover her nakedness – a nineteenth century restorer probably. Nathan could see her head moving now to the sound of whatever music she had playing in her ears that day.

He smiled to himself then abruptly turned away, got out his camera and started lining up the shots.

It wasn't until lunchtime when the two of them were sitting eating sandwiches in the snug that Hannah said something which finally broke the troubling dream for him.

'I'd dropped the brush on the floor and hadn't noticed.' She laughed. 'I looked everywhere for it in my trunk and there it was all the time, under the table.'

'What was that?' he demanded.

'I said I'd…'

'Yes, yes, I know. I heard.'

He stared at the fireplace and became aware of Hannah doing the same thing, trying to figure out what he was looking at.

'Are you all right?' she said.

'I need to get back into the storeroom. Today. This afternoon in fact.'

'Why?'

'I just want to look again.'

'There are too many people about.'

'It's Monday. The house isn't open. Even Rose isn't around today. It'll be fine.'

Hannah waved a sandwich at him. 'Well don't expect me to come up with some clever cover story for you. I'm all out of them right now.'

'It'll be fine,' he repeated. 'I'll explain later.'

'God, you're infuriating.'

He wandered to the office just after two and briefly made a pretence of studying the calendar on the wall. But the room was empty and he could hear no-one nearby. He opened the box in the desk drawer, extracted the key to the storeroom, and was out and back in the rear vestibule barely three or four minutes later. Letting himself in, he silently closed the door behind him and turned the key in the lock.

With his back to the door, he stood to let his thoughts settle. He'd brought his hand-held torch rather than risk the main light showing under the door into the darkness of the vestibule and he panned it round the room. Nothing much seemed to have changed and he walked across to the bookshelves. The inventory book was in the same place, as was Carrie's new folder.

He picked the book up, flicking slowly through the pages. His dream had sparked an idea in his head and he desperately wanted to prove it wrong. He came across the entry for the study of a young man by Carracci, found it again in the drawer of the plan chest and put it out on top. With the aid of his torch, he slowly studied its lines and the way the shading had been applied. He tried to look at it dispassionately, without prejudice. It had been done in red chalk on buff paper.

He left it out, checked through the inventory book again and found the entry for *Portrait, Unknown* by Michelangelo. *A drawing of a man's head in red chalk and highlights.* His heart felt leaden inside him. An image of his brother's boat came to mind and in particular the cosy kitchen-cum-dining area they'd sat in on the Saturday afternoon, drinking coffee and eating cheap beefburgers in toasted buns while they tried to patch up the tattered fabric of their relationship. Under the table, Nathan had seen a piece of red chalk on the floor, just a fragment, maybe a centimetre and a half long.

He hadn't thought about it at the time, had barely even noticed it, his thoughts too jumbled and his emotions too raw. But the image had stayed with him, buried deep within his brain and that's what he had been dreaming about. Red chalk. Why would Sam have red chalk? Marking something up on the boat before cutting it perhaps, or marking something that needed attention? He was clutching at straws. There could surely be only one use for red chalk of that particular muted hue. In any case there was something about the lines of that Carracci drawing that looked familiar…

He threw his head back and stared up at the ceiling, seeing nothing, trying to be objective and think it through. Sam hadn't been completely honest with him; he'd suspected it at the time but he was certain now. Maybe the whole story had been a fabrication. When Hannah had asked what Sam was like, Nathan had been quick to say what a multi-talented lad he'd been, able to turn his hand to all sorts and to do them well. He hadn't mentioned that Sam was an inventive child, quick to

213

come up with clever excuses when he was in a hole.

Nor had he said – he hadn't thought of it at the time – how good an artist Sam had been as a kid. The boy had never taken it seriously of course but when he was bored at school he used to draw little portraits of his teachers in the margins of his notebooks. And he could copy anything. Other interests had taken him over; he'd preferred his music to art and Nathan had thought no more about it. But now… Could he really be in league with someone from the manor? Wasn't that absurdly far-fetched? Of course it was; it was just a coincidence – it had to be. This was his brother he was thinking about. There was a big leap from a piece of red chalk and childish tall stories to serious forgery and fraud. And if he thought Sam was involved in the forgery then it followed that maybe he was involved in Carrie's death. Something hard clutched and twisted at Nathan's stomach making him feel sick. Surely not. Not his kid brother.

He took a couple of deep breaths trying to get his emotions under control. This wasn't the time for snap judgments but he did need to see Sam again, and soon. As soon as possible. Maybe tonight.

He replaced the Carracci and the inventory and stood behind the door, listening. He slipped out, locked the door and returned to the office. It was still empty and he replaced the key in the box.

Hannah looked round as he entered the workroom and pulled an earpiece out.

'So?' she said expectantly. 'Did you find whatever it was you wanted?'

'I just wanted to look at the Carracci again. I needed to check but I'm still sure it's a fake.'

It was true as far as it went. He sat down without offering anything more and pretended to focus on his work.

214

But he was aware of Hannah looking his way, her gaze drilling into him. She turned away but her silence said it all. She knew he was hiding something.

*

It was twenty past five when Nathan got in the car and set off for Pollersby. He'd told Hannah where he was going but not why, trying to imply – without explicitly saying so – that it was an attempt to build bridges with his brother. He hoped he was wrong about Sam; no, he was sure he was wrong – he had to be – but he wouldn't say anything to Hannah until he knew for sure. He'd spent all afternoon arguing with himself and struggling to concentrate on his work. His suspicions were too preposterous, he'd decided, but not so preposterous that he could dismiss them without talking to Sam first.

The traffic was busy and it was half past six when he parked the car and walked the short distance past the pub to the tow path. At a glance, he was pretty certain that the moorings were all taken which was a relief: Sam was still there. But when he reached the end of the path, the last boat was not the *Sally Ann*. He'd never seen it before. He walked slowly back, checking each vessel in turn but there was no sign of his brother's boat.

He swore violently, making a couple of heads turn on the nearest cruiser. Sam had lied: he'd had no intention of sticking around for a few days and now Nathan had missed him.

And he had no idea when or if he would see his brother again.

*

Hannah sat down to dinner with Sidony, Rose and Mortimer that night. Nathan didn't turn up and she found herself lying

215

for him again. He'd gone to see a friend who'd been staying nearby and was leaving tomorrow, she said. It was a last-minute thing. She apologised to both Mortimer and Netta while inwardly cursing Nathan for putting her in this position. Mortimer seemed completely unconcerned and Rose just looked sulky – she'd hoped to have a word with him, she claimed, but refused to say what about – while Sidony watched Hannah now and then as if guessing some back story to his absence. Hannah tried to make bright conversation to cover for it but suspected she was only making her discomfort, and the lie, more obvious.

After dinner, she went to the snug, flicked through the available television channels then gave up on finding anything to watch and settled to read, listening for the sound of Nathan returning while refusing to admit it to herself.

She gave up in the end, made herself a drink and went up to bed. Maybe Nathan had simply decided to stay over on Sam's boat overnight, but it was obvious from his strange behaviour that afternoon that something was going on, something that was causing him real concern. Had he really gone to Pollersby or was it all a lie?

Unable to settle, she abandoned the novel she was reading and picked up Carrie's notebook again.

*

The next morning Hannah found Nathan in the dining room alone, still eating his breakfast at nine-fifteen. He'd overslept.

'You look awful,' she said.

He put the last spoonful of cereal in his mouth and dropped the spoon in the dish.

'Thanks. In future, when I want my morale boosting, I'll remember to go elsewhere.'

She pushed the door to behind her and sat down in the

216

chair opposite him.

'So, tell me: what happened last night?'

He hesitated for the blink of an eye. 'Nothing. He wasn't there.'

'He wasn't there? So why were you so late? It can't have been much before midnight when I heard you come back.'

'Was it? I hung around a while, in case he turned up.' He shrugged. 'He didn't.'

Her eyes narrowed. 'And that's it?'

'Yes. Why? What are you getting at?'

'That you're still hiding something? That there's something I ought to know?'

He stared back at her, unblinking. 'There's nothing you need to know.'

'Fine. Glad we've got that straight.'

She leaned back in the chair, doggedly watching him. Now he was trying to ignore her and spreading marmalade on a piece of toast.

'You haven't asked me what I was doing last night,' she said.

He slowly raised his gaze to her face. 'No. But you look pleased with yourself so I guess I'm going to hear anyway. What were you doing?'

She sat forwards again.

'I was unravelling that cryptic phrase you found in Carrie's notebook. It's an anagram.'

Nathan grimaced. 'What's an anagram?'

'An anagram is when the letters from a word or phrase can…'

'I know what an anagram *is*,' he said impatiently. 'I meant what phrase in Carrie's notebook is an anagram?'

'Oh. *Sees a chart is ruined*. It's got nothing to do with charts, ruined or otherwise. The words *is ruined* mean that *sees a chart* is an anagram. I should have seen it before. It's a classic cryptic crossword device. Especially since Nigel said Carrie loved crosswords.'

'Did she?' Now Hannah had his attention. 'OK, so what does it mean?'

'Has a secret.'

'It means "has a secret"? Who has a secret?'

'I don't know. *BAON*, whoever that is. But it shows that we're on the right track. It's definitely a clue.'

'But we're no further on unless we can work out who *BAON* is.'

'Good grief, some people are never satisfied. I thought you'd be pleased I'd cracked it. OK, so only part of it. But I'll work out the rest.'

'Shh. Keep your voice down.'

She nodded, cross with herself. Her voice had risen in her enthusiasm.

'They aren't the initials of anyone here but Carrie didn't know many people outside her work so perhaps it's a nickname.'

'With four initials? It'd have to be a hell of a long nickname.'

'OK, well, yes smarty pants. Whatever it is, I'll figure it out. I thought I had it on the tip of my tongue last night but it wouldn't come. Anyway, I may find more clues yet.'

Nathan grunted and drank some black coffee.

'What is it?' she demanded.

'Nothing. It's just, well, don't get me wrong but not everything is a clue.'

'I know.'

Hannah had planned to tell him about another phrase she'd found, crammed into a margin on another page in the notebook – *mixed up with the ballet man* – but there was no point, not the mood he was in at the moment. Maybe when she'd worked out its significance.

'Did you hear that?' she said sharply.

'No, what?'

'I thought…'

She turned and looked towards the door, head cocked, listening. A moment later she was up and opening it, glancing each way along the passage. She could hear Rose saying something to someone through the open office door a few yards away and there was a noise coming from the kitchen at the other end. She was about to turn away when Sidony emerged through the sitting room door opposite. Her expression suggested surprise at seeing Hannah there and she held up a pair of glasses, looking sheepish.

'I keep forgetting where I've left my reading glasses,' she said. 'The penalty of getting old, Hannah.'

She walked away up to the office. She wore flat, soft-soled shoes. Silent. 'Easier on your feet when you're standing on them all day,' she'd once told Hannah.

*

Rose turned up at the workroom that afternoon, knocked once, then walked straight in, looked from Nathan to Hannah, then back again and sidled up to Nathan's table. Her attention caught, Hannah slipped both earpieces out and unashamedly turned to listen.

'*Ciao*,' Rose said silkily. 'I've come to ask a favour. It's about Saturday.'

Nathan regarded her suspiciously. 'What about Saturday? What kind of favour?'

'It's the annual Raft Race in East Ranling. You've seen the posters, haven't you? They're everywhere. Oh come on, Nathan, you must have.'

'I've seen them,' volunteered Hannah.

Rose cast her a venomous glance, then ignored her.

'Only my friend, James – you know, you met him that time on the quay with Debbie – he's gone and broken his leg, and he can't compete now so they're a man down. We need someone with strong muscles to help man the raft. It has to be a team of four.' She smiled pleadingly. 'You will help won't you?'

Nathan offered Rose a polite smile but shook his head.

'I'm sorry, no. I'm not…'

'Oh but you must. Please Nathan. It's in aid of a load of local charities. They rely on the money. And it's great fun too. You'll love it. All the competitors build their own rafts and they have to dress up. Each raft has a theme. Of course, James's raft is already built so you don't have to worry about that.'

'And what theme has James's raft chosen?' Nathan asked warily.

'The ugly sisters – you know, like in the pantomime Cinderella.' She laughed. 'They've hired these oversized dresses with big puff sleeves. And wigs. And beauty spots are essential. But you don't need to worry about the costume either. You'll fit into James's. He's fatter than you so it'll be fine.' Nathan didn't respond so she pouted at him. 'Please. It's all for good causes and our raft has already been sponsored. And everyone'll be there. Even Uncle Mortimer usually goes.'

'How did James break his leg?' asked Hannah.

Rose reluctantly looked across again. 'He had a fall from the raft,' she replied airily. 'They were practising and got too close to the quay and he slipped then got kind of caught up in something.'

'Great,' said Nathan, and caught Hannah's eye.

Rose glanced between them.

220

'It was just an accident,' she said defensively. 'Please, Nathan. They need you.'

In the end he gave in and Rose told him she'd be eternally grateful. She looked as if she was about to hug him, then glanced at Hannah and appeared to think better of it.

'Sounds like you'd better stay on the raft,' Hannah remarked after she'd gone. 'It's lucky you like boats.'

'Not that kind of boat. And don't even think about laughing.'

'Me? Would I?' She put her tongue firmly in her cheek, rammed the earpieces back in and returned to picking paint off the Rubens.

Returning to her room at the end of the afternoon, Hannah felt sticky and grubby and she grabbed her wrap and toiletry bag and headed for the bathroom to take a shower. Twenty minutes later, back in her room and in search of a fresh tee-shirt to wear, she opened the top drawer of the chest of drawers and her mouth fell open. All her clothes had been pushed to one side, crumpled up, and the same had been done in the next drawer down. And the bottom one too. Someone had searched through all her things.

Feeling a rising sense of panic, she went to the wardrobe. Stowed at the bottom on one side was her travel bag. It had been expensive, a considered extravagance since she moved around so much, but it had a clever arrangement of zipped pockets to separate out her belongings and protect them. It also had what the shop assistant had described as a secret compartment, hidden at the bottom of another long, zipped pocket. The bag had been moved too but when she delved into the secret compartment she felt a wash of relief to find Carrie's notebook still there.

She clutched it protectively. She'd thought she'd been fussing to bother hiding it but her instincts had been proved

221

right. The stairs opened out onto the landing a stone's throw from her door and the door didn't lock. It meant anyone could have been in her room. Absolutely anyone. They must have been looking for the notebook so it was progress of a kind. She'd made someone scared.

She was a little scared herself.

Chapter 16

Nathan arrived in East Ranling for the raft race just before eleven on the Saturday morning. The village was already crawling with people. A practice run with his fellow competitors the previous evening had left him sore and bruised but it had been surprisingly good fun, as well as an opportunity to burn off some deep-seated anger and frustration and occupy his mind with something nonsensical for a while.

Their raft had been built from layers of wooden pallets. A chunky wooden pole served as the mast from which hung a hand-painted flag proudly proclaiming them to be The Ugly Sisters.

It wasn't technically James's raft, it was Rob's. Rob was their skipper and a painter and decorator by trade, and he'd built the craft himself. It was rigid and it floated – two essentials as far as Nathan was concerned – and incorporated a wooden rim, designed to stop them falling off. Since that clearly didn't work, Rob had since attached two ropes to the mast as well as screwing a few hand grips to it, all in an attempt to keep all members of the crew on board.

It was the first time he'd built his own raft, he confessed, and it was a bit experimental, but on their last practice run they had managed to negotiate the whole course with all four men still there – a requirement for any team to win. Of course, without the other rafts getting in the way and the diversionary tactics of the other supporters, it would be harder in the actual race, Rob admitted.

'What do you mean by "diversionary tactics"?' Nathan enquired suspiciously.

Rob gave a light shrug. 'You know, people throwing wet sponges or flour bombs, things like that. Nothing that'll hurt, just things that'll put you off your game.'

The race course ran with the flow of the river from the road bridge near the inn to the footbridge by the boatyard, a distance of some five hundred metres. The distance wasn't the issue; the variable current as the river turned in a long arc was and the paddles they were using to propel themselves forward offered little control. The day was dry and bright but breezy and the wind added to the choppiness and unpredictability of the water.

Nathan changed into his costume at the rowing club along with the other competitors. He had a daffodil yellow dress and a powdered wig with little ribbons fastened in it – he didn't want to know where the wig had come from – but wore swimming trunks underneath. Rose did all their make-up and gave them each a beauty spot. She pressed Nathan's onto his cheek herself, just to the right of his mouth.

'Good luck,' she said, and gave him a quick kiss on the cheek. 'Go kill 'em.' She hesitated. 'Don't you think you'd be safer without the glasses?'

'I can't see without them.'

'Oh.'

Once dressed, Rob – attired in pink and a fetching wig of dark curls – gave them a team talk and last-minute instructions, repeating much that he had said the night before only with more urgency.

'Watch out for The Invincible Vikings,' he warned. 'They're the same team as last year and they played dirty then, no holds barred, trying to capsize the other rafts and stealing paddles. OK, I'll see you back here at one forty-five.'

Nathan wandered down into the village, trying to ignore the fact that he was wearing a huge yellow dress and a pair of trainers on his feet. The place had a party atmosphere with bunting stretched in loops between the buildings and along the riverside, and music blaring out from a loudspeaker system – sixties and seventies hits mostly.

A couple of mobile burger vans had parked up with people already queuing in front of them, but there were several stalls along the road too. They sold a wide choice of food between them: hot dogs, sandwiches thickly filled with roast meats, and pancakes, both sweet and savoury. One sold Indian curries with rice and poppadoms in take-away containers. The inn was running a stall too and Nathan saw Kyle – one of The Ugly Sisters – buying a beer and hoped his team-mates didn't down too many pints before the race or they'd probably fall off in the first ten metres.

Old-fashioned games booths stretched along the road too: skittles and hoopla and mophead throwing as well as card games and a tombola.

There were ten teams taking part in the race and the costumes gave the event a surreal atmosphere. Nathan saw a foursome of Elvis Presleys, a Humpty Dumpty and at least two King's horsemen, a few Santas, as well as Little Red Riding Hood and a couple of wolves. A female crew were attired as fairies wearing oversized tutus, wigs of blonde pigtails, wired to make them curl up at the side, and carrying wands. And he saw two of the notorious Vikings clad in hairy tunics and horned helmets and brandishing plastic axes.

'Very striking colour, I must say,' a cold voice said behind him.

Nathan turned. 'Alan. Hi. How kind of you to notice.'

225

'I'm afraid I couldn't miss you.' Alan produced a supercilious smile. 'All ready for the battle? You do realise it can get a bit heavy out there? Some of these guys don't take any prisoners.'

'So I hear, but all in a good cause. Not keen to get involved yourself then? Too rough?'

'Not my sort of thing. Hannah not here?'

'She'll turn up later.'

Alan moved away, easing his way through the throng. A few minutes later, Nathan saw him by the tombola, talking and smiling with Mortimer and the guy from the gallery. He was a smooth operator but after what Hannah had told him about Grace, he disliked the man more than ever.

Nathan bought himself a hot dog and ate it trying not to ruin his make-up. How did women put up with this stuff, he wondered? It made him think of Hannah – he wasn't sure why because she didn't wear much make-up – which made him think of what he wasn't telling her and the next minute he was dwelling on his brother again and the forged drawings.

It had been like this all week. On Monday night's abortive trip to Pollersby, walking back to his car a little before eleven, he'd bumped into Glenys's husband who'd been giving their dog a last walk. The man had immediately recognised him and asked if he'd come to see his friend again. Only John – he definitely calls himself John, Paul insisted – had been seen casting off and chugging up river on the Sunday. So he'd missed him again.

'Yes, John,' said Nathan. 'I confused the names. I saw him on Saturday, thanks to your wife's message. But I've got something I forgot to give him. Perhaps you could give me another ring when he comes back? I'm still at Ranling Manor. I'd be very grateful.' He'd hesitated. 'But I'd prefer it if you didn't mention it to him.'

Paul had agreed but looked both reluctant and puzzled. As well he might, Nathan thought, for what kind of friend has to be chased down in this way, swearing people to secrecy?

So now he was waiting on a phone call that would probably never come. Paul might think it too odd to fulfil his promise, or might warn Sam that he was being looked for, or Sam would simply not turn up again. Unless he had to of course. If he had a drawing to deliver perhaps, and Pollersby or somewhere nearby was the rendezvous. In fact maybe it would be better if he didn't see Sam again. At least that way he'd never know. There would be no moral dilemma, no issue of what to do about it.

Nathan looked round. He hadn't seen Hannah. Maybe she'd changed her mind.

'Wouldn't dream of missing it,' she'd said. 'But don't break anything. I don't want to have to explain it to Timothy.'

He wanted to tell her to stop looking for the fraudsters, at least until he knew where Sam stood. But then he'd have to explain why and he couldn't do that yet. Not that she'd probably stop anyway. He might have started her off on this quest but Hannah was like a terrier once she got going.

He glanced at his watch. It was one thirty-five. He'd better get back to the rowing club, leave his watch in the locker, and help the others get the raft launched.

*

It was one-twenty when Hannah finally made it into East Ranling. The traffic had been insane and the parking a challenge. She finally managed to squeeze her Mini into one of the last two spaces available behind The Boatman and hoped Brian and Alice wouldn't mind.

Walking down into the village was an assault on her senses: a bizarrely dressed crowd of people chattering and

227

laughing, bunting everywhere and a disconcerting mixture of competing food smells. She scanned the throng but couldn't see any sign of the daffodil-yellow dress Nathan had said he was wearing. A man was addressing the crowd over the public address system, exhorting them to spend money and to give generously in all the charity collecting boxes being carried through the crowd.

She worked her way along the food stalls and joined a queue for the freshly cut beef sandwiches. A few metres away Sidony was talking earnestly to someone dressed up as a wolf but, by the time Hannah had bought her sandwich, Sid had gone. She made for the quay but it was frantic with people jostling for position at the water's edge and she couldn't get near. Eventually she gave up. Standing slightly back of the crowd, Toby had his arm round a young woman and greeted Hannah as if they were long lost friends.

'I don't think you've met Amanda, have you?' He turned to the woman. 'But you've seen Hannah around, haven't you? One of our itinerant art restorers? Doing clever things to our art collection.'

Amanda offered a polite smile. 'Nice to meet you.' With the public address system in full voice it was hard to hear her. She leaned forward. 'It's a terrible crush, isn't it?'

'Yes, I'm not sure where to go to see the race.'

'I'd try the bridge at the end,' Toby bellowed. 'You'll never get a spot down here but the bridge would give you a good view of the finale. We've seen it all before.' He pulled Amanda closer. 'Thought we'd go and get a drink, didn't we?'

The bridge seemed like a good idea and the crowd did thin as Hannah left the centre and headed out but the numbers built up again at the course end. She found a place near the middle of the bridge's span and pushed in tight to the little parapet, eating her sandwich while she waited. With the long bend in the river, she wouldn't see anything until half way through but then she'd be perfectly placed. More people turned up and soon they were several rows deep, all elbowing for position.

At two o'clock a klaxon sounded and the race began amid a cacophony of frenzied shouting and the blaring of horns. On the bridge the crowd became restless, pushing and straining to see and a child leaned too far over the railing and was quickly hauled back by her mother. It was several minutes later when the first rafts became visible. Three had come round the bend in a line with two more close behind and, a minute later, still others a couple of lengths back. It was a fantastical sight – rafts made of wood, plastic bottles and even oil drums, some with decorative panels or carving, all with gaudy flags flying.

The Ugly Sisters and The Invincible Vikings were the second-tier rafts, and they were neck and neck and too close for comfort. The Vikings were trying to tip the Sisters' raft over and making a grab for their paddles. The shouting from the bridge hit a new level.

'Come on Ugly Sisters,' bellowed Hannah. 'Fight back. Give them a dose of their own medicine.'

They managed to disentangle themselves and as two of the leading rafts fell back, caught on a current, the Sisters and the Vikings edged forward, still only a metre apart. Hannah could see Nathan clearly, white with flour, hanging on to one of the ropes with one hand and desperately trying to paddle with the other as the raft bobbed and lurched. She leaned forward, shouting and waving, jostled on either side, her ears ringing from the noise.

And now three rafts were making for the finish line, all neck and neck.

'Come on Ugly Sisters,' Hannah screamed again.

The next thing she knew, she was over the parapet and falling, falling, falling…

The water hit her with a cold, hard slap. It engulfed her and blinded her and washed into her unguarded mouth as she dropped further and further down, feeling the air choke out of her lungs. Disorientated and confused, she forced herself to think, struggling to blink her eyes open. Somehow she managed to right herself and started kicking, clawing her way desperately back up to the surface, blinking against the water, trying to focus on the fractured light above her. Breaking the surface, she gulped at the air, then everything went dark again as the rafts closed in over her and something hit her hard on the head.

*

'I'm fine.'

Hannah was sitting in the St. John Ambulance. Nathan looked her over, trying to assess the damage. She had a dressing on her forehead and a bruise on her chin and she looked her usual truculent self except that she was extremely pale. She had been told to sit for a while.

'I could go now,' she said.

'You're fine when they say you're fine,' said Nathan. 'Stop complaining.'

It occurred to him that he was more traumatised than she was. It had been shocking enough to see a body drop into the water from the bridge but worse still to realise a couple of minutes later that it was Hannah. He was uncertain now about the succession of events after that. It had been so difficult to control the rafts in the moving water that it had been a scrabble between them to somehow haul her out. One of the wolves had immediately jumped into the water and Nathan had followed, his stupid dress billowing out and making movement difficult. Between them, they'd heaved her up onto the plastic bottle raft with Little Red Riding Hood and the remaining wolves.

Apparently someone had inadvertently hit her on the head with a paddle, stunning her for a minute, but she was quickly conscious again, moving and coughing then shivering. No lasting damage seemed to have been done, thank God.

The first-aiders finally let her go with advice and a list of things to look out for in case of delayed concussion. While she was being cared for, Nathan got into his dry clothes at the rowing club and no sooner was he back at the ambulance than Sidony turned up with some dry clothes for Hannah too. She'd seen it happen – 'Who didn't?' she'd said – and, as soon as Hannah had been safely pulled from the water and was clearly all right and moving, she'd driven back to the manor to pick some clothes up.

'They'll be too big for her,' she said, thrusting them at Nathan, 'but better than wet ones.'

He thanked her and she waved the thanks away and left, never one to waste words.

Nathan drove them back to the manor.

'Who won?' Hannah said after they'd been driving for a couple of minutes.

'Little Red Riding Hood. It was decided that they were in front before the confusion of you landing in front of us and the lack of one of the wolves was excused because he'd nobly jumped in to help.'

Hannah looked out of the side window and said nothing. Her unnatural quietness bothered him. Back at the house he insisted on installing her in the snug and making her a hot cup of tea, watching over her while she drank it, pulling the folded rug from the back of the sofa and draping it over her knees.

'Really, Nathan,' she said impatiently. 'This is unnecessary.'

'You need to stay warm. Would you like something to eat? Soup perhaps? Netta's not here but I think I've seen some

231

tinned soup in one of the cupboards.'

'I don't want soup, thank you.'

'Or something else that's soft. Rice pudding? Or would you rather have a sandwich?'

Hannah looked at him in disbelief. 'Will you stop fussing over me? I'm fine. It was just a shock. I'm fine, really.'

'Good. Well, good. I'm glad you've drunk the tea anyway. They said you should have hot drinks.' He hesitated. 'Do you want another one?'

'No, for goodness' sake.' She gave an amused smile. 'Look Nathan, sit down. Chill.' The smile faded. 'We need to talk.'

He perched on the arm of the sofa and looked at her warily.

'What about?'

She glanced towards the closed door then fixed her disconcertingly direct eyes on him, speaking softly.

'Someone searched my room on Tuesday.'

'Why? And how do you know?'

'When I went up at the end of the afternoon, I could tell someone had been through the drawers, clothes disarranged, that kind of thing. They must have been looking for Carrie's notebook.' She grinned, looking triumphant. 'They didn't find it though. I'd hidden it.'

'But no-one knows about it.'

'Except that I heard someone outside the dining room door when I was talking about it on Tuesday morning, remember? And then I saw Sid. I told you.'

Nathan frowned at her. 'Are you sure someone searched your room? Why didn't you tell me before?'

'Oh come on, you've been so preoccupied lately, it's been like talking to a brick wall. Anyway, I kept trying to persuade myself I was wrong.'

'So you think it was Sid?'

She shrugged. 'Yes. No. I thought so but now I'm not so sure. Honestly it could have been any of them. Alan or Rose could have been lurking in the passage and nipped back into the office. Or even Mortimer. I didn't get up fast enough. And it was Toby today who suggested I watch the race from the bridge.' She hesitated. 'The thing is... well, it all happened so fast and what with all the people around, I wasn't certain. And I didn't want to say anything till we were alone anyway. But the more I think about it the more certain I am.'

'What? Certain about what?'

'That my fall wasn't an accident. Someone pushed me – right in the middle of my back. I've rattled someone's cage. They're scared the notebook might give us some clue to their identity and when they couldn't find it, they targeted me instead. A warning probably.'

Nathan was on his feet again, agitated, restless. 'They could have killed you.'

'I suppose, but the water's pretty deep there.'

'Except whoever it was waited till the rafts were there. You could have broken your neck.'

Nathan began walking up and down. He'd developed a foul taste in his mouth and his fists were clenched into two tight balls.

'Of course, it might not have been anyone from the house,' Hannah was saying, apparently oblivious to his simmering anger. 'Given that we know whoever it is must have an accomplice. At least one if they're part of a bigger operation.' She frowned up at him. 'Will you please sit down? You're giving me a headache.'

He stopped and stared down at her.

'It was Sam.' He ran a distraught hand through his hair. 'I mean, I don't know that for sure but that's what I think...

233

dread.' He collapsed down onto the sofa beside her, leaning forwards, putting his head in his hands.

'Sam?' exclaimed Hannah, then dropped her voice. 'Why the hell should you think that?'

He straightened up, painfully aware that he couldn't put this off any longer, and explained about the red chalk he'd seen on the floor in the boat and his suspicions.

'It might sound far-fetched to you but he was a good artist,' he finished by saying. 'As a kid he could copy anything. Except that back then it was for fun or for a challenge.' He shook his head, staring down at his hands which kept clenching and unclenching. 'And he was a bit wayward though I'd never have thought he could be criminal. But if he's doing this, maybe he was the one who pushed Carrie. And then...' He stopped short, reluctant to even say it.

'Me?' offered Hannah. 'Did you see him today in the village?'

He looked up at her. 'No.'

'Then you're jumping to conclusions. You don't know enough. I have another suspect: the ballet man. Carrie had scribbled it on another page of the notebook: *mixed up with the ballet man*. It feels significant. I've been wanting to tell you.'

He frowned at her. 'Who's the ballet man?'

'I don't know but if we can figure it out, it might help us work out who *BAON* is.'

'These are probably just red herrings, Hannah. Jottings. Nothing to do with our problems.' He stood up again, his restless energy and anger getting the better of him. 'I'm going to see Sam and have it out with him. If he's involved he's going to tell me.'

He left before Hannah could try to talk him out of it. This had gone far enough.

234

'They raised a lot of money,' said Rose. 'I mean, apart from the end there – which of course was scary,' she added diplomatically in Hannah's direction, 'it was a good race. I think The Ugly Sisters could have won really. Should have, definitely.'

Mortimer looked at Rose benevolently. She sounded defensive, as if, because of Hannah's fall, she'd be blamed if she said anything positive about the race. Certainly most of the conversation so far had been solicitous enquiries after Hannah's health, though she didn't appear to have suffered any ongoing effects from the fall which was surprising.

It was Saturday evening and, with the exception of Nathan, all the household were gathered round the dining table. Sidony had even insisted that Alan and Grace should be invited to join them too.

'It's a special day, Mortimer.'

Hannah had given Nathan's apologies however, saying he'd gone out but without offering any details. It seemed odd timing and, when pressed, she'd said she wasn't sure where he was. To Mortimer that seemed unlikely.

So now they had Alan sitting there, looking supercilious as usual. And Grace, a sweet girl, but too quiet. If all Nathan wanted was to be somewhere else Mortimer felt a flash of sympathy for him. Sitting round this dinner table could feel like a penance sometimes what with the strained conversations, repetitive subjects and barbed remarks. If it weren't for Sidony… He glanced towards her but her attention was fixed on Hannah.

'It was good,' Hannah was saying. 'I'm afraid I might have ruined their chances though. Maybe next year. James will be back and competing again then.'

'I thought Nathan did very well,' said Sidony, 'thrown in at the last minute like that.'

'Thrown in,' said Toby with a smirk. 'Poor choice of words in the circumstances, Sid. I daresay it felt a bit like that, didn't it, Hannah, with all those people pushing and shoving?'

Sidony gave him a withering look and Hannah managed a weak smile. Neither chose to respond.

'What did you think of the race, Grace?' said Rose.

Grace opened her mouth to speak but didn't get the chance.

'Grace was working,' stated Alan.

'That's a shame.' Sidony offered Grace a sympathetic smile.

'I think we should probably change the subject,' remarked Mortimer. 'I'm sure Hannah would prefer not to dwell on today's events.'

He noticed Rose look at him with an odd expression but she looked down as soon as he caught her eye. Toby unconsciously filled the brief, awkward silence by recounting some issue with his car. Coming back from Cambridge on the Thursday, he'd had to call out the RAC. They'd managed to get it going but there was something wrong with the timing and now it was in the garage though the mechanic hadn't yet worked out what the problem was.

Toby drove a classic old sports car, creamy white with pale blue leather upholstery. It was a foolish choice as far as Mortimer was concerned and Toby looked ridiculous in it, pretending to be twenty years younger, wearing a flat cap and a tweed jacket and swanning around like something from a forties' movie. What's more the car hadn't been properly maintained – which was probably how he'd managed to afford it in the first place – and it kept breaking down.

After the main dish was finished and cleared away, Netta

came in with a strawberry cheesecake for dessert and Sidony offered to serve. Mortimer readily agreed. He hated serving desserts – he invariably dropped something – and he didn't want any in any case. His stomach felt churned up at the moment; nothing he did seemed to be going to plan. The conversation died and by the time they were all served and had started eating again, all that could be heard was the scrape of cutlery on china.

Mortimer laid his napkin on the table and got to his feet.

'Excuse me,' he said. 'I've got some work needs attending to.'

He was aware of raised eyebrows and several pairs of eyes exchanging looks as he left the room. They'd probably talk about him as soon as he was gone. Let them. None of them understood the pressure he was under. But at least they were all occupied and safely out of earshot for a while. Sometimes you just had to do things, he tried to console himself. It wasn't as if he'd ever wanted to do any of this.

He closed the study door firmly before picking up the phone and dialling.

'Hello? Mortimer Gyllam-Spence speaking.' He tried to sound more confident than he felt. 'I was hoping you might reconsider. I've another proposition.'

Chapter 17

'Timothy asked me to ring.' Daphne's dependable voice spoke calmly in Hannah's ear. 'He said he hadn't heard from you in a while and he wants to have an idea how much longer you'll be.' She paused and Hannah could imagine her there back in Oxford, looking towards Timothy's office door, wondering if he were listening in. 'Says he's got work queueing up.'

'When hasn't he, Daphne?'

Hannah glanced across at Alan who was at his desk, pretending not to listen. It was the following Friday morning and Rose had come to the workroom to tell them that Daphne was on the office phone wanting to speak to one of them and Hannah had offered to take it. Rose had not returned, presumably because she was hanging around Nathan again.

'That's exactly it, dear,' Daphne was saying. 'You're always in demand.'

'You can tell him we're making good progress.' Hannah realised Alan was now watching her. She met his gaze, blank stare for blank stare, and after a long minute's stand-off he looked away. 'Nathan is working on the Bonnington watercolour. I'm well on the way to finishing the Rubens. We've both got one more work to do. A couple of issues, I think, but shouldn't be too long now. Impossible to say exactly.'

'Timothy said – and I quote – get Nathan to help with the

oils when he's done with the drawings.'

'I see.' Hannah wasn't keen on that idea; she didn't like splitting the work on a painting with someone else. She was a bit possessive like that.

'Oh come on, Hannah, Nathan's not that bad. Speaking of which, is he all right? He sounded a bit flat when we spoke last.'

'He's fine, thanks.'

'Good. And what about the accommodation? Is it comfortable there? Everything all right?'

Hannah didn't immediately reply because Mortimer had just walked in from the house passageway. A moment later, Sidony came in through the door from the public hall.

'Absolutely fine,' Hannah said with forced brightness. 'No problems.'

'Silly me, there's someone there with you, isn't there?' murmured Daphne.

'Yes, that's right.'

One of the collars of Mortimer's shirt was neatly visible, the other was tucked inside his cardigan. Hannah watched Sidony move in and pull the collar out, smoothing it down into position to match the other one. She smiled at him indulgently as she took her hands away and said something Hannah didn't hear.

'You haven't got into any trouble, have you?' Daphne was saying in her ear. 'You don't sound right. You will let us know if you have any problems?'

'Certainly will,' said Hannah, producing a smile and hoping it reflected in her voice.

Daphne, not sounding convinced, told her to take care and was gone and Hannah replaced the receiver on the rest.

'We've got another school party coming round next Tuesday,' Alan immediately told her. 'I thought perhaps you could give your talk again.' He glanced at Mortimer as if belatedly realising that his employer was there. 'If that's all right with you, sir?'

'Good idea,' said Mortimer, in that abstracted way he had. 'Good idea. Great reports from your first talk. Went down well, I gather.'

Hannah nodded with something resembling a smile but her heart sank. Another talk. That was just what she needed.

She made her way back to the workroom where Rose left almost as soon as Hannah entered. Hannah waited for a minute then returned to the door and opened it again. Rose had gone.

'Your paranoia's showing,' said Nathan.

'Can you blame me?'

He shook his head.

'What did she want? Or was it just your undying affection?'

'Something like that, probably.'

'Timothy's pressing for us to finish. I told Daphne that we both still had another work to do after these. I didn't offer a timescale.'

Nathan nodded thoughtfully but didn't respond and returned to the watercolour on his table. It had apparently been hung in the exhibition room in the past but had fallen at some point and the frame ruined. Some of the surface of the image had flaked too and Nathan was involved in the delicate task of stabilising it.

Ever since admitting his concerns about Sam, Nathan had been easier to talk to, as if a boil had been lanced and the pent-up pressure finally released. But his brother hadn't been in Pollersby when Nathan had turned up there the previous Saturday and, despite a couple of speculative trips since, he still hadn't made contact with him. Nathan was desperate to talk to him and Hannah guessed that the looming end of their

240

stay here in Norfolk was only adding to his stress.

She installed herself in front of the Rubens again. After having removed all the old restoration she was now touching the last tiny dots of paint into the damaged area over Venus. With any luck, she'd finish the retouching later that day and get a coat of varnish on it too. She picked up the earpieces of her stereo but, before putting them in, turned to Nathan again.

'Why don't we go for a boat trip tomorrow? You keep telling me what fun you had as kids in boats.'

'I didn't think you were keen. And after last Saturday I wouldn't blame you.'

She produced a lop-sided smile, eyebrows raised. 'I'll try and stay in the boat.'

'Always a good plan.' He eyed her up thoughtfully. 'OK, it could be fun, but can we maybe do it on Sunday? I've got plans for tomorrow.'

'Pollersby again?'

He nodded. 'Sam's going to be back there again sooner or later, I'm sure of it.'

'How long can you keep this up for?'

'As long as it takes.'

*

It was the last weekend of June and a fine, sunny one. Nathan arrived in Pollersby early. He had decided to stay all day if needs be, maybe all weekend. The small village had swelled in the last few weeks, the nearby caravan site full and the river a busy thoroughfare of yachts and cruisers. It meant he didn't now stand out as a stranger to the same extent but he was determined to keep a low profile just the same, avoiding the pub and the very public, honeypot areas around it. He didn't want one of the locals to see him and protectively warn his brother off.

Over the preceding days he had pored over an Ordnance Survey map, examining the public footpaths around the village, looking for places to loiter without attracting too much attention. There was one which looped around the north side of the village, ending near the far end of the moorage by the river. He had seen the little track beyond Sam's mooring without realising that it went anywhere. With a backpack containing food and drink rations slung over his shoulders he set off to explore.

It was a beautiful, calm morning. Still barely nine thirty, he had the path largely to himself. It set off winding between fields of barley and wheat then tracked alongside an area of marsh and wetland with shrubs and trees to either side. The air was filled with birdsong: whistles and chattering, clicks and falling cadences. He saw a sedge warbler singing from a high twig of a willow, then a heron, flapping silently overhead. A large swallowtail butterfly flitted past.

It brought back all the bittersweet memories of his childhood again, competing with Sam to recognise each call and identify the birds with the help of their pocket guides, ticking off the ones they actually saw. The memories only fuelled his anger and frustration. That they should have come to this: sneaking and subterfuge, lies and deceit.

The path turned inland, snaking, and he'd left the marsh behind and now walked between scrub of hawthorn, bramble and alder with glimpses beyond to a meadow on his left. And suddenly he was close to the river. Though still masked by trees and shrubs, he could hear the chugging sound of boat engines and the low babble of voices. The path narrowed and wound between overhanging branches and he ducked his head, moving cautiously, until it emerged at the end of the little quay. A quick survey showed him that Sam's boat wasn't there and, more than that, there was no spare mooring. It was what he had expected but he had noticed somewhere he could wait just before the path narrowed, a small patch of bare ground where someone long ago had placed a basic wooden bench up against the fence, now weather-greyed and carved with initials, with a smattering of cigarette ends littering the ground beneath it. He went back and settled in for the wait.

Sam would come. He didn't know how he knew; he just did.

*

Nathan was getting stiff and sore. What's more he was tired and bored. He'd read a little, got up, walked around, visited the public conveniences just off the other end of the quay and checked the boats repeatedly. A couple of them had left to be replaced soon after by two more but there was still no sign of Sam.

By five-thirty in the afternoon, Nathan had run out of food and was nearly out of patience, questioning his sanity for doing this: he had no good reason to think he'd see his brother here again at all, let alone today. But still he waited because he couldn't bear to go and leave the issue unresolved any longer. He had to stay, just in case.

Even so, he was on the point of leaving when his vigil finally paid off. It was after seven when he heard the shouts of a boat crew getting ready to cast off then a boat chugging away. A few minutes later, another engine, with a slow, elderly throb, moved in. Nathan felt a tingle down his spine. He waited a few minutes, listening to the sounds of mooring up, trying to gauge his moment, then hefted his backpack onto his shoulders and walked through to the quay.

The *Sally Ann* was back, tied up to the same mooring as when he'd first seen it, as far from the buzz of the village as it could be. There was no-one visible on deck but this time

243

Nathan didn't bother to call out. He grabbed the guard rail and climbed on board.

*

'I wasn't avoiding you.' Sam flicked a glance Nathan's way but wouldn't meet his eyes.

He was opening a couple of bottles of beer, prising the caps off with an easy, unconscious hand.

'I've been busy,' he added defensively.

He handed one bottle to Nathan and took a swig from the other then wiped the back of his hand over his mouth.

'Doing what exactly?'

Sam shrugged. 'This and that. Like I told you last time.'

'So you did.'

Nathan's cynical tone was clearly starting to rattle his brother because Sam flicked him another edgy glance, frowning now.

'Have a seat.' Sam waved a hand towards the benches either side of the table. He took another swig of beer, warily watching Nathan as he sat down, then lowered himself onto the bench opposite. 'Is this just a social call? Only you seem to have something on your mind.'

Nathan snorted a derisory laugh. 'Do I? How observant of you. I always knew you were smart, gifted even, though…' He paused and looked round the tired old boat in a slow, pointed manner. '…it doesn't seem to have got you very far.'

'I explained that.'

Nathan bent down to look at the floor under the table; it was clear. He hesitated then got to his feet and crossed in a few short steps to a tall cupboard on the other side of the cabin, pulling the doors open.

'Hey,' said Sam, jumping up and rushing over. 'What do you think you're doing?'

244

'I'm looking for evidence. Oh here, what's this?'

Nathan bent over and pulled out an A3 artist's portfolio.

'Leave it,' said Sam, putting an ineffectual hand on his brother's arm. 'Nathan, please.'

But Nathan ignored him, shrugging the hand off, and took it back to the table, laying it flat and unzipping the three sides till he could flip it open. The pocket on one side was filled with sheets of paper, some new, many which looked old. But were they old or had they been treated to look old? The pockets on the other side held drawings. Nathan fumbled through them while Sam continued to protest in a half-hearted, plaintive way. There were sketches, practice sheets from the look of them, in a variety of styles and media, chalk and crayon, pencil and charcoal. Nathan could recognise drawings or part drawings in the styles of Toulouse-Lautrec, Fragonard and Ingres among many others, as well as, pertinently, both Tiepolo and Rubens.

Nathen straightened up and fixed an accusing look on his brother.

'I think it's about time you explained, don't you?'

Sam hesitated for the blink of an eye. 'I like to sketch. It's a hobby.'

'You used to be a better liar.'

'But it's true. It's a hobby. Why are you even doing this? What's got into you?'

Nathan ignored him.

'Well it's not in here so…' He scanned the room, looking back at the cupboard whose doors still lay open. He went back to it.

'It must be in here.' He bent over to look.

'What must?'

Nathan started poking about. 'In something protective, I hope, to stop the chalk from smudging and keep it safe.'

245

'What on earth are you talking about?' Sam's attempt at indignation failed.

Nathan straightened up and fixed a beady gaze on his brother. 'The Michelangelo of course. The one you're going to copy.'

He saw Sam visibly blanche and knew without a shadow of a doubt that he was right. It was a sickening feeling.

'Sit down, Nathan. Please? Can't we talk?'

'Only if you're going to tell me the truth.'

Sam's head swayed side-to-side desperately like wild animals sometimes do, trapped in cages. 'OK, OK. Yes.'

They sat as before, facing each other. Nathan waited while his brother fidgeted, looking at his hands, then towards the closed door, then back at his hands.

'How much do you know?' he said eventually.

'Oh no. You tell me. Tell me what you're doing and who you're doing it for.'

Sam gave a derisive laugh. 'Of course, just like that. You think it's all so simple, don't you? You come waltzing in here, holier than thou, pretending like everything's black and white. Have you ever been in a hole in your entire life, Nathan? You've never been stuck, desperate, not knowing which way to turn. Don't lecture me.'

'You've had choices, Sam, the same as everyone. You've chosen badly. You always refused to stick at anything. You've had the kind of opportunities some people can only dream about so don't give me the self-pity routine because I won't wear it. You could have come to me when you needed help; you chose not to.' Nathan thumped a fist down on the table making the forgotten beer bottles jump. 'Don't you dare suggest that any of that is my fault.'

Sam frowned, lips pursed and looked away. He ran a hand through his thinning hair and sighed, long and slow.

'You're right.' He massaged the back of his neck and appeared to be studying the table. Nathan wondered cynically what story he was cooking up now, what fairy tale he thought he might be able to sell.

'There's a group of people,' Sam said eventually. 'Let's call them a syndicate. They... they're interested in acquiring certain art works, then they act as dealers, so to speak, passing the works on to clients.'

'They sell them.'

Sam nodded. 'They... *persuade* people who have some artistic skill to help them achieve this.'

'They get them to copy the art works,' Nathan suggested, 'so that it's not immediately obvious that anything is missing and they're good copies but they wouldn't fool an expert.'

Sam looked up at Nathan in surprise. 'Exactly. But they need to have somebody on the inside of whichever collection they're targeting to effect a swop and they're clever at doing that – at finding someone who can be bought or blackmailed. They identify places with weak security.'

'And this is happening in several places at the same time?'

'That's what I hear. It's a large syndicate. That's all I know.'

Sam stopped talking as if he hoped that would be enough. As far as Nathan was concerned he'd only just got started.

'And what's happening here then?' he pursued insistently, stabbing the table with a determined index finger. 'They're targeting the collection at Ranling Manor but only the drawings, the work that's easy to take and replace and forge?'

'*I* don't know. I've *heard* that they are.' Sam paused. 'The word is that you don't ask too many questions about these guys. They recruit people they can manipulate but only tell them what they need to know. Most of the time they don't know who the other people involved are. The art work, whatever it is, is dropped off for the artist who's going to copy it in a specified place. Just a note or a call to say where. Then it's left there again a specified time later. Communication is all by note, you see, or a phone call, with fake names so no-one can grass on the others. No face to face.' Again he paused. 'That's what I've heard they do anyway.'

He picked up his bottle of beer and took a long pull on it.

'And the Michelangelo that's missing?' prompted Nathan. 'Where's that?'

Sam put the bottle down but continued to hold it as he met Nathan's gaze.

'I imagine the artist has it still to work from.' He produced a pinched smile. 'If he doesn't, he'll get into a heap of serious trouble, you see. It takes time to do a good copy. It takes practice so the artist is given a few weeks. They monitor it though. They don't like them taking too long – it makes discovery more likely – so there's a cut-off date by which it has to be delivered. Like I told you: it's just what I've heard.'

'Why doesn't the artist go to the police?'

'Because he doesn't know enough to break the syndicate, I imagine. And that leaves him seriously vulnerable if they find out he's talked.' He paused again, still holding Nathan's gaze. 'And they always find out. There's also the artist's family to think of.'

'And what about the art curator who conveniently died because she realised what was going on?'

'I know nothing about that,' Sam spat out vehemently.

'Are you sure?'

'Bloody hell, Nathan, what do you take me for?'

There was a brief, tense silence.

Sam got to his feet suddenly. 'Do you want something to eat? I've got sausages. And a couple of those potato sachets. I might even run to baked beans.' He started rummaging in the wall cupboards, pulled out a tin, then looked back at Nathan. 'Then you should go, for both our sakes.'

Nathan stared up at his brother, incredulous.

'But you haven't told me anything.'

'I've told you all I can.' Sam gave a resigned shake of the head. 'There's nothing else to say.'

They ate but he refused to discuss the matter further, despite Nathan's persistent attempts to make him.

'Now you should go,' Sam repeated, when Nathan had barely swallowed the last mouthful.

'I can't leave it like this,' said Nathan. 'I can't know that there's a huge crime going on and not do anything about it. And it's going to go on and on unless someone does do something about it.'

'You should never have got involved.'

'An innocent woman was murdered.'

'Was she? Do you know that?'

Nathan stared at him. A couple of minutes passed.

'What have you become?' he said.

Sam didn't reply.

'More people will end up dead. Don't you care?' Nathan stared at Sam who stared back. 'These things always snowball. It'll get out of hand. At least give me something to go on. Like where does the art work get left?'

'I believe it changes.'

'When will the fake Michelangelo be put back in the collection?'

'I don't think the artist would be foolish enough to give that kind of warning.'

'Soon?'

His brother shrugged.

They parted without embracing. In the couple of hours they had been together it felt as though the distance between

249

them had become a chasm, deep and wide. Nathan returned to his car and drove slowly back to the manor in a daze and still sat in his car in the parking area long after he'd killed the engine. Sam's account had a ring of truth to it, for all the veiled language, but still he wondered how much of it was Sam's all too plausible and imaginative creation. But Sam was clearly involved, right up to his neck. There could be no doubt.

The problem was, he didn't know what to do about it, either way. Sam's words: *They always find out. There's also the artist's family to think of,* kept running through his head. Was that just Sam, trying to stop his brother from rocking the boat, or a real and genuine threat?

Chapter 18

Hannah was knocking on Nathan's door at ten to eight the next morning. She'd not seen him at all the previous evening but she had heard him leave his room earlier that morning and cross to the bathroom. He'd been back in his room more than half an hour already and she couldn't contain her curiosity any longer.

'Who is it?' he called.

She glanced up the corridor but there was no-one in sight. 'Me.'

'Come in.' It was a tired, flat response.

He wasn't in bed but he wasn't dressed either. He was standing, shrugging a thin dressing-gown over a bare chest and a pair of night shorts. His hair was dishevelled, his face looked drawn and behind the glasses his eyes were strained and pinched.

'Don't tell me there's another fire,' he said acidly, pulling the dressing-gown belt round his waist and knotting it.

'Didn't you sleep?'

He raised his eyebrows. 'It's that obvious, is it?' He turned away, making a futile effort to pull the bed covers straight before sitting down heavily on top of them.

'What happened? With Sam I mean. I'm guessing you saw him.'

He sighed. 'Yes, I saw him.'

251

Hannah pulled the armchair round to face him and sat down, looking at him expectantly. 'And?'

'And... nothing. And I don't know what.'

'Explain.'

Another sigh and the familiar running of his hand through his hair.

'Well, he's got all the necessary gear there on his boat: practice sketches to copy Old Master drawings, all kinds of art materials and paper – some of it old or looking old. It's all pretty damning as far as I'm concerned but it's not exactly proof and he won't admit to anything. He confirmed the way these people work which is just as we thought, but pretends he only knows because he's heard it on the grapevine. I was so cross, Hannah, I could have...'

He broke off and was silent, putting a hand to restlessly smooth out the thin coverlet over the sheet beside him.

'I asked when the fake Michelangelo would be dropped off but he wouldn't play along. He implied that he's too scared both for his own skin and for his family.' He shook his head. 'The thing is I honestly don't know how much I believe. You know, I was so excited when I first realised I'd found my brother again but now it feels like I've met a stranger.'

Hannah got up, went to the door, looked out into the passage again, then resumed her seat.

'Did he have the Michelangelo?' she asked softly.

'I don't know. I didn't see it and without pulling his boat apart...' He shrugged. 'He wasn't about to show me, that's a fact.'

'So what are you going to do?'

'I don't know.' He rubbed at the stubble on his cheek with an agitated hand. 'I really don't know. It's a nightmare. I've been working it through every which way in my head all night and I'm no further on. *Someone* must know who's at the top.

Sam tries to make out it's all anonymous – I suppose he's covering himself – but it couldn't work that way, could it, especially if threats are involved? There must be some face-to-face contact. I suppose it's possible the artists don't know who they're dealing with but there must be middle men too. If Sam or whoever delivers a drawing to a specified place, assuming that's true, then someone else must be picking it up.'

'Yes, but that could be whoever from here is taking them in the first place.'

'You're right. I'm just trying to find a way to believe him and hope he wasn't involved with what happened to Carrie. I feel so helpless.'

Hannah was at a loss to know what else to say. She noticed the watercolour Nathan had bought for his mother had been taken out of its wrapping and was propped up on its side against the wall.

'You got the watercolour out again,' she observed, for something to say.

'I was looking for distraction in the night. It's a lovely picture. Very peaceful.'

'It is.' She went over to pick it up. 'I thought you were going to send this on to your mum.'

'I decided I'd rather give it to her in person. It's selfishness – I'd like to see her open it.'

She studied it a moment, admiring the cleverly laid subtle washes of colour, then slipped into work mode and automatically examined the frame, turning it over to scrutinise the backing. Anything rather than address the elephant in the room. How would she phrase it: have you thought of going to the police?

'What do you think about getting out on the water then?' she suggested instead, replacing the painting against the wall. 'We could do with a change of scene. It might clear our heads a bit.' She looked towards the door. 'And we can talk better. There's no chance of us being heard on a boat.'

'Sure. Why not?' He didn't move.

Hannah looked down on him, her nose wrinkling.

'You will need to wash and dress however. And a shave would be good.'

He raised bleary eyes to her face with the first flicker of a teasing smile. 'You mean you don't feel the primitive animal attraction I'm exuding?'

'Is that what it is? And to think I thought it was just sweat.' She went to the door. 'I'm going down for breakfast. I'll see you later.'

*

Rose knocked on the door of Mortimer's den and waited. It was barely ten o'clock but she knew he was in there. She'd been waiting for an opportunity – and the courage – to tackle him about the things her father had said and she'd seen him sauntering out here some ten minutes ago.

She didn't come over to the den very often. Mortimer didn't encourage visitors and in truth she found it an unnerving place. It was the trains, spinning endlessly round and round on their tracks. How pointless and how irritating, unearthly even. And Mortimer would often be sitting painting bits of scenery as if his life depended on it. Why? She liked her uncle but it gave her the creeps, a grown man playing with a train set and doing it with such intensity.

'Who is it?' came Mortimer's voice now from deep within the den.

'Rose.'

There was a pause before the door opened and Mortimer looked out at her suspiciously.

'Yes?' he said.

'I wanted to talk to you.'

'What about?'

She glanced round. There was no-one in sight.

'You. Mum.' She hesitated. 'Robert.'

He stared at her then stepped back to let her in.

As she'd expected the trains were running, producing a continuous soft hum. Mortimer obviously liked it. Perhaps if you spent enough time in here you didn't notice after a while. Rose walked to the little sitting area and, after a second's hesitation, sat down in one of the armchairs, perched on the edge of it like a schoolgirl in the headmaster's office. Mortimer joined her and stood looking down at her as if unsure what to do with her.

'Coffee?' he offered hesitantly.

'Sure.'

He busied himself with the kettle and a jar of instant coffee, dropped a spoonful of whitener into her mug and brought the two drinks over to the coffee table, then sat on the other chair. He was wearing that long cardigan again over a check shirt and his glasses were perched on the top of his head. He looked for all the world like an absent-minded professor, wise and harmless, but her father's words still stuck in her head: *He's not the pussycat everyone thinks.*

'So what did you want to talk about?' The tone of his voice was wary, challenging even, and her doubts crowded back in on her. She hesitated.

'You and Mum were an item a long time ago.'

He studied her a long moment. 'Ye-es, we were. But it was a very long time ago. Before your father started dating her. Who told you that?'

'Dad said. He said she stopped seeing you after her brother died.' She noticed Mortimer stiffen. 'He said that...'

She paused again.

255

'Yes? What did he say?'

'That you and Robert had argued before you went out on a boat together. The day he had his accident and drowned.'

Mortimer slowly leaned forward, picked up his mug from the coffee table and took a deliberate sip. He put the mug down again, very carefully.

'He says a lot of things, my brother, doesn't he? Likes the sound of his own voice.' He fixed her with a look. 'Did you believe him?'

'He didn't tell me. I overheard him saying it to someone else.'

Even as she said it, she realised she probably should have kept that to herself but she didn't want Mortimer telling her father that she'd told him. There again, he wasn't likely to do that in the circumstances.

'Who?' said Mortimer. 'Who was he saying it to?'

'Nathan. Over a drink. I don't know why.'

Mortimer's eyes narrowed. 'Did he say that I caused the accident?'

'No. Not exactly.' She shrugged one shoulder awkwardly. 'He sort of suggested that no-one asked too many questions. So, the thing is, what I wondered was, you know, what happened exactly?

'Exactly?' He snorted. '*I* don't know. One minute Robert was in the boat, reaching for his hat – a silly straw boater affair. It had blown off and was floating in the water next to us. The next minute he'd fallen in.'

'Couldn't he swim?'

'Yes. But something went wrong. There'd been a lot of rain for a couple of weeks and what with that and the wind, the currents were strong and there seemed to be an undertow.' Mortimer shook his head. 'I don't know. He might have got caught in the weed. I just know he didn't come up again. I got in the water to look for him and I kept hold of the boat for safety but I couldn't see him.' He produced another sad shake of the head. 'I couldn't see him anywhere.'

They were both silent.

'*Did* you argue?' she asked softly.

Mortimer frowned, picked up his mug again and cradled it, staring into the liquid.

'In a way. But nothing serious.' He looked up at her. 'People argue all the time, don't they? Your father likes to make it out to be something it wasn't. It's a game he plays.'

'And you and Mum... Does she blame you?'

'I don't know.' Another pause. 'I don't want to know. And I don't think you should mention it to her. It's a long time ago now.' He produced a tortured smile. 'Old wounds, Rose. Don't go opening them up again.' He paused. 'Tell me, what did Nathan say when Toby told him this story?'

She thought back. 'Nothing much.'

She left without drinking her coffee. Neither of them seemed keen to prolong the meeting. But she wasn't sure what she'd learnt exactly. She'd known for a long time that her father was, at best, an embellisher of the truth but perhaps his brother was too. Perhaps it ran in the family.

*

'Are you sure you know what you're doing?' Hannah called out.

'Of course.'

Nathan was sitting behind the wheel of their motor boat, focused on the waters around them, keeping track of the other boats moving in and out of the little marina. To judge from his straight back and the commanding looks to right and left, he could have been steering a huge cruiser on the Mediterranean.

They had hired the boat for four hours from a wiry, fast-

257

talking man who ran a small flotilla of vessels of varying sizes from a rental agency further up the river at Topingham. He had given them a five-minute explanation of how to drive the vessel, given strict instructions to keep to the speed limits and to the right, and told them that if they weren't back before their time ran out, they would pay a hefty surcharge. Now Nathan was reversing the boat slowly away from the boats on either side and into open water.

It was a small, neat day boat with an open-backed glazed cabin over two front seats and a couple of bench seats on either side at the rear where Hannah now sat, safely wrapped in a life-jacket. She hadn't thought her fall into the river would bother her but, getting into the boat, seeing the water chop and eddy around them, she had felt a moment's disquiet. The life-jacket was at least comforting.

They were away from the pontoon now and the throb of the engine changed as Nathan stopped reversing, slipped the throttle forwards and they began to move off. It was mid-morning already.

'Where do you think we should go?' she'd asked as they'd got in his car that morning.

'I don't know. Let's see where the boat takes us,' he'd replied enigmatically.

'Sometimes I could slap you.'

'Now, now.'

'But you've obviously got a plan. You could share it.'

'Would it mean anything to you?'

She hesitated. 'No, probably not.'

'Well then.'

Maybe, she'd reflected, she should have left him wallowing in his bad mood. Now, as they settled into a cruising speed, she picked up the map they'd been given and opened it out.

'So which way *is* the boat taking us?' she pressed him, staring at the map.

Nathan glanced round. 'South.'

'Ye-es, but...'

'We're not far from the junction with the River Bure. We'll turn onto it then pick up the River Thurne and head north.'

Hannah found where he meant, fingering the route, then relaxed and sat back. Nathan did appear to know what he was doing.

They were passing the last of the houses on the outskirts of Topingham, many of them huge, their gardens finely landscaped and running down to the water's edge, their river frontage boasting a boathouse and a boarded jetty. Then suddenly they were out into open country again, the banks a tangle of bushes and overhanging trees. Sunshine glinted off the water, breaking up into shards of light as the surface chopped and eddied; it was a beautiful summer's day. Hannah watched a pair of mallards paddling alongside them and a swan diving its long neck down near the bank, foraging the bottom. She felt the tension slip out of her shoulders and realised just how taut she'd been of late. This was just what she needed.

She got up and moved forward to sit in the seat beside Nathan.

'I'm beginning to see why you like the Broads and the boating thing,' she said. 'It's good.'

He looked sideways at her with amusement. 'I'm glad it has your approval.'

They reached the junction with the River Bure and Nathan swung them slowly left, heading east. Hannah watched the countryside drifting past, trees and shrubs giving way to reedbeds which swayed and rustled lightly in the breeze. Birds

259

sang and called from the reedbeds on each side; an occasional butterfly fluttered round the boat and away, and a procession of swans swam past, looking dignified and superior.

'Look at that.' Hannah pointed to a ruin on the river bank to their left.

'That's the remains of St. Benet's Abbey. It was a thriving Benedictine monastery until the Dissolution. That old mill was built much later.'

'Aren't you the knowledgeable one?'

'Don't mock.'

'I'm not. Honestly. I'm impressed.'

Nathan shrugged. 'Well don't be impressed either. I told you: we used to hang about here a lot.' He shook his head again, his expression darkening. 'It feels like it was in another life.' He turned to look at her. 'Do you want to take the wheel for a bit?'

'OK.'

He put the throttle into neutral but kept a guiding hand on the wheel until she was settled.

'It doesn't need much,' he said. 'Remember the speed limit.'

'It's OK, I remember.'

She focused on the river in front, frowning with concentration. After a couple of minutes she relaxed again – this wasn't so difficult – and they chugged on in companionable silence. They passed a small village where an old thatched inn nestled beside the river, managed to avoid a collision with a sailing yacht coming the other way and tacking into the breeze, then came to the junction with the river Thurne. Nathan took over again and soon after turned them into a narrow canal leading to a staithe where they moored up. A short walk took them into Shepston where they lunched at the pub.

They settled at an outside table, each with a half of lager and a ploughman's lunch. Nathan had gone quiet again and, by the time they'd finished eating and after a few dismal attempts at casual conversation, Hannah decided it was time they did some serious talking. She searched for a way in.

'I dated a guy once whose kid sister went off the rails,' she said. 'She started off shoplifting, silly small things just for the buzz of it, then got in with a bad crowd and it snowballed.'

'What happened?'

'She was found out in the end. Somebody talked and the police caught them – a small group of them – with stolen goods. Fingerprints matched, that sort of thing. She was still young and got away with a suspended sentence. Phil said it was the best thing that could have happened to her in the circumstances: it made her think and get her act together. I think she went into nursing in the end.'

Nathan nodded with a glum expression. 'I can't see anything like that happening here. We aren't talking about petty pilfering. We're talking serious fraud and murder.'

'You can't believe Sam had anything to do with Carrie's death. It was more likely to have been the hard guys Anders was talking about. He did warn us.'

Nathan grunted, took a mouthful of beer and flicked her an inquisitive look. 'So who was this Phil bloke?'

'I told you: a guy I dated briefly. I can't remember when exactly.'

'Been so many, have there?'

'No. I'm just not good with dates and years. It was ages ago.'

Nathan regarded her speculatively. 'Never been a serious one?'

She met his gaze for a second then looked away and picked up her own lager.

261

'Yes. I lived with someone for a while. My mother was scandalised because we weren't married.' She shrugged. 'I thought it was serious though. Turned out I was wrong. He got a job in South Africa. Didn't even tell me he'd applied. I had a job here and didn't want to go so he decided to go alone. End of story.'

'But then there's the doctor.'

She frowned. 'Do you mean Duncan? How do you know about him?'

'Daphne. I asked her if you were dating anyone. She said you'd been out a few times with a very smart doctor who'd taken you to some pretty exclusive restaurants. He's got a fancy house too, I believe. She'd looked it up to see where it was.'

She laughed. 'Typical Daphne. Yes, so? Why are you looking at me like that?'

'Still with him?'

'No. It finished not long before we came here. He was getting too serious. He's a nice guy but we just weren't... He kept trying to make me tidy. Imagine. Me. I'd have paint under my fingernails or in my hair and it seemed to bother him. Like a sign of some inner weakness, a character flaw.'

Nathan smiled suddenly. It was like a flash of sunshine on a cloudy day and it occurred to her that he hadn't smiled properly in days.

'Absolutely. You be untidy if you want to be. It's a huge mistake to try to be something someone else wants you to be. I've been there and it doesn't work.'

'I've decided not to try at all. I don't think I'm cut out for long-term relationships. Look at my parents. I haven't got the DNA for it.'

'I can't believe that.'

She looked up and their eyes met.

'Why?' she said.

'Why what?'

'Why did you ask Daphne if I was dating anyone?'

He shrugged, breaking the eye contact and focusing suddenly on the dregs of his lager. 'I like to know so I don't put my foot in it – with a colleague, you know.'

'Right. So what about you? I thought you'd be pretty sceptical about relationships after being cheated on like that. But I heard you were seeing a solicitor from that practice up the road from the studios.'

'Courtesy of Daphne?'

'Of course.'

'Did you ask her?'

'No-o, she volunteered it.'

'We really need to watch what we tell her.'

Hannah grinned. 'She'd find out anyway.'

'Well I'm not seeing that solicitor now,' said Nathan. 'Maybe I am a bit sceptical at that. Have you finished? We probably ought to be getting back to the boat.' He knocked back the remains of his lager and got to his feet. 'Coming?'

*

Nathan drove the boat on the return journey – he was happier that way – and Hannah sat at the back in the sunshine and watched the wildlife and the scenery going past.

They passed the little waterside village again with its thatched inn nudged up against the banks of the river and this time it was on their right-hand side and she could see it properly as they chugged past. The inn was old: long and low with neat, tiny windows and a picturesque drooping, mossy thatch. It was clearly popular too, the wooden tables and benches out on the quay busy with people dining and drinking in the warm sunshine.

263

She was going to point it out to Nathan when she saw someone familiar standing on the inn's riverside terrace, looking around as if he were waiting for someone. She stared, trying to place him, then became aware that Nathan had cut the throttle and the boat had slowed dramatically and was simply drifting on the current.

He laughed. 'There's a swan here in front of the boat that won't move,' he called back. 'Come on, girl, shift. We don't want to be fined for being late.' He turned round to Hannah. 'You daren't touch a swan, you know – they all belong to the Queen.'

Hannah barely heard him. She was too busy watching the man on the inn's waterside terrace. There was something about his behaviour that looked odd, she wasn't sure why. Then she managed to place him: the guy from the gallery. Thayne. She dragged at her memory to bring up his first name. Edward. No. Edgar, that was it. Edgar Thayne. Nathan had talked about him after buying the picture and for some reason it felt important but she had no idea why. Perhaps it just rang a bell because she'd seen the name of the gallery on the label on Nathan's watercolour that morning.

'Come and look,' said Nathan.

'Sorry?'

'Come and look. She's come alongside now. Hoping to be fed, I expect.'

Hannah got up and walked forward, craning her neck to see the swan who chose that moment to disdainfully paddle away.

Nathan laughed again. 'She didn't like the look of you, clearly.' He immediately pushed the throttle forwards and they moved off.

Hannah turned to look back at the inn which was rapidly receding into the distance, and Edgar Thayne who was

264

becoming just a shape: dark trousers and a pale short-sleeved shirt. He was still standing and just as the river started to bend, he turned again, as if someone had finally come to join him but she couldn't see who it was; Thayne was in the way. He was waving his arms about as though he was cross about something. Hannah frowned, staring intently over the stern of the boat but the inn had slipped out of sight.

'Are you all right?' Nathan glanced back. 'What are you looking at?'

'Nothing much. Just a nice old pub.' She sat down, but turned in her seat for a last look even though there was nothing to see.

'We're going to be a bit close for comfort with the time,' Nathan was saying. 'We should just make it if there are no more delays. I don't want to pay the surcharge.'

Hannah was aware of responding in some way but had no idea what. She had just realised the significance of the gallery man's name: Edgar Thayne. What had Carrie's note said: *mixed up with the ballet man*? The artist who produced all those wonderful pictures of ballet dancers was Edgar Degas. Edgar. The ballet man.

Chapter 19

Hannah turned to the table, jettisoned the soiled cotton swab she'd been using and picked up a clean one, wrapping it round the tip of the tiny wooden stick. It was Thursday morning and she did it without thinking, as she had been doing for the previous couple of days. She dipped it into the cleaning solution and turned back to the Guardi, an evocative scene of eighteenth-century Venice where, against a backdrop of a canal busy with gondolas, a wedding party had spilled out onto the street while people gathered to look on. The painting was dirty, much of the detail lost under thickened, yellowed varnish and grime. It also had a small tear in it. Stored badly, Carrie had surmised all those weeks ago when she'd first shown them the works that needed attention.

Carrie wasn't far from Hannah's mind now. As she sat meticulously rolling the cotton swabs over the surface of the painting to lift the dirt, her thoughts were mostly elsewhere. The figures she had seen at the waterside inn on the Sunday afternoon had stayed with her ever since. To start with she had doubted her decryption of Carrie's clue but she hadn't been able to shake it off, poring over the notebook again late each evening, sometimes even waking in the night with it still on her mind. Edgar was not a common name, especially not in a small rural community like this. And the cryptic note *the ballet man* was a perfect way of hiding the man's identity, only likely to be picked up by someone immersed in the art world. Carrie had been writing notes for herself, putting down ideas and working things out but not wanting anyone else to understand what she was doing should they accidentally get access to her notebook.

But where did that get them? Discussing what she suspected with Nathan wasn't an option. He was tortured right now and too personally involved. And she had no proof, nothing concrete to go on except a clue which it could reasonably be argued was open to interpretation. And suppose she was wrong? She needed more, something tangible.

She glanced across at him. He had started work that week on his last drawing, a charcoal by Ignace Henri Fantin-Latour which he said needed a lot of attention. All the same he too had a distracted air. For all the pleasure he might have got out of the boat trip at the weekend and their relaxed conversations, the issue of his brother's criminal activities was clearly never far from his mind. He was sitting now, staring ahead, glazed. Every now and then his face would contort, his lips moving as if he were having a silent argument with someone.

She focused back on the Guardi, gave the swab another roll, then jettisoned it. There had to be someone involved here, either living or working at the manor, someone who could take the drawings and replace them with forgeries. *BAON*. That was who she should be concentrating on but she was no nearer to working that out. If she had only seen the person with Edgar at the inn last Sunday, that might have solved the riddle once and for all. *BAON has a secret.*

She picked up another swab, dipped it in the solution and turned back to the painting. *BAON*. It felt like it was there on the tip of her tongue just waiting to surface. She tried to clear her head, listen to the music in her ears – a series of jazz piano pieces – and let her subconscious do the work for her.

It didn't. Nothing popped into her head. There was no blinding flash of inspiration. Nothing. Twenty minutes later, resigned to the inevitable, she decided that she would have to execute the plan she'd come up with during the previous night. It wasn't a perfect plan, she'd be the first to admit, in fact it was barely a plan at all but it was the only way she had a chance of working out which of the people at the manor was involved: she would have to search their belongings. The perpetrator must have something in their possession that would give them away. Which meant going through their rooms. And that wasn't going to be easy.

*

On the Saturday morning, Nathan drove into East Ranling. He found it both amazing and unsettling that it was the end of the first week in July already. In maybe just a couple of weeks they'd both be back in Oxford, but how could he leave with the issues round Sam still unresolved?

He left his car in the public car park and strolled into the centre. It was just after ten on a pleasant, intermittently cloudy day and a light breeze fluttered the bunting still strung around the village. He was at a loose end, unsure what to do with himself, restless and unable to settle, and wandered up the village street. The tea shop had a couple of tables free and he went in, ordered a coffee and sat, his thoughts tangled and knotted, hopelessly going round on a loop.

Everything was still up in the air. They were no nearer to working out who had been stealing drawings or who had killed Carrie and he could see no way of resolving it, certainly not in the time left to them in Norfolk. The only link they had was Sam and that, to Nathan, was a problem all its own.

He should go to the police, he knew that, but couldn't bring himself to do it. For one thing he'd be putting his brother's life in danger. And if Sam genuinely didn't know who was employing him, there would be nothing for the police to follow up. His brother would suffer while the real perpetrators went scot-free then dealt with him at a later date. Assuming, of course, that Sam was telling the truth, which was a big assumption. But these crooks would only get more ruthless with time. They'd get cocky and others would suffer and possibly die.

He could try and see Sam again though he doubted that anything would have changed. His brother would block and parry him at every turn; there'd be another row and Nathan would come away feeling worse than ever. He sighed and rubbed his forehead. His head hurt.

He left the tea shop and wandered along the river, idly watching the boats and the mallards and teal paddling hopefully towards anyone who paused near the bank.

Hannah had gone to Norwich again, shopping.

'Shopping? Again?' he'd made the mistake of saying.

'Yes. Why? Is there something wrong with that?'

She'd given him one of her *don't even think of messing with me* looks.

'No. Not if you need something.'

'Well, I do. And what about you, what will you do?'

'I don't know. I might go into the village. Or maybe go for a drive.'

'Good idea,' she said. 'Go exploring.'

Why? he thought now. Why was it a good idea? It wasn't like her to care what he did.

While his thoughts had been elsewhere his feet had brought him to the bridge from which Hannah had fallen. He stood where she had been that day and looked down. God, she had been lucky. His thoughts immediately clicked back onto who might have pushed her. Then back to Sam again.

269

He walked on aimlessly into the reserve. Maybe it would help.

*

Hannah let herself into Sidony's room, closed the door softly behind her and glanced round. It was the tasteful sort of space she would have expected of Sid: a neat, pretty but well-ordered room, the pale, floral curtains and a few luminous water-colours offsetting the darkness of the oak-panelled walls. The patchwork bedspread was made up of subtly coloured print fabrics to tone with the curtains. There was a low, upholstered armchair next to a small round coffee table, a set of bookshelves, a desk, a chest of drawers, and a wardrobe. Where to start? There was none of the clutter that tended to follow Hannah around. And what was she looking for anyway? She had no real idea. She started searching through drawers, attempting to leave each one as she found it.

In her pretence of visiting Norwich, she'd driven her car out of the car park early, parked it on a patch of waste ground off a lane about ten minutes' walk away, then waited a while before sneaking back. By the time she returned to the manor, Nathan's car had gone. Sid, she knew, was up in London for the weekend. There was no risk of her walking back in on her. Still, it was important not to hang about; she had thought of no plausible excuse for being there.

Sid was clearly a theatre buff and had collected programmes from a number of performances over the years, many in London, some closer to home. And among some lighter modern work her bookshelves were filled with classics of literature: George Eliot, Thomas Hardy, Ibsen, Shakespeare and Eugene O'Neill among others. There was a pretty, old musical box too, inlaid with exotic woods, but nothing that suggested some new flush of money. Hannah found no note arranging an assignation, no map indicating where a drawing might be left for collection. Nothing. Although there was a small locked drawer in her desk without a key. Was it hidden somewhere here? Hannah couldn't find it in the desk. There must be something important in there to warrant locking it. Or incriminating. She searched through Sid's clothes then stood and slowly scanned the room again but had no idea where the key might be. Damn. A few minutes later, she let herself out.

The room next door belonged to Rose. As far as Hannah knew, the young woman wasn't around either. Going to the kitchen with her used dishes after breakfast, Hannah had made a point of staying to engage Netta in conversation.

'It's very quiet this morning,' she'd said casually. 'Isn't there anyone else here this weekend?'

'Well, yes and no.' Netta turned to speak while she polished a glass with a soft cloth. 'Mr Nathan is here. Haven't you seen him? Miss Sidony has gone away up to London. Mr Mortimer is off to visit an old friend later this morning – the poor man's in hospital in Cambridge – and Miss Rose is helping out as one of the room guides. The drawing room, I think. Someone's gone down with the flu and they were short and Miss Sidony doesn't like to close any rooms off.' Netta half-smiled. 'I did hear Miss Rose complaining that it was all very well her mother having these rules but she'd gone swanning off to amuse herself. Of course, Miss Sidony didn't know about the staff shortage before she went or maybe she wouldn't have gone.'

'And what about Toby?' queried Hannah.

Netta gave a dismissive shrug. 'I don't know about him. He's often off somewhere at the weekend.' She leaned forward conspiratorially. 'Whether he's needed or not. Wrong, isn't it?'

'What about Alan? Is he working this morning?'

Netta looked at her oddly. 'I don't think so. He doesn't usually work weekends.'

Reassured that at least Rose was out of the way, Hannah now scanned her room. This room *was* cluttered. Rose had clearly ridden as a child. There were gymkhana rosettes and certificates fixed behind elastic on a cork noticeboard along with photos of sundry raft races and snaps of young people Hannah didn't know – friends presumably. Her dressing table was covered in enough cosmetics to make-up an entire theatre cast and to one side a jewellery box had become too small for Rose's collection and it lay open while necklaces, bracelets and earrings were strewn around it. None of it of any great value. And her wardrobe was crammed with clothes with still more draped over the armchair close by.

Rose had no bookcase but she did have two books – a teach-yourself Italian tutor and a small Italian dictionary – both stacked in front of a framed photograph of Florence, propped up against the wall on the chest of drawers. A couple of handbags had been left hanging around too, one of which had Rose's purse in it containing a small amount of money, a couple of bank cards and a few till receipts. And on her bed sat a fluffy donkey and a large teddy bear sporting a red and white bow tie. But Hannah's search revealed nothing suggesting involvement in a crime. Beginning to feel disheartened, she moved on.

Toby's room was muted and masculine and smelt of stale cigar smoke. Two leather armchairs faced an oak coffee table with an overspilling ashtray on it and against one wall stood a drinks cabinet with a variety of glasses and two bottles of spirits, more than half empty.

Toby had a bookcase too but his was filled with books about horses and, more surprisingly, art. Hannah studied them. They were both wide-ranging and well-informed. So it was an affectation when Toby claimed he knew nothing about art. Interesting. A couple of magazines on yachts had been abandoned on the coffee table and, perhaps more tellingly, a brochure for a yacht-building firm had been pushed into the bottom of the wardrobe. Was he thinking of commissioning one? An invitation to the private view of a one-man exhibition stood on the mantelshelf over a tiny fireplace and a small exquisite icon hung on the wall above. That was unexpected too. His clothes, when she searched them, exuded quality and he possessed a range of fine silk ties. All his belongings suggested either present affluence or the expectation of it to come and Hannah searched desperately for something incriminating.

But there was nothing linking him to Edgar Thayne and she reluctantly gave up and went to the door. This was starting to feel like a wild goose chase. Sticking her head out into the passage, she looked first one way then the other and found herself looking straight at Nathan as he reached the top of the stairs and saw her.

He frowned and walked towards her. Hannah calmly left Toby's room, closing the door behind her.

'I thought you'd gone to Norwich,' he said, drawing near.

'I changed my mind.'

'But your car's not in the car park.'

'No, it's not. Come to that, weren't you going for a drive?'

'I changed my mind too.' His eyes narrowed and he glanced towards the door she'd just closed. 'What were you doing in Toby's room?'

She checked back the other way again but could see no-one.

'Just having a poke about. Look, this isn't a good time for this conversation.'

'On the contrary, I think it's a perfect time for it.' He

leaned forward till she could feel his breath against her face as he spoke. 'You're playing with fire again, aren't you?'

'No-o. Rose is working as a guide in the house today and everyone else is out. I asked Netta.'

'Like I was out, you mean?'

She ignored him. 'Did you see Mortimer's car in the car park?'

He frowned. 'No. Why?'

'Good. He's gone to Cambridge then. His is the last room up at the front isn't it?' She took the few paces needed to reach it and opened the door, glanced round to make sure no-one else had appeared and went in. Nathan followed close behind.

'This is madness,' he said, carefully closing the door behind him.

Mortimer's bedroom was tidy, spare and unrevealing. A couple of old watercolours lightened the oak-panelled walls but it was clearly a room used simply to store his clothes and in which to sleep.

'Not that there'll be anything here,' she said. 'I'm sure Mortimer's not involved.'

'Of course you are. What are we looking for exactly?'

'I don't know. Something that suggests gain from fraud or, better yet, a link to Edgar Thayne: evidence of them meeting clandestinely, exchanging information about drawings, that kind of thing.'

Nathan's frown deepened.

'What are you talking about?'

'Edgar Thayne. *The ballet man*. Edgar as in Edgar Degas. *The ballet man*.' She saw enlightenment dawn across his face. 'Exactly. I saw him on Sunday when we were on that boat. At a riverside inn. That's when I realised. He was with someone but I couldn't see who.'

'And when were you going to tell me this?' he hissed.

'You don't think I'm involved? You didn't think I'd need to know?'

'Of course you're involved,' she hissed back. 'You're too involved. That's the point. You can't think rationally when you're so hung up about what your brother's up to.'

'Oh, so I'm not thinking rationally but you are I suppose, sneaking around these bedrooms looking for you have no idea what? God almighty. And it's only a theory, isn't it, and a bit tenuous at that? Edgar Thayne might have nothing to do with it.'

'That's why I'm looking for proof.'

'Doesn't being pushed off a bridge give you a clue that this is a dangerous situation? Suppose Netta was wrong? Suppose everyone hasn't gone out?'

'I was being careful.'

She started searching through the drawers of one of the cupboards, feeling under clothes, checking nothing had been hidden. She could feel Nathan watching her, silently criticising. She moved on to the wardrobe.

'You're wasting your time here,' said Nathan. 'If Mortimer's got anything to hide, it'd be in his study.'

She ignored him and carried on but knew he was right and finally gave up.

'All right, let's try his study, for what it's worth.'

'Now? You want to do it now?'

She'd already walked out, leaving him to close up, and made her way downstairs. He followed her right into Mortimer's study and shut the door behind him.

'Suppose Alan hears us,' he whispered.

'Netta didn't think he was working today.'

'Oh well that's all right then, if Netta didn't think so.'

Nathan shook his head despairingly but began looking through the desk anyway.

Hannah left him to it and worked her way along the book-shelves, using the neat wooden library steps for the higher shelves. She was looking for some kind of box file or folder but they were all genuine books, mostly quite old, and nothing looked suspicious. Her heart wasn't in it anyway.

'Well, well,' said Nathan softly.

'What?' Hannah joined him behind the desk to see what he was holding.

'This was at the bottom of this drawer, in a folder.'

He was holding a surveyor's map and the valuation of a section of land on the northern end of the manor's property, to the farther side of the private road leading to the car park. Hannah stared at it, taking it in.

Then the phone began to ring in the office next door and they both looked at each other and froze. It continued to peal.

'I told you Alan wasn't working today,' she muttered.

Suddenly the ringing stopped and they could hear a voice answering it.

'Rose,' mouthed Nathan. 'What's our cover story?'

Hannah produced a pained expression. 'We wanted to borrow a book?' she mouthed back, shrugging.

He rolled his eyes and still they waited. They heard what sounded like the end of the call and then nothing. A couple of minutes later, Hannah dared breathe again. She looked back at the map.

'That's the cottage Alan rents on that stretch of land, isn't it?' she murmured.

'Yes. Looks like Mortimer's thinking of selling it off, the land and the cottage. Alan won't like that. Nor the trustees I suspect, but he's hoping to raise some funds, I assume.'

Hannah nodded. 'So I was right: he isn't playing fraud games. He wouldn't be doing that if he was selling land, would he?'

276

'Maybe. Maybe not. Maybe it shows how desperate he's become. Anyway, I can't find anything else.'

'That just leaves Alan.'

'You can't simply go waltzing into his cottage.'

'I have no intention of waltzing.'

*

Alan's car wasn't in the car park and Nathan was almost disappointed: it would have stopped Hannah venturing further. As it was, she insisted on going to the cottage alone. Grace might be there, she said, and she knew Hannah; Nathan's presence would only complicate the issue.

'She's nervous,' said Hannah. 'And given the way he treats her, I think she'd feel happier talking to me. Not a man. No offence.'

'I don't like it,' said Nathan.

'Then go back inside. Do you want this resolved or not?'

The answer to that was too complicated. 'I'll wait in the car. Be careful.'

She gave him a baleful look and walked purposefully away.

He sat in his car, tapping a rhythm on the steering wheel with agitated fingers and glancing regularly in the rear-view mirror at the tree-lined path towards the cottage.

Hannah was insane. What did she hope to find? Whoever was swapping pictures in and out wasn't going to leave anything lying around for just anyone to find. Though she had been clever to work out *the ballet man* clue, he conceded.

If she was right.

Though the more he thought about the ingratiating, smooth-talking man who ran the gallery, the more he thought she might be. But if so, how did that play out? And where would that leave Sam? His thoughts drifted away again, back to an old, worn cruiser on the river at Pollersby and a man he wasn't sure he knew any more.

He caught a movement in the mirror and looked up. Hannah was already coming back down the path. Time had moved on without him realising.

'Well?' he demanded as she got in the passenger seat.

'No joy. Grace was there, doing the cleaning. Alan had gone out saying he might be back for dinner but not saying where he was going. Apparently he does that all the time and she doesn't dare ask any more. She let me look round. He has a little back room he calls his office and there's paperwork in there but nothing that I could see that linked him to the fraud. Or Carrie.' She frowned. 'He's a mean man, Nathan. I wouldn't put anything past him. I wish Grace would leave him. Why does Mortimer employ him?'

'Because he does the job that's required of him and says the right things when he needs to. People like that are clever and devious. He even puts on a smarter voice when he's in the office, have you noticed?'

She nodded, looking despondent. 'He's got a strongbox in his office that's locked. She's pretty sure that when he bought it there were two keys. She thinks he keeps one on him and hides the other one but she doesn't know where. I couldn't find it anyway. She said she'd keep looking.'

'But if he finds out she's been looking for it…' He didn't finish the thought.

'I know. I did warn her not to take any chances. Anyway, I'm going in. I need some lunch.'

'I'll be in in a minute.'

'You OK?'

'Sure.'

He watched her walk back up the path to the manor. It was at least a quarter of an hour later when he went in to the kitchen and began making himself a sandwich. Then Netta bustled in and fussed over whether he had everything he wanted.

'And by the way Mr Nathan, a letter came for you this morning. I didn't know where you were so I pushed it under the door of your room.'

He thanked her and took the sandwich upstairs. The letter might be from his mother or more likely it was a boring bill or advert that had been forwarded on.

But it was neither. The address had been hand-written in blue ink in an ugly, uneven hand and Nathan felt his skin prickle as he read it. He recognised the writing: disguised and painstakingly produced, done with a left hand by a right-handed person. Sam used to do it as a kid for fun.

The sandwich forgotten, he ripped the envelope open.

Chapter 20

On the Monday morning, Hannah left the silence of the workroom and made her way to the kitchen. There was no-one there and she put the kettle on, dropped a spoonful of instant coffee in one mug and a tea bag in another, then leaned against the units to wait. She had slept lightly and was tired. She was dejected that her bright idea of searching the rooms had come to nothing, frustrated that Nathan had come back and caught her doing it, and now irritated that he didn't appreciate that she was trying to make his position easier. She wanted to help.

If they had some evidence, surely it would work in some way to sort out the situation with his brother? It might even prove he wasn't involved. OK, so that wasn't likely. Sam had all the necessary materials to do the forgeries and clearly knew too much about it. But surely it would be better for Sam if the issue were brought to a head sooner rather than later? He was going to sink into ever deeper trouble the longer the scam went on. And if he'd been coerced into doing the work, admitted it and expressed his regret, the judiciary would be likely to treat him more leniently.

This had been the thrust of her argument to Nathan on the Sunday morning but he'd refused to discuss it with her, got cross and rudely told her to back off. Whereupon she'd informed him – among other home truths – that he was being obstinate, short-sighted and foolish, and they had barely spoken again for the rest of the day. And now the atmosphere in the workroom was thick with resentment. She'd apologise, except that she still didn't think she was wrong. Neither the problem, nor his anxiety and distress, were going to go away by Nathan sticking his head in the sand. But maybe she shouldn't have lost her temper.

She yawned as Alan walked into the kitchen, turning just in time to see him pointedly close the door behind him. He didn't speak, crossed to take a mug out of the wall cupboard, put a spoonful of coffee in it and turned to face her, legs apart and challenging. For a full minute he silently stared at her.

She felt a chill of apprehension but levelly met his gaze.

'Morning,' she said.

'You're leaving soon, I believe.'

'You are correct.' Nothing gets past you, she thought of saying, but didn't dare.

'Good.'

The kettle boiled and he immediately grabbed it and poured the hot water into his own mug then threw the remaining water down the sink, flicking her a twisted smile, daring her to protest. It was so petty, she didn't bother.

'It's as well for you that you're going,' he said, stirring his coffee. 'I heard last night from a friend that you've been trying to get pally with my Grace. He's just got back from a trip but he tells me he saw you in the village with her a couple of weeks ago. Having a very intense conversation you were, he said. So what was that about?'

'Do you know, I can't remember. But it can't have been that intense. We'd just bumped into each other.'

'Don't try to be smart with me, Hannah.' His eyes narrowed and he looked her up and down, lip curled. 'Her mixing with you explains a lot. She's changed lately, getting all independent and answering back. And I don't like that.

281

Friends like you she can do without. I'll not have you go putting ideas in her head. I'm warning you: keep away from her.'

'You are mistaken.' She spoke slowly, measuring each word. 'I don't know Grace well enough to call her a friend. We've seen very little of each other. But surely it's up to her who she chooses to have as friends?'

'Much more of your lip and you won't just be falling from a bridge. Stay away from her. I won't tell you again.'

The kitchen door opened and Sidony looked in.

'Am I disturbing something?' she said.

'Not at all,' said Hannah. 'Did you come for coffee?'

'Yes.'

Alan left with a curt nod in Sidony's direction and, while Hannah refilled the kettle and put it back to boil, Sidony put coffee in another mug.

'Everything OK?' She studied Hannah with shrewd eyes.

'Absolutely fine.'

Sid glanced towards the door which had now been left ajar. 'Alan's not always easy to work with. He's er... moody, I suppose you could say. Don't take it personally.'

'I don't.'

'Good. You know, I was watching you and Nathan this morning, over breakfast.'

Hannah frowned. 'Why on earth would you do that?'

'Have you worked together long?'

'A little over a year. I moved from somewhere else; Nathan had already been at Blandish a while.'

'So you were the new girl?'

'In a manner of speaking.'

'I thought so. That can make things a bit tricky to start with can't it?'

Hannah objected to Sid's maternal tone. Still rattled from

282

the confrontation with Alan, it was the last thing she needed.

'Are you trying to make a point here? Because if you are, I'm afraid I'm not seeing it.'

'Not really. It's just that I've watched the two of you together while you've been here and I can see you both sparring and jostling for position. You really don't need to. Don't look at me like that – I'm only trying to be helpful. People on the outside can sometimes see more clearly. Nathan likes you, that much is obvious. The way he looks at you sometimes...' Sidony pursed her lips up as though she might whistle. 'Why do you fight him so?'

'I don't fight him.'

'Of course you do. But he seems like a nice guy and he's good-looking and smarter than average, I'd say. Why not go with it and see where it leads? You like him, don't you? Come on, Hannah, don't be coy. Life's too short not to take these opportunities when they present themselves. Old rivalries are foolish. You're not star-crossed lovers, for heaven's sake.'

Hannah didn't reply. The kettle boiled and she turned away, pouring the hot water into the three mugs in turn. She held up the milk bottle to Sid who nodded and she added milk to both coffees, then removed her teabag and added a drop to the tea as well.

'First of all,' she said, 'I don't think it's any business of yours how Nathan and I interact – or don't. And secondly, given the relationship you've got with Mortimer, I don't think you're in a position to hand out advice.'

'What do you mean by that?'

'I mean that Mortimer thinks the sun shines out of you, has done for years and probably always will. I gather you were an item once upon a time then you dumped him for Toby but, let's face it, that clearly didn't work out, did it? And you're still incredibly fond of Mortimer, aren't you? You watch out for him and warn other people off hurting him. I've seen you fuss over him and straighten his clothes. You don't fool me.'

'I wasn't trying to fool you.' Sidony sounded cross now. She frowned. 'Mortimer still cares for me? I didn't know. Did he tell you that?'

Hannah nodded. 'But it's as plain as the nose on your face anyway. Don't you give me advice about relationships, Sid.' And she picked up her two mugs and returned to the workroom.

Nathan looked up as she came in, muttered a terse thanks for the coffee, and went back to work. *Nathan likes you, that much is obvious.* Really? thought Hannah. Could have fooled me.

She installed herself back at her work table and tried to concentrate. The cleaning had transformed the Guardi but it had revealed some areas that required attention. And she needed to find a piece of canvas from the supply in her work trunk that would be a good match in order to patch it.

Her mind struggled to focus though. She was worried about Grace. While she would escape back to Oxford, Grace would be forced to endure the brutish behaviour of that excuse for a human being.

And maybe she'd spoken out of turn to Sid. But that she didn't regret.

*

The note Nathan had received in the post lingered in his mind like an exam question you realise too late that you misunderstood. He was confused and uneasy and didn't know what to do about it. But if he asked Hannah's opinion she'd start off on her soapbox again.

It was Tuesday and they were still barely talking. And she was behaving oddly. While preparing a patch for the Guardi, teasing out the weave of the canvas to stop it leaving a hard edge, every so often her eyes would glaze over, the regular bobbing of her head to her music would stop and she'd stare into space. What was going on in that overactive, too eager brain of hers?

It wasn't until the end of the afternoon when she suddenly became galvanised. She'd been staring into mid-air again then nodded, just the once, waving the tweezers she was holding.

'Star-crossed lovers,' she exclaimed.

'What?'

She looked round and pulled an earpiece out. 'Hm?'

'What did you say?' said Nathan.

She stared at him as if she barely saw him.

'It's just…' she said dreamily. 'I think I've… Yes.'

She checked her watch, pulled the second earpiece out and dumped the stereo on the table.

'They'll all still be working.' She got to her feet. 'I've just got time.' She surveyed the disarray around her then turned to face him. 'Look, I need to go. I'll sort this out again. If I can find some real proof, will you listen to me then?'

'Proof of what exactly? How? Where are you going?'

'I've figured it out. I know where there might be something.'

Nathan glanced at his watch. 'It's too late to go poking about their rooms now. They'll be finishing any moment.'

'I won't be long. If I'm right, I won't need to be.'

'No, you're being rash.' He stood up, reaching out a warning hand. 'Don't…'

But she'd already grabbed her bag, marched to the door and glanced out into the passage. A moment later she'd gone, closing the door behind her and Nathan stood, open-mouthed.

*

285

It was half an hour later and Nathan was back in his bedroom when he heard a soft knock on his door.

He walked slowly across and opened it to find Hannah standing outside. He pulled the door back and she came in, stopped at the end of the bed and turned to face him.

'You're all right then,' he said coolly.

'Yes.'

'And?'

'And I think I've got something important. Are you prepared to listen?'

'Try me.'

She fixed him with a look. 'OK. I worked out the clue: *BAON*. It's kind of oblique but it'll make sense to you when I explain.'

And she did, showing how she got there, who the initials referred to and why.

He regarded her sceptically. 'Are you sure?'

'Of course I'm sure. Look at these. They prove I'm right. Once I worked it out I knew where to find them.'

She had a sheaf of papers in her hand and thrust them at him.

Nathan frowned and read the top one out: '*RUNNING LATE. CUTTING IT FINE. USUAL PLACE FRI 12.30.*' He shuffled to the second one: '*THERE MAY BE PROBLEMS. SPEAK SOON.*' And the third: '*SUN 1 PM. NEED TO TALK.* That's clearly an assignation.' He scanned through the remainder.

'You see. They're from Edgar.'

'You can't be sure of that. All capitals and nothing personal about any of them. They could mean anything. If this was Edgar Thayne he was being very careful not to give himself away.'

'Look again at the one at the bottom of the pile.' She

poked a finger towards the note. 'See? He used the back of a sheet from an invoice pad – well, part of it anyway. Look at the other side of it. The printed columns? And there's the slight imprint of some writing from another sheet and a price.'

Nathan brought it closer and peered at it. 'Yes. There's something. It says… "…*lour*." Watercolour maybe. Then "…*ing Broad*" and, yes, that might be a price.'

'You see? I'm sure if you compare it to the copy of the invoice Edgar gave you when you bought your watercolour, you'll find it matches.' Hannah sat down on the end of the bed. She looked weary suddenly. 'But you're right, he was being careful. He realised his mistake and didn't use any of that paper again. I checked.'

He grunted. 'It's hardly proof though. Lots of people in small businesses use the same kind of invoice pads.'

'I know. He's shrewd. He's very guarded with his language. But it's enough to show the police, to open their eyes to what might be going on.' She paused, looking down and picking at the ends of her fingers where bits of the resin adhesive she'd been using on the canvas patch still stuck. 'Nathan, I'm sorry. I know this is difficult for you. I do. I just thought…'

'I know. You don't have to explain.'

He walked across to his bedside table, picked up the paperback on it and pulled a small piece of paper from between its pages. It had clearly been torn from a larger sheet. He held it out to her.

'Read this.'

'It's almost illegible.' She peered at it then read aloud: '*The "new" Michelangelo will be returned on 12th July*.'

She frowned then turned the paper over to look at the back. It was blank.

'Where did this come from?'

'It arrived in the post on Saturday. I don't know what to make of it. Is it help, or is it a warning? It's from Sam, I suppose you've realised that. That's his "disguised" writing. I've seen it before.'

'I wondered.' She read the note again. '*The "new" Michelangelo*. The forgery presumably.' She looked up. 'I think it's help. He's telling you that the forgery will be put back on the twelfth.'

'Friday.'

'Exactly. He's put the ball in your court.'

'Great. Really helpful. But how does he know that?'

'Maybe because he's going to hand it over at the last minute. The syndicate insist on pictures being replaced in a certain timescale, isn't that what you told me?'

'Yes.' He hesitated. 'But it might be a trap.'

'By Sam? You can't think that.'

Nathan ran a hand through his hair. 'I don't know what I think any more.'

They were both silent. Hannah stared at the note.

'You know we should go to the police, don't you?' She looked up at him. 'Carrie got herself killed just for suspecting these people. You told me that yourself.'

Without explanation she got up and went out and round to her room. She came back a minute later with a small business card and handed it to him.

'He gave me that at my interview after Carrie died. I could ring him.'

'Chief Inspector Crayford?' He shook his head. 'No. We can't. Not until I know how involved Sam is.'

'But how are you going to do that?'

'I don't know,' he barked, and began to pace up and down, flicking the card against his fingers.

'But we've got something definite for them to go on now.

288

And that note is anonymous. There's no link back to Sam.'

'Of course there is. He's involved so there must be. Fingerprints perhaps or someone who saw him post it. Me. I'd have to explain how I came to have it.'

'But Sam wants you to catch these guys or he wouldn't have sent it.'

'No. Or rather yes.' He stopped pacing suddenly and faced her. 'Yes, that's it. We do what he's suggesting. We lie in wait ourselves until they appear with the picture. There's no need to mention the note to anyone. We catch them in the act. Then we tell the police.'

Hannah stared at him, her face creasing into a deep frown.

'Er... and how's that going to play out?'

'I don't know. We need an admission, I suppose. We'll play it by ear.'

Hannah pulled a bemused expression. 'Play it by ear?'

'Don't pretend you haven't done that before, Hannah Dechansay.'

There was a long silence.

'All right,' she said slowly. 'It's your call. But don't you ever call me rash again.'

Chapter 21

Hannah sat on the toilet seat lid and fidgeted. It was made of wood and very hard. At least it felt hard when you'd been sitting on it as long as this. She wanted to cross her legs, just to change the pressure on her backside, but there wasn't much room and she thought she'd probably kick Nathan if she did. Not that she could see more than the faintest outline of him but she knew he was there: she could feel his legs against hers if she didn't sit still and she could feel his heat. It was like playing a rather dangerous game of sardines.

It was the Friday and they were squashed into the cloakroom under the stairs in the rear vestibule of the manor.

'We'll have a stakeout after work,' Nathan had said. 'The cloakroom's the perfect place to do it. It's almost opposite the storeroom.'

'But it mightn't happen till the middle of the night.'

'Possibly. I think it'll be earlier – probably as soon as the house goes quiet.'

'Or it might happen during the day.'

'Nah. Still, we can leave the workroom door open then we'll hear if someone goes in. Maybe it wouldn't kill you to forswear your music for once? But they're not likely to try in the day. Too many people about.'

Suddenly it seemed that Nathan was an expert and perfectly understood the thought processes of the criminal mind perpetrating the fraud. She hoped he was right. She didn't fancy spending the better part of the night in this cloakroom. And she'd chosen not to ask again what exactly they were going to do if the drop went ahead. Get an admission, he'd said. It sounded easy but sitting here, it didn't feel that way. It could go horribly wrong. Would Edgar be around too, perhaps waiting nearby? Or maybe a couple of people. Was Edgar actually involved? She had begun to doubt herself. Whoever turned up, it was unlikely they would roll over and admit everything. This could be unpleasant.

But here they were in this cramped little cloakroom with the door open a crack. It let in just a suggestion of the weak light that filtered into the vestibule from the glazing either side of the back door. Nathan stood with his nose to the crack. He'd insisted that he had no problem standing, that he preferred it. There wasn't room for them both to stand – the stairs rising above them drastically reduced the headroom – so Hannah sat and waited and hoped that the drawing was returned that night and that she hadn't gone numb by the time it happened.

She leaned forward to touch Nathan's arm. 'What time is it?' she murmured.

Nathan lifted his wrist and angled it at the crack in the door to catch the light on his watch.

'Seven twenty,' he whispered back.

They'd been there barely two hours but it felt like four. She thought longingly of the meal they'd told Netta they wouldn't want tonight because they were going out. They hoped to survive on two chocolate bars and a bottle of water.

She fidgeted then nudged Nathan's arm again.

'Can I stand for a bit?' she muttered. 'It's your turn to sit.'

'It would be better if I...'

'I have to move.'

'OK, OK,' he hissed.

The back door creaked very slightly. Hannah hadn't really noticed that it creaked before but it was so quiet here now, so still, that every tiny noise seemed magnified. The last time she'd looked at her watch it had been eight thirty-five. It felt like an age ago but was probably no more than a quarter of an hour. She and Nathan had been taking it in turns to stand and sit for the last hour and a half but she was the one now standing by the door.

She craned her head to the crack and listened. The storeroom door wasn't quite visible from where she stood but she was sure there was someone out there in the hall. She could feel a presence and hear indistinguishable sounds of movement. Was that a key turning in a lock? She reached back without looking to tap Nathan and found his hand reached up to her arm, tugging on her. He must have heard them too and probably wanted her to let him get to the door but there was no way he could – any movement would simply telegraph their presence.

She stayed motionless, listening, heard the storeroom door close and waited a second then turned her head.

'Someone's gone in,' she whispered. 'Better wait a minute.'

'Did you see who it was?'

'No.'

A minute later she cautiously pulled the door back and, without waiting for Nathan, walked across to the storeroom door. She paused and looked round. Nathan had gone straight to the back door for some reason. Had he heard something? Was Edgar there too? She hesitated, irresolute, but they'd come this far. Nothing ventured... She opened the storeroom door. It was dark inside but she could see the flash of someone's torch. She flicked the light switch and stood, dazzled for a second by the sudden light.

'Rose,' she said evenly. 'What are you doing?'

Mortimer's niece was standing by the plan chest, dressed in black trousers and a thin black sweater with a dark green scarf tied round her blonde hair. A drawing had been put down on top of the chest and she was holding the old inventory book, apparently checking the entries, when Hannah walked in. Her astonishment was clear but she quickly regrouped.

'I'm putting this picture back, of course. What does it look like I'm doing? Anyway, what's it got to do with you?'

'Did you forget where you got it from?'

'No. Well yes, as a matter of fact.'

Nathan now walked in to stand beside Hannah and Rose's defiant expression crumbled a little.

'Nathan?' she said. 'I don't understand. What's going on?'

'I'm afraid you've been rumbled, Rose.' Nathan went over to the plan chest, picked up the drawing and examined it, then turned it to glance at the back. He kept hold of it. 'This isn't the original drawing. It's a good copy certainly but it's not the original. You see, Carrie knew that some of the drawings were fakes and she'd noticed that the original of this Michelangelo drawing was missing too. We've been looking into it.'

'No, no you're wrong. That's not true: Carrie knew nothing. She was just nosey and interfering. I borrowed this to have a look at and I was about to put it back. I mean, it kind of belongs to me anyway, doesn't it? I'm family. Anyway it might all be mine one day. I can borrow my own things.'

Nathan continued as if she hadn't spoken. 'Of course fakes – good fakes like this one, that is – only come to light when a picture is up for sale and is scrutinised by an expert.

293

You thought the exchanges would never be discovered.'

'No, you're just making this up.' She gave a brief, desperate laugh. 'What is this Nathan? What are you doing? And give me that drawing. It's not yours.'

He handed it back.

'No it's not. But none of the art works here belong to you either, not yet. And that *is* a forgery. I know it is.'

'So what if it is,' she hissed, glancing uneasily at Hannah. 'OK yes, it is. But I've only taken a few old drawings. That's not doing you any harm is it? I only wanted some excitement. I wanted something to change. Come on Nathan. It's harmless. Don't do this to me. We're friends, aren't we?'

'It wasn't harmless to Carrie,' he said coldly.

She raised her chin defensively, but looked scared now. 'I don't know what you mean.'

'I think you do. Carrie found out too much. She was becoming a threat, wasn't she? She had to be got rid of.'

Hannah glanced anxiously towards the door. She was sure she'd heard a noise in the passage outside.

'I don't know anything about that,' said Rose. 'I was as shocked as anybody when Carrie died.'

'That's because you've got an accomplice,' said Hannah. 'Someone to liaise with the forger, someone to organise the pick-ups and get a cut of the money from the sale of the originals. I bet you didn't get much of it though, Rose, did you, despite doing the dangerous part and stealing the pictures.'

'I did OK,' said Rose sullenly.

'Edgar Thayne's your accomplice, isn't he?' said Hannah.

Rose stared, open-mouthed. Beneath her make-up her skin had blanched leaving her cheeks incongruously rosy with blusher.

'How did you know that?'

The door opened and two men walked in. Hannah looked

round in amazement: it was Chief Inspector Crayford and Sergeant Harris. She looked across at Nathan. He must have rung them after all.

The inspector slowly surveyed the room and its occupants. Rose still had the fake Michelangelo in one hand and the inventory book in the other.

'Rose has the forgery, Chief Inspector,' said Nathan.

The inspector put on a pair of gloves. 'May I?' He held out his hand.

Rose reluctantly handed him the drawing.

'Thank you. I daresay you'll remember me, Miss Gyllam-Spence. I'm Chief Inspector Crayford and this is…'

'I know who you are.'

'We were alerted that this drawing might be put in here tonight so we were waiting outside. I'll take that book as well please. Thank you. Rosamund Gyllam-Spence, I'm arresting you on suspicion of theft and fraud. Sergeant, will you do the honours please?'

'No, no, you've got it all wrong,' said Rose.

The sergeant was already taking her by the arm. 'You do not have to say anything,' he intoned, 'but anything you do say will be taken down and may be given in evidence. Do you understand?'

'Yes, I understand,' she said belligerently.

The inspector studied the drawing a moment then slipped it into a large folder he'd brought with him.

'Get off me,' Rose protested, trying to shake the sergeant's hand off and failing.

'We'll be asking Mr Thayne all about the thefts too,' said the inspector. 'He'd just finished packing when we called to see him and he's at the station now, answering a few questions for us. He had a surprising amount of cash in his house, some of it in Argentine pesos, and a single airline ticket to

Argentina. So with no immediate intention to return, it seems.'

'Argentina? Why would he… ? No. A single ticket? No. He couldn't. Not without me.' Her voice began to rise. 'How could he do that? After everything he promised me. He was going to take me away. We were going to travel, see the world. He promised me we'd go to Italy.'

'He appears to have had other plans.'

'No.' She glared at him. 'You're lying.'

'I'm afraid not, Miss Gyllam-Spence. We'd also like to question you about the death of Carrie Judd.'

She visibly shrank back at the suggestion.

'No, no, no, that had nothing to do with me. That was Edgar. All Edgar. I only found out much later and I told him he shouldn't have done that. That was going too far. He panicked, you see. I'm not going to be blamed for that, especially when he's going to dump me. What a bastard. Wait till I see him. I'll admit to taking the pictures but I had nothing to do with Carrie. It was him. He said so. I'll tell you everything.'

She turned to Nathan, reaching out her free hand in a supplicant gesture. 'You see, I only wanted to get away. You should have helped me. I never liked Edgar that much. I just wanted to travel. He knew I wanted to go to Italy.'

'You can tell us all about it at the station, Miss,' said the sergeant.

She was still trying to shake his hand off and fulminating about Edgar as she was led out.

'Thank you for your help,' said Chief Inspector Crayford. He looked from Nathan to Hannah and smiled. 'Both of you. I'll need statements from you but in the morning perhaps? And we'll need to have access to this room. Nothing must be touched.'

'Of course. Rose left her key.' Hannah pointed. 'If you

want to lock up and take that.'

'I will. Then I need to speak to Mortimer Gyllam-Spence.'

'He's probably in the dining-room,' said Hannah. 'Or maybe his study. I'll show you.'

'It's all right, thank you, I know the way.' His expression was grim. 'I'll find him.'

Nathan and Hannah walked into the rear vestibule and watched the inspector lock the storeroom door then cut through into the private quarters. Even after he'd gone they both stood as if rooted to the spot.

'So you told him,' said Hannah. 'That was... courageous.'

'I don't know about that. I do know it was the worst thing I've ever had to do. But I decided you were right, that maybe Sam wanted me to do it. I just hope I've done the right thing.'

'I'm sure you have. Do you think they've...' She hesitated, reluctant to say it.

'What? Caught him?' He shrugged. 'I don't know. This isn't the end of it, I know that.' He looked round. 'Look, let's get out of here. I've had enough. I think I'm going to go for a walk for a bit, try and clear my head.'

'Sure. I'll see you tomorrow.'

Nathan nodded blankly, then wandered off and Hannah walked through to the kitchen. Netta had cleared up and gone. Hannah found some cold pork in the fridge and made herself a sandwich. She wondered what would happen next. Nathan was right: this couldn't be the end of it.

Chapter 22

'And you didn't see fit to tell me about your suspicions?' demanded Mortimer.

'We weren't sure enough,' said Hannah. 'It wouldn't have been right to accuse her until we were sure.'

'So you skulked around to catch her in the act? Was that an appropriate way to behave – here, living under my roof?'

Mortimer had turned up at the breakfast table first thing on the Saturday morning, looking more dishevelled than usual, and ordered Hannah and Nathan to come and see him in his study. This minute. And that's where they were, standing watching him alternately stand and pace, then sit behind his desk. He was sitting now, his reading glasses perched on top of his head.

'I'm sorry, but we didn't have a choice, sir,' said Nathan. 'I told you Carrie had concerns about the collection, that there was something wrong with some of the pictures, but you didn't believe me.' He hesitated. 'Or chose not to. I didn't feel I could come back to you with it unless we had some concrete proof. Unfortunately, the only way to get that was to be there when the thief tried to replace the stolen drawing.'

'You're blaming me now?' said Mortimer, getting to his feet again and glaring at him. 'You're going too far, young man.'

'No, sir. Not at all. I understand the pressures you're

under.' Nathan hesitated again. 'And it's an impossible situation when you have to suspect your own family. I know that.'

Mortimer stared at him, frowned, then collapsed into the chair again.

'Yes, yes, it is. I didn't want to think it could be someone here. I'm sorry. I admit I rather turned a blind eye. I didn't want to know.' He sighed and seemed to deflate before their eyes as his anger dissipated. 'It's a terrible business and that's a fact. Rose... She's not a bad girl but she's lost her way. I can see that and I'm partly to blame no doubt, but Toby hasn't... Well, that's not something that concerns you.'

The study door was flung back and Sidony came in, wild-eyed.

'What's this Netta's saying about Rose, Mortimer? She's been arrested? It can't be true. Where is she? What's it all about?'

'Ah Sid, you're up then. Now calm down. She's all right but, yes, she has been arrested. I hardly slept last night, wondering how to tell you.' He examined her face anxiously. 'You know the issues Nathan raised about the collection all those weeks ago?' Mortimer offered Nathan an apologetic look. 'Well, it seems he was right, after all. It's a horrible mess and Rose has managed to get herself mixed up in a nasty fraud involving forgeries and I don't know what. It turns out she's admitted it too. You were out last night when the Chief Inspector was here, telling me all about it. I've been trying to get my head round it ever since. I wasn't sure what to do for the best.'

'And what's your part in this?' Sid turned her accusing gaze on Nathan, then Hannah.

'We suspected something,' said Nathan. 'It hasn't been easy to figure out what was going on exactly.'

'It's not their fault, Sid,' said Mortimer. He flicked them a wry glance. 'I dare say they suspected all of us at some point and didn't know what to do about it.'

'I am sorry for the way it's turned out,' said Hannah. 'Truly. In the circumstances, I think we should leave. We'll find somewhere else to stay until we've completed the last two pictures. Of course, we'll keep out of your way as much as possible.'

'Unless you'd rather we left altogether?' added Nathan.

'Leave without the job being finished?' Mortimer said indignantly. 'No, no. Anyway, we've got a contract. Of course you must stay. I spoke in haste before. I was angry and upset and not thinking straight. I realise now the dilemma you must have had. And of course it had to come out eventually. Poor Rose. But she was the one in the wrong, I do see that.'

'Mortimer, for God's sake will you tell me what is going on?' exploded Sid. 'Where is Rose now? I want to see her.'

'Of course. Sit down my dear, please. Nathan and Hannah were just leaving.' He nodded towards them then transferred his attention back to Sidony. 'I'll tell you everything that I know. Really, she's all right. It's just... well, very unpleasant.'

Nathan and Hannah discreetly withdrew and returned to the dining room where they sat down again in front of their half-finished breakfasts.

'Awkward, isn't it?' said Hannah, picking up a piece of cold toast. She put it down again.

'Very.' Nathan regarded his cup of coffee with distaste. 'This is cold.'

'So's my tea.'

'What if we worked today? The inspector said he'd want to interview us anyway and I'd rather stay occupied.'

'I was thinking the same thing. Presumably he'll just turn up at some point. We might as well work.'

300

They took the remains of their breakfasts back to the kitchen, made fresh drinks and took them through to the workroom, casting a glance at the locked storeroom door as they went.

Hannah sat down in front of the Guardi canvas. The patch was firmly in place now and she'd already started infilling the paint losses with a tiny brush and minute dabs of paint. She glanced across at Nathan. He was staring at the Fantin-Latour drawing on his table: a charming image of the artist's sister reading a book, rendered in charcoal and white chalk. It had been badly buckled and he'd spent a lot of time trying to flatten it. Apparently it was now as flat as he could make it. He just needed to get on with cleaning it and cutting a new mount. They were well on their way to being finished. Timothy would be pleased.

Nathan looked up suddenly and their eyes met.

'I wonder where he is right now?' he said.

'Sam?'

He nodded. 'It sticks in my throat, you know, the fact that we parted on such bad terms. I wonder if I'm going to see him again.'

She thought of several things to say – encouraging, well-meaning remarks – but they were all platitudes and she rejected them. The moment passed and they both applied themselves to their work.

*

It was the end of the afternoon when Sidony turned up at the workroom looking less crisp and efficient than usual and not a little shamefaced.

'I'm sorry to disturb you. Toby's away for the weekend and Mortimer and I were hoping you'd both join us for dinner this evening.' She paused. 'I'm sorry for the way I reacted earlier. Now that I've heard the whole story, I realise that of course you are not to blame for what has been going on. We'd really like to hold out an olive branch, so to speak, and just talk, settle the air. You'll understand that it's been… a shock. You don't have other plans, do you?'

'No.' Hannah glanced towards Nathan. 'We don't have any plans, do we?'

Nathan shook his head.

'Have you seen Rose?' said Hannah. 'How is she?'

'They let me see her for a few minutes this afternoon.' Sidony slowly took a breath, her lips pursed as if mastering herself. 'She's all right, all things considered, and we've got our solicitor involved. Mortimer is blaming Toby and he's blaming himself but I know I'm at least partly to blame too. Anyway, I shan't bore you with our family problems. We'll see you later. Shall we say seven o'clock in the sitting room for aperitifs?'

'Have the po…?' began Nathan.

'Yes, that'll be fine, thanks,' Hannah said loudly over him. 'We'll see you then.'

Nathan glared at Hannah as Sidony walked out.

'Did you have to interrupt?' he complained bitterly. 'I was only going to ask if they'd said anything more about Sam.'

'I know. But you asked the Chief Inspector only this morning. And maybe it'd be better not to flag up your relationship with him too much. Not here with the Gyllam-Spences. Or at least not now. Their olive branch might wilt a little. After all, the police don't seem to have told them. We'll find out soon, I imagine.'

He let it go. She was probably right: they'd find out something soon enough, good or bad.

*

302

Mortimer was in his bedroom wearing only underwear and his light summer dressing-gown when he heard a knock at the door. He glanced at the clock beside his bed. It was still only six-thirty. He'd showered and had been sitting by the window, trying to fill a few minutes before dinner reading a new book he'd bought on the history of steam trains, but it wasn't going well. He kept rereading the same lines, his thoughts elsewhere.

'Who is it?' he called out.

'Sidony.'

Without hesitation he got up, pulling the gown tighter and knotting the belt more firmly. He couldn't remember the last time Sid had called at his room. In a reflex movement he checked his reflection in the mirror on the wall and smoothed down his hair before opening the door.

'Sid,' he announced superfluously. 'What is it?'

'I just wanted to talk.' She looked unusually flustered. 'I mean, I know we talked earlier but there's something else I've been meaning to speak to you about for days.' She stopped abruptly. 'Perhaps this isn't a good time.'

She pulled back a little as if she might turn away but he put out a hand to stop her.

'No, this is a good time. Of course it is.' He stepped back and pulled the door open wide. 'Come in. Please.'

She walked in diffidently and glanced round. Suddenly he realised the place looked shabby and dull. He hadn't bothered with his room for years; there had never seemed much point. What did she make of it? It occurred to him that he ought to offer her some sort of refreshment, anything really, but – unlike his brother – he didn't keep drink in his room. It was just somewhere he dressed and slept.

'Do sit down.' He gestured to the armchair he had just vacated. He only had the one; he never entertained here.

'Thank you.'

She sat, looking awkward and prim. After a moment looking down at her indecisively, he sat on the side of the bed to face her, carefully rearranging the dressing gown over his thighs.

'It's nice to see you,' he said, just to fill the silence, then wished he hadn't. What a foolish thing to say.

'Mortimer.' She turned her head and fixed him with her grey eyes. They looked troubled, as well they might in the circumstances. 'Someone said something to me...' She shook her head impatiently. 'This is ridiculous, I'm being coy. And at my age. And that's the thing, we're neither of us getting any younger, are we, so this needs to be said now or never, really.'

She frowned and looked away, through the window which offered a view to the front of the manor and the manicured lawns reaching down to the road. If you watched long enough, you'd see, over the flat lands to the south, the sails of an occasional yacht on the river in the distance.

'Then say it,' said Mortimer. 'My dear girl, what is it that's eating you up so?'

Sidony looked back at him, still frowning.

'Well, you see, I suggested to Hannah that she ought to realise how much Nathan liked her. That she shouldn't always be at loggerheads with him.' She paused.

'I see. And does she like him?'

'Yes. Well, at least I got the feeling she did. I'm sure she does. But then she retaliated and said I shouldn't be handing out relationship advice when you and I...' Sid stopped to point an agitated index finger between Mortimer and herself. '...couldn't sort out our own relationship. She knew we'd been an item years ago and said that she could tell I was still very fond of you. She was right, Mortimer. I am.' She hesitated. 'More than I can say, if I'm honest. Does that shock you?'

Mortimer began to think he was dreaming. He'd had a bad

night and now he'd gone to sleep and was dreaming.

'No, of course it doesn't shock me,' he murmured. 'I mean, are you, really?'

'Yes, really. And she also said that you'd told her that you were still very attached to me. So the thing is, Mortimer, was she right? I mean, this... this issue with Rose has just made me think how foolish I've been over the years. I should never have married Toby and left you like that. I was upset about Robert but I never blamed you for it. I just... I really don't know what I was thinking back then. I never cared for Toby the way I do for you. Anyway so much time has passed and I thought, if it's not too late to put at least this right...'

Mortimer was on his feet before she'd finished speaking. He reached a hand down and when she took it he pulled her to her feet then held her close, hardly daring to speak. He could feel her heart thumping in her chest pressed against him. It was wonderful just to hold her. He dreaded waking up.

'I didn't know,' he said in the end. 'I didn't know.'

He released his grip, took her face in his hands and kissed her softly on the lips.

'I adore you, Sidony Pettiver.'

'And I adore you,' she murmured. A moment later she abruptly pulled away. 'But I must go. We have to go down and entertain our guests.'

'Ah yes. The matchmaker and her friend. Perhaps we shouldn't be too hard on them.'

'No. Perhaps not.'

He squeezed her hand. 'Don't worry, we'll do our best for Rose. I'm sure they'll be lenient when they know the full circumstances.'

She raised his hand to her lips and kissed it, gave a wan smile and left.

Mortimer stood watching the door, then took a wedge of

the skin on his forearm and pinched himself, hard. It hurt. No, he wasn't dreaming after all.

*

Nathan combed his hair in front of the tiny mirror on the wall in his room, bending his knees slightly to see the top of his head. He didn't know what to expect from the evening. Having dinner with Mortimer and Sidony wouldn't have been his first choice in the circumstances. Whilst it might be intended as a goodwill gesture, it was still likely to prove uncomfortable.

Chief Inspector Crayford had interviewed Nathan and Hannah separately that morning. The questions had been thorough and business-like but the information the police inspector had been prepared to offer in return had been limited. The sergeant and a constable had been to Pollersby very early in the day but had found no trace of either Sam or his boat.

'You haven't heard anything more from him, Mr Bright?' the inspector enquired, eyeing him keenly.

'No. Nothing.'

Did the inspector believe him? He had no idea. Nathan wished he had heard from Sam. Probably. Or maybe not. He wanted to know he was all right but he felt pulled in two and unable to resolve it in his own mind. He didn't want to have to shop his brother for a second time. His head kept telling him he'd done the right thing; his heart swore he was a traitor.

He glanced at his watch: it was time to go down. He could hear sounds of movement next door and Hannah's door closing. He met up with her in the passageway.

'Into the lion's den?' she said lightly.

He pulled a face and didn't reply.

It was hard to place the atmosphere in the sitting room when they went down. They'd expected tension – given that Sid's daughter was now in a police cell that was only natural

306

– but there was something else as well. Something surprisingly warmer and more cheerful. Mortimer and Sidony were standing side by side in front of the cold fireplace, each cradling a drink.

'Ah good,' exclaimed Mortimer with more than usual vigour, 'you're here. What can I get you to drink?'

They both opted for gin and tonic and made brief, stilted conversation with Sidony while he poured it.

'Do sit,' offered Mortimer, waving an arm. 'Let's keep this informal, hm?'

There were three two-seater sofas arranged in a U round the fireplace. Mortimer and Sid sat on one while Nathan and Hannah shared another. There was a strained silence as if everyone was trying to think of something safe to say.

'You said you'd seen Rose earlier, Sid,' ventured Hannah. 'Is there any chance of her being released on bail?'

Trust her, thought Nathan, to grasp the nettle.

'We don't know yet,' said Sidony and produced a weak smile. 'I hope so. She's very contrite and trying to cooperate so perhaps that'll help. The police told me she's made a statement admitting to stealing the drawings – a number of them by different artists – and replacing them with fakes. She says she never met the forger or forgers and didn't know who they were. She keeps insisting that the idea came from Edgar Thayne and that he was the only one she dealt with. That he made a point of courting her till she agreed to help and then it became a kind of game. Well it was for her anyway. Passing notes; pretending to not like each other; secret assignations.' Sidony shook her head in exasperation. 'The silly girl. He was just using her. But she keeps insisting that Edgar killed Carrie.'

She shuddered, half closing her eyes, and Mortimer reached across and put his hand on hers before fixing his gaze first on Hannah, then on Nathan.

'I believe we ought to be grateful to you,' he said. 'On reflection we realise that it's just as well you found out what was going on before Rose got any more involved. These are dangerous people she got mixed up with.'

Sidony nodded agreement. 'The police gave us to understand that there's a whole network of them working similar scams. Though I understand Edgar Thayne is not being cooperative at the moment.' She regarded them quizzically. 'I have to admit that I'm curious how you came to suspect Rose at all. I feel so helpless, so ignorant of it all. And to think it was happening right under our noses. Perhaps you could explain? We know that Carrie had suspicions and she alerted you to them.'

'And when you came to me, I dismissed the idea, didn't I?' said Mortimer. 'I'm sorry about that. I did glance around but have to admit that I didn't search thoroughly. I was sceptical and didn't want any unnecessary scandal.'

He turned and looked at Sidony.

'I was also a bit preoccupied. I've been looking into selling off some land to help make ends meet. It'd have to go past the trustees in the end of course but I've been putting out feelers to see what we could get for it, see how much interest there might be.'

'But you never told me,' Sid said indignantly.

'I didn't want to cause any trouble about it until I knew it was worth pursuing.' He grimaced. 'Alan's cottage was part of the package, you see.'

'Oh Mortimer.' Sidony looked at him accusingly. 'That's not going to go down well.'

'No, well… we can talk about that again.' He looked back at Nathan and Hannah. 'Tell us how you realised Rose was involved. I'm curious too.'

'It was Hannah really,' said Nathan. 'She's the crossword

308

geek. She worked it out.'

All eyes turned to Hannah who coloured slightly.

'I'm not a geek,' she protested. 'It was Carrie's notebook that offered the clues. She'd kept a workbook, jotting down anything she needed to remember. It was pretty haphazard but I noticed some odd notes crammed in the margins, like afterthoughts. They didn't make much sense which is why I noticed them, I suppose. One of them was: *mixed up with the ballet man*. I saw him one day and realised she was referring to Edgar Thayne. Edgar Degas, you see – the artist who painted ballet dancers.'

She looked from Mortimer to Sidony and back again. They returned her gaze blankly.

'I guess it's a bit of an art specialist sort of clue. But then there were some letters: *BAON* and *sees a chart is ruined*. That was an anagram. *Sees a chart* turns out as *has a secret*, you see. Do either of you do crosswords? No. Well, it's a common device. And I couldn't get the initials until something you said Sidony.'

Sid gave a short laugh. 'Me? What did I say?'

'You referred to star-crossed lovers and that brought it up for me. The famous star-crossed lovers are Romeo and Juliet, aren't they? We studied it at school. In Shakespeare's play, Juliet dismisses the idea that Romeo's name is important. It's a well-known quote. She says: *that which we call a rose, by any other name would smell as sweet*. BAON. By Any Other Name. A rose. Carrie loved Shakespeare's plays, you see. Her husband told me so.'

Nathan smiled at their dazed expressions. 'No, I wouldn't have got it either. I've decided you have to have a brain that's wired differently to most normal people.'

Hannah gave him a withering look then ploughed on. She had got the bit between her teeth now, speaking quickly, all

309

bright-eyed and enthusiastic.

'I also guessed that, for the scam to work, there had to be some communication between Edgar and whoever else was involved, perhaps some notes or letters, anything written down that might be indicative. Then I remembered seeing that Rose had a print of the Duomo in Florence propped up against the wall panelling in her room. It looked slightly odd, I thought, with other items to do with Italy by it, as if it had some significance – like a shrine or something. And Mortimer, you'd told me there were secret panels in the wall panelling at odd places around the house. Hiding places, I assumed.'

Hannah smiled apologetically.

'So I went snooping and found a loose panel behind the picture of the Duomo. That's where her notes from Edgar were kept. Like a treasure, I suppose. She had a bunch of letters there from her old Italian boyfriend too.'

'Oh dear, it was there, right under our noses,' said Sidony. 'We've been so stupid, Mortimer.'

'Yes, I know.' He squeezed her hand. 'But I think we've talked about this enough. We could talk about it forever I'm afraid and still struggle to understand how it could happen. Shall we go through and eat? Netta will be waiting for us, I'm sure.'

The conversation over dinner was circumspect and careful, everyone at pains to avoid mentioning anything related to paintings, drawings or Rose. They talked of boats and steam trains and the nature reserve – Sidony had finally seen the elusive crane and there was even talk that a second had been seen; a mate perhaps – and Sid asked where Nathan and Hannah might be travelling to next.

'We don't know,' said Nathan. 'Wherever the work is. We might be going in completely opposite directions next time. Perhaps… I don't know, Edinburgh and Canterbury, say.'

'Or somewhere in Europe,' added Hannah. 'Or maybe just staying in Oxford for a while.'

The meal came to an end and they returned to the sitting room where Nathan helped Netta bring through a tray of coffee before she went home. They had all barely sat down with their cups when the front doorbell rang.

Mortimer looked at the clock over the fireplace and frowned.

'A bit late for visitors, isn't it?'

'Perhaps it's the police,' said Sidony anxiously.

'Or Netta?' suggested Hannah. 'Forgotten something maybe?'

'I'll go if you like,' said Nathan, getting to his feet. He wanted to go. He didn't know why but something told him it was important that he should go. Important to him, personally.

'Well...' began Mortimer.

Nathan was already out of the door and walking at speed along the passage to the office, then through into the front hallway. He shot the bolts back, turned the key and yanked the heavy oak door open.

There was no-one there. He stepped outside, looked around and peered into the darkness but, though there was a half-moon high in the sky, patchy cloud obscured it and he could see no-one. But, turning back, he found a large envelope propped up by the side of the door and immediately looked round again, out over the lawns and the path to the entrance. The cloud shifted a little and, for a brief moment, he thought he saw a figure moving quickly away. Someone keeping to the side of the lawns under the trees, someone who was now climbing over the front garden wall.

Then the cloud moved in again and the figure was lost to view.

'What is it, Nathan?'

Mortimer had come to the door.

'Someone's left a package.' He pointed and Mortimer picked it up.

'It's one of those stiffened envelopes. And they didn't stay? How strange. Let's take it inside.'

Nathan scanned the grounds once more but there was nothing to see. Mortimer took the envelope through to the office and carefully unsealed it. Meticulously wrapped in tissue paper inside was the stolen original drawing by Michelangelo.

Portrait, Unknown.

Chapter 23

The days slipped inexorably by and the restoration work was nearing completion. Nathan took his time over the Fantin-Latour, dragging it out. He suggested that both he and Hannah should leave at the same time, that it would be neater and more convenient for everybody that way. Though it was almost certainly true, Hannah guessed the real reason was that he still hoped to hear news of Sam. What news they did hear came via Netta, surreptitiously, when she was sure that no-one in the family was within earshot.

'Irene says everyone in the village is talking about it,' she whispered to Hannah in the kitchen on the Tuesday morning. 'They're saying that Edgar Thayne keeps claiming that Carrie's death was an accident, that he just wanted to talk to her but she panicked and fell into the water. I find that hard to believe, don't you? Of course it wouldn't explain why he didn't raise the alarm, would it? And that's not what Miss Rose is saying by all accounts. Surely the police'd believe her rather than him any day. I know I would.'

It was a mystery to Hannah how the village came to know so much about it.

'Everyone's concerned about Mr Mortimer,' Netta confided again on the Wednesday, this time to both Hannah and Nathan as they made sandwiches for their lunch. 'He's well-liked you know.' Netta moved across to close the door, but spoke in a whisper nonetheless. 'He's not the most organised of people but he is kind. He can't remember people's names for love nor money but he always lets on, you know, very friendly in his own way, just as if he does. They like that.'

'And have the police found out any more, do you know?' Nathan asked casually. 'I mean, about the other people involved in the scam?'

'Oh you mean like the chap who was faking the pictures? No, I don't think so. They found his boat, over Great Yarmouth way, they say. It was empty. He'd done a runner.' Netta shook her head. 'They'll never see him again, will they? I wouldn't be surprised if he hadn't gone down to Felixstowe and caught a ferry to the continent. Everyone's just amazed that that last picture got returned. Our Rita said it was like something out of a movie.' Netta sniffed disdainfully. 'But then she watches a lot of movies, does our Rita.'

'And what does the astonishingly well-informed village have to say today?' Nathan asked Hannah on the Thursday morning when she returned to the workroom with two hot drinks.

She put the coffee down on his table then leaned against it, arms folded.

'There appear to be a number of different viewpoints. The absconding forger has bolted up to Scotland and then to one of the islands – the Hebrides seem to be the front runner. *Or* he's skipped to London and is laying low with a bunch of accomplices, planning the next job. *Or* he's somewhere in rural Wales. *Or* he's flown to Spain and is already living the high life. Take your pick. Clearly no-one has a clue and I suspect that includes the police or Irene would be sure to know. Personally I think Spain sounds good. Sunny.'

She hesitated. 'What do you think?'

'I think it's not something to joke about.'

'Excuse me but you asked. And you can't expect to take all this gossip seriously. I mean, seriously, you don't do you? They don't know what they're talking about.'

She went back to her seat by the Guardi where she was doing the final check over the surface to find any last issues which needed resolving. She picked up the earpieces to ram in her ears. Today she was listening to Fleetwood Mac.

'I'm jumpy,' Nathan said tersely. 'I can't stand this not-knowing.'

'I'm jumpy too.' She flicked him an apologetic smile. 'That's why I make crass jokes. Sorry.'

*

By the Friday, they were all done. The art materials and tools had been packed away into their respective trunks, Daphne had been informed and had arranged for the carrier to pick them up, and Mortimer had been promised a full written report on the work that had been carried out.

Out of the blue, Nathan and Hannah had been given a free night's accommodation at The Boatman before they left Norfolk for good. They'd had dinner at the inn on the Wednesday night and when they told Brian March about their imminent departure he'd immediately offered them their old rooms back for the Friday night. With the staircase rebuilt and the rooms all redecorated, he and Alice were planning to open up for letting again the following week.

'You can still smell the paint I'm afraid but take it as our apology for all the trouble you were caused.'

It was mid-afternoon on the Friday when they left the manor. Netta said she was sorry to see them go but there was no sign of Alan or Sidony when they called at the office. Mortimer was on the phone and covered the mouthpiece to bid them farewell. He looked flustered and distracted and quickly returned to his call.

'I wonder what will happen to Rose,' Hannah said as they walked out to the cars. 'And then there's the manor. Do you think it'll stay in the family, what with all the financial problems and now these thefts?'

'I'm sure Mortimer will sort it out somehow,' Nathan said drily. 'I told you before: he may come across as eccentric but he's sharp enough when he wants to be. And like Netta said: everybody likes him. They'll all bend over backwards to make sure he and the manor come out of it all right. I mean, he's been talking about having the bail money almost sorted.' He laughed. 'Where did he get that from?' They reached the car park. 'Anyway, I'll see you at The Boatman.'

He felt in the pocket of his jacket, checking the letter was there. It was and still sealed up. He wanted to be alone when he opened it. Hannah was already in her car and she gave a brief wave and was gone, heading off to the village. Nathan followed on a few minutes later.

It wasn't until they had both checked into their rooms and he'd closed and locked the door that he took the envelope out of his pocket. When he'd gone into the office that morning it had been visible in the tumbling pile of post on Rose's desk and he'd grabbed it before anyone else noticed. Not that there was anything noteworthy about it: the long thin white envelope simply had his name and the manor address typed on the front. But it wasn't a bill and it had been posted in Norfolk and he didn't know anyone in Norfolk who'd be likely to write to him. Except perhaps...

He worked an index finger under the flap and ripped it open. The letter inside had been handwritten on a sheet torn from a block of drawing paper.

Dear Nathan,

I had to write, to try to explain. I couldn't before, you must understand that. I am sorry. Now I'm not sure where to start. It was as I told you – I developed a gambling problem, partly from boredom with my job and the rest of my life at the time. It's no excuse of course but I was never cut out to be a teacher and I wasn't a very good one. I ended up owing money to the wrong people. And unscrupulous guys look for idiots like me, people who have weaknesses they can play on and manipulate. I was prime for it.

I'd done some drawings for friends. At least, I thought they were friends. Pictures in the style of whichever artist they fancied. I didn't do them as fakes. They were just for fun and little thank yous for odd favours given like a good night out or a night spent on someone's sofa. When my debts got too high to cope with and I started getting threats, I moved to Norfolk and bought myself a cheap boat. I thought I'd lie low for a bit, sort myself out. But somehow these characters got to see some of my drawings and managed to find me. They 'persuaded' me to do one for them which they used to replace an original somewhere. I don't know where. It snowballed. Once I'd done it, I was sucked in. They made it clear I was already a criminal and I felt it.

I only ever met two of these guys, ages ago now. They weren't management; they were enforcers. I hope to God I never see them again. I don't know their names or their operations with other people, I just know that I was simply one spoke in a very big wheel. They already had the Thayne guy lined up. I don't know what his weakness was. Money probably. I didn't meet him – I only found out his name by snooping – but I was told about him and how to arrange collections and drop offs. We had a few places and kept

317

mixing it up.

Well there you are. Sordid, isn't it? I can't tell you how confused I was when you turned up at the boat. I was thrilled to see you and yet terrified that the whole operation would come out and we'd be blamed and killed. They threatened to harm my family several times when I wavered. I believed them.

I've managed to put a few savings by, hidden from them thank God. A friend is typing the envelope for me and posting this. By the time you read it I shall be abroad. I intend to find an honest way to make a living but I'll have to keep my head down. If they find me... They have long memories, those guys.

I hated not being able to tell you the whole story. I hated not seeing you and Mum all these years. I hope my help has at least done something to tip the balance back a little. I hope more than anything that you can forgive me. One day maybe we can meet up again. I'll cherish that hope.

Give my love to mum. Perhaps tell her a whitewashed version of the truth, something she can live with and still understand why I'm not around.

> *Till the next time.*
> *Always your loving brother,*
> *Sam.*

Nathan sat on the side of the bed, still clutching the letter. Tears rolled down his cheeks and he brushed them away with the back of his hand. This was what he'd wanted: some genuine contact, something to show that Sam forgave *him* but also that he recognised that he had to change something in his life. It was a step in the right direction. Nathan shook his head,

318

punch-drunk with all the emotions coursing through him. He felt he'd found his brother again, the real Sam. And yet, running away? Abroad? Was that the answer? Shouldn't he have gone to the police and cleared the slate once and for all, though presumably the 'enforcers' would still have found a way to get to him. At this moment Nathan had no idea what course of action would have been best but there was nothing he could do about it either way.

He read the letter through again, then carefully folded it and put it back in the envelope. After a few moments' thought he took it out again, pulled a match from the complimentary matchbook left in the room, struck it and set the corner of the letter alight. He laid it in the ash tray and watched it burn and shrivel to a brown crisp then went across to the bathroom and flushed it down the toilet. There had been nothing in it that would help the police and no indication of where Sam would be. That letter had been personal.

He wasn't going to tell Hannah. It was between him and Sam. If she didn't know, she didn't have to lie.

*

The two bars of The Boatman thronged with locals and tourists alike. It was nearly nine o'clock on the Friday evening and, with the setting of the sun and a threatening sky, most of the drinkers had abandoned the tables on the quay and had come inside. The babble of chatter and laughter was punctuated with the clink of glasses and the shouting of order numbers as meals were brought out from the kitchens. Alice March, holding a plate of steak and chips in one hand and a plate of fish pie and vegetables in the other, emerged from behind the bar and called out 'number 64', scanning the room. Her skin glistened and she had an impatient, weary air. Someone raised an arm and she went across to deliver the meals, no doubt glad that

319

they stopped taking food orders at nine.

Sitting at the table in the window that had been reserved for them, Hannah turned back to look outside but it was impossible now to see anything other than her reflection. She thought she looked tired too or perhaps drunk. She felt a little drunk. She and Nathan had already had two drinks apiece when they'd first come down to the bar – celebrating the end of an assignment – and Nathan had suggested sharing a bottle of red wine while they ate. The food was all gone now but still they sat with the remains of the wine and she had to admit that she felt good. It was such a relief to be back here and away from the stiff, strained atmosphere of the manor's dinner table. She glanced across at Nathan. He looked more sober than she felt.

'It is the problem with this job,' she said as if he'd been privy to her thoughts. 'I mean, I like the travelling. It's interesting. And I like staying in different places, grand houses and that. But it's difficult not to get caught in the middle isn't it? Other people's agendas, their family politics. All that. And look, now we're going to have to come back at some point to give evidence at a trial.'

Nathan looked at her with amusement. 'So you're thinking of giving it up and taking a regular job again, are you? Back to working in boring old galleries and stuffy collections? None of this life on the road and professional independence?'

She narrowed her eyes and pointed a warning finger at him.

'If you're trying to get rid of me, it won't work. Just because you can't work out a simple cryptic clue when you see one, there's no reason to blame me.'

'I don't blame you. Not at all.' He hesitated, fingering the stem of his wine glass. 'In fact, I think we work quite well together.'

Hannah picked up her glass and drank the last of the wine in it. 'Maybe.' She paused, frowning. 'But *do* we have professional independence? Don't we just do what Timothy wants?'

'You're joking, right? You never do what Timothy wants unless it suits you too. I don't suppose you've done what someone else wanted your whole life.'

Her frown deepened. 'That's harsh.'

He grinned.

They both became introspective. They'd talked off and on all evening, had exhausted discussion of the robberies and Rose, of Hannah's fall into the river – presumably pushed by Edgar but they'd never know for sure – and about the apparently burgeoning relationship between Mortimer and Sidony. Nathan had conjectured what their next commissions might be and seemed to be smitten with the idea of buying a boat of his own one day. What they hadn't talked about was Sam.

'What will you tell your mother?' Hannah suddenly demanded.

Nathan stared at her for what seemed like ages.

'I don't know. I've been thinking about that. Sam seems to have disappeared. I hope he's safe. But not telling her that I've seen him and that he was well would feel too cruel. She needs to know.' He shrugged. 'Though not the whole truth. I'll maybe just keep to his story about owing money to some dubious characters.'

'And you don't think she'll see through that?'

'Of course she will. She's no fool. But she'll probably be able to live with it, for now at least.'

He poured the remains of the wine into both glasses and Hannah held hers up.

'To Sam. May his road be safe and kind, wherever he

goes, and may it lead him back home soon.'

Nathan smiled ruefully, lifted his glass and clinked hers.

'To Sam, my incredibly troublesome kid brother.'

It was something to ten when Hannah, the wine all gone, announced in a loud voice that she was going up to her room.

'I'm drunk,' she said. 'I need tea. I don't want to wake up with a hangover tomorrow. Too many road miles to do.'

In the end they went up together and Nathan stood outside her room while she found the key to the door and opened it. She turned to look at him.

'Good night.'

'Good night.' He didn't move. 'And thank you.'

'What for?'

'For bothering about my little brother. For trying to help. For not giving him away. I'm really…'

He leaned forwards, his face so close to hers that she could feel the warmth of his skin, could see tiny flecks in his greeny-brown eyes that she'd never noticed before. And his lips were tantalisingly near.

'I'm really grateful,' he muttered and his head seemed to sway slightly.

It occurred to her that he was in fact drunk too.

He put a hand on the wall behind her to steady himself but didn't move, his eyes fixed on her face. He reached his spare hand up as if he was going to touch her cheek, but didn't and let it fall again.

'You're welcome,' she said incongruously, still transfixed by his lips. So temptingly close.

She ran a tongue over her own lips then locked eyes with him.

She cleared her throat. 'So I'll… erm… I'll see you at breakfast then, shall I? Eight o'clock?'

He straightened up, awkward suddenly.

'Yes. Breakfast. Of course.' He nodded, hesitated for the blink of an eye, then disappeared into his bedroom.

Hannah went into her own room, closed the door behind her and leant her back against it.

'That was close,' she murmured. 'What were you thinking, Hannah?'

Chapter 24

It was mid-afternoon on the Saturday by the time Hannah arrived back at her little semi-detached house in north Oxford. A pile of junk mail and free newspapers was scattered across the floor inside her front door. The forwarding service she'd paid for had expired some ten days previously and she hadn't bothered to renew it so there were a couple of bills too. And a letter. She didn't recognise the writing but it wasn't likely to be urgent and she put it to one side to open with the bills later. She started to unpack and sort things out, feeling the usual post-return dislocation. Her body might now be in Oxford but the events, sights and sounds of Norfolk still inhabited her head.

It was nearly six o'clock, with everything put away and the washing machine on, when Hannah made herself a mug of tea and finally sank into her sofa with the unopened post. The bills fortunately brought no surprises and she picked up the letter. It had a recent Lancashire postmark but she didn't know anyone in Lancashire that she could remember. She ripped it open. Inside was a lightweight greetings card with a picture of a crane on the front, one of the ones they sold at the nature reserve shop in East Ranling. Inside was a handwritten note.

Dear Hannah,

I escaped, just as you said I should and I wanted to thank you for giving me the courage to do it. I knew I should but your words of encouragement meant a great deal and were just enough to give me the resolve. It took a bit of planning but Alan was going out more and more – I know now that he was seeing someone else – which gave me the chance to slowly get my things out and then to leave.

After our conversation I made enquiries about jobs in wildlife management and I've just been interviewed and got one here in Lancashire at a wetland centre. I start next week and someone's kindly given me the use of their sofa bed till I can find a place to live. I'm a long way from Norfolk and from Alan and I feel happier than I've felt in a long time.

I wish you all the best for the future and hope that we might meet again one day. Thank you again.

> *All my best wishes,*
> *Grace*

PS I've sent a letter to Mortimer Gyllam-Spence too telling him about Alan's past. I didn't tell him where I was of course but I thought he should know.

Hannah smiled as she put the card down.

'Good on you, Grace.'

*

Back at the restoration studios on the Monday morning, Daphne gave Nathan and Hannah her usual cheery welcome, glad to have her 'wandering restorers' back home and keen to hear all about their trip. They'd arrived within minutes of each other but had hardly managed to exchange more than a few words with Daphne before Timothy lurched out of his office, clutching a pile of papers.

'Good, good, you're back.' He came to join them. 'No problems, I trust?'

He looked from one to the other, searchingly.

'The work went well,' said Hannah.

'Definitely,' agreed Nathan. 'Went well. No problems.'

'That's what I like to hear.' He waved the papers at them for emphasis. 'Steve's working through a mountain of jobs in the workshop upstairs. He'll be glad of your help. These are the pictures that are waiting.'

He thrust the pile of papers into Nathan's hand and retreated back into his office.

'We'll tell him again,' said Nathan.

'Absolutely. There's no hurry.'

Daphne's eyes narrowed. 'Tell him what?'

'It's a long story,' said Hannah.

Nathan leaned over the desk conspiratorially.

'It's all about stolen pictures, Daphne, and forgeries and a poor woman who happened to be in the wrong place at the wrong time.'

Daphne turned to look at Hannah.

'No,' said Nathan, 'not Hannah for once. Though she did manage to get on the wrong side of someone and ended up being pushed into a river. From a bridge. It's a gift she has for rubbing people up the wrong way. If only I had pictures.'

Hannah sighed. 'I'll tell you the real story later, Daphne,' she said, already walking away to go upstairs.

Nathan turned back to Daphne and winked.

326

Geographical note

The landscape in which this novel is set, the Norfolk Broads, lies in the east of England in the mainly flat lands situated between the city of Norwich and the North Sea. The Broads are actually of man-made construction, formed during medieval times when the land was dug for peat to burn as a fuel. The digging continued for three hundred years and more and, when it stopped, the workings slowly flooded to create the network of rivers and lakes (the 'Broads') that we know today.

Though once used for the transport of goods and food, the waterways are now predominantly enjoyed by boating enthusiasts. The area is also a carefully managed and protected wetland for wildlife where previously rare creatures have been reintroduced and protected and now thrive. Visitors have the opportunity to see a wide range of birds, both native and migrating, otters, water voles, dragonflies and butterflies. In the spring, the shy and elusive bittern may be heard booming and, if you're lucky, even seen. It is a naturalist's paradise.

A Crack in the Varnish

Kathy Shuker

Hollywood actress, Esther Langley, has a home in the hills of Provence, an old converted abbey where she keeps her precious art collection. Now she has four paintings in need of restoration: one modern work, fire-damaged, and three crumbling old masters. It looks like a straightforward job for an experienced art restorer like Hannah Dechansay, and who wouldn't relish a few months in Provence?

But living and working on Esther's estate isn't easy. It's a tortured household, haunted by a tragic death. There's guilt and recrimination in the air and relationships soon start to unravel. Was the death an accident? Everyone has a different version to tell. There's something sinister going on and everyone, it seems, has something to hide.

Available as an eBook and in paperback, both standard and large print.

For more information about Kathy's books, please visit:
www.kathyshuker.co.uk